NEVER MARRY YOUR BROTHER'S BEST FRIEND

LAUREN LANDISH

ALSO BY LAUREN LANDISH

Big Fat Fake Series:

My Big Fat Fake Wedding || My Big Fat Fake Engagement || My Big Fat
Fake Honeymoon

Standalones:

The French Kiss || One Day Fiance || Drop Dead Gorgeous || The
Blind Date || Risky Business

Truth Or Dare:

The Dare || The Truth

Bennett Boys Ranch:

Buck Wild || Riding Hard || Racing Hearts

The Tannen Boys:

Rough Love || Rough Edge || Rough Country

Dirty Fairy Tales:

Beauty and the Billionaire || Not So Prince Charming || Happily Never
After

Pushing Boundaries:

Dirty Talk || Dirty Laundry || Dirty Deeds || Dirty Secrets

CHAPTER
ONE

CARTER

"SON OF A BITCH!"

I slam the door to my office behind me, well aware that it was a second too late to muffle my outburst. I snarl over my shoulder, muttering under my breath the way my grandma taught me to do when you don't have anything nice to say. "Cam's nose is so far up Dad's ass, he can probably tell what he ate for dinner last night."

I can't help that Cameron is the golden child—the oldest, most brilliant, the most like our father and grandfather. Except we all know Cam's flawed in the worst way possible with a soul-deep scar from the accident that took his wife and left him a single parent.

That's not something we discuss out loud, even in an empty room under our breath. But Cameron's ever-present ability to stay in Dad's good graces and make me come out looking like a hack? That's fair game.

I throw the report Cameron presented onto my desk, glaring at it as if my brother can feel my anger through its perfectly formatted brilliance. I pace left, glare, then right, sighing as I try to find fault with any detail of his plan. But there's none. I know it. Cameron wouldn't have presented it otherwise.

He might be an ass, but he's a damn good businessman.

The door opens behind me and Zack comes in.

"Fuck off. Not now."

Considering he's my best friend, he doesn't take the slightest offense. Nor does he listen. Instead, he walks in like he owns the place. He doesn't even work here, and the meeting for our private real estate company is supposed to be over dinner tonight, so he shouldn't even be here.

Not that anything like that has ever stopped him. I don't think Zack has met a single obstacle in his life that he didn't tackle with single-minded, obstinate determination. Or steel balls, whatever the case may call for.

"Whoa, who pissed in your grits this morning?"

His humor makes me even angrier. Launching in without preamble, I inform him, "Cameron did a big-ass, full-court presentation today. I had no idea he was even working on anything, but then he goes and throws out a whole business plan with plotted out progress points and fully developed return on investment figures like he shit it out after his morning Metamucil."

I wave a hand at the report on my desk, shooting it another sour look for good measure. I hope Cameron feels the glare like a solid kick to his family jewels. Not that he fucking needs them. He's head-down, focused on work or his daughter, twenty-four-seven. I'd be surprised if he ever distracts himself with something as frivolous as jacking off.

Zack picks up the paperwork and helps himself to one of the chairs in front of my desk, flipping pages as he scans to get the gist of Cameron's new grand plan. "Venture capital?" he surmises as he throws it back to the desk carelessly.

"Yeah, some hotshot chef's opening a restaurant. Somehow, the damn thing already has a waiting list before they've even begun construction. It's a 'sure bet', or at least Cam thinks so." I add finger quotes to make sure Zack understands how idiotic this proposal is. I would never admit it, but I'm pouting.

Normally, I'd be laughing that he brought in an investment into a restaurant because generally, they're risky, but I'll admit this is gold. But only to myself, not to Zack.

My grandfather began the family business decades ago with a

profit-sharing deal with a friend, and it's grown exponentially since then. We have our well-manicured fingers in business deals around the globe, in everything from real estate to stock markets to small start-ups to portfolio management.

We're the archangels of angel investors. Anything we can do to make money, or make someone else money, which in turn also makes us money, is our specialty. And in a business that traditionally has more misses than hits, we have a remarkable 'batting average'.

Because of deals like Cameron's Hottie McHottie chef.

I also have a side hustle business with Zack, using my funds and his brains. Not that he doesn't have money or I don't have a brain, but we started it long ago when my focus was on making my way in the family business and he needed an influx of start-up cash.

Zack holds up his hand, rubbing his fingertip against his thumb. "Want me to play you a sad song on a tiny violin the size of your teeny-tiny dick? You can cry your whiny tears 'til you blow snot bubbles out of your nose." His voice is gratingly pitying as though I'm a fussy toddler demanding their way.

"My dick is not teeny-tiny," I correct, focusing on the most important part of what he said and purposefully ignoring the rest as I plop into the chair next to him.

"That's the spirit!" Zack cheers sarcastically. "Not that there's a need to go crossing swords with your brother, but you're too good to pout about a done deal. What you need is a deal of your own. Not coincidentally, that's why I'm here." He holds his hands out wide like he's God's gift to fix my bad mood.

I can sense the carrot he's dangling, and while there's a part of me that wants to be angry—fine, *jealous*—a bit longer, I can't deny the appeal of the next new thing. Dad definitely bred that into Cameron, but he also put a good dose of those genes into me too, along with a fair amount of brotherly competition.

"What've you got?"

"A little birdie told me about a widow—" he starts.

"Weak," I interject. "I need something big."

"As I was saying," Zack continues, not slowing down, "portfolio management for a widow with a huge estate. I'm talking property, an art collection worth well into the eight figures, investments, and more."

Looking his way, I concede. "I'm listening."

Zack grins triumphantly, knowing he's got me solidly wiggling on his hook and he's a patient and skilled fisherman. "She's only considering outsourcing, but I think you could sway her with that magic charm of yours. Seems to work with every other woman between twenty-two and ninety-two."

I flash him my signature smile. "Now who's jealous?" He doesn't answer, merely stares back, waiting me out. "Fine, tell me more. Please."

Pleased as punch with himself, he reels me in slowly. "Elena Cartwright, seventy-five, but spry and sharp. Her estate is out past Pearl, about ten thousand acres. But who's counting at that point?" He rolls his eyes, well aware that my family owns that much too, though not in one plot. Land like that comes from more than three generations of wealth like us Harringtons, but Pearl is far enough away that I don't know the Cartwright legacy.

He continues, "She lost her husband, Thomas, three years ago and has been grieving ever since. Though not too upset to manage the portfolio with her financial advisor. But he's in over his head and knows it. More importantly, she knows it. She's looking to the future."

"Her future?" I ask incredulously. "Didn't you say she's seventy-five? She should be sitting on the porch, drinking a sweet tea, and singing the praises over witnessing another sunrise."

"She probably does a fair amount of that, but she's also been the brains behind the latest generation of Cartwright success. She's not an empty-headed placeholder, which you'd do well to remember," he warns.

"Noted. So, what's the catch?"

"The way in."

I knew it. If it sounds too good to be true, it's damn-near always a guaranteed loss.

"Thomas Cartwright was the art collector, and an artist in his own right. Elena is his biggest fan. The art is your way in."

"I know approximately less than fuck-all about art," I argue.

Zack kicks out, knocking my foot off my knee. "No shit. I have a plan for that." The full effect of my scowl lands on Zack, who seems completely unfazed. "Luna."

I know the word, Latin for moon, but I'm not sure why he's suddenly speaking a dead language.

"My sister, Luna," he explains slowly. "She knows more about art than anyone. We can get her to tutor you or something, at least give you some talking points to get Cartwright on your side."

The suggestion might as well be for me to speak to Elena Cartwright in a dead language because there's no way Zack's little sister will help me. I've been friends with Zack for over ten years, since our freshman year of college. And though I've met her at a handful of birthday parties, I've heard plenty of stories about how eccentric Zack's sister is.

Some of the tales are simply the difference in ages, since Luna is almost nine years younger than Zack, but others highlight that sometimes, siblings can be polar opposites. And given that Zack and I are two peas in a pod, I'm sure Luna wouldn't care too much for me, either.

I look at him as though he's lost his damn mind because I'm considering the fact that he may actually have.

"Don't give me that," he orders, despite my not having said a word.

"You think she's going to help?" I ask doubtfully. But it really doesn't matter. Even if Luna were to agree, it's unlikely I could learn enough in a short amount of time that'd fool someone passionate about art.

He smirks confidently. "I might know a thing or two about a thing or two, not that I'll tell you. It'd make a crappy secret if I go blabbing it all over town."

"You plan to blackmail your sister into teaching me enough about art that I can charm an old lady into choosing me to manage her portfolio." It's not a question, I'm simply repeating the plan concisely so I can evaluate it.

"Yep." Zack looks self-satisfied. With that, he gets up and pops me in the shoulder. "See you at dinner tonight."

Alone, I glare at Cameron's report once more. I hope Zack's intel on this Cartwright deal is right because I could really use a win.

CHAPTER
TWO
LUNA

"*NEVER BE ENOUGH* . . . *never enough . . . for me . . . for me-ah!*"

The lyrics turn to humming as I focus on the precise linework of my illustration. A little thinner here, a little thicker there for perspective. And . . . voila!

"Okey-dokey, Daddy choke me, page fifteen is in the *books*." I laugh at my own Dad-slash-Daddy joke as I scroll to the next page on my tablet. I've done plenty of work with paper and pencil, oils, and acrylics over the years, but this tablet has become an extension of my creativity, allowing me to bring my alter-ego to life. "Alphena, let's show Bradley who's boss."

Alphena is the headlining character in the graphic novel I've been drawing since I was in high school, though she's taken on a life of her own more recently. A little Alpha bitch, a bit of Greek goddess Athena, and a lot of me blend to create a character that attacks the patriarchy and makes the world her oyster.

If only I were this bold in real life, but that's never been the case. In reality, I'm quiet, almost shy. Even when my mind is throwing out ideas about what I should have said, my mouth stays tight-lipped. My art is where I can let loose, where my mousy becomes mighty.

On this page, Alphena is smack-talking a guy who's

mansplaining the electoral college . . . incorrectly. *"No, Braaad. That's actually not how it works, in fact. Try a basic Google search and you'll see that I know more than cooking and cleaning. I retained my sixth-grade government education, something you seem to have forgotten."* I'm in the zone, so when my phone rings next to me, I ignore it. Then my text alarm goes off, and I narrow my eyes, staying focused on the tablet screen. When it rings again, I groan in irritation and set down my pen.

My eyes roll of their own volition at my annoying brother's name on the caller ID. For all the sass Alphena has, I answer the phone relatively politely. "What?"

"Good to talk to you too, dear sister," Zack responds dryly.

"Mm-hmm. What do you want?" My brain is ninety percent work and only ten percent paying attention to Zack.

"What makes you think I want something?"

"Call. Text. Call. Unless something's wrong with Mom—which I know it's not because I talked to her earlier today and she was lamenting that you never call—you want something."

He can't fault my logic. "Valid. I want to take you to dinner tonight. I have something I'd like to talk about."

"I'm busy. Maybe next week?" I'm putting him off for tonight, and then next week, I can do it again. It's not that I don't want to see Zack, but he always picks fancy places where I'm uncomfortable and then plies me with unsolicited advice about how I should work with him. For some reason, he wants to shape me into a miniature version of himself, despite being well-aware that I would consider that a painful realm of hell. All the hand shaking, brown nosing, and negotiating he does? I would live in a panicked state.

My life is art, not in a poetic sense but a literal way.

To pay the bills, I work at the local museum doing tours of their collections and occasionally teaching a community outreach program class. It's enough social interaction to last me a lifetime and works because I only have to talk about what I love. Besides, the tour is mostly scripted, and I have it memorized.

To feed my soul, I create Alphena. Between the two, I don't

have time to care about much more, especially whatever angle my brother's working.

"Tonight, Luna. You name the place."

Interesting. And suspicious. "Anywhere? My choice?" After a beat, I clarify, "And you're paying?"

"Yeah, of course." The small chuckle he swallows down is one I've heard before, when he's commenting on my lack of salary compared to him. That's more like Zack.

"Fine. I'll meet you at Fairy Tales, then." I can already taste the coffee and sandwiches, and most importantly, smell the books in my greedy little hands.

"Seriously?" he scoffs. "I'll buy dinner anywhere you'd like, and you want to go to a cheap café you eat at once a week?"

I smile an evil smile as I reveal my plan. "I'm going to add a significant stack of art hardcovers to that dinner bill you're footing."

"Deal. I'll see you there at seven," Zack answers too easily. "Bye, Sis."

I look down at the phone in my hand, noting apprehensively that Zack has already hung up. He's up to something, clearly. But I'm getting books I could never afford out of the deal, so it can't be too bad of an arrangement. It's only dinner, right?

I go back to page sixteen after setting an alarm to remind me to stop working to get to Fairy Tales on time.

———

"Shoot, shoot, shoot." My alarm went off, but I only had a tiny bit left so I kept working, and now I'm late. Not that Zack will be surprised that I got lost in my art again. He's used to my 'five minutes' being more like thirty. Or more.

I swing the door open and run smack into a guy carrying a huge paper bag of books. "Oops, sorry," I tell him, already ducking inside and away from the guy's scowl as I push my glasses back into position. The smell of books rushes through my nose and straight into my blood. I feel . . . at home here.

In the café, Zack is sitting at a table in the middle of all the action, staring at his phone. A definite change from my usual hidey-hole in the corner where no one interrupts my reading and quiet dinners, but I'm not going to ask him to move because he'd totally give me a hard time about it. Leaning against the chair across from him, I drawl out, "What's so important that you're willing to come here to see me?"

Unbothered, Zack looks up with a smile. "Have a seat."

He kicks the chair out next to him, but I see the flash of disappointment on his face when he takes me in. My baggy overalls, tank top, and Converse aren't exactly Zack's style. In contrast, his hair is styled perfectly, his glasses spotless, his button-up shirt tucked in, and though the rest of him is beneath the table, I know he's wearing slacks and dress shoes. The quintessential businessman to my creative artist. For siblings, we couldn't be more different.

"Let me order first." I hold out my hand for his card, which he hands over wordlessly. My brother is nothing if not predictable, and an agreeable Zack doesn't bode well.

I spin and head to the counter. "Hey, Lydia. How're you?"

Lydia is here most weeks when I come, and we've gotten to be friendly, which mostly means she talks and I listen. Lately, she's been telling me about the guy in her economics class she's crushing on. After hearing the tea, I order one of my own. "Chai tea latte and a Greek salad, please." I swipe Zack's card, but as Lydia hands me the receipt, she gasps.

"Who's that?"

Without looking, I answer, "My brother."

"No, I recognized him. I mean . . . *him*." She purses her lips, indicating the table behind me, and I glance back.

"What the—" I gasp, spinning back around so he doesn't see me staring.

Him is my brother's best friend and business partner, Carter Harrington, who's sitting at the table with Zack. Carter looks like a model in an Armani photo shoot wearing a black suit, blue shirt, and dark blue power tie. Even from here, his blue eyes pop, his tan looks island-vacation fresh, and his jaw is sharp and square.

"Don't get excited," I warn Lydia. "Carter's the devil in disguise." When she leans forward eagerly, I know it's my turn to return the gossip. "He's my brother's best friend, richer than God, handsome and knows it, bossy because he assumes he knows best, and an all-around annoyance. And he's *not* supposed to be here."

Lydia raises one brow as she leans around me to peer at Carter and Zack. "Well, I for one don't mind that he showed up uninvited. Especially when your negatives are rich, handsome, and bossy." She ticks the traits off on her fingers, adding, "Girl, that's what I'm looking for in a man. I can teach him everything else he needs to know."

She forgot annoying, but I don't argue the point. It doesn't matter when her eyes are more glazed than a dozen Krispy Kreme donuts. Returning to the table, I throw out a hand to indicate Carter and speak only to Zack. "Is *this* why you're bribing me with dinner and books?"

"I can hear you, ya know?" Carter responds. Out of the corner of my eye—because I'm not giving Carter Harrington a moment of my full-eyed attention—I can see that he's grinning in amusement at my irritation. *He probably gets off on it*, I think wryly.

I don't react, keeping hard eyes on Zack. He's the one who owes me an answer. "Sit down. Please. And yes, this is what I want to talk to you about. I mean, *he* is."

Slowly, I lower to the chair with a 'nope' already on the tip of my tongue for whatever Zack wants.

"Thank you," Zack says with a placating nod. "I've called you both here tonight to discuss an opportunity," he starts, sounding like a salesman on late night television. Although, if he starts trying to sell me some ever-sharp knives, I might be buying, because I might have an immediate use for them. "Luna, I found a potential client for Carter, but he needs help. That's where you come in."

"I'm not interested." I cross my arms over my chest, trying to become small and invisible. But I shoot a look of distaste at Carter despite the fact that he's barely spoken. His mere presence annoys me. Actually, his existence on the planet.

"I'll pay you," Carter offers.

Nostrils flaring, I stare at him. As if I want his fucking money.

Zack holds his palms up to slow my impending implosion. Yeah, I implode, not explode like most people. I hate it, but it's how I'm built. "Not like that. He means he'll pay you to tutor him." I flick my eyes to Zack, silently questioning his sanity. "About art."

Wait. What?

"What?" I echo my own thought.

"Carter is approaching a potential client who is particularly art savvy, a topic he has admittedly minimal knowledge on. Luckily, I know someone who knows more about art than virtually anyone in the world." He smiles charmingly. "You," he clarifies as if I didn't know he was talking about me.

A laugh pops out before I can stop it. "Me? Help Carter?" Unconvinced, I wait for the punchline or a camera crew to pop out and say 'gotcha!' When neither is forthcoming, I realize Zack is serious. "No thanks. Like I said, not interested. Lydia," I call out, "can you make my order to go?"

Lydia, who's apparently been watching the whole show of Zack's big reveal, drops surprised eyes to Zack and then to Carter. "Uh, sure."

Carter leans back in his chair, completely unaffected by my denial. His eyes sparkle and his white teeth flash as he baits me. "Am I so repulsive that you won't even hear me out?"

I'm quiet, my brain spitting piss and fire that my mouth would never say, even though I've been waiting for a chance to tell Carter what I think of him. Except this time, the words pour out in all their flat and dull honesty. "Physically, no. And you know it, which is part of the problem. Emotionally, I'm pretty sure you have the maturity of an eighteen-year-old boy on a Spring Break weekend, so despite your business success, I have no interest in helping you scam someone into signing their life and funds away to you."

Whew! Guess I've been holding on to more than I thought about my brother's best friend.

There's a flash in Carter's eyes, but I must've imagined it because he doesn't have the emotional depth to feel hurt. Especially based on an insult from someone like me.

"Luna! That's not what he does and not what we're asking you to do!" Zack hisses.

Carter holds up a hand, and to my chagrin, Zack leans back and gives him the floor. "I'm hearing that you think I'm attractive and successful, but immature and immoral." I'm actually surprised he could hear the negatives through the fog of his inflated ego. When I stay silent, he continues, "Give me the chance to prove you wrong. Please. I'll make it worth your while, I promise you that."

With that solemn vow, he stands, gives Zack a nod, and struts out of the café. I definitely don't notice that his long legs eat up the ground toward the bookstore door. But Lydia must because she yells, "Come back anytime! Especially Mondays and Thursdays for the dinner shift!"

I glare at her, and she shrugs. "He's cuter than Economics Alex, and definitely richer. Can't blame a girl for trying."

"She's got a point." Zack's agreement only adds to my annoyance. "I don't know why you've never liked Carter. He's a good guy."

I press my lips together, fighting the urge to argue with him. Zack depends on Carter to fund their real estate business, so he's loyal. But when you get into bed with the devil, you're going to get burned. No matter how many times I've warned Zack, he doesn't see it.

"Agree to disagree."

Zack sighs heavily. "Look, I'm asking as a personal favor, plus I'll buy you all the books you could ever want, and Carter really will pay you. All he needs are a couple of tutoring sessions on art so he can approach this potential client. I know you don't care, but he needs a win."

My brother cannot be serious right now. But he seems to be. "Carter's whole life is one big Powerball lottery prize."

"I'm surprised at you," Zack says with a judgmental frown. "You know better than anyone that money isn't everything and doesn't make you happy. Like you, you might struggle some-times, but you stay strong on doing what you love because it's what makes you happy. I've always admired that."

That was actually . . . sweet, which is not something I'm used to hearing from my brother.

"For people like Carter and me, closing a solid deal is what makes us happy."

There go any warm fuzzies I might've been developing. That's part of the problem I have with Carter. He's turned Zack into whoever this is sitting across from me.

"Do it for me, Moony," he asks sweetly. "Please?"

Ugh. He pulled out the nickname only he has ever been allowed to use because he's the one who gave it to me. Appar-ently, I went through a bit of a nudist phase as a toddler and liked to run around the house naked. That, coupled with my name, earned me the nickname 'Full Moon', which was short-ened to Moony over time. And using that means he's pulling out the big guns.

I roll my eyes dramatically. "Fine, but no promises. I can't possibly make him an expert in a "couple" of tutoring sessions. Tell him to meet me at my place tomorrow at eight P.M. sharp. I'm only doing this for you, and I already regret it."

"It'll be fine. He just needs to be conversational. And thank you."

Zack stands, probably trying to make a run for it before I change my mind, but I clear my throat. "Unless you're leaving your card with me, we have some shopping to do before you go."

He laughs and throws a twenty on the table for Lydia. Considering he only got a cup of coffee and she packed my salad and latte to-go, that's generous. I hate to admit it, because I do live frugally to be able to chase my passions, but money is a necessity and Lydia will be grateful for the tip on a slow Monday night.

But my Mama didn't raise a fool, and I'm still getting the new books Zack promised me. "Come on, the art history section is back here."

CHAPTER
THREE
CARTER

I LOOK UP and down the hall as I wait for Luna to answer her door. The building isn't what I expected for Zack's little sister. He owns several rental properties, a couple of Airbnbs, a commercial strip mall that's fully occupied, and his own home. Yet, his sister is living one step above a dorm. It's clean, but bland and basic.

The door opens, and I forget all about the boring building. She's . . . *a vision.*

"What're you doing here? Our session isn't till eight."

Her hair is piled on top of her head, her black-rimmed glasses are slid down her nose, her pink sweatpants are slung around her hips, and her cropped gray T-shirt has fallen off her shoulder to reveal the straps of a white sports bra. For some reason, there's also a black smudge on her right cheek.

And it's cute as *fuck.*

"Huh?" I ask in confusion. She makes it sound like I'm interrupting something in her busy schedule. There's only one issue with that. "It's two minutes after."

"What?" Her brows scrunch together in confusion as she looks over her shoulder. She must see a clock somewhere because she shrugs carelessly. "Oh. I was doing yoga, and then I got caught up with work, I guess. Come in."

Inside, I'm greeted with a tiny studio filled with a hodgepodge of furniture that reminds me of a post-college dumpster diving collection. Not that I ever did that. My college experience was one of private apartments decorated by the designer my mother hired, and since then, my homes have been the same.

But where my homes have abstract, forgettable art to fill the walls, Luna's apartment is filled with canvases in a myriad of styles. From here, I can see every wall of the small space, each of them covered floor to ceiling with colorful pops of eye candy. There's so much to look at that I can't even absorb it all at once. "Interesting place."

"Interesting," Luna says, though I'm not sure whether she's echoing me or making her own comment on my judgment. She walks past me into the single room. "Have a seat."

She gestures to the small couch that's covered in a patchwork quilt and takes the chair for herself, curling up cross-legged in it. Behind her glasses, her gaze is hard and accusatory, but I don't know why.

"Thank you again for doing this. It'll really help me out," I try, hoping to garner some favor.

"Zack told me to name my price, so . . . so it's five hundred dollars an hour."

I cough, choking on my own saliva. "Five hundred an hour?" Finding my voice again, I snipe, "I wasn't expecting you to be a gold digger."

Her cheeks flush immediately. "I'm not, but I'm also not stupid, and Zack has beaten negotiating tactics into my head since I was a kid. You need me more than I need you," she explains, but she shifts in her seat, telling me that she's not as confident as she's trying to appear. "I could just as easily work tonight. Plus, you can afford it."

"You're taking advantage of me because I'm wealthy?" Despite whatever Zack has taught her, Luna has always seemed like more of an intellect than a financial whiz, so I'm surprised she's going straight for my wallet.

"No. I'm charging an extra handling fee because I have to *handle* being around you." As soon as the words leave her lips, she slaps her hands over her mouth. From behind her spread fingers, she tells me, "Sorry, that was rude. I shouldn't have said it aloud."

Unperturbed, I laugh at her reaction. "Am I that annoying?"

She shrugs, her eyes dropping to her lap where she's wringing her fingers.

"Do I make you nervous?"

"No." Her answer is quick, and a total lie. "Agree to the price and we can get started."

I stall as long as I can, but she's got me dead to rights. I want the Cartwright deal, which means I need to learn something useful about art, and Luna's my only and best option. "Deal."

A high-pitched squeal erupts from Luna as she kicks her feet wildly, fluttering them in the air. I think it surprises us both, but she composes herself quickly and says, "That'll help with my publishing costs."

I have no idea what she's talking about, but if it makes her willing to help me, it works for me.

Hopping up, she grabs a stack of notecards from the mess of a countertop that seems to serve as a makeshift desk. When she sits back down, I can see that they're some sort of study guides. That she took the time to make them tells me that while she might not want to do this, she is taking it seriously. It's a good sign.

"Are those for me?" I ask, pointing at the cards.

She hugs them tightly to her chest as though I've suggested taking her kidneys out and leaving her in the bathtub to bleed out alone. "No, these are mine from college. Art 101."

I hold up both hands to show that I have zero intention of snatching the cards from her grasp.

"Okay, first let's see where you're at knowledge-wise. Tell me three painters you know," she says, sounding like a teacher.

And like a fool, my brain completely blanks. I'm not overly informed about art, but I have the same general education about it that most folks do. "Uhm . . . Michelangelo?"

"And?"

Luna already looks disappointed in me. The frown on her full lips only deepens when I go silent, my eyes rolling back as if I can find additional names in my brain. "I know this. Like, the Mona Lisa. It was made by . . ."

"Painted by, not 'made'. Machines are made, cakes are baked, paintings are painted," she corrects, holding up a finger.

"Right, the Mona Lisa was painted by Da Vinci!" I'm ridiculously excited to remember something so basic.

"That's two, and good job on knowing both the artist and the art. One more?" she prompts with a smile.

"I'm not a toddler," I snap. "I don't need pity praise." I don't say it, but it sounds like something my mother would do with us kids when we were little. No matter how good or bad we were at something, in our mother's eyes, we deserved a head pat of congratulations. I'm sure she meant it to be encouraging, and when I was younger, perhaps it was, but somewhere along the way, I realized that doing my best wasn't much different from barely squeaking by in her eyes. Fastidiously, I adjust my watch and the cuffs of my shirt until they're perfect, consciously avoiding explaining my reaction to Luna's simple words.

She studies me with interest. "I wouldn't have thought a guy like you ever got nervous."

With my hackles already up, that hits harder than it normally would, digging in deep. Pressing my lips into a flat line, I question, "A guy like me? What's that supposed to mean?"

"I didn't mean—" She stops herself. "Well, maybe I did. But you're just all . . ." She waves her hands in my direction. "Hot shot, big wig, thirst trap. It's kinda nice to see that you're not perfect." Her head drops a bit, her eyes falling back to her lap where the notecards rest.

"Definitely not perfect," I reply, using my time to correct her. "Obviously, given that I need art tutoring and can't think of three painters when put on the spot."

Self-deprecation isn't my style, but I'm being truthful. I hope Luna can respect that at least.

She looks up, meeting my eyes, and I can see her thoughts whirling behind hers. I'm not sure how we've gotten off on the wrong foot, but we have. I resort to my usual charm and say teasingly, "And don't think I missed you calling me a thirst trap."

"Of course that's all he heard," she whispers to herself. Louder, she asks, "Can we get back to these?" She holds up the flashcards, and I nod, thankful for a truce.

I still feel like there's some unspoken issue between us, but she's helping me and that's all I need. I don't need Zack's little sister to like me or for us to become besties. We have nothing in common, she's ridiculously young, and Zack would kill me anyway.

But an hour later, I'm honestly impressed with Luna. Her knowledge of art is expansive and her passion for it is beyond obvious. She speaks of brushstrokes the way most people talk about their children—fondly, in depth, and emotionally.

On the other hand, I'm struggling. Majorly.

We've been through the same set of basic flashcards multiple times, and while I thought I was doing well for a bit, Luna recognized that I'd only memorized the order, not the actual answers. She shuffled them, and suddenly, we were nearly back to square one.

"What's this one?" she asks, holding up a painting of a group of white-collared men gathered around the deathbed of another man, his arm dissected.

"Renoir," I say with surety.

Luna pushes her glasses up onto her head, looking at me closely. "Seriously? Renoir and Rembrandt both start with R, but that's about where the similarities end. A trick I used with the outreach kids is to remember that Rembrandt has a D in his name, so his paintings were darker. Literally, the backgrounds are darker and there's an ominous nature to them. Renoir sounds a little like air, and his paintings are light as air, showing the activity of a bustling Paris. Does that help?"

I flop back on the couch, a concerning creak sounding out from somewhere under the quilt. I consider that I might end up on my ass in more than one way . . . from Luna's couch breaking beneath me and with Mrs. Cartwright if I can't sort this out.

I rub my eyes with the heels of my palms, appreciating the

sparkles behind my lids as much, if not more than, all the art flashcards. "This is never going to work. It's going to be worse than my just admitting I know nothing about art. I wish you could just come with me. You could do the art talk, and I could do the money talk."

Luna laughs, thinking I'm kidding.

But . . . I sit up suddenly, struck with my brilliance. "That's it! It's perfect!"

Still shaking her head at the idea, Luna says, "No way. Nopity, nope, nope. No freakin' way, count me out. And did I mention . . . no."

I stand up, the idea taking shape in my mind. "We could say that you're my assistant and working with me for the portfolio management presentation."

Luna stands up too, her beloved cards falling to the floor. She's a good foot shorter than me, but that doesn't stop her from putting her hands on her hips and squaring up. "Your assistant? Why? Because I'm young? Or because I'm a woman?" She shakes her head, the messy bun on her head flopping around wildly. "I shouldn't be surprised from you."

"What?" I have no idea what she's upset about. I only meant that could be a cover story so she could go with me to Mrs. Cartwright's for the meeting, but she's acting angrier than a honey badger.

She's mumbling under her breath, and I strain to make out what she's saying. It sounds like, "Assistant? Unbelievable! Just because I have a vajayjay doesn't mean all I'm good for is taking notes and looking pretty. Not that I'm pretty."

"You're very pretty, Luna," I reply, surer that I heard that part correctly than the rest of it.

She stomps her foot like a pissed off gnome. I definitely do not notice that it makes her shapely thighs and voluptuous breasts wobble as she does it because Zack would cut my dick off for looking at his little sister that way. Still . . .

"You should go now," she orders flatly.

"Wait. I'm sorry. We were doing well with the cards. Maybe we can flip through them a bit more?" I bend down to pick them up, but the suggestion falls on deaf ears as Luna strides toward the door, giving me her back as answer.

"Tomorrow, then?" I try as she opens the door. I consider that she might actually bodily shove me out and for a moment think that I'd like to see her try. Her fire is intriguing, especially when it pops up unexpectedly, taking her from quiet and bookish to badass and confident in an instant. But I squash that idea down quickly.

"I work tomorrow. Good luck scamming the old lady out of her money, Carter."

And with that, she yanks the cards from my hand and shuts the door in my face. I stand there in shock, not sure how everything went wrong. Well, it started wrong, but we were doing well there for a while. Until it all went haywire again.

But Harringtons aren't quitters, and if I let a small setback derail me every time one came up, I'd never be a successful businessman. I saw Luna's passion for art and her need for money, and I'm not above using those things to persuade her to continue to help me.

CHAPTER
FOUR
LUNA

"WHEW, I'm glad that tour is done!"

School field trip groups are typically my favorite visitors to the art museum where I work, because the younger kids are so unfiltered and the older kids are usually art lovers already.

But the group I had this afternoon was a doozy. One kid kept trying to touch the paintings, and another was making inappropriate comments about every centuries-old sculpture. He even pretended to spank a dyad's ass.

And the poor teacher was trying to be in five places at once with octopus arms to keep each kid safely corralled while preventing damage to the museum's pieces.

So I'm admittedly grateful to see that particular school bus pulling away.

"Well, I hope your tank still has some gas in it, girl. You've got a four o'clock tour now," Maeve informs me.

Maeve is basically the boss of the museum. She usually stays buried in the administrative tasks, keeping us funded and running. But it's not unusual to see her walking the floor, her colorful outfits almost works of art themselves. Today, her gray hair is pulled back to give her teal hat the spotlight, which matches her multi-colored wrap dress and contrasts with her bright red loafers and lipstick. She's what every cool sixty-year-old woman dreams of being on their best day.

Shoot, she's what I dream of being at twenty-three.

"A four o'clock? That wasn't on the schedule this morning." I look at my phone to confirm. Nope, schedule clear. And after the insanity of my last three-hour tour, I was looking forward to a cold cereal dinner with a fruit punch, truly like a real adult after a long day, not another couple of hours of WWE-meets-art lecture with kids who scatter like wolf spider babies.

Please let it be a couple of tourists who want a show-and-tell tour.

"It was booked today, actually. A private tour at that, with a special request for you as the guide," she confides slyly. I know what she's thinking . . . the cost of a private tour will be a boon for the monthly museum budget.

But I have a sinking suspicion that I know exactly who would book a private, last-minute tour with me.

An hour later, my suspicions are confirmed when I arrive at the main desk only to find Carter there, leaning against the counter and at least halfway to charming the panties off the receptionist with his toothpaste-commercial smile and naughty-glint eyes.

Before he notices me, I take a moment to look him up and down. He's objectively attractive, of course, but I've always felt that there's something dark beneath his squeaky-clean exterior.

For him, I think he's dressed casually in slacks that are likely part of his daily suit and a button-up shirt that he's undone at the throat after ditching the tie. Vaguely, I wonder if he ever gets down and dirty, and an image of him climbing into bed in one of those old-man, two-piece matching pajama sets makes me giggle internally.

Right at that moment, it's like he senses me because he looks my way, catching me grinning like a loon right at him. Of course, he thinks I'm smiling because he's here, the idea that I'm laughing at him never once occurring to him.

"Well, hello, Luna," he drawls out, seeming pleased to see me. Or tickled that he's busted me mooning over him like the receptionist and every other woman he encounters.

Prickles run along my arms, and my own response to his

honeyed voice saying my name all sexy like that annoys me. "What're you doing here?"

His blue eyes go frosty, but he shrugs as though my challenge is no big deal. "Getting the help I need. I don't give up easily, or ever." He shoots a cheesy wink at the receptionist who's probably sitting in a puddle of her own making.

I take a big breath to steel myself. "Fine. We'll start with the medieval torture devices."

We don't even have those, but right now, I'm wishing we had an entire wing of them so that I could put Carter on a rack and stretch him until he was as long and elastic as Gumby.

"For my use or yours?" Carter quips with a sly lift of his brow. When my jaw drops in shock, he holds his hands up and grins that panty-melting smile. "No judgment if that's what you're into."

"I could be into that," the receptionist offers with a twirl of her hair.

"Argh,' I growl. "Come on."

I lead him to the Impressionist section first, showcasing the single Monet painting we've acquired that is the capstone of our collection. In full tour guide mode, I tell him, "This was loaned to the museum by an anonymous donor. It's been on display here for over ten years and seen by thousands of visitors. If you'll notice, looking at the piece overall, the way he used light and shadow creates a sense of vibrant movement even though the subject is a still-frame capture." I pause, waiting for Carter to agree, and once he nods, I continue. "Moving closer, you can see that the way he does that is through small brush strokes going all different directions to create that fluidity. For example, here." I point to the lower portion of the painting where there's a section of greenery in the foreground that appears to be blowing in an invisible wind.

"I can see what you're talking about." Carter seems surprised himself, but no more so than I am. It gives me a little hope as we walk through the rest of the Impressionist area, moving into post-Impressionist and then toward more modern artists. He's an attentive student, and as we go, I forget my official tour guide capacity and start talking about the art for real with Carter, sharing my thoughts, not just quoting the approved speeches about each piece.

Standing in front of a Picasso, Carter tilts his head left and then right, looking at it with a furrowed brow.

"What does it make you feel?" I ask.

"Huh?" Carter says, now looking straight on at the piece.

"All art is created from emotion. The artist sees something, whether with their eyes or their mind, and feels something within their soul. The art, or painting in this case, is merely the method the artist uses to convey that emotion. There's no right or wrong answer, though, in what the viewer feels when seeing the art. That's the beauty of it."

"I feel . . ." He pauses and then admits, "confused."

I laugh lightly. "That's completely valid. Especially with pieces like this that challenge what you see with your eyes. I mean, obviously, people don't look like this, exactly, but it was Picasso's perception of them. Take the line of the eyes here. Most people have eyes that are unilateral." I hold my hand flat at my eye level, showing that mine are even. "What could he be saying about this person by painting their eyes off a linear line?"

Carter pops off. "That he was drunk, high, or both, and seeing double?"

Disappointment floods me. He's been doing well, listening and responding thoughtfully, but I'm trying to push him beyond the technicalities of the art. If he truly wants to impress his client, the deeper meanings will be key. He can't just read the name on the painting and start repeating a Wikipedia page by rote memory. Well, I guess he could, but something tells me that won't be enough for this client.

He could just smile at her and she'd probably hand over the passwords to her whole portfolio.

"Try again," I challenge. "Think deeper."

His lips purse, and I realize that what I said could be easily misconstrued. Thankfully, he doesn't make a juvenile joke about 'I'll show you deeper' like most man-child types would.

"Okay, the eyes are—as my grandma would say—cattywampus. I'm trying to think what she would say about someone like that." I watch him as he stares contemplatively at the painting, and his entire mood shifts into something serious and introspective, which is somehow more attractive than his typical gregarious charm. "Someone who always thinks there's something better around the corner. Like they're here with you" —he points at the painted eye that seems to be in the correct placement and then moves to the other— "but they're always on the lookout for something better or different. Distracted by what could be or what they could have. Like being with you in the moment isn't enough."

My heart skips a beat as my jaw drops. "Wow," I say breathily. "That's . . . really good."

"You don't have to seem so surprised. I'm not all dashing good looks and Southern charm. I've got a brain in this head too." He taps his temple with one of those panty-melting smiles, seemingly not offended at my over-the-top reaction, but it feels a bit forced and there's a blankness in his eyes that wasn't there a few moments ago when he was talking about the meaning in the Picasso.

"No, I didn't mean . . ." He gives me a sharp look, and I confess, "Okay, maybe I did. I'm sorry. I shouldn't have assumed you couldn't grasp what I was talking about. That was rude of me."

"Apology accepted." He dips his chin once, and with that, it's like the whole thing never happened. He says brightly, "Where's your favorite piece in the whole museum?"

Interesting. It seems Carter has a deeper side than maybe I'd considered, but he keeps it hidden away. I can understand that. It's not like we're besties. I'm just a means to an end for him, but for a moment there, I could see more to him. And that 'more' is way more interesting than Carter's usual façade.

"This way," I tell him, leading him toward the piece that I love the most in the entire museum. I'm actually a teensy bit curious what Carter's take will be on it.

Please don't let him say something stupid like 'I could do that in five minutes' or 'he really put his all *into it' about the white splashes.* I hear comments like that too often, and they infuriate me with their dismissiveness of the talent behind the piece.

The large Jackson Pollock is a relatively new addition to our collection, and anytime I have a few moments, I like to sit and study it, finding something different in the layers of wild colors each time. It gives me a lift when I begin to feel like my work is never going to be enough, or seen, or valued. I pour all of myself into Alphena, and somehow, the chaos on the Pollock canvas makes that feel like a normal and reasonable thing to do.

I stand in front of the piece silently, hoping that Carter can see some of the magic he saw in the Picasso painting in this one as well. Unexpectedly, Carter drops to a knee beside me, and at first, I think he's fallen. Maybe he passed out or spontaneously hurt his leg?

I gasp, "Are you okay?"

He looks at me from a crouched position and reaches for my hand. I reach back to help him get up, still confused on how he ended up on the floor, but he doesn't stand. No, he holds my hand in his warm, large one and gazes up at me with a strange look in his eyes.

"Luna, thank you for sharing your days with me, and your nights. I hope to share a lifetime of them together with you as my wife. Will you marry me?"

"What?" I manage to squeak out.

Did he bump his head somehow? Is he having a stroke?

My focus shrinks and time rolls in slow motion. I watch as his Adam's apple bobs up and down with a thick swallow, and then he smiles and tiny lines sprout beside his eyes, which are so blue and locked on me in a way that makes my whole body freeze in place. Squeezing my hand, he repeats more clearly, "Will you marry me?"

That's what I thought he said, but it makes absolutely zero sense. We barely know each other and don't even like each other. We're ridiculously incompatible, my awkwardness and his smooth charm a piss-poor fit. And again . . . *what?*

Through the fog of my confusion, I hear a voice cry out, "If you don't say yes, I will, honey!"

I look around to see that we've gathered an audience of onlookers who have their hands clasped over their mouths or at their chests, eyes wide with excitement over witnessing what must look like a romantic proposal. It's my worst nightmare come to life, or one of them, at least.

I can feel my mouth opening and closing as I look back to Carter. "I . . . I . . ."

He pushes a ring onto my left ring finger and then stands, grabbing me around the waist in one movement. He spins me in a circle wildly, my feet flailing through the air. Applause surrounds us and then . . .

Carter. Freaking. Harrington. Kisses me. Right on the lips, like he has any right to.

My first thought is that he's a great kisser—his lips soft, his mouth warm, and his breath minty. My second thought is . . .

"Put me down!" I shout, slapping at his shoulders.

The onlookers laugh, and a lady says, "Let him pick you up while y'all can still do that." I glance over to see her smiling lovingly at the wrinkled and hunched man at her side.

Carter chuckles at the woman's comment like this whole thing is some big joke and whispers roughly in my ear, "Smile, Luna."

The heat of the words and the gruffness of the order surprise me, but what surprises me more is the shiver that runs down my spine. I look at Carter, whose lips are entirely too close to mine again. I wiggle, looking for the stability of the floor because the foundation of my world has gone wobbly.

I don't like Carter Harrington, so why is it suddenly so hot in here? And why did he propose to me?

Carter lowers me but keeps me tucked into his side with a tight arm around my shoulders, smiling at the crowd like he's the mayor as he accepts their congratulations and well wishes. I'm too awkward and too confused to move away, my feet frozen in place and my face a mask of puzzlement.

That only gets worse when Zack steps out from around the

corner with a victorious smile. "Got it!" he shouts, holding up his phone.

The crowd begins to dissipate, leaving the three of us alone with the Jackson Pollock painting that I'm definitely never going to look at the same way again.

"What?" I push away from Carter, feeling like Zack caught us doing something wrong. I won't admit to anyone, not even myself, that I feel the loss of the weight of his arm around my shoulders. And I totally don't stumble as I put space between us because my whole world just went . . . what did Carter say his grandmother called it? Cattywampus—that's it. That's what I am. But I'm fighting my way back to even-keeled with every passing second.

Carter flashes me a sheepish smile. It's one I'm sure has gotten him out of trouble his entire life, but it's not working on me. Not now.

"I got to thinking last night after we talked. I do wish you could be there to help me, but if not . . ." He pauses and gives me a hopeful look as though I've reconsidered and decided to go along with his plan for me to be his assistant. I cross my arms in response. "Right, so if you're not there, I can at least say that I have an art-loving wife. And now I have a sweet story, with video proof, of how I got engaged on a private tour at the museum in front of her favorite piece in the collection."

I stare disbelievingly at him, trying in vain to process how something so outlandish could possibly seem like a reasonable idea to him. I mean, I'm the creative type and he's all-business, so it'd seem like the roles should be reversed here, but somehow, he's the one living in a completely upside-down, alternative universe.

"That's your grand plan? Instead of bonding over art itself, you're going to . . ."

I trail off, and he nods. "Say you're my wife. So any mistakes I make, I can play off as 'must've misheard the wife' and it becomes endearing rather than stupid."

"That's ridiculous."

"You mispronounced brilliant," Carter corrects me.

"It was my idea," Zack adds. "Carter told me about the assistant thing, and really, there's no need for it to be such a thing, Luna. He just needs a good sales pitch." He makes it sound like I overreacted to something completely sensible.

I'm not a sales pitch. I don't have any skin in the game with whatever stupidity Carter is going to pull. I trust there to be karmic justice sometime, when he'll have to answer for his own lies and scheming. But Zack? It hurts that he can reduce my love of art . . . no, my existence . . . down to 'useful as a sales pitch'. It shows just how far under Carter's spell he's fallen and how far guys like them will go to seal the deal.

I'm furious. I can feel the heat rushing through my veins and hot tears threatening to spill. Not because I'm sad. I'm just one of those unlucky people who cries when I'm angry. I hate it. It always makes me feel like I look weak at the moment I'm trying to appear strongest.

I manage to squeak out to Carter, "You're exactly who and what I thought you were. I'm disappointed that you fooled me for even a moment into thinking you might be something more." He's gone stone still, other than the clenching of his jaw. To Zack, I ask, "You came up with this? Business at all costs, I guess, huh?"

And with that, the tears escape so I whirl and run away. I'm sure it looks like I'm some tantruming child pitching a hissy fit with my outburst, waterworks, and escape for the hills. But it can't be helped.

CHAPTER
FIVE
CARTER

I REVIEW the file in front of me once more, then close my eyes. I'm ready for this. I've prepped the same way I have for every other deal I've sealed over the last decade. I just really need a win right now. Especially after the mess I made of things at the museum.

I knew Luna would be surprised at the fake proposal. That was the point. Now, if I need to show a cute video of my art-obsessed wife, it'll look like I'm a romantic husband who swept her off her feet. I'm all about putting my best foot forward, especially for a deal like this.

But her reaction shocked me. Neither Zack nor I expected her to freak out so badly. Especially when everything had been going so well for the tour. I was having fun with Luna, listening to her talk about the art and seeing her in a new role where she's comfortable and confident.

And then it all went to shit.

But it'll be worth it. It has to be. I still agree with Zack's assessment that this is my best option given the tutoring was a bust. And though he assured me that he'll make things up to Luna, I expect an extra 'tutoring' invoice from her for her trouble. I'll have to send it with some big apologies and maybe a Jackson Pollock coffee table book to smooth things over.

One little in with Mrs. Cartwright. That's all I need and this will be worth it. I can do the rest of the job of securing this deal with my skills, experience, and hard work. I'm ready for this.

I pick up my phone and dial, waiting nervously for the call to be picked up. I'm doing this myself, not having an assistant or associate reach out, because I want Elena Cartwright to know that I intend to provide the best degree of personal service I'm capable of. Plus, I know the value my last name and our company name carry and intend to leverage them as heavily as possible. "Hello, this is Carter Harrington with Blue Lake Asset group calling for Elena Cartwright, please," I tell the woman who answers the phone.

"Good news, young man . . . you've got her." She laughs, but it ends with a bit of a cough.

"Oh, good to speak with you, ma'am. I understand you are considering a new portfolio management firm," I say politely. "I would love to meet with you to see if our firm would be a good fit for your needs."

"The first thing I'm looking for is someone who'll leave all that pomp and circumstance behind. I don't need all that razzle-dazzle. Just call me Elena."

I blink in surprise. The older generation, particularly those with wealth, tend to want all the fanciness and then some. But I can be chill if that's what Mrs. Cartwright—I mean Elena —prefers.

With a chuckle, I mimic her casual tone. "Well, I can sure do that."

That seems to be the right thing to say because it opens the floodgates, and suddenly, Elena is telling me all about her portfolio, from properties to funds and more. Zack said she knows her stuff, but she's surprisingly well-versed on the details for someone with such a large and varied estate. And talking through what has been previously effective lets me see where I can offer something different to improve things for her.

"At this point, I'm not worried about much, darling. I've got more money than I could ever spend."

"Of course! You and Mr. Cartwright worked hard so your family could be well-cared for in generations to come."

"We made dang sure of it, I tell you that for sure. I've always handled the financial stuff, but Thomas had a good head on his shoulders too. But his true love—other than me, of course—was art. I can't tell you how many times that man painted me," she says wistfully.

I hope she means in a regal, Southern matriarch way, but her tone makes me think there are nude paintings of Elena Cartwright over their marital bed. *Draw me like one of your French girls* and all that.

The very idea is jarring.

But she's given me the opening I need. "I can understand that. My wife, Luna, is quite the art lover too. She's always going on about Rembrandt this and Pollock that, but my favorites are her own pieces. To see the way she creates . . . it's beautiful, magical."

I may not have seen anything Luna has personally painted, but the way she brought the art in the museum to life, I can imagine her doing the same with her own work.

"Oh, darling. That makes my heart melt like butter on a hot biscuit." She sounds a bit choked up, and I say a silent thank you to Luna. "I tell you what, let's have us a bit of dinner this weekend and we can talk about my portfolio. Do you need to check with Luna's schedule to see when she's available?"

What? Why would I need to do that?

And then it hits me.

Elena means dinner with me . . . and Luna. My wife, Luna.

"Oh, I'm not sure she can. She's so busy, you know, and I try not to bore her with too much work talk," I say, hoping Elena can be charmed into meeting with only me.

"Nonsense. If she's an art lover, she'd never forgive you if she missed out on seeing Thomas's collection. I wouldn't want you to be in the dog house. Why, I remember one time Thomas went to town with a friend. They were going to play a round of golf or something, I forget what. But they went to the movie theater instead, and he saw that tornado movie without me. You know the one with that cutie-patootie Bill Paxton? He knew how much I liked that fella, so whoo-boy, I was hotter'n an August day in

Atlanta. Made that man sleep on the couch for two solid nights."

"You didn't," I tease, following along with her dramatic storytelling.

"You betch'ur bottom I did, but do you know how he got out of the doghouse?" She pauses, and I can sense her smile through the phone. "He set us up a little picnic out back at sunset, and we had ourselves ice cream sundaes for dinner. He knew that ice cream is the way to my heart because we'd gone for milkshakes on our first date."

"Sounds like he was a good husband, even though he didn't take you to see *Twister*," I agree.

"Oh, he took me, alright. I made him go watch it again. With me."

I laugh in surprise. For such a wealthy, influential couple, it sounds like the Cartwrights were remarkably normal. Maybe even a bit simple in their lives together.

"That's why I'm tellin' you, you'd best bring your Luna to see this art or you're going to be sleeping on the couch and planning ice cream dates." Her voice has gone from congenial to hard, as though testing to see whether I'll accept her wise advice.

I don't think. I don't consider. I certainly don't plan, which is my *modus operandi*. But nevertheless, the words spill out. "Of course, I'm sure she'd be thrilled to come."

———

I knock on Luna's door with my heart in my throat and my head buzzing. I've fucked up and I know it, but I'll fight to see if there's any way at all I can rescue this messy situation I've gotten myself into. Hopefully, Luna's calmed down and Zack's smoothed things over with her too because I'm about to throw a whole new cow in this tornado a la Elena Cartwright.

But it isn't Luna who answers the door.

"Who're you?" a tall, slender brunette demands. She's about

Luna's age and dressed in wide-legged slacks and a tank-style blouse. Her makeup is expertly applied and her hair looks as though she's had it professionally styled. The only thing missing to complete the picture of the perfect businesswoman are the shoes, as her bare toes wiggle on the wood floor of Luna's apartment.

"Uhm, I'm looking for Luna." I glance around, double checking that I haven't gone to the wrong apartment, but behind the woman, I can see Luna's art-filled space.

"Didn't answer the question. Try again." The order is mildly softened by the glint in her eyes as she openly assesses me with a look up and down.

"That's Carter Harrington, Zack's friend and all-around annoying scammer in a business suit," Luna's voice calls out, sounding flat and dull.

The woman in the doorway goes near feral in an instant. Stabbing a perfectly manicured finger into my chest, she charges, "You're the asshole who fucked over my friend and made a fool of her at the one place she feels most at home? Should've known."

She's much harsher than Luna, but the insult doesn't hurt nearly as much as Luna's does.

"I didn't make a fool of her," I argue. Deciding I need to handle this at the source, I push past the woman and into the apartment to find Luna sitting on the kitchen countertop.

She's wearing shorts and a baggy T-shirt, and she looks lost —her skin bare and pale, her eyes vacant, and though she's sitting cross-legged and upright, there's something that makes it feel as though she's shrinking away from me.

"Luna? What's wrong?" I go up to her, setting the bag I brought with me on the counter next to her. My first instinct is to gather her in my arms, which surprises me. I'm not usually overtly caring that way, but something about Luna in this moment makes me want to pull her into me and press my lips to her hair soothingly.

But she flinches away from me. "Seriously?" she says quietly.

"I was hoping Zack had—"

She huffs. "Zack and I are fine. You and I are not."

Okay, apparently Zack only fixed one problem. I don't know how he did it, but I wish I had a secret Luna language book right about now so I could do the same.

"Back away from her and no one gets hurt," the woman from the doorway orders as she holds up karate hands.

"Samantha, Carter . . . Carter, Samantha," Luna says, gesturing from the woman to me and back.

"I'd say nice to meet you, but that'd make me a liar and I pride myself on honesty, so . . . yeah, hard no to that." She frowns at my outstretched hand as her hands go to her hips. "Because from what I hear, you pulled a ridiculous stunt . . . proposing to Luna, who you hardly know, at her job, where she felt pressured to go along with it so she wouldn't look stupid to her coworkers and the guests, and catching it on video, with her wearing what is unanimously voted the ugliest outfit in existence—I added that part myself—and ruining her favorite piece of art with a super stressful memory, just so you can get some poor old lady to give her money to *you*. Am I wrong?"

She sneers as though my very existence is distasteful and whatever I could say is most certainly going to be a lie.

"Well, that's not exactly—"

Luna cuts me off before I can even start. "I don't need you to protect me, Sam, even if you're on a pretty good roll—and absolutely accurate."

I can feel that the horrible summarization Samantha gave is likely word-for-word how Luna described it. She said she was disappointed in me. Honestly, at the time, the words had next to no impact on me.

I might be seen as successful, and my mom might give out praise for merely breathing. But in my family, it's well known that I run a far and trailing second behind my brother Cameron, especially in my dad's eyes, so I'm quite accustomed to ignoring disapproving comments. I should've given her words more consideration, not because of what she said but because of what it took for her to say them.

I swallow my pride and say the one thing I never admit. "I'm sorry. I did have fun with the tutoring and the tour, despite initially thinking art would be boring. I think that's because of the teacher." I smile, hoping to salvage things with Luna. I have zero hopes that she's going to help with my fake-wife situation with Elena at this point, but I would like to leave things friendly so that this whole mess doesn't affect her and Zack's relationship. And so that his birthday party next year isn't a completely painful clusterfuck.

"Keep it coming," Samantha tells me, waving her hand. "More groveling, Prince Charming. I'm sure you've got it in you —somewhere in that tall . . . muscular . . . Greek god body of yours." Samantha's eyes are tracing every inch of me with appreciation bordering on ogling. I don't think I could feel more exposed if I were a Thunder Down Under stripper on-stage in a G-string.

Luna laughs lightly, covering her mouth, but Samantha seems to have given her a boost. "Yeah, whatcha got?"

I glance between the two women, so different but asking for the same thing. With a resolved sigh, I go all in with full theatrics, dropping to the floor—on both knees so that there's no mistaking what I'm doing this time and clasping my hands in a pleading move.

"Luna," I say seriously, my eyes locked on hers. Slowly, as though she's a wounded bird that might fly away if startled, I place my hands on her bare knees. When she allows it with a tiny smile, I begin . . .

"I'm soooo sorry," I wail dramatically, flinging my head into her lap, my cheek pressed to her thigh. Though I'm close to a danger zone of contact, I look up at her from the submissive position with puppy dog eyes. "I never meant to hurt you. Please forgive me. I will never look at the scattered chaos of a Pollack again without thinking of you and our broken engagement," I howl as I shake her in my grip.

"Shh!" she hisses, but she's laughing as she swats at me. "My neighbors are going to call the cops if you keep that up!"

But then, we both laugh, and it feels like things might be okay. I sit back on the floor, my legs stretched out in front of me as I lean on the cabinets opposite Luna. "Also, someone very wise told me that one sure-fire way to get out of the doghouse was an ice cream sundae, so there's a couple in there." I point at the bag I dropped on the counter.

Samantha grabs it first. "If you think for one second that you're getting one of these, you are sorely mistaken."

Before I can argue or agree, Samantha already has both sundaes open and is licking the whipped cream off the top of one. Luna snatches a spoon from the dishes drying by the sink and digs into the other one.

"I wouldn't think of depriving y'all of a sundae." I wait a couple of bites and then ask, "Is it working?"

Luna flashes a look to Samantha, who lifts a shoulder. "You said he's a good kisser."

"Sa-man-tha!" Luna shouts, and that must be all the neighbors can handle because there's a loud *clunk* against the wall.

"Sorry!" Luna yells over a hunched shoulder. But she laughs like she's not that worried. "I'm always quiet, and the one time . . ."

"Did you say that?" I ask, curious beyond belief.

"What?"

"That I'm a good kisser."

"Maybe." She eats a bite of ice cream slowly, her cheeks hollowing as she sucks it from the spoon and her eyes fall as though she can't admit that while looking directly at me. It's sexier than it should be and my cock notices how much shapely leg her shorts reveal and that she's definitely not wearing a bra beneath her T-shirt. "Did you really enjoy the tour?" The question is weighted with meaning.

"I absolutely did." There's also a lot rolled into my simple statement. Warning sirens go off in my head, reminding me about who Luna is and who I am, so I back away from whatever's happening between us strategically. "But I still think Picasso was drunk as hell."

"He was a drinker, actually, but I wanted you to think beyond the obvious," Luna tells me with a sly smirk. "That's why I'm a good teacher."

"You are," I agree.

Despite my efforts, something electric and hot passes between us when our gazes lock. It feels important that Luna looks better than when I first got here. There's brightness in her cheeks, life in her eyes, and she's smiling now.

"Aww, aren't you two adorable," Samantha sing-songs.

"No," Luna says, shaking her head, "it's not like that."

"Yeah, not like that," I agree too quickly.

"Mm-hmm." Samantha doesn't sound convinced. "So, what happened with the old lady?"

Shit. I don't want to say that things have gotten so much worse, especially when Luna isn't mad at me. Because once she finds out what I've done, she's going to hit the roof. And Samantha is currently blocking my escape out the front door. She also sees me checking for an emergency exit and tilts her head, glaring at me as she holds up those karate hands again. "Like a Band-Aid, just rip it off, man."

"It went great, but also . . . horribly?" That's the best way I can describe it. Luna copies Samantha's previous waving hand gesture, silently telling me 'more'. Gritting my teeth, I confess, "I talked to her and things were going well. She's not as formal as I expected, but then . . . I told her about how much my wife loves art—"

"You actually told her that?" Luna gasps. "After everything I said at the museum?"

I shrug grudgingly. "It was the plan."

"Plans change!" Luna answers.

"I know." I look at the ceiling, hoping for divine intervention to explain to me how in the hell things got so out of hand.

"And then what?" Luna demands quietly.

"She invited us to dinner, said she'd love to show her husband's collection to an art lover."

Samantha laughs bitterly. "You mean your *wife*, the art lover?"

Luna is shaking her head with wide, horrified eyes. "I'm not doing that. There's no way."

"I know. I'll tell Elena that you're not feeling well or something," I promise.

"Another lie?"

Luna's accusation makes the dark pit in the base of my stomach grow bigger and deeper, and it hurts more than the routine comments my family make. I don't know why that's so, but the pain in her eyes is so different. It makes me want to soothe it in any way that I can.

"You're right. I'll tell Mrs. Cartwright that I'm not married," I vow stiffly, knowing I'll do no such thing. But Luna will never know one way or another, because after this, we'll go back to seeing each other occasionally with Zack as a middle man.

The idea is oddly discomforting.

Luna smiles, but then concern mars her brow. "Wait . . . Cartwright? Not as in, Thomas Cartwright?"

"Well, as in Elena Cartwright, but yeah, her husband was Thomas Cartwright. He was the art collector and his wife is managing their portfolio."

Luna hops from the counter and crouches down in front of me, her eyes completely wild as she plants her hands on my shoulders. "*The* Thomas Cartwright?" When I don't answer, she starts mindlessly shaking me and rambling rapid-fire, "Holy shit, you should've led with that, man. We could've avoided all this mess! Isn't the first rule of business to know what the other person values?" She pauses but doesn't seem to want an answer, so I stay quiet, having learned my lesson about the trouble my mouth can get me into. "Let me clue you in . . . I value Thomas Cartwright's private art collection that's rarely been seen in decades but is reported to have pieces from all the masters. Just hanging on the walls of his house, like they're no big deal."

She stands, pacing in the small space as she waves her hands around. I think she's picturing the supposed art and not trying to slap me, or at least I hope that's the case.

"Oh, yeah, that? It's a Degas." Hand flap. "Have you seen my Warhol? Right over here next to the Pollock!" Double hand flap. "I've considered bidding on a Kara Walker, but I want to find the one that inspires me."

That last one had a hand flip but it was more of 'fancy brag-gart at a cocktail party' type, especially given the forced tone. I've known more than a few of those folks. Carefully, I question, "Does that mean you'll come with me? As my wife?"

I feel like it's the most dangerous question I've ever asked, and I'm still stupidly sitting in the floor with Luna and Samantha between me and the door. There's a distinct possibility that I might be nothing more than a chalk outline on the kitchen floor by morning.

Nah, both of them are smart enough to hide your body so they don't get caught.

The unhelpful thought doesn't give me any peace as I wait for one or both women to attack me for daring to ask the question. I fight the urge to cover myself and at least protect my most sensi-tive of parts.

Luna freezes, looking down for a long moment as if consid-ering her answer carefully. When her eyes lift to meet mine, there's doubt, but she nods. "I can't believe I'm going to do this, but for someone like me, seeing those pieces is akin to a chance to hold the Holy Grail. I can't say no."

"Ooh, get it, girl!" Samantha squeals, now supportive of the whole lying situation if Luna's good with it.

CHAPTER
SIX
LUNA

"I'M gonna wear the little black dress I showed you," I tell Samantha again. She shoots me a dangerous look and I clamp my mouth shut. That lasts all of ten seconds before I remind her, "It fits, and it's perfectly respectable."

"You mean boring," she corrects, and then, with a sense of finality, says, "And still, no. You've worn that to a funeral and two weddings."

She leads me down the sidewalk of the fashion shopping district, stopping in front of stores that I would never give a second glance. Mostly because even the mannequins in the windows seem to be judging me with their faceless, eyeless aura of superiority. Admittedly, they're dressed better than I am, and I pulled on non-painty, non-lounge clothes today in an attempt to rise up to Samantha's style level.

I glance down at my black jeans, Converse, and plain green T-shirt and then over to Samantha, who's wearing leopard print trousers, a black V-neck blouse that shows a bit of cleavage, and red peep-toe shoes.

"Hey, do you have something going on today?" I ask, realizing she looks dressed for more than a day of shopping. I hope I'm not interrupting her day, but a sizable portion of my mind is also thinking that maybe I can still get out of this expedition and just wear the black dress. "If you have a date, we can skip this." I'm trying to be a good friend, but so is she.

Samantha and I met when she came to the museum for her Art 101 class, and she basically adopted me as her friend by force, for which I will forever be grateful. After double majoring in Psychology and Biology, she's now well into her graduate program specializing in sex therapy and likes to make me blush by sharing too much about her studies. Through her, I know way too much about kinks for someone who doesn't know if I even like vanilla. All jokes aside, she takes her schoolwork very seriously, saying she wants to help people live a full and fulfilling life. She leads a much more exciting life than I do for sure, dating guys of every type, which she says gives her 'stimulating intel' for the future. I wonder who she's seeing today.

"Not till later. You want to *come?*"

"Eek!" I exclaim. "No, no, no."

"Consent is key," Samantha agrees sagely.

"What if I don't consent to going into the store and trying on dresses that aren't going to fit anyway?" I'm exposing a bit of my own insecurity with the question. Places like this store don't dress people like me—short, curvy, and plain. They're for people like Samantha, who truly wakes up looking like a goddess.

Samantha opens the door and nearly shoves me inside. "Nice try, but this is your best option. Let's go."

I stumble over my own feet and right into the saleswoman inside, who I think has been watching me try to talk my way out of this.

"Ladies." Not exactly a friendly greeting, but before I know it, Samantha is explaining to her what I need.

"A fancy dinner?" the saleswoman repeats. She's staring at me as though my version of 'fancy' and hers couldn't possibly be the same thing. "I'm sure I can find you *something.*"

She gives me a shrewd look, and I feel like she's taking my measurements as accurately as if she had a tape measure choking my curves. But despite her words, she seems less than confident about fitting me.

Now that Samantha's gotten me in here, I'm committed to

this, and I stand up as straight as I can, still only reaching the lithe blonde's chest. "Can we skip the whole *Pretty Woman* moment? I have a black Amex card, courtesy of my dinner date, so if you can find something here . . ." I trail off and look around doubtfully to throw out the challenge, "I would appreciate it. Otherwise, I'm sure Samantha can find somewhere else willing to take my money."

The saleswoman takes the rebuke congenially, her customer service mask never slipping. "No need for that. I'll pull you some options if you'd like to look around."

Samantha claps her hands giddily. "Ooh, the claws are out! Let's get this party started! Bring the champagne too, Brenda."

"I'll do that first. I know how you are, Samantha," she teases with a wink, seeming much friendlier and more helpful now.

When she disappears, Sam starts shopping in force. Walking to the nearest rack, she begins flipping through the dresses. "First off, good job standing up for yourself with Brenda."

The compliment is appreciated. Sam knows that on the pages of Alphena, I can do or say anything, but in real life, it's another matter altogether. One I'm working on. But she's not done. "Second, you need something that'll knock Carter on his ass."

"What? No, I don't," I warn. "I need something appropriate for dinner. That's it. Carter has nothing to do with it."

"Your husband has nothing to do with it?" Samantha taunts.

Husband.

My fake husband, Carter Harrington, my brother's best friend.

This is nothing like me. I don't do wild, outlandish things. I'm boring as hell, disappearing into a world of my own creation with Alphena for days or weeks on end.

Panic shoots through me. "Oh, my God!"

Brenda pops up like a groundhog from a rack across the room. "Everything okay, ladies?"

Samantha waves her off. "Yeah, we're good. She just realized that she's gonna need to shave her kitty cat before dinner."

Brenda blinks, clearly shocked but fighting to keeping a

neutral face. "I could have the drugstore deliver . . . uhm, supplies?"

"You're a doll, but no need. The dinner is tomorrow. She'll take care of things tonight."

With a grateful nod, Brenda disappears back into her search.

"Samantha." I shake my head, my eyes unfocused as I realize the full scope of what I've promised to do. In the moment, the possibility of seeing the art got to me, but this is so much bigger than that. I have to play the part of Carter's wife. And I couldn't be a worse match for a man like Carter. Nobody will believe he and I are a couple.

"I told you this whole thing is absurd," Samantha says, "and that's saying something, when even I'm reigning you in. I'm usually the one telling you to get out there and experience life, not just draw about it."

"I don't know if I can do this," I confess.

"Not like this, you can't," Brenda interrupts, walking up with an armful of dresses. "But there's not much you can't do in the right outfit. Let's go."

Numbly, I follow her to the fitting rooms and let her help me into a dress. I instantly feel like I'm playing dress-up in someone else's closet, but Brenda exclaims, "This is so you!"

She doesn't even know me. That's obvious given this red dress with a neckline somewhere below my sternum.

Back in the shop, Samantha bursts out in laughter. "If you were going to a strip club, that'd be perfect. But for dinner? Absolutely not. Your tits, while fabulously motorboat worthy, are one breath away from popping out. Venus may've free boobed it, but you cannot."

Around 'strip club', I'm offended, but by the time Sam mentions Venus . . . "You do listen to me when I talk about art, don't you? That's so sweet." Touched, I place my hands over my heart and find bare skin. "Oh!" My breasts are not just showing off, they're showing *out*.

"Of course I listen," she preens. "Now take that off." She wiggles her fingers at me to shoo me back to the fitting room, and I hear her tell Brenda, "Less slutty, more sensual."

I try on a few more dresses, each of them okay but not *it*. Until the last one.

"Carter's jaw is going to hit the floor when you walk out in that. It's perfect."

When I look in the mirror, I think Samantha and Brenda might actually be right. I never think of myself as a sexy woman, but in this green dress, I am. My curves are whiplash worthy, my breasts are pushed up to be shapely but not overly exposed, and my ass is guaranteed to bounce a quarter. Best of all, the knee-length skirt and short sleeves keep it modest enough for dinner at the Cartwright estate.

When Brenda walks off to look for jewelry, Samantha purses her lips. "Okay, you've got the body armor for dinner, but are you sure about this?"

Looking at my reflection, I'm more ready than I was before we got here, but still . . . "No, not at all sure. But ugh . . ." I groan. "Sam, some of the pieces in this collection haven't been seen in decades. The list of what Thomas Cartwright purchased, as well as his own paintings, is more supposition than fact. The last time I saw even a guess at a list was when *Art World* did a story about an insurance company agreeing to cover the collection, and a few of the pieces were named. Now I have a chance to see them first-hand, with Elena Cartwright herself as a tour guide. As crazy as it is, I have to do this or I'll never forgive myself."

Samantha tilts her head, mulling over what I've said. Finally, she says, "Okay, if you say so. But I'm not talking about the art. I'm talking about Carter. You're stepping into dangerous territory with a man like that. I mean, he's . . . him."

"I know, and I'm me," I say bitterly, turning away from the mirror. "I'm out of my league."

"That's not what I mean and you know it," she corrects firmly. "I'm worried about Carter."

"You think I can't handle him?"

"I think he's a do-or-die businessman who's obviously willing to go to major lengths and lie through his professionally-whitened teeth without losing a wink of sleep at night. But that's not how you operate. I want you to be careful with him. Don't get caught up in this husband-and-wife act."

"I'll be careful," I vow. "This is solely about the art for me. I have no plans of falling for Carter Harrington. He's too old for me and too focused on business. He's one of those guys who only date gorgeous, debutante types and probably think graphic novels like Alphena are silly stories for kids. I honestly don't like him very much."

"But he's, and I quote, 'a good kisser'," she reminds me.

"A kiss doesn't have to mean anything." I shrug noncommittally.

Samantha frowns. "You're lying to the wrong person here, Luna. A kiss is the physical meeting of two souls, sharing time, heat, and space. Their breath becomes one as their bodies react to one another. Don't simplify or degrade something so vital."

Her words are poetic and make my whole body go liquid, but she's missing a key factor. "If the people are kissing as part of a relationship, whether a momentary or permanent one, that's true. But a kiss can also be just a kiss. No meaning, no souls, no promises. Just a touching of lips, no different from bumping into someone on the sidewalk."

Sam sighs heavily, unconvinced but not willing to argue further. "Be careful."

"I will."

The promise is heavy, even as I pay for the dress, shoes, and jewelry using Carter's Amex card, but I keep reminding myself . . . the Thomas Cartwright collection.

CHAPTER
SEVEN

CARTER

STANDING outside Luna's door once again, I feel like my world has become some over-scripted pseudo-reality show in the last twenty-four hours. I've gone above and beyond for deals before, but this is so much more. No matter, though, because I'm doing this, as crazy as it is.

I knock on the door, and in the few seconds before I hear Luna turning the lock, I have one last thought of making a run for it and calling the whole thing off.

But before I can, the door swings open.

"Wow, you look great." The words pop out of my mouth before fully forming in my head, but they're true. Luna is wearing a dark green dress, showcasing an hourglass shape she usually hides beneath the oversized overalls and frumpy uniform. Her hair is down and curled, her lips glossy, and behind her glasses, her eyes are almost doe-eyed with liner and lashes.

In an instant, her smile falls. "You don't have to sound so surprised. Come in while I grab my purse."

I can't help but notice the way her ass sways left and right with every step of her clicking heels on the wood floor as she strides to the kitchen. And of course, she catches me looking when she spins back around.

"Seriously?" she huffs, totally busting me.

Shrugging innocently, I reply, "What? I'm just appreciating my wife, and I said you look great."

"Don't even start. And it's not what you said, it's how you said it," she says quietly. I open my mouth to ask what she means, but she cuts me off with an outstretched palm. "Can we just go?"

"Sure." I agree because it seems like the safest bet before we go to Elena's and have to sell being a happily married couple. I offer my elbow, hoping some gentlemanly charm will help, but she struts right past me and out the door. Though, if I'm not imagining it, she's swishing her hips a bit more now that she knows I'm watching.

She locks the door behind us and then downstairs, she snorts when she sees my car parked on the curb. "Should've guessed."

"What?" I question, not sure what's irritated her now. First off, the Mercedes CLS is a perfect vehicle for me and my lifestyle, sporty and powerful enough that I can pass anything I need to on the highway, but safety conscious, with airbags everywhere and antilock intelligent brakes. The thing's even eco conscious, with a hybrid drive that lets it get good in-city gas mileage. And it's not too crazy looks-wise either, in perfectly glossed black and chrome, with a smoke gray leather interior.

I could have easily bought something more expensive. So what's Luna's issue?

"That'd you'd drive a car like this. Fancy, but not flashy. It's just . . ." She pauses, searching for a word as her eyes lock on mine, delving into my soul. "You."

Feeling unsure, I reply, "I'm going to choose to take that as a compliment."

In the car, things don't get any better as I get down to business. "I figure we need to have our story straight in case Elena asks any questions. I looked up how Thomas and Elena Cartwright met to see if we could work in some similarities for connection. It was pretty straightforward—they met through friends, dated for a short time, married, and lived together for almost fifty years of wedded bliss, by all accounts. They never had children, but Thomas has a niece he doted on as almost a substitute child. The Cartwrights are known business minds, with a variety of investments, but they're also philanthropists, working with everything from children's hospitals to women's causes in developing countries."

"And art," Luna reminds me. "That's why I'm doing this."

Despite her direct hit to my ego, I tease, "And here I thought you wanted to spend the evening with me?"

"You thought wrong." She looks out the window, watching the city fly by. "So the story is . . . we met through my brother, dated, and fell in love. You proposed at the museum and we married after that. You work for your family business and I do tours at the museum. Probably best to keep it as true to life as possible so we don't misspeak."

I nod and then remember. "I told Zack about the deal too. He was surprised you agreed but said he was fine with it."

She turns her head slowly, and when I glance over, her lips are pressed into a thin line.

"What?" I ask, splitting my attention between her and the road.

"You asked my brother for permission when he has absolutely nothing to do with this? I don't need his or anyone else's permission for anything." Her tone is no-nonsense, and I'm left staring at the back of her head when she whips around and resumes staring out the window. Her lips move slightly, as if she's talking silently to herself. Or possibly preparing a speech to rip me a new one.

I decide that it might be in my best interest to keep my mouth shut and not argue that talking to Zack about taking his little sister out to dinner, even on a fake date, much less in a fake marriage situation, is completely reasonable. He's my best friend, and the last thing I would do is disrespect him by seeing his sister behind his back, especially for something outrageous like this.

We ride in silence for several minutes, the only sound the interruption of the automated voice giving me directions. "Next exit, 126 miles."

Shit. It's a long drive to the Cartwright estate, at least three hours, and I think we're going to be traveling in utter and awkward silence. Still, I set the cruise control and think of turning on the sound system. I could use a few hours of surround sound. But that would require talking to Luna about what she'd like to listen to, and the vibe she's giving off tells me her answer would be the sound of my balls being chewed on by rabid toy poodles or something like that.

When my phone rings, I'm actually thankful for the distraction. I hit the button to answer and my brother's voice sounds out.

"Carter, man . . . I need your help."

I groan in annoyance. Kyle always needs something, usually a swift kick in the ass, and he manages to blow up his life at the most inopportune times. He's the youngest Harrington, and as the baby of the family, you'd think he was coddled, but you'd be wrong. He was basically left to his own devices growing up and used our parents' money to get into and out of trouble.

Drag racing? Yep. Both illegal street ones where he pretended to be in *The Fast & The Furious* franchise, and even some on a track . . . where he wiped out a half-million-dollar Lamborghini Huracan.

Out of control parties? Of course.

Brought home by the local police? So many times I lost count.

But did he ever pay a ticket or fine, or spend time behind bars? Absolutely not, despite it being warranted a few times. And since becoming an adult, there's no telling what he's done because he sure wouldn't share it with us.

"I'm sure you do. What's wrong?"

"Where are you? Any chance you can swing by for a minute?" He's trying to sound casual, but there's a thread of distress in his voice. And I'm already calculating the time it'll take to get to Elena's if I add in a stop at Kyle's. The dinner is way more important, but he's my brother, even if we're not the closest.

"I have an important dinner tonight. Can it wait?" I ask hopefully.

Kyle laughs roughly. "If it could, would I be calling you?"

He's closest with my sister, Kayla, and likely always calls her first. She was the one to play second mother to him when they were little. As they got older, he became Kayla's protector. Thankfully, he didn't take her along on any of his paths to hell. At least that I know of. But they forged a connection that's beyond what any of the rest of us siblings have.

"Fair point. I'll be there in fifteen, but it needs to be quick. I can't be late, not for anything," I warn.

I hear Kyle sigh, and the line goes dead.

"What's that about?" Luna asks curiously.

Kyle's drama seems to have drawn her attention away from the window, at least, but we don't share family secrets, and despite Luna being my 'wife' for this occasion, I can't reveal too much. Not that I know anything in this particular situation.

"With Kyle, honestly, there's no telling. He might need money or he might want to show me his new motorcycle, or anything in between. He's . . . unpredictable." That's not enough to describe Kyle, but it'll work as a warning for the few minutes Luna will be around him.

Luna lifts her brows as she comments, "Is that the worst thing someone could be in your world?"

"No," I argue, "but you don't know him. He's always going off on tangents and wild goose chases. It isn't a healthy way to live." I'm hoping Luna can read between the lines a bit, but she takes me literally.

"Says you. Did you appoint yourself chief decision maker on how everyone else should live their lives? Because if so, you should probably rethink that," she says matter-of-factly. Her fire is back in full-force, and though it's exciting, I wish it wasn't directed at cutting me off at the knees.

I shove my hand through my hair in frustration. "Fuck, you're probably right, but that doesn't change where we're going or what we're doing." I solidify the declaration by pressing the pedal down, speeding toward Kyle's, as Luna resumes staring out the window.

I pull into Kyle's in record time to find him in the driveway tinkering with his motorcycle. I bite back the snarky comment that tries to escape, but Luna has no such desire.

"That's your brother? He doesn't look anything like you." She's leaning forward like getting four inches closer to the windshield will let her get a better view of Kyle, who's wearing low-slung jeans, thick-soled boots, and no shirt, leaving his nipple piercings quite visible. Before I know what's happening, I stick my arm in front of her and press her back to the seat. If we'd been coming to a sudden jolting stop in traffic, it would've been perfectly normal. But at a standstill in Kyle's driveway, it's definitely not and Luna looks at me in shock. "What was that for?"

"Saving you from yourself," I explain. "Kyle doesn't look like the rest of us because he's nothing like us. It's not only that he's unpredictable, he's—"

"Hot?" Luna suggests softly.

Jealousy rears up inside my gut. Luna's not mine beyond this play act tonight, but I don't like her lusting after my brother. Especially one who is my polar opposite, though I'm not going to examine why that in particular bothers me.

I glance out the windshield myself. I know that Kyle is attractive. He's a Harrington, with all the genetic benefits that implies. But instead of the dirty blonde and blue-eyed, tall and lean-muscled version the rest of my brothers grew into, Kyle is shorter, wider with muscle, and has darker hair that he keeps long and messy. Though he has blue eyes, they're not the deep blue the rest of us have but rather an icy blue.

But the true difference is in presence. We're mostly cultured, having grown up with Dad's expectations of what being a Harrington means. Kyle skipped all that, officially left home at eighteen, though he'd been gone long before that, and he lives a life filled with grease, motor oil, and roughness for no reason that I've ever been able to discern.

He's every girl's dream bad boy . . . except that he's actually bad.

That Luna finds that the least bit attractive irks me. "You can put your tongue back in your mouth. He probably still has last night's *frosted flakes* on his dick."

"Huh?" Luna looks at me in surprise, then waves her hands. "Never mind, I don't want to know, and if I do, I'll ask Samantha. Not you."

Shit. I guess that was a bit crass, but it was the jealousy talking.

"Sorry. Stay here. I'll see what the big emergency is," I tell her brusquely as I open my door. "Hey, man, what's up?" I say to Kyle by way of greeting. "Like I said, I'm in a rush."

"Yeah, yeah . . . you're always in a rush. I have a life too, you know." He's risen to his full height, which puts him at six feet, still a couple of inches shorter than me, but with his arms crossed over his chest, he looks ready to take me on, especially given that I'm in my nicest gray suit for the dinner. "I need you to . . . whoa, well *hellooo* there."

Kyle's looking over my shoulder, and there's only one thing he could be seeing. Luna.

"Hi, I'm Luna," she says, and I can hear the . . . *sweetness* in her voice. I never get that, goddammit.

"I told you to stay in the car. This won't take long."

I don't have to see her to know she's doing something behind my back because Kyle is fighting a losing battle to hide a smirk. "Well, I guess I'm too unpredictable and don't like being told what to do," she challenges.

I turn to face her fully, and her bratty grin melts when she sees the thunder in my face. "We'll see about that," I warn.

"Hey, I'm Kyle. This guy bothering you?" Luna looks past me to Kyle but thankfully shakes her head.

"More like the other way around."

I feel like I'm on the outside of whatever conversation they're having, and somehow, the butt of the joke too. "What do you want? No time for shooting the shit."

Kyle plops down onto his motorcycle sideways, his feet spread out to brace himself. "The two of you are going to dinner? No offense, Luna, but you're not his usual type."

She laughs, and that hurts. "I know. I have a brain, my own boobs and nose, and this is . . ." She looks around as if someone might overhear her revealing a deep secret. "My natural hair color."

She flips her brown curls over her shoulder dramatically, and Kyle's deep chuckle pisses me off, but not nearly as much as Luna talking shit about who I typically date. "It's not like I only date blonde bimbos."

"Of course not, dear," Luna says in a patronizing tone, patting my arm before she flashes a conspiring look to Kyle.

Kyle grins. "Ooh, I like this one, Carter. Are you sure you can handle her? If not, I could take her off your hands and show her a good time." He licks his lips, running his thumb over his bottom one as he leers at Luna.

Luna turns her fire on Kyle, rolling her eyes as she says, "For all his audacity, you're an arrogant asshole. Neither are exactly sexy. To me, at least."

Wisely, I choose not to remind her that she was drooling over him mere moments ago.

Kyle shrugs off the dismissal. "I wasn't expecting you to hop on my dick. I just like giving my brother a hard time, especially when it seems like he's crashing and burning already. Can't say I'm disappointed to see the show. It's some pretty entertaining shit."

I've had enough of this. We have places to be. Returning to the issue at hand, I demand, "What do you want?"

Kyle lets out an ear-piercing whistle, and the storm door swings open so hard that it hits the porch wall. "Uncle CJ! You're finally here! I've been waiting forever and ever!"

My niece, Grace, is running at me full-force, and I brace for impact instinctually. "Hey there, Gracie girl! How's my sweetheart?" I pick her up and spin her around, her legs flying out behind her in a move we've done since she was little bitty.

"Good!" she shouts as she laughs. Putting her down, she informs me, "Uncle Kyle says you're taking me home because he has work to do."

Shooting a deadly glare at Kyle, I answer Grace, "Oh, he did, did he?"

"Yeah, you can drop her off at Mom's. Cameron's gonna grab

her from there after dinner, but I can't put her on the bike yet. Cam's orders."

Kyle seems to think I'm going to drop everything and handle this.

Of course he does. The selfish prick. At least he followed Cam's rule on the bike.

Admittedly, we all help take care of Grace. She's like the family mascot, always hanging out with one of us. It started when Cameron lost his wife and Grace was just a baby. He understandably needed time and couldn't handle everything amid his grief, so we all stepped in to help, and as much as Cameron annoys me by being the golden child at work, I would never take it out on Grace. She's blameless for her dad's assholery.

But not today.

"Kyle, I can't. This dinner is important. Call Mom and have her come pick up Grace," I suggest reasonably.

"Gotta go, man. See ya later, and" —he shoots a wink at Luna — "hopefully, I'll see *you* sooner." Somehow, without my noticing, Kyle has already straddled his motorcycle, and he starts the engine, drowning out my arguments with the roar as he revs the throttle. He pulls off, shouting loudly, "Bye, Gracie-Face-y!"

"Bye, Uncle Kyle! Be safe!" she yells, her hands cupped around her mouth needlessly because this little girl has lungs so big the neighbors two streets over probably heard her, even over Kyle's bike. "Ready, Uncle CJ?" Seeming to only now notice Luna, she holds out her hand. "I'm Grace Harrington, nice to meet you."

Cameron's taught her well, especially for an eight-year-old. Luna, charmed it seems, shakes her hand politely. "Luna Starr, nice to meet you too."

Grace looks gobsmacked. "Is your name really Luna Starr? Like moon and star? That's cool. I wish my name was cool like that."

Luna bends down, getting on Grace's level. "Your name is pretty cool too. Are you graceful, by any chance?"

Grace shakes her head so wildly that her blonde curls fly back and forth. "Nope, Mee-Maw H says my name is *ironic* because I never met a piece of furniture I don't walk straight into."

"Well, that only makes it better. Keeps people guessing," Luna says, making Grace beam with pride. "We should probably go if we're adding another stop," she tells me.

I plaster a smile on my face, never wanting Grace to feel as though she's a bother. "Yeah, let's go, Gracie. It's a drive, so hop in."

But someone else hears me say 'drive' and also hops in the car. "Nutbuster, get out of my car!" I shout at Kyle's dog, who's climbed in Luna's open door and is sitting happily in the back-seat, ready to go for a ride.

Rrrarf!

"Did you say the dog's name is Nutbuster?" Luna asks, her brows scrunched together as though sure she must've misheard.

I sigh in response. "Technically, his name is Peanut Butter," I say about the brown, long-haired dog who's probably drooling and shedding all over my back seat. "But when he grew, he stopped right at" —I hold my hand groin high to explain— "and he's a bit overly welcoming. By the time he racked us all a few too many times and we'd have to greet him with our hands over the crown jewels, the name stuck."

"What're crown jewels?" Grace asks. "Can I wear them?"

"No," I say sharply.

Softer, Luna says, "I don't think you want these jewels, honey. They're all wrinkled and hairy and gross. A lady like you deserves a tiara."

"Ooh, can I get a tiara, Uncle CJ?" Grace asks. Thankful to not be talking about testicles, I quickly nod in agreement. "Woohoo! Let's go to Mee-Maw H's, then."

Before I know it, Grace and Nutbuster are in the back seat, buckled in and ready to go, and I'm looking at Luna in confusion. "How're we going to do this?"

"Breathe, Carter. It's not on your plan for the day, but it's fine. Let's go so we're not late to the Cartwrights'." Her tone is soothing and calm, like this is no big deal, like flirty asshole brothers, no-filter kids, ball-busting dogs, and fake marriage dinners are just another Saturday. As ridiculous as that is, she does help me settle down a little.

"Okay, this is fine, totally fine," I repeat, more for myself than anything. Getting in the car, I back out of Kyle's driveway, cussing him a blue streak but only in my mind so that Grace doesn't learn those words . . . from me.

Once we're on the road, I call my mother on speakerphone, hoping to warn her that we're doing a drive-by drop off, but it goes to voicemail. "Uh, hey, Mom. I'm bringing Grace by. Kyle said she was hanging out with you until Cam could pick her up later. See you in a few."

I hang up, but there's something gnawing at my gut. Kyle wouldn't have pawned Grace off on me and lied about the plan, would he?

He's Kyle. Of course he would.

"Shiii—"

"'take mushrooms," Luna says loud enough to drown out what I was going to say. "What's wrong?"

I dial Cameron and end up with his voicemail too. "Cam, Grace is with me and I'm not sure where I'm supposed to take her. Kyle said Mom's, but you know how that goes. Where are you? Call me."

I look in the rearview mirror and see Grace's smile as she pets Nutbuster. This is not how today was supposed to go. Not at all. And one look at the clock tells me that I'm running out of choices.

I run through the list of Grace-sitter options beyond Kyle, Cameron, and Mom, which is basically the rest of my family.

My brother Cole? He doesn't live far, but then I remember that he's out of town this weekend, so he's a no-go.

My brother Chance? He teaches Saturday classes and turns his phone on silent to ensure he's not interrupted. Plus, the center where he teaches is in the opposite direction.

My sister Kayla? Yes!

I dial her number and she actually answers. "Kayla! Where are you? I need a favor . . . I'm begging you."

"And hello to you too. Yes, I'm doing fine, thank you for

asking. How are you?" she replies, sweet-sarcastically correcting my rushed non-greeting.

"Sorry, but Kyle tricked me into . . ." I freeze when Luna swats my arm with the back of her hand and shoots a pointed look toward the back seat. "I mean, uh . . . I picked up Grace from Kyle, and he said Mom was taking her, but she's not answering her phone. Do you know where she is?"

"Well, I have good news and bad news. I do know where Mom is because she's next to me. Unfortunately, we're in Westport today." That's an hour away, meaning there's no way I can get Grace to her or Mom.

Resigned, I sigh. "I'll figure it out. Somehow. By the way, maybe forget you have a younger brother because I'm going to kill him."

Kayla laughs, thinking I'm kidding, but honestly, I might throw a punch or two Kyle's way if I can sneak attack him. I hang up with Kayla and look at Grace again.

"Change of plans, Gracie. You're going to go with me and Luna," I tell her. Before she can ask a million questions, I fill her in on the fancy dinner with the fancy lady at the fancy house with all the fancy things that we do not touch. "It's like a game. Be on your best behavior and practice all your manners so Uncle CJ can work, and I'll get you that tiara we were talking about. Deal?"

She tilts her head and then whispers to Nutbuster, "What do you think?" She leans the other way, acting like the dog is whispering to her, and then nods. To me, she says, "Deal . . . with the caveat that the tiara is purple and real. Not one of those plastic ones."

"Are you negotiating with me?" I can't help but laugh. She is her father's daughter. "And how do you know the word 'caveat'? You're eight, not eighty."

She shrugs casually, but her smile gives it away that she's proud her vocabulary surprised me. "I listen."

"Okay, deal. One purple, real tiara for your absolute bestest behavior." I reach behind me, and though we can't officially shake, she grabs my pinkie finger with hers to pinkie promise.

"Can Peanut Butter have a tiara too?" she adds.

"Pushing it," I warn. But when she crosses her arms over her chest, I acquiesce. "If you're extra-extra-extra good, I'll get him one too."

She hugs the beleaguered dog and he licks her face. With a smile, I try to think of a way to spin this, but Luna interrupts my whirling mind. "Keep it simple, stupid. K-I-S-S, just like our background story. She's your niece that you needed to watch. It makes you seem like a family guy the same way" —she drops her voice to a whisper— "a wife does."

She has a point. I nod, visualizing the introduction and how Elena might respond. "Okay, KISS, got it," I echo vacantly.

Before I forget, I call Cameron back and leave another message. "Hey man, Mom's a no-go for babysitting tonight, but Grace is with me. We'll be out a little late, so she can stay at my place. I'll bring her back tomorrow or Sunday, whatever's good for you. No worries, we'll just hang out and play the Royal Family because she's already talked me into a tiara."

When I hang up, Luna is looking at me strangely. Before I can find out why, Gracie asks, "Did you hear that, Peanut Butter? We're having a sleepover at Uncle CJ's!"

CHAPTER
EIGHT
LUNA

"*WE DON'T TALK ABOUT . . .*" Grace sings and then waits for me to join in.

"*Bruno . . . no, no, no!*" I finish with a big flourish, having fun singing the entire Disney repertoire with her. Grace has an arm thrown over Peanut Butter, happily singing to him in full-blown Mariah Carey mode despite his howls begging us to stop. Grace explained it's his way of singing along with us, but I have serious doubts about that.

The little girl is an absolute hoot. She's infinitely better than either of her uncles, and the drive that had seemed extraordinarily long before has flown by with her constant questions, song requests, and storytelling.

Surprisingly, Carter has had a faint ghost of a smile on his lips the whole time. He's even joined in on the fun, sort of, answering some of her questions with playful answers of his own. He doesn't go so far as singing, but I'm pretty sure I heard him humming. He's so uptight and work-focused that I would've thought he'd be annoyed by a child's antics. But my assumption was obviously wrong.

"We're almost there. Ready?" Carter asks us.

"I'll be super-duper good, Uncle CJ." Grace holds up her hand as she makes the solemn vow.

I shoot a smile at Grace and mimic her move. "Me too.

Super-duper good."

"Okay," Carter says easily, but his fingers haven't stopped nervously tapping on the steering wheel. We pull up in front of a pair of tall gates that are already open. "Elena's expecting us. Showtime."

On the other side of the gates, there's a long and winding drive leading to the front of the house. Though it's not like one I've ever seen.

"Is that a house for one person?" Grace exclaims, pressing her nose and hands to the window. "You could fit my whole school in there!"

"Right?" I whisper. It's more like a mansion or estate, or whatever's bigger than that, and my heart begins thumping in my chest. I don't belong here. No dress is enough armor to make me fit in at a place like this.

Carter parks and comes around to open my door like a gentleman. Taking my hand, he helps me out, and the touch of our hands reminds me of the role I'm playing. I look up into his eyes, and there's an instant where I forget that I'm mad at him and this feels like a date.

Grace and Peanut Butter explode out of the car with a whoop of laughter, shattering the moment. "Let's go, Peanut Butter!"

The dog heads straight for a pair of meticulously pruned rose bushes by the front steps and lets loose with a long stream of pee. I swear I hear him sigh in relief.

"No, bad dog!" Carter hisses, but there's no stopping the yellow waterfall hitting the pristine flowers, the leaves flapping backward with the force of the golden shower.

A tall man comes around the corner, surprise widening his eyes when he sees us, but his expression quickly changes to anger when he sees Peanut Butter. "*No*! Rosalia! You're killing her!" he yells sharply.

Who's Rosalia?

The man waves wild hands, trying to shoo the confused pooch away from the bushes. "Git!"

"Peanut Butter, come here. Get away from the mean man!" Grace cries, running toward them to throw herself between the dog and the man, holding her arms out protectively. "Don't you be a meanie!"

Gathering Grace and Peanut Butter and shoving them behind his back, Carter tells the man, "Excuse us, so sorry."

His attempt to diffuse the situation is in vain, though, because the man has given his full attention to the rose bush, which he's caressing tenderly with gnarled hands and sweet-talking. "Oh, Rosalia. What has that monster done to you? I'll get you some fresh water to drink, would you like that?"

Oh-kay, I guess the bush is Rosalia?

"What's all this racket out here?" a woman says from the porch. "Bernard? Are you okay?"

She's older, wearing a loose-fitting bronze pantsuit, kitten heels, and a worried look as she scans the yard, her silver bob swinging back and forth with the movement.

"That dog tried to kill Rosalia." The man points an accusing finger at Peanut Butter, snarling his lip.

"It was a long drive, so he really had to go," I explain apologetically.

"No big deal. The poor baby had to piddle." She's telling Bernard, but Peanut Butter has climbed the steps and is sitting politely at the woman's feet as though he recognizes a kind spirit. She reaches down to pet his head and he leans into her touch. "My bladder's the size of a walnut too."

Standing back up, she greets the rest of us. "You must be Carter. Thanks for coming all the way out here. I hope it wasn't a trouble, other than the peeing." She laughs at her own joke, petting Peanut Butter again.

Carter takes a few steps up to the porch and offers his hand. "Happy to come out anytime, Mrs. Cartwright." He pauses, drops his chin, and then smiles. "I mean, *Elena.*"

Ooh, he's good. That was a pure act of fertilizer-grade manure with the name misspeak, playfully coy while also being old-fashioned polite. He's shoveling it both ways.

"And you must be Luna, Carter's lovely wife. You should hear him talk about your artwork. They say what a man says when you can't hear him is as close to the truth as you'll ever get. If that's the case, he's quite smitten with you, dear." She winks at me theatrically, and I freeze.

When Carter glances back at me, there's a slight blush coloring his cheeks. It's kinda adorable, and then I remember that whatever he told Elena was fake as hell. I play my part, though, stage whispering as I tease, "You should hear what he says when we're alone."

Elena laughs, thinking I'm being cheeky, but my true target is Carter and the things he's said that weren't so kind. If he can shovel two ways, then so can I.

"I'm Miss Grace Marie Harrington, eight years old, third grade. And that's my Uncle Kyle's dog, Peanut Butter," Grace offers with a ladylike curtsy. She sounds like she's introduced herself on countless Miss America pageant stages until she adds, "But we call him Nutbuster."

Carter chokes. "Oh, Gracie, Elena doesn't want to hear that."

But Elena's chuckling and petting the nut-busting dog again, not offended in the slightest. Instead, she curtsies back to Grace, holding out the leg of her pants. "Pleasure to meet you, Miss Harrington. Now, how about you call me Elena and I call you Grace, and we can go inside where it's cool, m'kay?"

"Okay, Elena," Grace parrots.

"Oh, Bernard . . ." Elena says to the man who's still scowling at Peanut Butter, "Would you mind taking this sweet, good boy over to the barn? I bet he'd love to play in the hay and have an oat cookie or two. If that's okay?"

That last bit was directed to Carter, who nods to Bernard gratefully and then adds, "I really do apologize. We had a bit of a family emergency, and I—"

He holds his hands out wide, gesturing to Grace and Peanut Butter. But this is Elena's show, and she waves it off. "Nonsense, the more, the merrier!"

"Yeah, Uncle CJ, me and Elena are cool." Completely comfortable having crashed Carter's meeting, Grace takes Elena's hand and they walk into the house together like insta-besties.

Bernard pats his leg, content with his orders. "Wanna cookie, boy?"

That's all it takes for Peanut Butter to trot off after him, leaving just me and Carter behind. He looks back and forth between Peanut Butter and Grace, though, concern on his face for his two charges. It's actually admirable.

And a bit adorable.

"We got this," I tell him gently as I hold my hand out. He takes it, and together, we walk inside. The house is impressive, with soaring ceilings, marble floors, intricate moldings, and antiques. But beyond the air of fanciness, what draws my attention is the art on every single wall.

"Is that . . ." I can't get the words out as I rush to a piece in the foyer, dragging Carter along. "The colors, the texture, her expression." I clamp my hands over my mouth as tears unexpectedly fill my eyes. This artwork is everything I'd dreamed, only better.

"Oh, you found our Eakin piece. It's not a classic—or not yet, at least—but Thomas really enjoyed the emotions in her eyes."

We all stare at the art for a moment in silence, feeling connected to the woman in the drawing.

"She looks sad, like she's gonna cry," Grace whispers.

Bending down, I nod agreeably. "People do cry when they're sad, but there are happy tears too. And I'll tell you a secret, I even cry when I'm mad. Do you think she might be crying for another reason?"

I can feel Carter and Elena's eyes, but I'm in tour guide mode with Grace because you never know what will spark a child to have a life-long love of art.

"Elena? Dinner's ready." I look up to see a square-shaped woman with blonde hair slicked into a military tight bun standing by a doorway. She's wearing black pants, a black polo, and black kitchen clogs. Clearly, she's house staff.

"Nelda, this is Carter, Luna, and Grace. Could you be a dear and get us an extra setting on the table?" Elena subtly tilts her head toward Grace.

"Of course," Nelda answers. "Should I make an alternative meal for the young lady? We're having salmon."

Grace looks up at Carter. "That's the pink fish?" When Carter nods, she speaks directly to Nelda. "I like salmon."

Of course she does. I think I've had salmon once in my life at a museum event where I mostly hid in the corner and prayed no one would ask me questions. But this little girl knows pink fish from other fish and can talk to strangers with ease. I make a mental note to see if I can use Grace as a character inspiration in my graphic novel.

Instead of the dining room, Elena takes us to the kitchen where a round breakfast nook table is set for dinner with family-style serving dishes in the middle. Nelda quickly adds another setting as Carter pulls out a chair for me, and then, in a move that startles me, he slides the napkin into my lap. It feels intimate, and when I glance up, Carter's eyes are stormy. The second I meet his gaze, he jerks his away as though burned and finds his own seat between me and Grace, with Elena sitting across.

"I hope you don't mind eating in here. The dining room is so stuffy, and between you and me, I need glasses and a hearing aid to talk to people at the other end of that thing." Elena holds her hands up wide, demonstrating how big the table is.

"No, of course not. This is perfect," Carter says obsequiously.

Elena picks up a platter from the assortment in the middle of the table and leans toward Grace. "Would you like help getting the salmon on your plate? Sometimes, they like to swim away."

She laughs at her own silly joke, and Grace grins as she nods. Once everyone has filled their plates, Elena says, "Tell me about Blue Lake Assets, Carter."

She takes a bite of broccoli salad as he sets his fork down and dabs his mouth. Carter's clearly ready for the question, and his voice is sure and steady as he answers. "My grandfather started it decades ago, and my dad is CEO now. My brother, Cameron, my sister, Kayla, and I work there. It's a family legacy we're proud to stand behind. Our specialty is that we don't lock ourselves or our clients into a single investment vehicle. It's specific for each person's needs and wants."

As Carter attempts to sell Elena on his family's company, I only understand about a fourth of what he's talking about. It's English, and I know the words themselves, but all together, not a bit. He's going heavy on the family angle, driving home that this is no small potatoes offer but rather a close connection between the Harringtons and Cartwrights.

He's a good salesman, I remind myself. *Does and says whatever it takes, no matter who it cuts, as long as he ends up in the plus column.*

I thought Carter would be all dry facts and figures, and though he does discuss those, he also adds in a story of his own first account acquisition.

"I put ten thousand in the stock market based on a tip I thought was a sure thing." Carter laughs and then Elena joins in. "We both know there's no such thing, but then I was young and cocky, sure I had a money maker."

"What happened?" I ask and then clack my mouth shut, realizing I should know this story as his wife.

Carter plays it off excellently, almost as if we've done this pony trick before. "What always happens if you don't invest wisely and manage your assets. I lost the funds. But I learned a valuable lesson, did better, and by the end of the next quarter, that investor had his original funds back plus a significant increase."

He and Elena go on to talk shop for a while, and the whole time, I'm watching Carter work his magic. He's engaging, intelligent, a bit arrogant, and all around, a good businessman. If only he weren't such an asshat personally, he might even be attractive beyond his classically good looks.

But he is an asshat. A two-faced one.

I've heard it with my own ears and seen it with my own eyes. I can't let this sexy, smart, gentleman version make me forget.

CHAPTER
NINE

CARTER

"THIS IS ONE OF MY FAVORITES," Elena says wistfully, pointing at a small painting on the wall. "It makes me think of the beach, with sand beneath my feet and a drink in my hand."

Elena's been great company all evening, but she must be losing it because this painting is definitely *not* a beach or anything remotely ocean related. In fact, the dark purple, black, and neon green abstract remind me more of *Halloween*. Or maybe *The Joker*.

"Interesting," Luna replies. "What about this piece makes you think about the beach?"

What a polite way to ask whether someone is batshit crazy.

Luna's usually on the quieter side, but when the subject is art, the words come out easily and effusively. The conversations aren't one-sided, either. She asks us questions and shares her thoughts. It's a sight to behold when her eyes light up with every new piece, and I find myself holding my breath and watching her instead of the art, waiting for her commentary to see the art through her eyes. And to piece together an opinion of my own because I'm discovering more and more that art and I are not friends. I think some of the works are pretty or well-done, but I don't have the same visceral reaction Luna and Elena do.

Elena touches the frame gently. "Thomas and I went on a vacation, something we rarely did. There was always a reason—a meeting, an investment, something specific we wanted to see or do—for any trip we took. But he surprised me, smack out of nowhere, no birthday or anniversary or holiday. He booked the whole dang thing and took me to the Seychelles." Her eyes go misty and vacant like she's not here with us but traveled back in time to that trip.

"Aww, that's so sweet," Luna coos. "Did you find this at a gallery there?" she guesses.

Elena shakes her head, coming back to the present a bit. "No, we went for a walk and found a young lady sitting on the beach, painting her heart out with everything from her fingers and brushes to a palette knife and even sand. Thomas asked if we could sit a spell with her while she worked, and we had such a great visit." Her eyes drift over the colors. "I thought it was odd that she wasn't painting the beauty in front of her, but something else instead. When I asked why, she told us that even in paradise, people dream of more. She dreamed of space . . . said she'd wanted to go to the moon ever since she was a little girl. Of course, she didn't have the opportunity to do anything like that, but she could imagine it even from her paradise prison."

She smiles at us warmly. "Space was Sandrine's dream, but that beach with Thomas was mine. This reminds me of that."

"I wanna be a horse acrobat," Gracie pipes up. I'm honestly surprised she's been listening so closely to the art tour, but Luna somehow keeps it interesting for us all. "I saw it on TV, and I've been telling Pegasus about it."

"Pegasus is her horse," I explain.

Elena bends at the waist to get closer to Grace. "Then you'd best keep working at it, and one day, you'll do it."

"And now when you remember this painting, you'll dream those big dreams too, like Sandrine," Luna tells Grace, tapping her temple.

We all look at the piece once more, and then Elena claps her hands. "Ooh, let me show you one Thomas painted, m'kay?"

"It'd be an honor." Luna might as well have hearts popping out of her eyes and she's bouncing on the balls of her feet in excitement. In her heels, it makes a *tippy-tap* sound. It's a little ridiculous considering it's a bigger reaction than she had to the Degas we already saw, but also quite adorable. And it seems to please Elena, which is supposed to be the point.

Elena laughs as she tells me, "Carter, can I give you a piece of advice from an old lady?"

"Only if you know one," I reply with a lopsided grin.

She swats my way, hitting at the air. "Flatterer. My advice is, you'd best keep this wife of yours happy with all the art she wants to see and make. Look how she is over seeing some old man's doodles."

I look at Luna, and she catches her breath, going statue-still. Too soon, she drops her eyes to the floor, but I can see the slight lift of her lips. I need to see that smile. Placing my finger beneath her chin, I lift her head back up, willing her eyes to mine. "She is quite beautiful."

It's the truth. Luna's not a classic beauty, certainly not one of the blonde bimbos she all but accused me of dating. But there's a magnetism inside her that draws people to her, even me. I don't know how I never noticed it before.

The smile takes over her lips, lifting them fully. Her inner beauty radiates, and I feel lucky to be so close to it. And then I see the shutters close deep in her eyes when she remembers what we're doing. She thinks I'm faking, but I meant it. She is beautiful in a distinctively unique way all her own. She laughs awkwardly, the sound choked, and turns back to Elena. "You're right, he is a flatterer. But I really would like to see one of Thomas's paintings before we go."

Go? I'm not going anywhere until the deal is done. But a quick glance at my watch shows that it is late, and Grace is yawning widely. I bet she'll be asleep in the car before we're out of the driveway.

Elena leads us to a large library where a poster-sized canvas portrait of a much younger version of her likeness hangs on the wall. It's surrounded by simply framed sketches, clearly precursors to the final creation. "See? An old man's doodles."

Thankfully, she's fully dressed in the painting. However, I will admit that Elena was a good-looking woman in her youth.

Luna nearly has her nose pressed to the glass of the sketches. "You can see the eraser marks and sketch lines." She looks back at us excitedly, and I can imagine her saying 'are you seeing this?' but she whirls back around, moving to the next one. "Did he always sketch this many versions before beginning on the canvas? Or only for special subjects?"

"Just for me. When he did other work, he would dive straight in, sometimes not even knowing what it was gonna be. He used to tell me he'd work on it until it felt done." She smiles at the portrait, almost laughing at her image. "But me? He'd have me sit and pose. We'd talk while he sketched. I think that was his trick to spend time with me, but whoo, I always felt like such a silly goose sitting there like a statue while he studied my every flaw."

"He didn't see flaws," Luna corrects wisely. "He saw the woman he loved."

I hear Elena's swallow of emotion as she takes Luna's hands, patting them gently. "Thank you, honey. That's sweet of you to say."

A soft snore from behind us gets everyone's attention. Grace has curled up in one of the chairs, her head resting on the arm and her eyes closed. It tugs at my heart. She looks so innocent and sweet when she's asleep. Nothing like the wild child she can be in her waking hours.

"Looks like she's arted out," Luna whispers. "I suppose she's got to build her art muscles some more."

"It's so late. Y'all should stay here in the guest rooms and do the long drive back tomorrow when you're fresh," Elena suggests. "Your pup will be fine staying the night too. We've got plenty of chicken around, maybe some hamburgers that can be cooked up."

"Oh, we couldn't impose like that," I tell her, but I'm disappointed that I'm not leaving with a hand-shake agreement on her portfolio management. "We don't have an overnight bag or anything, and Grace can sleep on the way back."

"It's no bother. It'll do this old house some good to have a little life in it for the night. It's usually just me and the staff. And I've got everything you could need. Thomas bought mono-grammed T-shirts and sweatpants for the guest rooms, and the bathrooms are fully stocked." She's thought of everything, but then she really puts the cherry on top of her offer. "In the morning, after breakfast, we can look at more of Thomas's collection and maybe talk a bit more business, too."

She flashes a wink, knowing she's got both of us by the short hairs. I don't look at Luna because I don't want to give her a chance to say no. Instead, I nod graciously, accepting her offer. "We'd be delighted. That's really kind of you."

When Elena steps over to a desk phone to place a call, Luna steps in front of me, giving her back to Elena, and though her eyes are wide and angry, her voice is barely above a whisper. "What the hella-rama-ding-dong?"

"I couldn't refuse. She's willing to talk business in the morning. And more art," I remind her, hoping she doesn't walk out the front door and ditch me.

"Elena?"

I jerk in surprise and realize a tall, thin man in pajamas and a robe has appeared silently in the doorway.

Well, shit. I guess for all Mrs. Cartwright's sweet talk of her deceased husband, she has a new special friend.

"Oh, I am so sorry for bothering you, Stanley. Why didn't you say you were already lying down? I could've gotten them set up for the night myself," she fusses. Okay, so I was wrong. He's not her boyfriend but rather another member of the house staff.

"I wasn't asleep yet." He smiles, but his bloodshot eyes give away that he was definitely long gone to Snoozeville. "I'm happy to show them to the guest rooms."

Elena clucks. "This is Stanley. Stanley, this is Carter and Luna, and that little cherub over there is their niece, Grace. Bernard has their dog, Peanut Butter, out in the barn too."

I'm not used to shaking hands with men in their pajamas, but in this case, I'll definitely make an exception. I hold my hand out, and he looks at it in surprise but takes it slowly. His grip is stronger than I expected. "Nice to meet you, Carter."

"I don't know how he keeps this place running, but he's been doing it for decades at this point. I couldn't do much of anything without Stanley," Elena gushes.

Elena bids us good night, promising that Grace will get chocolate chip pancakes in the morning, and with Stanley's help, we manage to get Grace and Peanut Butter into a guest room. Grace is remarkably easy to coerce into bed despite it usually being a three-ring circus to get her to lie down at night. But one mention of pancakes in the morning and a reassurance that we're right down the hall make her snuggle in with the dog, both of whom close their eyes quickly, though I don't think Stanley is particularly excited about having a dog and a child in one of the luxury linen-covered beds.

Stanley then shows us to our room, pointing out the king-size bed, dresser full of clothing, and doorway to the bathroom. "If you need anything, pick up the phone and dial six-two-six. It's my direct line and I always answer. If that's all?"

"Thank you so much," Luna says kindly. "We'll let you get back to bed."

Stanley still looks at me for confirmation, and when I nod, he closes the door behind him. Alone, I sigh in relief. The sound seems to set Luna off because she starts pacing around the room, muttering under her breath. "This is such a mess, all because Zack said he'd buy me books. Stupid, stupid, stupid. I could've stayed home, in sweats, and worked on Alphena, but *noooo*, I got greedy. And now look where I am. Alone with Carter freaking Harrington, as his *wife*. Like that's remotely believable."

At first, I'm amused by her useless rambling and pacing and the way she's nearly vibrating with emotional energy. But then I hear what she's saying. I take her arms, stopping her steps, and say firmly, "Luna. Stop. Look at me."

A soft gasp escapes her lips as fiery eyes flash behind her glasses. She holds my gaze for a moment, and then, as her cheeks go rosy, she looks at my shoes.

"This is crazy, I know," I admit. "But I couldn't say no."

To me, that's obvious. The deal isn't closed and I very much need it. It's taken on a life of its own in my mind, a symbol of my success, a competition between me and Cameron that he doesn't know is happening. But I do, and I'm going to win. And I'm already in this far. What's a few more hours and breakfast?

"This is more than we agreed to," she argues with the floor.

I swallow, not sure how to explain why I'm willing to go to such lengths to her. I don't discuss our family dynamics, not with anyone. Well, Zack sometimes, but we talk more about last night's game or upcoming deals than our deep, dark emotions. It's just not what guys do.

"It is. I swear I'll make it up to you somehow. But for now, let's stick with the plan. Bed, breakfast, portfolio talk, art tour." I tick off the agenda items on my fingers, and she lifts her eyes to watch.

I feel the submission in her body even though she doesn't say a word, so I turn her to the dresser. "Let's find some pajamas."

She nods woodenly but lets me guide her over, where we discover Elena was right. There's every size of T-shirt, sweatshirt, and sweatpants in the drawers. Not to mention socks, underwear, swimsuits, and flip-flops, all neatly folded and placed. Luna grabs an oversized sweatshirt and socks, holding them to her chest as though they're a shield. "I'm changing in the bathroom."

When she closes the door behind her, I fight to keep my chuckle quiet. She acted like I asked her to strip right here in front of me or might follow her in to sneak a peek.

Instead, I grab a pair of sweatpants of my own and make quick work of changing before she comes out. I'm still hanging up my clothes when the bathroom door opens.

"Want me to hang up your dress?" I offer. But when I turn around, Luna doesn't have her dress in her hands or anywhere else. It's just her . . . in a sweatshirt that hangs long, cupping the fullness of her hips and then the middle of her thighs. Her socks are pulled up, hitting just below her knees.

There's only a small strip of her legs showing, but I can't tear my eyes away from it. It's like a magnet, pulling me in while at the same time powering . . . thoughts. Ones I shouldn't have, not about Luna.

"I hung it up in there." She points over her shoulder with her thumb and then starts gnawing on the digit nervously. "Uhm, where are *you* sleeping? You're not sleeping with me."

"There's a couch right there." My voice is too low, too rough when I think about us in bed together doing everything but sleeping, but she doesn't notice, thankfully.

"Okay." She agrees easily but then moves toward the couch herself, pulling a quilt from the foot of the bed.

I can't help but grin. There's something quaint and cute about the way she looks padding across the room in a long shirt with a blanket in tow. "I meant that I'll sleep on the couch."

"Oh." She freezes like a deer in the headlights before redirecting to the bed. She climbs up, throws the decorative pillows to the floor to make room for herself, and then pulls the bedding back. The whole time, she's on her knees, her ass sticking out, and my palms itch to grab her, dent the supple flesh there, or maybe see what it takes to make it flush like her cheeks did.

The dirty turn of my thoughts shocks me. I mean, this is Luna. She's not my type, and she's Zack's sister. Hell, if she breathes one word of what's happening tonight to Zack, he'll skin me alive and I won't even try to stop him. But she's also voluptuous in a way that makes me want to suffocate in her breasts and drown between her thighs.

Wait, what?

"You don't think she'd expect us to have sex, do you? Like as a young, newly married couple?" The words pop out as a result of the path my mind has disappeared down. As if Elena is outside our door listening or something.

From her spot on the bed, Luna says dryly, "I'm not having sex with you."

"We could fake it," I suggest, grinning foolishly, continuing down this nonsense path. This is a bad idea, a really bad idea. But also, maybe a brilliant one. If we needed to sell the husband-and-wife image, this surely will.

Luna pushes her glasses up her nose as she looks at me carefully. "What do you mean?"

I don't explain. I climb on the bed with her, making sure to stay on top of the covers, but when she gasps in surprise, I wink and rise to my hands and knees beside her, on my own side of the bed. I shake the bed back and forth a few times, testing to see if it squeaks.

No luck. This is no IKEA bed. This is one of those heavy-duty, luxury deals meant to last until doomsday, and then some.

I shake it harder, finally getting a little movement, enough for the headboard to touch the wall. It's not a bang, exactly, but when I do it again, the rhythm is unmistakable.

"Carter!" Luna hisses, her eyes widening in horror.

I stifle a laugh at how scandalized she seems. Instead, I grunt a little before groaning out, "Ohhh, Luna."

"Don't say my name like that!" she whispers hotly.

"Like what?" I keep my pace. *Bang, bang, bang.*

"All grunty, groany caveman like that. It's gross." She wrinkles her nose in distaste, but I can hear something in her tone. The lady doth protest too much. It makes me grin harder and bang a little louder.

Keeping my voice down, I ask, "Are you a prude in bed?" Offended, she pulls the blanket up to her chin and I smirk triumphantly. "Figured."

I keep a steady tempo, changing my position every few moments to make the headboard banging sound different. I even find a spot in the mattress that does creak a little, and I bounce on it. "That's it . . . good girl. Take all of me. I know you can," I order, as though someone is obeying. "Squeeze it for me . . . fuck yeah." I'm enjoying the play of emotions that cross her face—horror, interest, desire, denial.

Luna's grip on the blanket has gone slack, her tongue slipping out to wet her lips. "Is that what you really say when you're . . . doing that?" She makes a gesture, motioning to me.

"Depends on what they like," I answer quietly. "Why? Was I wrong? Does sweet, little Luna like a bit of dirty talk in her fucking?"

Her cheeks flush and then her fire is back. With a determined set of her jaw, she kicks the covers off, plants her feet on the bed, and starts bouncing on her own, her hips bridging up into the air before dropping to the mattress. "Oh, Carter! Yessss," she moans in a voice a solid octave higher than her own. "Make it hurt, baby!"

I'm shocked to the core for a solid two seconds before I realize she's playing along.

Two more seconds of watching her hips rise and fall, her tits bouncing with every move.

She lifts one brow, challenging me.

I join in, and it quickly turns into a competition of who can say the most outlandish thing as we bounce and bang in a ridiculous simulation of sex that's louder and more acrobatic than any I've ever actually had.

"Make that pussy suck me dry. I wanna fill you up, breed you with my seed." *Bang, bang, bang.*

She whispers, "Gross." Louder, for the show, she cries out, "Choke me, Daddy!"

Those words coming from Luna's mouth surprise me. In my mind, I can see my hand wrapped around her throat, putting the slightest pressure as we get closer and closer to coming simultaneously. And even though we're faking, my dick is rock hard. Strictly biological, I assure myself. It's not because I want Luna. That would be an unbelievably huge mistake, especially for a one-night stand.

I mean, seriously, this is damn near phone sex levels of hot, everything but the skin contact, so a physical reaction is only logical. Or at least that's what I tell myself.

"Can I come? Please?" *Bounce, bounce, bounce.*

The words roll off her tongue easily, and I wonder if there's something about Luna Starr that I never considered. Her sex talk, even if fake, has a decidedly submissive tilt, and I like it . . . a lot.

I realize I need to answer to keep up appearances, but I desperately want to know what Luna looks like when she comes.

Even if it's for show. "Come for me, baby. Come right now on Daddy's cock."

She sobs out a very believable keening whine, slapping the mattress with her hand. Her eyes are closed as she acts out, and I watch with focused concentration, noting the color on her cheeks, the hitch in her breath, the bounce of her breasts, and the way her sweatshirt has climbed up her thighs with her movements.

"That's it, good girl," I croon. I grip the blanket myself, not to hide from Luna but to stop myself from reaching out to touch her skin.

Her eyes flutter open and she grins. "Your turn," she mouths.

Oh, yeah. Right. I plant my feet and hands on the bed, pumping my hips so that the headboard hits the wall rhythmically again. "Fuuuck, Luna. You feel so good."

I grunt a few more times, letting the last one trail off, and then I lie belly down on the bed so my erection can't be seen.

Luna collapses to the pillow too, arranging her hair beneath her head. We're panting from the exertion despite not getting any real action. Our eyes meet, and there's something deep in Luna's that I can't identify. Lust? Anger? Disappointment? Embarrassment?

"You okay?" I ask gently.

"I usually take my glasses off. Guys don't like them, but it's nice being able to actually see," she confides as she pushes her glasses higher on her nose. Realizing what she shared, she covers her mouth to conceal the escaping giggles, crossing her legs and rolling a bit.

I can't help it, I start laughing too.

"Glasses could get . . . messy," I joke back, and Luna has to bite her sleeve to stop her howls of laughter.

"Still better than in your eyes," she adds, making a windshield wiper move over both lenses, and that's how I end up half-dressed, in bed, post-fake-coital, laughing my ass off with my best friend's little sister, who is also my fake wife.

Life is weird sometimes.

"Seriously, though. If any guy tells you he doesn't like your glasses, he should not get access to your pussy," I say firmly. "Your glasses are cute, and most importantly, they're you."

She seems shocked at my opinion on the situation, but it's pretty obvious if you ask me.

"Well, not like I'm in any position to turn guys down, though," she laments.

I grab the other pillow, propping my chest on it. It pushes my hips into the bed, and I note that at least my dick has gone soft now. "What the fuck does that mean?"

The demand is sharp as I search her face for what she's talking about. She sinks into her shoulders and sighs. "Look, Carter. I know you're supposed to be my fake husband and all, but we don't have to do this." She waves from me to her. "We're in different worlds—financially, professionally, personally, physically. It's okay. I'm happy with myself for the most part, but other than Elena, who might be blind as a bat for all we know, no one would believe we're a thing."

Her shrug is one of resignation and her tone of quiet acceptance. But I don't get it . . .

"We are different," I start, and I see her cringe, waiting for whatever she thinks I'm going to say. "But different can be good," I finish. "I don't really get why you cry when you see a painting or don't always say out loud what you're thinking, and I definitely don't understand how you can get art from your brain out to the real world. It's magic, it's witchcraft, it's something I absolutely can't do."

"Sure, yeah," she says dismissively. "But people don't want—"

"I wasn't done. Last but not least, quit saying you're not pretty or that this is unbelievable." I use her earlier words so she knows I heard her. "You're beautiful, and anyone who doesn't see that is an idiot." I don't add that I was one of those idiots a few short days ago. "Any man would be lucky to call you his."

She scans my face, searching for the lie, but I'm telling the truth. Finally, she says, "I don't understand why you need this deal so badly. Your life is charmed. You're one of those people born with a silver spoon, but you're making it hard on yourself, going to extremes like this whole fake marriage thing for a deal. This would be a lot even for someone who had nothing."

"Easy is boring. I need to prove myself," I confess.

Unconvinced, she asks, "To whom?"

"To my brother, my dad, my family. Hell, probably even to myself a bit. There's a lot of pressure that comes with that silver spoon. So much that I feel like I'll choke on it sometimes."

The confession surprises me more than her, I think. I hadn't realized I felt so trapped by my family's competitive nature. Probably because it's been bred into me for generations. I could use one of my mom's easily given reassurances right about now, but she saves those for Grace these days, trusting that her adult children have their shit together. If only she knew how much that's not true.

"Hmm, you're maybe not as bad as I thought you were." Luna smiles to soften the not-quite-a-compliment but then yawns.

"Apology accepted. I'll move over to the couch so you can get some rest." I shove the pillow back toward the head of the bed, but she stops me.

"It's fine. This bed is huge. You stay on your side and I'll stay on mine." She draws a line down the center of the bed with her hand.

"My back is gonna thank you in the morning." We both get rearranged so that we're under the blankets, but not touching, with a few inches of no-man's land between us. As I reach over to turn off the lights, I chuckle and murmur, "Good night, wife."

She laughs and answers, "Good night, Carter."

I flick off the light with the remote on the nightstand, and we go silent, waiting for sleep to come. Luna succumbs pretty quickly, and I should be thinking about Elena, this deal, and how I'm going to get that handshake in the morning before we leave.

But all I can focus on are Luna and her soft breathing.

CHAPTER
TEN
LUNA

I WAKE UP, or maybe I'm not awake because this must be a dream. I'm floating on a cloud of the softest, fluffiest cotton and there are warm, strong arms wrapped around me. There's also a very hard something pressed between the cheeks of my ass.

I arch my back into the sexy feelings as I sink into the dream with a moan. It jumps, and I'm about to open my knees in invitation when the arms tighten into a delicious hug that pulls me against the hardness forcefully. "Good morning, beautiful." I shudder reflexively, heat pooling between my legs that has nothing to do with the high thread-count duvet.

My brow furrows as the dream turns confusing. That voice is oddly familiar . . . but why? Or who?

Logic is overwhelmed by sensation, and I grind back against the firmness, moaning in desire. Just a slightly different angle and I'll be able to get . . .

My mind screams at me, forcing me awake.

Carter?

Oh, fuck.

Carter!

I flail wildly, kicking the blankets off in an effort to get away as fast as possible. "Get off me!"

"Wha—?" he stutters, clearly half asleep himself. And he's an octopus, pulling me back in with his arms and legs until we're snuggled together with my face buried in his bare, muscled chest, his arms encircling me and our legs entwined. Trapped, I freeze as he presses a kiss to the top of my head. I wiggle, and he looks down at me with half-open eyes. He's probably seeing double or still asleep because he smiles and in a sleep-rough voice says, "Mmm, hey, Luna."

I squirm, and my knee catches his morning wood.

"Ugh! Fuck!" He grunts as he doubles over into a fetal position, cupping himself.

But at least he lets me go, and I scoot to the other side of the bed, putting space between us. "Carter!"

"Why'd you rack me?"

"Why are you holding me hostage with your super-strong arms and stupidly big thing?" I gesture toward his groin, getting madder when he grins.

"Thing?" He chuckles, shifting himself in his sweatpants and still looking decidedly uncomfortable. "Seriously? What are you, twelve?"

I sit up, crossing my arms over my chest and frowning at him. "Twenty-three," I remind him even though I know the question was rhetorical.

"Last night, you're all 'choke me, Daddy' and now you can't even say cock or dick?" he teases, and I can't help it, I flush at the memory. Yeah, it was play acting . . . but it felt good doing it, too.

"That was different," I argue. Carter raises a single brow in challenge. "Leave me alone."

I get out of the bed, twisting and turning my sweatshirt to get it back down around my thighs, but I'm pretty sure I flash a fair amount of butt cheek in the process. Stomping to the bathroom, I can feel Carter's eyes following my every move, so I give him a solid glare as I shut the door behind me.

As soon as I do so, I lean back on the door, my pulse racing. He's getting to me, and I can't allow that.

I sigh and go over to the toilet to sit down. Taking care of my morning business and then washing my face, flashes of last night come back. I stare at myself in the mirror in shock. I actually did that. Me, Luna Starr, had fake sex with Carter Harrington.

I'm mad at myself, completely embarrassed, and also, way deep down in a secret space I won't tell a soul about, a little disappointed it was fake. Not because I want Carter but because the way he was bangin' around and the things he said were definitely turning my core to liquid, and now I'm left tense and frustrated. Samantha would tell me to rub one out really quick, but I can't . . . not here. Not when he could hear me. I would die of mortification.

And then another thought strikes me. What if Carter's taking care of his own morning business out there? And I don't mean peeing. The man had a whole bonfire's worth of wood in his sweatpants.

I wouldn't mind seeing that!

I tell my inner ho to shut up, even though I'm already imagining Carter taking himself in hand, stroking hard and fast, and coming on the bed right where I slept last night as he grits his teeth so I won't hear him say my name.

No, bad Luna! You're not some orgasm-starved nympho who'll do anything for a hit of dick.

As if he can sense me thinking of him, Carter knocks on the door. "Luna?"

I startle hard, sure that he somehow knows what I'm thinking. "What? Can't a girl use the bathroom in peace?" My voice is too sharp even to my own ears, an obvious tell that something's up.

"You good?" Carter asks, and I swear I hear his smug grin in the two little words.

"Yep, fine. *Just* fine. Totally all good here." I bury my face in a towel, wishing I had one tiny ounce of cool in me, but I don't. Never have, never will.

"Uh, okay," Carter stammers, probably thinking I've bumped my head in here and concussed myself. Or more likely, that I'm in the middle of 'handling' things the way I figured he was. "I'm going to go check on Gracie. She sleeps like the dead, so she's probably still conked out, but Peanut Butter probably needs to piss too," Carter says through the door. He clears his throat and adds, "That'll give you some privacy to do . . . whatever."

He totally thinks I'm rubbing one out.

"Sure, yeah. Thanks," I squeak. "Oh, make sure Peanut Butter doesn't get the rose bushes again." The advice is unneeded, but I don't know what to say. How do you go from 'get your cock off me' to taking the dog out?

A moment later, I hear the door to the room open and close.

Slowly, I crack open the door, peeking out.

Empty. All alone.

I start toward the dresser, but the mess of pillows and sheets on the freshly slept-in bed catches my eye. And then I glance at the door. If Carter already thinks I did jill off, then what's the harm in actually doing it? At the least, it'll take the edge off and clear my head so I can think properly at breakfast.

I don't decide. I act. I rush over to the door, peek out to the hallway to make sure it's clear, and then close and lock it. Locking it is key because if Carter actually walks in on me . . .

I hop in the bed, grabbing the pillow that still smells like Carter and not examining why that's so sexy. Nope, not doing that right now . . . and probably not later, either.

I lie face down, gathering the pillow in one arm to bury my nose in his scent, and slip my other arm underneath my body. With my hips lifted and my knees parted, there's a delicious sense of vulnerability as I feel my lips spread to the air of the room.

I grin into the pillow when I feel my wetness coat my fingers. This is gonna be quick, what Samantha calls the 'Hundred Flick Dash'.

I close my eyes, and though it'd be a nightmare in real life, in my mind's eye, I imagine Carter walking in on me . . .

"What the fuck?" His exclamation is in surprise, but his eyes are hungry for me, enjoying the view.

"Carter!" My fingers stop as I blush furiously.

"Sorry, I . . . fuck, that's hot," he whispers, and I can tell he's not lying. The circus tent in his pants confirms that. "I came back to get my phone, and I heard . . . something. I wanted to make sure you were okay."

"I am." At least I think I am, given the way he's licking his lips.

"Don't you dare stop," he says, stepping closer to the bed. "Let me watch you get yourself off. Show me how you like it."

"Look. But don't touch."

"Deal," Carter says, climbing onto the bed. He sits down behind me, his ass on his heels and off to the side a bit so he can see my pussy and my face as I curl to the side to see him too.

He's straining to get out of his pants, the long, thick rod visible in his sweat pants.

"Let me see you too," I say with a confidence I don't have in the real world.

Carter yanks his T-shirt over his head and hooks his thumbs in his waistband to drop his pants below his butt, letting his cock free. His body is chiseled and lean, his muscles strong and powerful without being body-builder pumped, his deeply ridged abs narrowing to a happy trail that leads to the very definition of proud manhood, standing straight up and rock hard.

He licks his hand and does one full stroke, looking at me as if he's waiting to see if I protest.

When I don't, he wraps his hand around his cock and pumps slowly. "Be a good girl, Luna. Work yourself for me."

"Mmm . . . is that for me?" I ask as I slip a finger inside myself, shuddering at the feeling. I do it again, the heel of my palm bumping my clit as my finger thrusts inside and I watch Carter stroke himself slowly until precum oozes from his tip.

"That's for you," he says, and I'm tempted to ask for a taste . . . but he uses it to spread over his head, giving him a slicker grip. "And when I spill cum everywhere, it'll be for you too. You're driving me fucking wild, Luna."

I fuck myself with my fingers, hard and fast, the bumps to my clit a shock of pleasure each time, getting me closer and closer.

"You're the hottest thing I've ever seen. Pussy in the air, begging me to fill it with my big cock. Fuck, I'll grip your hips, slap your ass, and slam so deep inside you, you never forget what it feels like to be filled with me." Carter strokes himself mercilessly, his words turning us both on.

"Do you want that?" he demands.

I bite my lip and nod, too focused on my hand's rhythm to find words.

"Not good enough. What are you going to do to me? Tell me."

I wrench open my eyes to meet his. He wants me vocal, as aroused by the words as by my telling him what I want. I gasp, stuttering out, "Suck you, swallow you. Till I'm a mess of drool and cum. Even tears, because I choked on you."

It's too much for us both. His chest is rising and falling erratically, and I'm moaning softly on every exhale, right on the edge.

"Together."

We synchronize our strokes, my fingers and his hand moving in time together. As he strokes, I stroke, my pussy gripping my fingers like it would the beautiful cock just a few feet away. We watch each other, and I can see the precum starting to spill over his hand. My thighs tremble with the oncoming climax and I move my fingers to my clit, focusing where I need it most.

"I . . . I want it," I gasp. "Mmm, Carter . . . yeah . . ."

The line between fantasy and reality blurs as I come back to consciousness, in the here and now, with my face smashed into the pillow's fluffiness. Hopefully, it muffled any sounds I made because I kinda got a little carried away there. Okay, a lot carried away.

"Oh, my God," I pant quietly into the empty room.

I collapse to the bed, groaning in frustration. What just happened? Did I seriously jill off while thinking of that asshole?

Yep, you did. And it was the hottest fantasy you've ever had. Don't pretend you're not gonna pull that one out of the old mental spank bank later for a round two.

I roll my eyes at my own inner ho, who got her way this time, and get up. I need to get ready or Carter's going to come check on me, and I don't think it'll be like my imaginary scene. I wash up, find a ponytailer in the fully stocked bathroom that makes an easy messy bun, and pull on a fresh sweatshirt, pants, and flip-flops. I can't meet my own eyes in the mirror right now, so I trust I look okay. I definitely feel more human and have my mental and emotional shields up. I'm going to need them after last night . . . and even more so, after this morning.

In the hall, I hear voices and follow them to the kitchen.

"Good morning," Elena greets me. She's sitting at the table

with Grace, a huge stack of pancakes already on each of their plates. "Have a seat, and Nelda will get you set up in a jiffy."

"Incoming," Nelda warns a second before setting a stack of chocolate-laden pancakes in front of me. "Say when." She shakes a large bottle over the pancakes, covering them with powdered sugar.

"Keep it coming." I wave for more, and keep waving, waving, and waving. Finally, I say, "When."

"A woman after my own heart." Elena laughs, seeing my pile.

The French doors open, and Carter comes in with Peanut Butter on a rope leash. But he has zero control on the slick tile floor, and the dog makes a direct beeline under the table, pulling a stumbling, slipping, and sliding Carter along for the ride.

"Nutbuster, get outta there," Carter pleads, his eyes disappearing below table level as he squats down. We all peer under the table at the big dog sprawled out ungracefully, his nose at Grace's feet.

Carter apologizes to Elena. "So sorry, he's a bit overly loyal."

But considering Grace is slipping the dog a slice of bacon while Carter's not looking, I don't think loyalty is the issue. Grace sees me fighting a grin and puts a finger to her mouth, telling me to keep quiet.

"It's okay. Not like he's on one of the fine rugs," Elena says. "Tile mops easily."

I don't know many wealthy people—in fact, probably only one, Carter—but Elena is definitely not what I expected. She's so casual about everything, almost . . . normal, except she's in a house large enough for hundreds of people to live in. I get the feeling that even if Peanut Butter were pooping on one of the fine rugs, she'd say it was no big deal because a rug is just a 'thing' and not nearly as important as a cute doggie answering nature's call.

Carter plops into a chair with a huff. "Glad you think so. I'm afraid Bernard nearly had my hide in addition to Nutbuster's this morning. I kept him away from the roses," he says, cutting his eyes my way pointedly. "But I guess the peach tree is off limits too? I think his exact words were, 'If my peaches taste like piss, I'm gonna hang your ass in the hayloft as bait for the mice.'"

Elena laughs loudly. "Oh, I love that man's turn of phrase. He's quite imaginative."

"I'm not sure he was kidding," Carter says sullenly. But his eyes light up when he sees the pancakes. "Thank you, Nelda. These look delicious." His manners are back on point now that we're in public and he's in business mode. He takes a bite and moans. "Tastes delicious too."

There's a little small talk before Carter expertly transitions the conversation to Elena's portfolio. "I'd be happy to coordinate with you to ensure your money is working how you'd like it to. There're all sorts of options we can discuss, but the most important thing is that you team up with someone who understands you and your hands-on style. I'd like to think that's me."

For all Elena's easy-going nature, she also knows when to show her hand and when to hold it. "I think it might be, but I'd like to review your management proposal with my current financial advisor. He's ready to move on from the amount of work I take." She pats her silver bob carefully with a smirk as though she's the problem, not the size of her portfolio. "But I've worked with him for enough years to trust his opinion."

Carter's bright smile fades by a few degrees, but quickly, he forcefully turns it back on full-throttle. "Of course. That's a smart plan. I'd be happy to meet with both of you if that'd be helpful. I can answer any questions you might have."

"That's mighty kind of you. I'll get that scheduled."

There's an awkward moment of silence, and I rush to fill it, wanting to help Carter if I can but also show my appreciation. "Elena, I have enjoyed seeing so much of Thomas's collection. It's so special, with pieces I haven't even seen in books. Have you ever considered doing an exclusive exhibit at the museum? It would be a great way to honor him." I wave my hands through the air, sort of doing the 'premiere rainbow' move. "The Thomas and Elena Cartwright Collection."

Elena, who's licking syrup off her finger with a smack, says, "I hadn't thought of anything like that. The art is mostly a part of the décor at this point. It's there, I see it, but I don't *see* it, you know?"

Nodding in understanding, I add, "It could be as large or small as you'd like, showing whichever pieces you'd feel comfortable not being in their 'home' for a little bit. We could even do the plaque info together, telling people exactly what you'd like to share about each piece."

"I'll have to give it some thought. I don't know if I could be apart from any of them. They're like Thomas's babies." Elena puts her hand over her heart, and her smile turns sad. "It feels good to have them surrounding me, like he's still here in a way."

"That makes perfect sense. No pressure at all, just let me know. I'd love to work with you to share his love with the world, but only if you're comfortable with it. I'm honored to get to see his 'babies' at all."

It's the absolute truth. There are pieces I saw last night that will stay with me for the rest of my life, and while I'd love for others to have the same opportunity to see them, I'm protective of my art too, both my own and what I've collected from other artists.

Elena pats my hand. "Will do, honey." Changing the topic, she says, "You know, if y'all are done eating, I believe I promised a bit more of a tour. I thought Miss Grace might like to visit the barn?"

Elena and I have no idea of the bomb she just detonated, but Carter plugs his ears quickly as Grace squeals, "Yeeessss! Do you have horses? And goats? What about chickens?"

Grace is up from the table, tap dancing her feet and ready to go while she interrogates Elena about the full roster of animals in the barn around a mouthful of pancakes. "My barn has a mouser cat named Cricket. Do you have a cat?"

She doesn't wait for an answer before she keeps speed-talking, hopefully swallowing somewhere along the way. "Pegasus is afraid of Cricket 'cuz Cricket tried to jump up on Pegasus's back for a little ride around. Weird that she'll let me on her back, but a tiny cat? Nope, not having it." She shakes her head, already walking out the back door, still rattling on.

Elena's listening, walking with Grace's hand in hers, and Carter and I abandon what's left of our pancakes to follow a few steps behind. "Sorry you didn't get the deal yet," I whisper. "You okay?"

His jaw tenses but he nods. "Yet is the operative word. I haven't given up. I've barely started to woo her." A few more steps, and he takes my hand in his. "You know what that means, right?"

Dumbly, I ask, "What?"

He stops, guiding me to do the same. Toe to toe, he tips my chin up so our eyes meet. "It means," he says in rough whisper right next to my ear, "that you have to be my wife for a bit longer." He presses a soft kiss to my cheek while I freak out on the inside, my brain beginning to process this new information.

What? No! That's not part of the deal. I've seen the art, and now we're done. This sham marriage is finished, and I can go back to my quiet life.

"Aww, you lovebirds are adorable as two June bugs in a jumper, but you'd best come on or me and Miss Grace are gonna beat you to the barn." With that, Elena and Grace start galloping toward the barn like they're horses, Peanut Butter nipping at their heels as they go. Elena is remarkably spry for her age, though Grace is several feet ahead.

"That wasn't our deal—" I start, but Carter cuts me off with a press of his finger to my lips.

"Please, Luna."

I know he's asking me to agree to be his fake wife until he gets this deal with Elena, but it feels like he's asking for much more than that. "I . . . I . . ."

"Don't answer now. Let's make sure Grace hasn't talked Elena into giving her another horse. Just . . . later, okay?"

He leads me to the barn with my hand firmly in his. With every step, my mind whirls more and more. How did this happen? It's gone from tutoring to pretending, and I was kinda onboard with that because of the art.

But now? Having met Elena, it feels so much more wrong, and guilt is growing quicker than a weed in my heart. She's so sweet and genuine, and we're deceiving her. And for what, a deal? I hadn't thought past the dinner, but what if Elena does decide to work with Carter? Are we going to have to keep the charade going?

Where does it end . . . our eventual fake divorce?

I don't get the chance to tell Carter what I'm feeling or what I'm thinking because Grace and Elena are feeding cookies to a pair of horses in neighboring stalls. "Oh, wow! They are . . . big!" I murmur in surprise. The light brown horse closest to Grace towers over her by a couple of feet at least. "Is that safe?"

I don't know who I'm asking, but all three nod at me and Carter looks amused by my concern. "Here, you can do it too," Elena offers, holding out a cookie to me. "They're all big babies."

I recoil, shaking my head as I look at the huge beast. "That's okay. Thank you."

"This ol' fella is a gentle soul. He's a big softie, I promise." Elena proves her claim by petting him on the nose, rubbing from between his eyes down to *boop* his snout. He snuffles and wiggles his lips, baring long, yellowy teeth.

I make an embarrassing sound of fear as I step back quickly.

Grace laughs. "What's wrong? Ed's sweet." She's backing up her claim by playing with his mane, which hangs down low where she can reach. "He's smiling at you."

Between Grace and Elena, I'm feeling backed into a corner.

"Have you ever seen a monster smile right before he eats you? I think that's what Ed's doing," I counter.

Carter whispers, "W-W-A-D?"

I wrinkle my nose. "Huh?"

"What would Alphena do?" he explains. "You write this badass who tackles life, and she's supposedly based on you, so surely, you're not scared of a horse who only wants a cookie?"

"You're using my alter-ego against me?" I accuse. But I hate to admit that he's got a point. Alphena would never let a horse stop her, never let fear hold her back. But Alphena is only part of me, the me I want to be. The real-world me is eyeing Ed like he might jump high enough to clear the gate of his stall and tackle me. But for what? All he seems to want is a cookie. Grace is right about that.

"W-W-A-D," I repeat to myself over and over as I step closer by inches. Elena hands me a cookie, which I hold between delicate fingers. I curl my other fingers down in some small effort to save them if this goes awry.

I can probably draw with my middle finger as long as I keep my thumb.

"W-W-A-D?" Straightening my back, I meet Ed's eyes . . . well, my two eyes look deep into the one of his on the side I'm standing on.

"Ed, want a cookie?" I ask, sounding like I'm asking a parrot named Polly. I hold out the cookie, my shoulders scrunched up protectively as I lean away just in case. "Here, horsey, horsey. Who's a good horsey?"

Ed slowly leans forward, nibbling the cookie for a moment with careful eyes on me before taking the whole cookie. "Oh!" I'm partially terrified, partially excited, and completely surprised that I survived with all my fingers intact. "I did it!" I tell my audience of three, who seem to be fighting back laughter at my dramatics over something they were doing easily.

But I've never been around horses. That's not the life I lead.

Maybe I can use this as inspiration for an Alphena episode, though. Alphena tackles her greatest fear . . . moose. In her back story, Alphena was driving through Michigan to go Polar Bear skinny dipping on the Canadian border when a moose stepped out of the fog at a gas station to literally try to mate with her car while she was inside getting peanut butter cups and beef jerky. Alphena stopped the moose by shouting and shooing it off, but she had hoof-sized dents and a broken hood ornament as souvenirs for her troubles.

Yeah, I can see it . . . Alphena feeding a moose at a rescue sanctuary, getting over her fear just like I am . . .

"Good girl."

Carter's praise hits me unexpectedly, sounding so much like

last night, and the rumble of his voice is echoed deep in my belly by butterflies banging around. "Uh, thanks . . . babe."

Grace gives Carter a strange look, and I step to his side, snaking my arm around his waist before Elena catches on to my stuttered endearment.

Thankfully, Grace has the attention span of your average eight-year-old, and when Peanut Butter runs by chasing a blowing leaf, she runs off after him.

Crisis averted! For now . . .

CHAPTER
ELEVEN
CARTER

I'M DISAPPOINTED that Elena isn't ready to sign a deal with Blue Lake Assets, and by extension, me. But I understand her desire to sleep on it and meet with her current money man, so I keep a salesman's smile on my face while Elena shows Grace through the barn, then walks us through the statue-filled garden and the pool house. It's completely oversized like the estate itself, with several bedrooms, a large living room and dining room space, and a bathroom centered around a spa tub. She's not showing off but rather showing Luna more of Thomas's art. It seems to be tucked into every nook, every possible cranny.

Even the bathroom has art, sculptures that resist the humidity and have Luna marveling. Because of that, it's hours before we start making our way back toward the main house, but I'm in no rush. The more Elena talks, the better my chances are with wooing her. And the more Luna enjoys seeing the art, the more likely she is to keep helping me.

We're in what qualifies as the back yard when a young boy, probably close to Grace's age, runs toward us. "Ann-Elle! Ann-Elle!"

I blink in surprise, listening carefully because it really sounds like he's screaming 'anal' over and over. It takes me a good second to decipher that he's saying 'Aunt El', as in Elena, but with a bit of a drawl.

The screeching is enough to scare Peanut Butter, who's not exactly a fearless dog anyway, and he yelps as he bolts away with his tail between his legs. Right into the swimming pool with a big splash.

"Nutbuster! Get outta there!" I shout, adding to the racket. Running after the damn dog, I can still hear Elena as the boy nearly tackles her in a hug.

"Oof, well, hello there! I wasn't expecting to see you today, Jacob," Elena tells the boy breathlessly. "Where's your momma?"

He starts jumping up and down excitedly. "Talking to Mr. Stanley. Are we swimming?" The boy—Jacob, I guess—sprints to my side, bumping me out of the way to step past me into the pool up to his knees, fully dressed, shoes and all.

"Probably don't wanna do that, man. If I know moms, yours is gonna have your hide," I warn. But he shrugs me off, either not believing me or not fearing his mother.

"Here, doggy, doggy!" he shouts, his voice still gratingly high. What is up with this kid's vocal cords?

Grace has followed—thankfully staying dry on the pool deck next to me—and informs the boy, "His name's Nutbuster. He's my Uncle Kyle's dog. Nutbuster, get your butt over here."

Squatted down and leaning over the water, I've managed to grab Peanut Butter's collar and guide him toward the pool steps, where a waiting Jacob wraps his arms around the dog's neck, getting his shirt soaked and burying his face in wet fur. *Blech!*

"Why don't we get on up to the house? We'll get y'all cleaned up and dry," Elena tells the kids and dog, and then she looks to me and Luna. "And you can meet my niece, Claire."

Elena's suggestion is met with more wild jumping, and then Jacob takes her hand, roughly pulling her toward the house. He's a bit rambunctious, and that's saying something considering I'm used to Grace's exuberance.

I glance at Luna to see if she's on the same page, but she's holding Grace's hand and being carried away toward the house too. I guess one way or another, she's onboard.

"Guess it's you and me," I murmur to Peanut Butter. He gives me a doggy smile, barely warning me before he shakes wildly, sending water droplets everywhere. "Ugh, seriously?" I growl, trying in vain to shield myself from the onslaught but mostly only stopping it from hitting me in the face. Peanut Butter barks happily, looking after Grace.

"Let's go." One pat of my leg, and we cover ground easily, catching up despite with a few more shakes from Peanut Butter.

Going through a side door into a mudroom of sorts, Elena calls out, "Claire? Where you at, sweetie?"

But Elena waits for no one and she's opening cabinets, pulling out towels, and roughly drying Jacob off. Once his hair is standing straight up, she hands him a stack of folded sweats and he disappears into a small bathroom. I've got Grace toweled off too, but thankfully, she doesn't need a change of clothes, and the dog that started this whole wet mess is somehow mostly dry.

A woman I assume to be Claire comes into the mudroom. She's in her late forties, her blonde expertly managed to hide any grays, her face a skillfully done Botox mask, and her designer outfit is from this year's Dior collection. She's what my mother would politely call 'well-maintained'.

"Right here, Aunt Elena." Her voice is warm honey, but when she sees Luna and me, it turns to steel. "Hello. Nice to meet you."

She's lying, but I'll win her over. I always do. I offer my hand. "Nice to meet you, Claire. I'm Carter Harrington and this is my wife, Luna. My niece, Grace, is around here somewhere . . ." I trail off teasingly, looking around as though I don't see Grace, who's standing beside me. "Here?" I lift one arm, glancing to my right, then the other, glancing to my left and spinning in a circle as I look behind me.

"She's right there," Jacob calls out, pointing as he comes out of the bathroom in the fresh clothes.

Grace joins in with a laugh. "I'm right here, Uncle CJ!"

"Oh, there she is!" I boop her nose and then glance up to the women. Luna and Elena are amused, smiling warmly, but Claire is staring dead-eyed. If her eyebrows moved, I think she'd have one up by her hairline and one scrunched down toward her nose.

As it is, they're completely frozen in perfect arches. Hard sell, I guess, but I'll persevere as always.

Either that or the Botox has done its job a bit too well.

"Not that I ain't pleased as punch to see you, but I thought you were doing that big showing this weekend?" Elena asks, looking worried.

"I was," Claire answers reassuringly, "but when I called to chat, Stanley said you were entertaining visitors." Still talking to Elena but looking at me, she warns, "I wanted to check in on you."

I understand her cold shoulder reception now. She thinks I'm one of the gold-digging weasels who prey on widows and widowers during a time of vulnerability. Protecting her aunt is her responsibility and honor. "That's very kind of you."

"She's good like that," Elena agrees. "I'm fine, Claire. But you look like you need some lunch. Come on, Nelda's probably got a spread all ready."

She doesn't wait for Claire's agreement. She marches off toward the kitchen with Jacob's hand in hers on one side and Grace's on the other. "I bet she made us a treat. She's good like that. Nelda knows this old girl likes a sweet tea and a cookie every afternoon. You two probably eat healthy stuff like carrots and don't like cookies at all, right?"

Jacob and Grace shout nearly in unison, "Yes, I do!" Jacob then commences bouncing like a kangaroo and yelling, "Cook-ie! Cook-ie!" Each syllable is a hop with an ever-increasing volume. "Cook-ie! Cook-ie! Cook-ie!"

Rather than be annoyed by it, Elena hops with him, though her hops are less sure-footed. Grace gets into it too, hopping along. Thankfully, she doesn't add to the cacophony Jacob is creating all on his own. Cameron would *love* it if I brought Grace back with that new habit.

In the kitchen, Elena leads Jacob and Grace to hop up into chairs at the counter as she points to the table for us. I hold out Luna's chair for her and then wait for Claire and Elena to sit before sitting myself. In the melee, Peanut Butter scoots under the kids' feet and lies down, knowing where he's most likely to be fed, intentionally or accidentally.

Elena was right. Nelda has laid out quite a well-appointed charcuterie board. And yes, there are cookies. Following Elena's lead, I make a plate of small bites for Grace. When both kids have been served, I make another plate for myself.

"Mr. Harrington, what's your business here?" Claire asks coldly.

"Claire!" Elena scolds.

I hold out a staying hand to Elena. "It's okay." After nodding respectfully to Claire, I add, "I came to meet with your aunt on business matters and stayed for the sweatpants and cookies."

I grin impishly, hoping to garner at least the tilt of a smile, but Claire's lips stay perfectly flat. If anything, they press together. "Cute. I'm sure that works for you quite often," she says snidely. "However, I'm disturbed that you think charming wit will prove effective in allaying my concerns, rather than simply being transparent."

"Me-oww," Luna mutters under her breath, so quiet that only I can hear her.

Elena is more upfront. "Claire, don't be such a Rude Rhonda. Carter's been a perfect gentleman, not some high-pressure used car salesman."

"That's not what I *hear*." She looks me up and down with a frown of disgust.

Luna lets out a squeak at the obvious entendre, her chin dropping and her cheeks flushing instantly. I place my hand on her thigh without thinking, needing to make sure she's okay. She looks at me desperately, a plea in their brown depths.

"I'm sorry if we were a bit . . ." I glance to the children and then back to Claire. "Exuberant?" I don't know what else to call it. Luna and I were obnoxiously loud last night. It started in an attempt to sell the marriage farce, but it turned into out-of-control fun, something I haven't had in too long. "We were—"

"Newlyweds," Luna blurts out.

"What?" Claire asks, giving Luna her attention for the first time.

"We're newlyweds," Luna repeats. "It's hard to . . . I mean, *difficult* to not . . ." She's stumbling over her words, but her gaze is strong as she gives Claire her full focus. Finally, she gives up, sort of flailing her hands together. "You know?"

Elena pats Claire's hand. "Dear, I think what she's saying is . . . have you seen this fine specimen of a young man? And this beautiful, sweet woman? They're in love, and that means a little lovin'." Her eyes go soft, and she stares up toward the light over the table. "I remember when Thomas and I were newlyweds. Why, there wasn't a flat surface in our house we didn't christen. Tables, beds, floors . . . walls." She confides to Luna, "Thomas was strong and I was a wee thing like you back in those days."

Luna shifts uncomfortably, and I squeeze her thigh beneath my palm, stilling her with the punishing pressure.

"Aunt Elena, I don't think anyone wants to hear about you and Uncle Thomas' *sex life!*" Claire mouths the last bit more than speaks it, glancing at the kids.

"Hmph, well I'm not the one gossiping with Stanley about guests' activities after they've retired to their private spaces for the night, now am I?" Elena pops a cube of cheese in her mouth, having gotten the last word. "Besides, it's how we all got here on this planet, ain't it?"

Claire's eyes narrow, but she does stop talking about sex, at least. Mine and Elena's.

"Nutbuster, get your butt down! You're smashing my balls!" Jacob shouts, pushing at Peanut Butter, who's stood up and placed his feet on Jacob's thigh, at an apparently sensitive location, to beg for food.

"*Eh-eh.*" I make the disapproving noise Kyle has used for Peanut Butter since he was a puppy, and the dog looks my way instantly. "Down."

I point to the floor, and the dog settles back under the kids' chairs.

"Jacob! What did you say?" Claire demands in a high-pitched voice, clearly more upset about the words than the dog.

Jacob looks over his shoulder to his mom, sensing that he's in trouble. "Uh, she said it first."

He points at Grace, throwing her in harm's way without remorse to deflect trouble from himself. I damn near hear the sound of the bus rolling by as he does.

"She did?" Claire turns a mom-glare on Grace, but no one gives Grace shit on my watch except me.

Leaning to the side to interrupt Claire's visual warpath, I ask calmly, "What's the issue?"

"That language!" Claire exclaims. "Obviously."

She's reacting as though Jacob dropped some F-bombs over his crackers and pepperoni slices. Her hand is literally on her chest, grasping for invisible pearls, and her mouth is gaping like someone's going to throw in a three-pointer with a cheese cube.

"What's she talking about?" Grace asks Jacob. "You just said Nutbuster was smashing your balls and told him to get his butt down." She looks confused as she repeats what Jacob said and finds no issue.

I sigh. "If I may . . . Nutbuster is what we call Peanut Butter. It's an affectionate nickname. And he did say butt, not ass. That's better."

Grace holds her hand up and quotes, "Tush . . . Bootie . . . Badonkadonk . . . Butt . . . Ass . . . *Culo*. In order of badness. I can use up to butt now, ass at thirteen with friends and at sixteen with family, and *culo* after I'm eighteen and only if I'm being dirty. Never in front of Daddy, Maw-Maw H, or Paw-Paw H."

"Grace!" The scold is met with her throwing her arms out like 'what, you know I'm right'. What the hell is Cameron teaching her? Or more likely, Kyle? Hell, probably Cameron's multi-lingual nanny too.

And why is *culo* worse than ass? Actually, that's one I probably don't want to know the answer to.

"He also called his *testicles balls*," Claire corrects, her nose curling as she whispers the words as though they're both offensive.

"That's what they are, Mom. Nobody says *tess-a-culls*. Even Dad calls 'em balls," Jacob adds. "Or his nuts."

Shrugging, I offer, "He's not wrong. I've got four brothers

and I can count on one hand the number of times I've said 'testicles', but balls, nuts, moose knuckle, and *cojones* are all common." I'm taking a risk—a huge one—at offending Claire, but I'm depending on Elena losing the battle she's fighting with the laugh that's trying to escape.

"Ooh, moose knuckle! I like that one!" Jacob tells us, and Peanut Butter barks in agreement.

That's all Elena can take. She bangs the table with a palm as a loud belly laugh escapes, her eyes squinch shut, and her mouth drops wide open. "Oh, my word! That's the funniest thing I've heard in a month of Sundays. You asked for it, Claire, and Carter delivered with bells on. Or balls, in this case."

I chance a smile and then laugh along. Luna places her hand over mine in a move of solidarity, and it suddenly feels less punishing to have my hand squeezing her thigh and more sexy, especially as my pinkie moves an inch higher of its own volition.

Though there's laughter around the table, I still hear the tiny hitch in Luna's breath and it makes my heart stutter.

But as the laughter fades, Claire straightens her back, visibly resetting herself. "If we could stick to the topic at hand . . . Carter, we won't be needing your services."

CHAPTER
TWELVE
LUNA

BEEP-BEEP-BEEP, *beep-beep-beep.*

"And break for fifteen." I stand from where I've sprawled on the floor for the last forty-five-minute work sprint and stretch my arms overhead.

"Let me finish this chapter. I'm on a roll," Samantha argues with her nose buried in her notes.

That's not what we agreed upon, and we're sticking the plan. Past history has proven we do best with forty-five/fifteen-minute cycles. It's how we can work successfully for the whole evening, which is what we both need to do tonight. Me, on Alphena. Sam, on coursework for the test she has next week.

This interruption is key to her studying, even if she doesn't think so. She's spread out on the couch—laptop, papers, highlighters everywhere—so I plop right down in the middle of the tornado.

"Hey!"

"Break. Time." My declaration is met with an exasperated sigh. "You know you need it. Don't ignore your body's signals." It's a direct quote from her, one she's told me numerous times, but that doesn't mean she likes me throwing it back at her.

She glares at me for a long moment where I think I've won, then she leans back against the arm of the couch and a slow smile steals her lips.

Uh-oh. When she looks at me like that, I'm in trouble.

Deflect! Save yourself!

"Hungry? Thirsty? I've got Raisinets, popcorn, wine, La Croix . . ."

Samantha wrinkles her nose. "I hate that shit and you know it. La Croix is water that they wave fruit over and pump full of more air than a puffer fish's ass. And raisins are not candy, no matter how much chocolate you cover them in." I have a split second of thinking I've gotten away with the deflection before she shatters the illusion. "Body signals, that's the topic at hand."

"Nope, I happen to love Raisinets." I make a run for the kitchen, but with the size of my apartment, I'm not exactly far away and Samantha keeps talking.

"You owe me a story. How was dinner with your husband?"

I shove a large handful of candy in my mouth and gesture that I can't talk right now. I should use the time to think of how to explain the craziness of the dinner with Carter, but instead, what pops out as soon as I can talk is . . .

"We had fake-sex."

And also, a stray Raisinet that was somehow going ninja on my tongue. I cover my mouth with a hand, chewing and swallowing as quickly as I can without choking.

Samantha sprints across the room to my side. "You had sex with Carter Harrington? Seriously?"

She picks up a candy and beans me in the forehead with it. Luckily, I catch it on the drop and hold it in my hand with the others. "Fake sex," I repeat, "Not peen in vag. That's your specialty."

"Details, Luna," she says, not offended at all by my comment. "Are we talking dry humping, fingering, or what?"

"Samantha!" She tilts her head in a threat to continue listing sexual acts until I start explaining or die of embarrassment. Given the heat of my cheeks, death by mortification is entirely possible, so I spill my guts. "We had dinner and it was fine. Except we had to take Grace and Peanut Butter. But still, fine. And the tour was amazing. Thomas's collection was all I hoped and more. Surprisingly, I think my favorite was one of his personal works. It was beautiful in a different way than I expected. The technique was flawless, but it was the emotion in every stroke that showed how much he loved Elena, his wife."

Samantha holds up a finger, halting me. "Who are Grace and Peanut Butter?"

"Carter's niece and his brother's dog. There was a family mix-up and he ended up emergency babysitting, so we had to take them with us to dinner."

"To a business dinner? Oh-kay, you know that's weird, right?" When I nod, she rolls her eyes. "But then y'all did dinner, a tour . . . unless there's something I need to know there, get to the fake sex part. I want to hear all the *wet, juicy, sloppy details*."

"It was late. Elena suggested that we stay over and leave the next day." I pop a Raisinet into my mouth, chewing thoughtfully. "Once we got in the bedroom, Carter made a joke about them expecting us to have sex and that we could fake it. I thought he was nuts, but then he crawled onto the bed with me and started banging the bed against the wall. I kinda had to go along."

Another Raisinet, and I chase this one down with a swallow of wine. Samantha waits impatiently, now nibbling popcorn faster than a chipmunk stuffing its cheeks for winter.

"It was ridiculous. But it was kinda . . . fun?" I tilt my head, thinking back. "I said some stuff that was . . ." Shyly, I smile and meet Samantha's eyes. "Kinda kinky. Stuff you told me about, and Carter seemed to like it. He said some stuff too."

"Did you like what he said?" Samantha asks carefully. She's not quite in professional mode, but almost.

Chewing slowly, I confess, "I did. But we didn't . . . do anything. Or not anything sexy. We didn't even touch during the fake sex. But we talked after, and he was different than I thought. He puts a lot of pressure on himself . . . and he called me pretty." I shouldn't have told her that part, but it blurted out before I could squash it down.

"Shit. I told you not to fall for his act, Luna, and you went and fell anyway with the slightest compliment from a man who

gives them out like a shady masseuse gives out hand jobs."
Samantha shakes her head, frowning in disappointment.

"It wasn't like that," I argue.

"It wasn't?" she questions. "Are you sure?"

I drop my eyes to the rapidly disappearing candies in my
hand and then toss the last few back in one go. "I didn't fall for
him. I just maybe-sorta-kinda don't hate him as much as I did.
And there was no hand job involved—for either of us."

"Luna, he's no less of an asshole than he was before. He's
pulling a fake marriage charade for a business deal and he fake
fucked you to really sell it. Who cares if he's slightly human deep
beneath all that?"

Maybe I do.

The words are on the tip of my tongue, but I don't say them
aloud. Mostly because I'm not sure whether I believe them
or not.

Carter was different than I thought, but he also assumed I'd
continue the farce until Elena agreed to the deal, which was not
what we discussed. And there's a definite sense of 'poor, pitiful
prince' to his worries about impressing his family.

But there was something surprisingly sexy in the way he
looked at me sometimes . . . in his hand squeezing my thigh . . .
and in waking up in the cage of his arms with him pressed to my
back. Or maybe I'm horny and the mere proximity of a man is
sending me into a stupor?

Beep-beep-beep.

"Saved by the bell," I sigh gratefully as I realize the alarm
means it's time to work again. "Forty-five minutes and we'll
reconvene."

"Of course," Samantha huffs. "This isn't finished."

Despite claiming that, she does return to her spot on the
couch and drops her eyes to her notes as she grabs a pink high-
lighter. "Note to self, get Luna a new toy so she doesn't hop on
Carter's dick and get her heart broken in the process."

"Samantha!"

She shrugs, not embarrassed in the slightest to be talking

about letting your fingers do the walking. I eat two more Raisinets before I sit down to work on Alphena some more.

I'm on page twenty-three now after several sleepless nights of work. Not sleepless because I couldn't actually go to sleep but because every time I did, Carter was waiting in my dreams. Only the sex wasn't fake. It was very, very real, and I'd wake up hot and liquid, so burying myself in work was preferable to burying my fingers in myself.

As I focus on Alphena, I can't help but ask myself WWAD? What would Alphena do with this whole situation? Would she take the fake marriage in stride and continue helping someone in need or protect herself and walk away before it all blows up in her face? Maybe she'd fuck him for fun, her heart clad behind some Alpha-bitch armor?

Or maybe take the biggest risk of all and see if there could be anything real with Carter?

I honestly don't know.

CHAPTER
THIRTEEN
CARTER

THERE WAS a time that being invited to my father's office felt like a privilege. I was eager to learn or to show off. But somewhere along the way, it morphed into a summons to my doom. Dramatic, but it's one of the few things that makes me grit my teeth instantly because there's no winning in Dad's office.

It's his domain, his den, his realm of complete authority. And while he means well, without the balance my mother provides, I always feel as though I'm being called to the principal's office after sending my underwear up the flagpole. Not that I did that. That was my brother Cole. But we all learned from that disaster exactly how fast the vein in Dad's forehead can pump.

I tilt my head left and right, popping my neck, and prepare to enter his inner sanctum. From her desk, his secretary smiles blandly. "He's waiting for you."

"Scale of one to ten?"

"Mm, three. You're good to go."

I appreciate her comment and give her a small smile to let her know. The assessment lets me know that I'm not walking into an ambush.

I open the door and realize I asked the wrong question, or not the follow-up I should've . . . is he alone?

My dad is sitting behind his desk, which is one of those old-school, oversized, dark walnut numbers, in a tufted, dark green leather chair. He's the epitome of a powerful CEO, practically ready for a *Forbes* photographer at any moment, and exactly what I expected. However, sitting across from him is my brother, Cameron, whose eyes are stone-hard as they meet mine.

Damn, what's his issue? You'd think he'd be a little grateful that I took care of Grace on the fly when he was out doing God knows what. I'll never resent Grace for needing me anytime or for anything, but Cameron? Another issue altogether. We give each other shit freely and easily, competing against each other while simultaneously being willing to kill for one another.

Shutting the door behind me, I take my time striding to the other chair in front of the desk, reading their faces. "Hey, Dad, Cameron."

"Have a seat." Dad holds out a hand like I don't know where I'm supposed to sit, like we haven't had a hundred meetings with the three of us in this triangle of a power dynamic.

Appearances are key, so I lean back in the chair, resting an ankle on the opposite knee. Outwardly, I'm unconcerned, chill as a Choco Taco in a January blizzard. "What's up?"

Dad's eyes flick to Cameron and then back to me. They've been talking about me, that much is clear.

"Dad wants us to work together on my venture capital deal," Cameron says flatly, obviously not on board with that plan in the slightest.

"The restaurant one?" Now I'm the one looking between my brother and dad. "Why?"

This is where Dad steps in. "It's a big investment that needs close monitoring. I thought having two Harringtons involved would make that more manageable."

I lean over to Cameron, talking as though Dad can't hear us. It's a trick we've done since we were kids that lets us say things out loud that we would never say directly to Dad. "Does he think you can't handle it? Your plan was spot-on."

Cameron leans in too, the trademark Harrington grin on his face. "You read my plan?"

I lift a wry brow in answer. He knows I obsessively scoured the damn thing after the meeting. He would've done the same thing if I dropped a surprise investment opportunity with zero notice. Actually, maybe I should do that with Elena's deal? That'd show them I can bring value to the table.

His grin grows with my lack of admission.

"I'm good, though I'd never turn down some help. But I think this one is about you, man." He jerks his head toward Dad.

Me? Why?

Choosing the direct route instead, I ask Dad, "What's the deal? It sounds like Cameron's got the restaurant under control."

Dad's shrug is noncommittal. "Like I said, it's a big job, and you don't have anything specific on your plate right now, so I thought you could help out. You always push each other to do better."

This is one of the ways Cameron and I started our perpetual competition with one another. As the second oldest, I wanted to do everything my big brother did when we were kids, and as the oldest, he wanted me to leave him alone. Our parents cultivated our relationship as brothers by encouraging us to play together, whether in the yard or on a baseball diamond, and later, to play against each other in school, in business, and in life. The result is a rivalry built on shared experiences and a love that we show by giving each other massive amounts of shit whenever possible.

"Putting one and one together, I take it you think I need Cameron to push me right now?" I summarize bluntly. Because I don't have time for games and double-speak right now. I'm too busy with my notes and follow-up from dinner at Elena's.

Not that Dad knows that.

Dad chuckles. "You don't have to make it sound like a bad thing."

"Seriously? You're basically forcing Cameron to let me tag along on his big deal like some pitiful puppy no one wants."

"Woof, woof." Cameron's sound effects are not needed, and I shoot him a warning glance that he thankfully accepts.

"If you don't have anything going on, help Cameron." Dad's declaration is final, or at least in his mind, it is.

"And if I have something going on?" I challenge. I'm playing with fire because I don't want to spill my guts about the possibility of the Cartwright deal, not yet, but I can't work with Cameron and give Elena the time she deserves.

Cameron clears his throat, but it doesn't cover his scoff and I glare at him openly now. Shut the fuck up, Cam.

"Yeah, Gracie said you had *something* going on." He backhands my arm like we're frat bros, which we definitely are not. "By the way, next time she's hanging out with you, could you *not* take her to your latest's house for an overnight? All I heard was Elena-this and Elena-that. If Gracie doesn't know about my dating life, I definitely don't need her knowing about yours."

Shit, there's a lot to unpack there, but I start with . . .

"Your dating life? I thought you'd taken a vow of celibacy."

It's borderline and I know it, but it's been a long time since the accident that took Cameron's wife, and to be honest, even though we argue and compete with one another, I worry about him. He buries himself in work, not because he loves it but because it's a distraction from the loss I'm sure he still feels acutely. As an unspoken rule, we don't discuss the accident, never mention his wife's name, or note that Grace is the spitting image of the mother she doesn't remember. His mentioning a dating life, even as a joke, is . . . progress? At least in a twisted way.

"Yeah, well, if I'm celibate, at least you know I'll never fuck you over. Can't say the same for you."

"Who's Elena? Someone we should meet?" Dad asks, skipping over the brotherly shit-stirring. He's always worried about who we date and spend time with, wanting to make sure they're 'worthy' of a Harrington, and in some cases, that no one leads us astray. I think he fell down on that gig by the time Kyle came around, but for the rest of us, it was a constant Q-and-A about anyone we mentioned. Which is why we don't mention anyone we date to family, especially our parents. Mom would have the wedding half-planned before the introduction was over and Dad would be running a Pentagon-level background check.

"Maybe, but not like you're thinking," I venture carefully, not wanting to say too much, too soon.

"She must be something real special for you to not bail on the overnight after Kyle saddled you with a tagalong. Sorry about that, by the way. Grace said y'all did some sort of museum visit to look at boring paintings, the pancakes were yummy, and that she got to pet a horse?"

"Again, yes . . . but not like you're thinking." He's fishing for information that I don't want to share, but not answering is like chumming already-shark-infested waters. Because Cameron is definitely a shark, but Dad is the head shark of us all.

"Elena who?" Dad asks, suddenly intrigued.

"Thanks," I mutter to Cameron. I could say that Elena is someone I'm casually seeing. Lying is becoming my SOP when the situation warrants it. But I don't.

"Elena Cartwright. Strictly professional, I assure you."

Dad's eyes narrow, and if his head were transparent, I think I'd see a tiny elf erratically flipping through file cabinets, looking for an encyclopedia entry on the name Elena Cartwright.

And I see the moment the elf finds the correct file when Dad's eyes widen and the proverbial lightbulb over his head lights up. "What in the Sam-hill are you doing with Elena Cartwright?"

"When there's something to know, I'll tell you. Until then, I've got it handled." I try to sound confident, maybe even arrogant. Dad respects both. Cameron respects neither, at least not in others.

"*You* had dinner with the matriarch of one of the wealthiest families in the state, and now you're holding out on us. Spill your guts or I'll spill them for you." He makes a slicing motion across his waist, as though he would have the courage to attack me physically. We both know his daggers are verbal.

"I've got it handled," I repeat.

"Look, I've heard of Elena, so I know what she's capable of. Why are you talking to her?" Dad asks again. Except it's not a question this time.

I don't want to say. I've already said too much, and if I spill any more, there's no way I'm going to be left alone to handle this. But Dad isn't the type you tell no. Especially about business.

Resigned, I sigh and search the ceiling for how best to say this, where I come out the hero for having brought the Cartwright portfolio to Blue Lake Assets all by myself. No shared credit, no shared responsibility.

"Carter." Dad's patience is waning, the vein in his forehead starting to pulse.

Meeting his eyes, I say proudly, "I'm talking to her about taking over her portfolio management."

Dad leans forward in interest. "Are you serious? Her portfolio is massive, diversified, and . . . seriously?" His brows are climbing his forehead as he tries to decide whether I'm telling tall tales or the truth.

I smile triumphantly, though I haven't sealed the deal yet. I know Elena is going to sign with me. She has to after this weekend.

For a long moment, I wait for Dad to return the smile. He's got to be proud of me for chasing down this opportunity. It's not a make-or-break for Blue Lake Assets because we're so large ourselves, but gaining Elena Cartwright's portfolio as a client would be a massive win for us. Which means it's a huge win for me.

Because this is my deal. Even if it's in the early days.

Dad stands up, coming around his desk and leaning back on the front of it between Cameron and me. With his arms over his chest and his feet crossed at the ankles, he says, "This sounds like an exciting prospect. Good job, Carter."

I beam at the approval. I hate to admit it, but I do. I've worked hard for so many years to please my dad, to feel worthy of the Harrington name, and in one little sentence, I feel like I've finally done that.

"We'll have dinner with her. The whole family shebang. We need to woo her, really show her what the Harringtons and Blue Lake are all about," Dad decides.

And just like that, the balloon of pride filling up inside me pops, leaving strings of latex self-doubt and frustration in its wake. "No, Dad. This is my deal. I'm handling it, and it won't include the five-ring circus we call a family."

"This is a potential Blue Lake Asset deal, and if a little Harrington is good, a lotta Harrington is better. We're not a five-ring circus. We're a close-knit, passionate family who happens to know a thing or two about making people money. That's what Elena Cartwright cares about."

I hear what he's *not* saying loud and clear. He doesn't think I can do this on my own. He thinks I'm not good enough to secure the deal alone and is taking over because he thinks I'll fuck it up.

"You have no idea what she cares about. *I do.* I've done the research, put in the hours." I almost admit that I've gone above and beyond to a point that no one else in the family would be willing to do.

"Then I'll ask her what she cares most about . . . at dinner," Dad says. "Any food things I should tell the chef?"

Once my dad has made up his mind, there's no changing it. I think I could literally switch out his brain with a new one, and he'd wake up from the transplant surgery still planning a dinner for Elena. But I have to try.

"Dad, stop. I've got this under control. Sometimes, going in full-throttle isn't the move, and finesse isn't exactly your style."

"I was finessing before you were a thought in my ball sack, Son. Now what should I tell the chef?"

"Yeah, that's some smooth moves, Dad." I glare at him mockingly, hoping he'll see reason and yield, but he stares back, giving no quarter.

"She likes horses, pancakes, and art," Cameron offers, and when I sharply cut my eyes to him, he shrugs. "At least according to Grace."

Dad nods, as if it's everything he needs. "This is happening with or without you, Carter."

I feel like this whole thing is being taken from my hands no matter how much I scramble to keep ahold of it for myself. I weigh my options, wishing I'd kept my mouth shut in the first place. But that bell can't be unrung.

So, what are my options? Say nothing and play second-fiddle to Dad when he contacts Elena. In that case, even if Elena signs with Blue Lake, it won't be my acquisition, it'll be Dad's. Or give in and try to hold on to some degree of control of this deal.

"I don't know if she's allergic to anything, but she must prefer chicken or pork because there was no red meat at our dinner, breakfast the next day, or the lunch charcuterie board."

Why am I sharing this and how the hell did this happen? This is supposed to be my big deal, and now I'm discussing menu options like I'm Martha Stewart or some shit. Next thing you know, I'll be making napkin origami swans.

"It's settled then. Carter, get with Elena and invite her for dinner as soon as possible and then let me know what night. I'll need a full run-down of everything you've got so we're on the same page. Cameron, looks like you're back to working on the restaurant alone."

Dad claps his hands sharply and strides back around his desk, returning to his chair. I guess that means we're dismissed.

In the hall, Cameron whistles quietly. "Damn, man, I had no idea that's what you were working on. Grace kept talking about Elena, and I thought you had a new hook-up."

"You thought I'd take your daughter with me to a hook-up? I'm not a monster."

Cameron smiles a small smile. "I trust you with Grace, implicitly. You probably more than anyone else. You won't try to put her on a motorcycle . . . Kyle." He holds up a finger. "Or take her shopping—"

"Kayla," I complete for him, and he holds up another finger.

"Or let her eat her weight in sugar."

In unison, we say, "Mom."

"For fuck's sake, you showed Gracie art and horses, let her sleep with Nutbuster, and fed her 'shark-coochie'. She thinks you're the best."

"Because I am," I volley back. "To be clear, I'm pretty sure she meant charcuterie."

"I know, but don't you dare tell her how to say it correctly. I haven't had to put a sandwich together in months, and it cracks me up every time she says that's what she wants for dinner."

I can see the light of humor in his eyes, and it reassures me in a deep part of my gut. We all worry about him, but finding joy in little things like your daughter's mispronunciation of a difficult word is a good sign.

"Does she have you playing Royal Family yet? I might've gone a bit overboard on the tiara, but she earned it. Not to mention, she negotiated for it like a damn pro. She'll be interning before she's eighteen at this rate."

'A bit overboard' is being kind. By the time I took Grace home, she'd talked me into a plastic rhinestone-encrusted tiara with purple silk roses and curled ribbons that hung down her back plus a gold one with rainbow rhinestones for Peanut Butter.

"Yeah, since Peanut Butter left his at our house . . ."

He pauses and together, we say, "Kyle."

Cameron continues, "That one is mine for now, but I only warrant a loaner and have to share it with the dog."

I smile but don't give him a bit of shit because we'd all do the same for Grace, and he says, "Good luck on this Elena deal, man. I think you might need it with Dad acting that excited."

His expression says I'm gonna need a hell of a lot more than luck. I might need a genie and three wishes, and even then, I may not be able to get in front of the steamroller better known as Charles Harrington the Second.

"Shit. I'm fucked, aren't I?" I ask, not sure if I want him to tell me the truth or a white lie that'll make me feel better.

"Completely and thoroughly, six days a week, and twice on Sunday," he answers.

Yeah, the white lie would've been better.

CHAPTER
FOURTEEN
LUNA

"LUNA!"

The yell through my door is accompanied by loud banging that scares the snot out of me. I startle, a squeaking noise escaping as I instinctively try to hide in the corner behind the couch.

Do I have an outstanding warrant I don't know about? Is the SWAT team gonna bust through my door? Maybe they'll go away if I'm silent?

"Open the door, Luna!"

"No Luna here!" I call out in a falsely low voice. Ugh, I sound like a voiceover dub for an anime or something.

And they clearly aren't buying it either. "Not funny. Open the door, *wife*."

Wait, what?

There's only one person who would call me that, but it doesn't sound like Carter out there. Unless he drank three espresso energy drinks, followed them with enough sugar to make an elephant get the jitters, and then got a case of mad cow disease.

I climb out from my hidey-hole and peek out the peephole. It's Carter, but not like I've ever seen him. He looks . . . shook. Curious, I open the door. "You look like—"

Carter pushes past me, barging into my apartment.

I glare at his back and mutter, "Well, come on in, I guess."

He pays no attention to my sarcasm as I wave my hands around, mimicking a welcoming host. As I close the door, Carter helps himself to my refrigerator. Grabbing one of the craft beers I keep stocked for Zack, he twists off the cap and takes a long draw from the bottle.

I tilt my head, watching as his Adam's apple bobs with every swallow and an intrusive thought of what it would feel like to lick over the stubble on his jaw and down to kiss his neck pops into my head.

What!?

I don't want to do that. That's ridiculous.

Ahh, maybe this is a dream.

That could be true. Since I got back from Elena's, sex-filled nightmares where Carter and I turn that fake sex very real are disturbing my sleep. This is probably one of those. I must've fallen asleep while working, and voila . . . Carter appears. I wonder if this'll be the one where he holds my jaw while feeding me. And I *don't* mean food.

"Feeling better?" I ask.

He swallows once more and then licks his lips. Wiping the slight sheen from his mouth with the back of his hand, he looks at me with eyes filled with torture. "All day, all night, I've played out every scenario possible, every variation. I've been over it a million ways, maybe more. I want you to know that. You have to understand. There's no other way."

He's ranting wildly as though I have any idea what he's talking about.

"What? I've never seen you like this. You're scaring me." I take a slow step back as tingles of fear dance over the nape of my neck. He looks crazed and desperate—his normally neat hair mussed, his tie gone, his dress shirt untucked and unbuttoned at the neck—but it's his eyes that bore into mine that look the most different. Carter always seems confident and in control, even when unexpected things are thrown at him. But right now, he's looking at me as though . . .

I'm his salvation?

I'm no such thing. I couldn't save someone else from a fly. I can't even save myself from myself.

He covers the space between us while I'm still frozen in place, too stupid to run and too intrigued to speak. He drops his beer bottle to the counter and firmly grabs around my upper arms with both hands.

I feel the pressure and realize that this is no dream. I'm wide awake and completely confused. "Carter—"

"You have to help me, Luna," he says, his voice low and rough and desperate . . . and sexy as fuck. "Please."

The plea in his voice strikes directly into my heart. "Yeah, sure. Whatever you need."

I don't know what I'm agreeing to, but it can't be worse than what I've already done. Right? And I'm pretty sure there's a rule about disagreeing with crazy people when they have ahold of you. As in, don't do it.

"Really?" He shakes me a little bit, lifting me to my toes. My hands find their way to his stomach, pressing for balance as I look up at him. There's a spark of electricity in the space between us.

"Of course?" The questions are bubbling up, but I don't have a chance to ask.

"Yes . . ." The word of relief becomes a breath as his lips meet mine. It's so much like my dreams that I fall into it at first.

He tastes like beer and bad decisions. Especially when his mouth moves against mine and his hands move from their squeezing grip on my arms to a gentle caress of my jaw, keeping my face tilted up to him as he moves me the way he wants to.

But this is real.

I should stop him. Deep down, I know that this is a bad idea for so many reasons.

But Carter Harrington is a good kisser. I was definitely right about that, and that's enough to make any reasonable thought fade away given how pent up I am and how, despite my stubborn avoidance and denial, this has been coming since that first night of tutoring.

So I kiss him back, hoping I'm half as talented as he is. Hell, I'd settle for a quarter as good, considering the difference in experience between the two of us.

But I don't need practice to know that the heat building in my core is fiercer than any I've ever felt. I take the opportunity to answer my own earlier question and lick along his jawline, the blonde stubble prickling my tongue, and then place an open-mouthed kiss to the side of his neck when he lets his head fall to the side. I feel the pulsing of his heartbeat in his throat and I answer with a moan of my own.

It's the last bit of control Carter lets me have. He lifts me in a swoop that makes my stomach flip and sets me on the counter, pressing my legs open to accommodate him between my knees. Before I can say a word, he returns to kissing the stuffing out of me.

I whimper when his hand encircles my neck, not squeezing but just letting me know he's there and in charge. "Do you like that?" he groans against my mouth. "My good girl, Luna?"

A sound of needy hunger is all the agreement I can make, but it's not enough for him.

"Tell me." He kisses my cheek, a soft press of his lips that contrasts with the squeeze of his hand. "Tell me," he repeats, his breath hot on my ear, and then he nips my lobe with his teeth.

"Y–y–yes." If he'd been looking me in the eye, I don't know if I would've been able to admit that. But with the tip of his tongue teasing over the shell of my ear, I couldn't lie if I wanted to. He rewards me with another kiss, and his free hand grips my hip, squeezing the flesh there more sharply than my neck, and I squirm, delighting in his touch.

"You like it rough? Want me to bend you over this counter and take you from behind with one hand on your ass and one on your throat while I slam into your pussy?" He lays sweet kisses over my face as he asks the filthy question, painting a picture I won't soon forget.

It reminds me of the way he spoke when we faked sex, and it

sounds amazing, sexy and wonderful. But I've never done *that*, and I need a second to think.

"I–I–I don't know?"

That's not the answer Carter's looking for, and the moment of craziness breaks. His hand gentles on my throat as he presses his forehead to mine, moving his head left to right as though he can't believe he kissed me.

"You're a lifesaver." He sighs, the tension palpable between us.

"I am?" I whisper, wishing he were still kissing me. Which is weird because I don't even *like* Carter Harrington. At least not in *that* way.

But my body sure does. I'm vibrating with heat and want.

His thumbs brushes over my cheeks, and he pulls away, leaving warm traces on my skin that tingle without his touch. His hands run through his hair, mussing the strands even more, and his eyes take on the desperate glint once again as the haze of our kiss fades.

"It's all fucked up. So fucked. And I need your help, Luna. You said you'll help."

He's desperately reminding me, as though I haven't been paying attention since he came in. "I will, but with what? What's going on?"

"You're not gonna believe this. I still don't." He tells me about his day at work and how his dad has taken over wooing Elena Cartwright for Blue Lake Assets.

"That's your contract, though." I'm defending him as though I'll benefit in some way from his getting the deal with Elena.

"I know, but nobody argues with Dad. He thinks he's doing the right thing. I spent the whole evening going over it, looking for any way around him or a way I could get Elena to sign without a family dinner. But there's no way." He shakes his head vacantly, his mind not here in the kitchen with me but likely going over the options he's already considered and rejected.

"Now what?" I ask, trying to fill in this very unclear picture. "Do you need to call Elena?"

His eyes meet mine and he says flatly, "I did." Adding in a

high-pitched voice I think is supposed to be Elena, he says, "She was *completely delighted* to be invited to dinner, said she's looking forward to *meeting the man in charge of Blue Lake*, and the *fella who taught me how to work an investment portfolio*." He shrugs, blinking as he does so. "I didn't tell her that I learned a lot from Dad, but it was really Professor Malkin in college who taught me the most about diversified portfolios."

"So she's coming to dinner. That's good, isn't it?"

I'm trying to keep up with his manic switches from ranting to kissing me and back to ranting, while consciously ignoring the heat between my legs. Carter stops pacing and pins me with a hard stare. "She said she's looking forward to dinner with us again. *Us*, as in you and me."

Finally, I realize why he's freaking out because I begin freaking out worse than he is. I hop down from the counter, brushing past Carter as I look for an escape that my small apartment doesn't provide. "No way, nope, nuh-uh, not doing that again."

"You have to. You already said you'd help me," he informs me, seemingly thinking I've forgotten my response from mere minutes ago.

Trust me, bucko. I won't be forgetting anything about tonight.

"Help you? I thought you meant like you wanted me to go over art with you some more!" I can hear how ridiculous that sounds once I say it aloud, but I can't sit with sweet old Elena Cartwright and lie to her again. I feel guilty enough as it is.

"Please," Carter begs, making puppy dog eyes at me. "There's no other way. I've been over it again and again." He huffs a bitter laugh. "Believe me, I've looked from every angle, from the KISS solutions to the ridiculous. None of them will work."

Plopping down onto my couch, I cover up with the blanket there, needing to put barriers between us after what just happened. I can't tell him no when I can still taste the beer from his kiss. "Can't you tell her I'm busy that night or something?"

Carter shakes his head. "That'd only bring up more questions."

"More questions than showing up to dinner with a wife your family knows nothing about?" I ask incredulously.

"If we come in together, Elena knows and likes you, and they'll just think we're together. They wouldn't dream of arguing in front of a potential client. It would serve no purpose." He seems sure, but I can't imagine a family where a surprise wife wouldn't be cause for alarm and a whole laundry list of questions.

He drops to the floor in front of the couch, his hands gathering mine in his. Looking me in the eye, he says earnestly, "Please."

I stare at him for a long moment, wanting to say no.

He moves closer, until our lips are mere inches apart, as he whispers, "Please, Luna. I need you. Please."

His kiss this time is gentle, his tongue probing as his lips move over mine. It feels as though he's savoring me, and I get lost in him. I lean forward, hungry for more, and he weaves his hands into my hair, holding me in place as he takes my breath. And along with it, my doubts and worries.

"Okay," I whisper against his lips.

I'm not sure why I agree. The smart thing to do would be to leave Carter alone, walk away from this fake marriage thing he's still running on Elena, and tell Zack he owes me an entire library worth of books.

"Really?" He breaks the kiss, pulling back the slightest bit so I can see his smile is hopeful and full of promise. He rises to the couch, sitting next to me. His eyes are clearing, his focus centering.

I can't think of an argument, or at least not one I haven't already tried, so I nod silently, though I do wonder if I'm getting played by Charming Carter the same way he's playing Elena.

"Thank you. I don't know what I'd do without you."

I'm not sure about any of this, but he sounds so deeply grateful that I can feel a blush heating my cheeks.

"I need to give you the rundown on my family so you're ready." He's back to all business in a blink, and my head spins.

How can he do that? Go from kissing to clear-headed?

"Ready?" I will never be ready for this. I'm the antithesis of ready to meet my fake husband's family, especially when they're the freaking Harringtons and I'm an awkward, introverted artist whose idea of fancy dress is non-paint-spattered overalls. In a moment of wishful thinking, I ask, "How bad could they be?"

"They're not bad, exactly, just Harringtons, and that comes with a lot of baggage. A *lot* of baggage," he repeats.

"You're coaching me on how to meet your family as your fake wife, and you think *they* have baggage?" I question.

He chuckles at the dig. "I really appreciate this." His eyes drop to my hands, where I'm fidgeting with the blanket. "And I'm sorry for . . . before."

He's talking about the aggression in the kitchen and how it differs from the sweeter kiss we just shared. But if we're getting to know each other, I need to be honest with him. "I'm not."

He gives me a cocky, heated smirk, and I wonder if I maybe should've kept that to myself. "Let's start with the easy ones," he says instead of torturing me with that info. "You've already met Kyle . . ."

"Wait! Let me get my notecards so I can study before dinner." This will be so much worse than a test or memorizing the tour information. I will need to know these people backward and forward and respond to them in real time as if we've been family for a while so that I can fool Elena. And pray that Carter's right about his family not questioning my sudden appearance in front of a guest.

With notecards and my favorite pen in hand, Carter tells me about his family. He's right . . . they're a lot. And I have to have dinner with them as Carter's wife.

I'm in so much trouble.

CHAPTER
FIFTEEN
CARTER

IF DAD'S office at work is hell, his home office is purgatory. It's equally his domain, but there's no façade of professionalism, and the only hope of rescue is Mom, and she tends to stay out of office politics and projects as much as possible.

And this is firmly into the realm of a company project, at least in her eyes.

"What else do I need to know? Any updates?" Dad asks. He's been a bulldog on this, and his questioning's been relentless. We're sitting in leather chairs in front of the empty fireplace, a pre-dinner scotch in each of our hands. I take a sip, stalling as I take Dad's measure.

I think every teenage boy comes upon an age where they think they could out-man their father. I was fourteen when I thought that day had come. I don't remember what we were fighting about, but I'd yelled, been disrespectful, and thrown out those infamous words, *'wanna take this outside?'* and though Dad hadn't wanted to, he'd gone with me, a resigned look on his face.

I was wrong, and the fist-sized bruise he left on my gut after I'd tried and failed to land several punches was proof enough.

As I got older, I realized that real power wasn't in whether or not I could take Dad on mano-a-mano. It was in money, influence, and control, and he will always have more of those than I do. At least at Blue Lake.

But this time, he's the one who's underestimating me.

"I still don't agree with this. You're stomping right into and over my prospect when your heavy-handed approach isn't warranted."

I'm trying hard to not sound like a whiny seagull—*mine, mine, mine*. Not sure I'm succeeding, though.

"Noted," Dad says agreeably but then adds, "It's still happening. But consider your objection on the record."

He's such a steamroller. A charming one, but a steamroller, nonetheless.

Mentally, I evaluate the imaginary chess board we're sitting at, searching for my best play. The end goal is to bring Elena on as a client. It'll be good for Blue Lake, good for Elena, and admittedly, good for me. It'll prove that I can stand up next to Cameron as the next generation of Harringtons, bringing in business, managing clients, and increasing revenue.

My best move is to make sure that tonight is a resounding success.

"Elena isn't your usual fundraiser elbow-hobknobber," I remind him. "She's got more money than God but lives casually. You're more likely to find her in the barn with her horse than attending a gala. She literally told me to drop the pomp and circumstance, so don't overdo it. It's a sure bet to turn her off Blue Lake."

Dad scoffs. "Everyone likes a little pageantry to make them feel important. Don't worry about me. You just make sure you don't *underdo* it. This could be a big deal for us."

He doesn't understand at all. Not Elena, and not me. He's usurped this deal without giving me a chance of succeeding on my own. And I was doing well with Elena without involving the family.

I just needed Luna. I still need her.

Once more, I consider my decision to spring Luna on my family in the middle of everything. Of course, the most obvious answer would've been to tell them about the fake wife situation ahead of time and hope they'd play along, but there's no way that would've gone well. I can almost hear Dad yelling at me about treating this opportunity like a joke.

Which I'm not.

Having Luna arrive a few minutes after Elena is my best choice. No one in my family will risk being the fool who doesn't know who Luna is during a professional dinner. We're trained to nod along with whatever Dad says, and they'll do the same for me. I hope.

Mom comes in, her full-circle, knee-length skirt swooshing as she walks to Dad's side. "Hey, boys, enjoying a last-minute scotch?"

I hold mine up in answer. Mom perches on the arm of Dad's chair, wrapping her arm around his shoulders. If they weren't my parents, they'd be an adorable couple people would aspire to emulate—wealthy, attractive, intelligent, and one hundred percent in love. Sickeningly in love. To the point that we know not to drop by unannounced or walk into any room without making an obvious noise first.

I learned that the hard way.

"Not as much as I'm enjoying you," Dad growls, gripping Mom's hip. She pushes her blonde hair behind her ear, giggling.

"Could you not?" There's only so much staring at my glass of scotch I can do.

"You should be so lucky to be this gross when you're our age," Dad taunts.

The doorbell rings, and I'm saved by the bell, literally. Setting my scotch on the table, I bolt for the door. "I'll get it!"

One of the staff will already be on standby to open the door as people arrive, but I'm taking the opportunity to get away from parents who are likely gearing up for a pre-dinner make-out session.

Walking into the foyer, Grace sees me and shouts, "Uncle CJ!" She runs at me with both arms outstretched, and I bend down to do our usual pick up-and-spin greeting. "Wheeee!" Her squeal echoes in the high-ceilinged space.

"Put her down, Carter. I don't want her to get riled up before she's got to be on her best behavior." Cameron says the last part to Grace, likely reminding her about the conversation they had in the car about manners for a family dinner with a guest.

I let Grace's feet touch the floor as she tells Cameron, "I know, Dad. I'll be the bestest ever. I always am, you know that." She's nodding her head up and down with surety, but I could name at least a handful of people who'd disagree with that.

"You ready to see Elena again?"

Grace screws up her lips, tilting her head. "D'pends. Are we having shark coochie again?"

I glance to Cameron, who's wearing a smile that matches my own. Both of us are fighting laughter. "Not tonight, Gracie girl. Maybe another time."

"Promise?" She holds out her pinkie finger expectantly.

I wrap my finger around hers. "Promise."

"With tiny cookies," she amends.

I nod. "Circus cookies. I know your favorite."

Grace pulls me into the sitting room, and Cameron follows closely behind. But Grace quickly abandons us for her collection of Barbies that fills a basket in the corner.

"How much shit is Dad giving you about this whole Cartwright deal?" Cameron says low enough for Grace to not hear.

"Not as much as he's going to," I mutter cryptically. "Have my back?"

"Always." I'll give it to Cam. He might give me shit, and I give it right back. But if I had to go into a life or death knife fight with anyone on the planet, I know who I'd pick to be by my side. No matter how much we bicker and compete, at the end of the day, Cam's my ride or die.

We watch Grace playing for a moment, and then she yanks us down by our hands to sit at her kid-sized table. "You, be Princess Pony. And you, be Dino Dylan. He's Barbie's boyfriend." She shoves figurines into our hands, and though Cameron and I are equally annoyed, we play along.

"Remember when we used to pop firecrackers in back,

behind Mom's garden? How'd we end up playing Barbies?" Cameron groans.

"You had me," Grace answers flatly, seemingly not listening but as usual, hearing everything.

The front door opens again, and Kayla and Chance appear. Though Kayla is Cole's twin, she's more likely to be with Chance at any given time. They're perpetual sidekicks. I'd call them partners in crime, but Chance wouldn't consider speeding, much less any actual crime, and Kayla pretty much does whatever the fuck she wants. Usually, we don't even know what she's up to because she holds her cards close to the vest until it serves her to lay them out for show. I should've taken a play from her rule book with this whole Cartwright deal.

Though this is our parents' home, I turn into the host of this shindig. "Hey, y'all! Thanks for coming!"

Chance looks at me like I sprouted a second—or third—head. "Dad said there was a dinner. We're expected to be here, so here we are."

He holds his hands out, sounding slightly annoyed at Dad's non-invitation, but there's no way he'd go against the old man. I get it, Dad's done this to all of us at one time or another.

Kayla rolls her eyes at Chance's good soldier response. To me, she says, "It's Dad's dinner, but it's your deal. We gotchur back, Carter. Whatever you need."

Like Cam, I'm glad to know that Kayla's here for me. And it helps that she calls it my deal.

"I'm gonna hold you to that," I warn.

Kayla gives me a slightly confused, slightly questioning eyebrow but says nothing as she sits down in another kid-sized chair at Grace's table. Picking up a Mandalorian figurine, she deadpans, "Play or play not, no try."

Grace laughs and joins in with Kayla, but not before gesturing to Cameron and me to return to our roles and handing Chance a tree.

"What am I supposed to do with this?" he asks. Cameron glares at him, silently telling him to figure it out and not fuck around with Gracie. Minutes later, we're at Grace's mercy as she directs us in a scene of her making. At least I've got a chair to sit in. Chance is kneeling on the floor, dancing his tree across the table and singing a song about the parts of a tree to the tune of *Head, Shoulders, Knees, and Toes*.

But the show really begins for me when Elena and Claire are shown in. Grace pipes up immediately, "Elena!"

She runs to the woman, hugging her around her middle. Elena's charmed and hugs her back just as tightly. "Well, hello, sweet Grace. How're you doing, darling?"

"Good. You wanna play Barbies?"

Cameron interrupts, "Grace, I think Mrs. Cartwright has better things to do right now."

While I'm not so sure of that, we all rise, thankful to be released from Barbie hell.

Grace's face falls, her bottom lip poking out. Elena bends down a little to stage whisper, "You'd best pop that lip back in. He's wrong, I don't have anything *better* to do, but I have to play adult right now instead of Barbies. So annoying."

Grace laughs. "Playing adult sounds boring."

"It is sometimes," Elena agrees.

Switching gears from fun uncle to business, I hold my hand out to Elena for an easy shake and then to Claire, who shakes it reluctantly. "I wasn't expecting you. Thank you for coming."

Through gritted teeth, she says, "Stanley said you'd called and invited Aunt Elena to some dinner." She flashes her fingers around like this dinner party is a waste of time.

"Damn, Stanley really needs a life of his own, doesn't he?" I joke.

"He looks out for Aunt Elena," Claire says stonily. "He always has."

Okay. Elena was definitely fond of Stanley, but he's sounding a bit stalkerish if you ask me. I introduce Elena and Claire to my brothers and sister, and then, as they come in, to Mom and Dad. "Elena, this is my mother, Miranda, and my father, Charles. Mom, Dad . . . this is Elena Cartwright and Claire Reynolds."

Mom is in full hostess with the mostest mode, a role she's especially good at. She's done this song and dance enough times over the years for Dad's various business partners that she could probably pull this off in her sleep. She can make anyone feel like the guest of honor.

"It's so good to meet you, Elena," Dad says, his blue eyes twinkling. "I hear lovely things about you from Carter."

They keep talking, with Dad layering on charm, compliments, and Southern hospitality like Elena's a Sunday supper peach cobbler that needs ice cream and whipped cream, plus a sprinkle of pecans. And for all Elena's request for nothing fancy, she's eating up Mom and Dad's attention like they're long-lost friends catching up on a lifetime of happenings.

Meanwhile, Claire stands by, silently scowling. I consider talking with her? Sort of like 'if you want the girl, be nice to the best friend' advice that I learned back in my high school days . . . except this involves money and not pussy. But Claire doesn't seem open to any conversation and is listening to Elena as though she might spill family secrets at any moment.

"Why do you keep looking at the door?" Kayla whispers out of the side of her mouth while Dad is holding court.

"What?" I ask quickly. "No, I'm not."

I was totally looking for Luna. I'm worried because she's late. I told her to be here a few minutes after the scheduled arrival time, but it's several minutes past that now. It's entirely possible that she got caught up in her work again and won't realize that she's late until hours from now. It's also possible that she changed her mind and will no-show on me.

But though those options are reasonable, there's a seed of worry too. She planned to drive herself out since I needed to be here early. What if she had car trouble? Or got in an accident?

The concern for her takes over, and I can feel my heart speed up. I should call her. Just to check if she's okay. And on her way.

I need her.

Kayla places her hand on my shoulder. "Dude, where'd your brain go? Are you having a panic attack? Go in the hall and put your head between your knees or something."

"What? No, I'm fine. I'm just . . ."

What? Freaking out that my fake wife isn't here?

"You're not. No need to lie to me."

There's a saying my grandmother used to tell us—that some men were all hat and no saddle. It meant that a man was all about show and not about the real deal. Kayla is the opposite— all saddle and no hat. She has no time for niceties and white lies. She would despise what I'm doing with Luna.

But she also doesn't want me to tell her false pleasantries when I'm clearly not okay.

"I'm worried," I confess, not divulging why.

"You should be." She points at Dad and Elena, who are acting like best buds. "Dad's stealing your deal and you're over here letting him. Go get your client, man."

She's right. She always is. "Thanks."

Mission renewed, I interrupt them as Dad starts on the story of how he turned a dilapidated boat into a million dollars. "Elena, is Dad telling you war stories about his days in the trenches of corporate life? He's got some whoppers."

"No, but I'd love to hear them. I can see where you get your charm from, young man." Elena smiles warmly. "And your good looks."

She looks to Mom, even though I'm basically a cut n' paste of Dad. Small talk is an annoying but necessary fact of life, and I launch in with her, talking about piddly nothings for a bit while still watching the door like a hawk.

But eventually, I hear the front door open and nearly run toward it with palpable relief. That lasts for all of two seconds until Luna appears in the sitting room doorway . . . on the arm of my brother, Cole.

He's wearing black jeans, a white button-up that's undone at the neck, sunglasses pushed up on his head, and a stack of bracelets on each wrist where his sleeves are rolled up. Luna has on a pretty black dress that's relatively basic except that in its plainness, it makes her whiplash curves all that much more standout.

For all intents and purposes, they look like a couple arriving for dinner. Which is definitely *not* the plan.

"Luna." It's a bit sharp, but I don't like seeing her hand in the crook of my brother's elbow.

She looks at me and then at the assembly of people. I can see the color drain from her face and the nerves rising as she bites her lip. "Uhm, hi!"

Her voice is bright and high with nervousness. I walk right up in front of her, and her hand falls from Cole's elbow and to her side as she looks up at me, eyes wide with panic and mouth dropped open.

"Hey, babe. I was worried about you." And then, right there in front of my family, I kiss Luna like I own her. Like she owns me—body, heart, and soul. It's quick but impactful. My family holds their collective breath.

"Oh, y'all are just the cutest things ever," Elena says, echoing her earlier sentiments about Luna and me. "When you get done saying hello over there, I need a hug, ma'am."

Luna laughs, and when she moves to hug Elena and exchange pleasantries, Cole's eyes are the first I see. The questions there are big, but him I can ignore. When I turn around, Mom and Dad are looking at me in shock. *That* I can't ignore.

CHAPTER
SIXTEEN
LUNA

A FEW MOMENTS AGO . . .

I'm standing on the steps of Carter's family house. It's huge and fancy, but that's not why I'm frozen like a statue outside, muttering to myself.

No, I'm frozen because on the other side of this door is the biggest lie I've ever told and the scariest thing I've ever contemplated doing. I hate crowds, hate meeting new people, hate knowing that I'm going to be judged as a 'weird artist'. It's why I stick to my small group of people. Carter's already forcing me to grow for this fake marriage thing, but at least the nerves over dinner with Elena were balanced out with the excitement of seeing her art collection.

Here, there's none of that. This is just pure, unadulterated fear shooting through my veins.

"You going in?" a voice asks from behind me. I didn't hear anyone approach, so I jump a bit, which is met with a male chuckle. "Sorry, didn't mean to scare you."

I force a smile, starting my role a moment before I'd planned. "It's okay . . . Cole." I recognize him from the pictures Carter showed me, but even if I hadn't seen a single photo, I'd know this man is a Harrington. They mostly look alike, almost copy-paste versions of their dad. Well, other than Kyle, but Carter assured me that he wouldn't be here even though they invite him. 'Family drama', he called it.

Cole's brow scrunches as he looks at me more closely. "Have we met?"

"Oh, I'm Luna. I'm Carter's . . ." I pause, not sure if I should say wife. Part of Carter's plan is that there will be a bit of mob mentality when his entire family is around us, and they won't question us with an audience. But out here, it's only me and Cole, and I know introducing myself as Carter's wife will definitely lead to questions I can't answer. I lick my lips and repeat with more resoluteness, "I'm Carter's."

Humor lights up Cole's eyes, and he holds out his elbow politely. "Well, alright then. Looks like I'm gonna be glad I didn't skip this family shindig after all. Shall we go in, Luna?"

I take his elbow gently and let him lead me inside. Truthfully, it's kinda nice to not walk in alone. Right up until Carter barks at me, "Luna!"

I think I wave stupidly. Or maybe I say something? I'm not sure because I'm lost in Carter's blue-eyed, stony stare as he strides over to me, a man on a mission. I watch his lips move, but my ears are full of staticky noise, so I don't hear what he says. I'm on short circuit until Carter kisses me.

I swear he must've taken a class or something because every time his lips meet mine, it's like my brain cells go into a frenzied chorus of 'ahhhhh' and hip-humping horniness that basically makes them ping off the inside of my skull.

When he lets me go—which might be a second later or might be an hour, I truly don't know—he pushes me toward Elena. At least she's a friendly face and has her arms outstretched, so I know what to do. I hug her as she tells me how good it is to see me again.

Now it's up to me.

My eyes tick around Carter's family, recognizing them from his descriptions and the photos he showed me. I mentally flip notecards in my head in an attempt to keep from freaking out because almost all of them are looking at me or Carter with shock, horror, or some mix of the two, and being the center of attention is one of my most common nightmares.

Absently, I rub my hands on my thighs, the smooth dress fabric reassuring me that at least I'm not naked in this version of the nightmare.

What would Alphena do? W-W-A-D?

I start with the easiest of the bunch, bending down to Grace.

"Gracie, Gracie, Bo Bacie," I sing-song to Grace as we do the complicated routine of high-fives that we choreographed in the car on the ride home from Elena's.

She laughs before finishing, "Little Luna foo-foo, hopping through the forest."

We do bunny ear fingers and then wiggle them against each other. It makes no sense to an adult, but it works for us. I look up to Cameron and smile. He seems stunned, probably at both my appearance and the song and dance with his daughter, but he fixes his face quickly. "Hello," he says politely.

I swear he mutters under his breath, *"Loo-na* and *El-a-na?* I thought she was saying the same name, just misspeaking sometimes."

He thought Luna and Elena sound alike? That's kinda funny. But nothing else about this meet-and-greet is.

Next, I smile at Kayla. "Hey, Kayla," I say, side-hugging her in greeting.

To her credit, she hugs me right back the way Carter said she would. "I'm gonna need answers from someone later," she speed-whispers in my ear.

Counting my greeting with Cole as I was walking in, I'm three for three with the siblings without hyperventilating. My internal Alphena is doing a little badass comic book cheer.

I wave at Chance, who Carter warned me would be a hard sell and a poor reaction and someone to avoid. Then it's time to focus on the big bad in the room. "Hi Mom, Dad. So good to see you."

Charles Harrington looks at me carefully, his eyes scanning mine. I catch Miranda looking past me to Carter. There's a moment of horrid anticipation where I think my stomach contents might come right up and spill on their shoes and the very expensive rug beneath them. And considering I didn't eat breakfast or lunch today because of nerves, that would not be a pretty sight.

Miranda must see something in Carter's face because she reacts first.

Placing her arms around my shoulders in a friendly hug—as though we've done this dozens of times before—she says, "Hey, sweetheart, so good to see you too."

I let out a relieved sigh in her arms.

They're going along with it! I can't believe it! The next thought I have is, *This family is reeeally weird.*

There was a tiny part of me that honestly thought Carter might be playing a prank on me. Like I was going to walk in, expecting to act like his wife, and the whole family would shout 'gotcha' and I'd be the dummy. I guess as long as Ashton Kutcher were here, I wouldn't mind being *Punk'd* though.

That doesn't seem to be the case. If anything, Carter and I are the ones punking them.

Carter's dad, Charles, isn't nearly as easy as Miranda. His curious look has turned downright hostile. "What's going—"

Carter puts his arm over my shoulders, pulling me to his side so fast that I almost lose my balance in the heels I rarely wear. The move is intentional, showing that I belong with him. Or rather, to him. At least in this context. His tone is equally sharp. "Dad, whatever issues you have with my *wife*, now is not the time. *Luna* and Elena enjoyed talking about their shared passion for art, and if Elena chooses to work with Blue Lake, it will be partially because of Luna's love for all things artistic."

Carter makes it sound like Charles and I have some sort of sordid, drama-filled history while dropping all sorts of hints to his father about what I'm doing here without spelling it out on an airplane banner. Carter told me that his dad is brilliantly smart and adaptable, but whether Charles takes the hints and plays along is another matter entirely.

Carter and Charles enter into a stare-down competition with me trapped between the two of them. I have one savior in this room, and I bury myself into Carter's side, my hand on his abdomen, where I can feel the hard muscles beneath his shirt, and my eyes are locked on his chest, which is rising and falling steadily. His breath keeps me from going into a full-blown panic attack as I pace my breathing to match his.

"I could use a drink. Anyone else?" Kayla says brightly, breaking the standoff. She pulls me away from Carter, and I flinch at the loss of his protection, but it seems she truly does have my back because she guides me over to the corner to a bar. Quietly, she asks, "Are you old enough to drink? If not, for fuck's sake, tell me now so I can go ahead and murder my brother."

I know I look young, but it didn't occur to me that they might think I was underage compared to Carter. I was strictly concerned about the unknown wife situation. I nod, confirming, "I'm twenty-three."

Kayla opens a bottle of red wine with a 'POP!' that covers her curse. "Twenty-three?" she repeats. "Do you have like . . . a safe word or something with him for whatever the hell this is?"

I blink, my feet stepping away from Kayla instinctively. "Uhh . . ."

"Of course not," she sighs, gritting her teeth as she pours wine into glasses. "He's put you in the middle of some serious shit. If you need an out, meet my eyes and blink twice." Her warning is delivered with a dramatic demonstration of blinking.

With that, she leaves me alone, turning to hand out glasses of red wine to her family. Her words rattle around in my brain, making me question everything Carter's told me.

Why am I doing this again?

I should leave, walk right out the door without looking back and go home to Alphena where I belong. There's a mirror above the bar, and I meet my own eyes in the glass. I look scared, but my makeup is perfect thanks to Samantha's help. That small detail gives me a tiny boost of strength, and when Carter turns, his eyes find mine instantly in the mirror. That's another boost.

Picking up the other glasses, I offer them to those not holding one from Kayla's distribution. It's not my place, but I need to do something to keep my hands busy and my feet from running for the door. With my breath stuck in my chest, I hold a glass out to Charles as a pseudo olive branch.

"Dad?" I say questioningly, my voice breaking on the single syllable.

My nerves make it sound as though I'm scared of Charles—which I am, but not for the reason Carter made it out to be.

From off to my side, Elena drawls, "If I's you, I'd take it."

Unspoken is the threat that she'll leave if he doesn't. Charles looks from the glass, to me, to Elena, and then to Carter. Finally —*finally!*—he takes the glass, purposefully not touching my hand. He doesn't make a toast or drink the wine, but rather just holds it.

"Good to see you too, Luna." The words are pulled from Charles's throat one at a time. Miranda bumps his hip with her own, and he smiles reflexively, but it doesn't reach his eyes.

It's a signal to everyone that whatever's going on, we're all moving forward with it, and small talk starts up again. I take a big breath, forcing a smile to my lips and hoping it looks natural.

We did it!

Carter pats my butt, and I jump, squeaking in surprise. When I look up at him, he winks cockily.

Did he seriously have no doubts? Is he not near DEFCON one right now?

I know I'm full-blown freaking out on the inside, and only my past experience with hiding nervous meltdowns is keeping me vertical.

Thankfully, now that I've been accepted, at least momentarily, I don't have to actually speak. I'm virtually forgotten as Charles holds court, chatting with Elena while Claire looks on like a sourpuss.

"Sorry for your loss. I can't imagine life without my Miranda." Charles looks to his wife warmly before returning his gaze to Elena.

Pressing her lips together, Elena nods solemnly. "I miss him every day."

"Me too," Claire interjects. "My uncle was a good man. He cared about others."

Claire cuts her eyes to Elena and resumes her silent grumping. She very clearly is implying that other people don't care the way Thomas did. I can only guess that she's talking about Elena, but that doesn't make sense. Elena seems so sweet and has been nothing but kind.

Charles agrees. "Family is the most important thing we leave behind."

He glances at Carter, and I wonder if Charles is threatening his son, but Carter doesn't seem worried in the slightest. Even so, I have an urge to stand in front of Carter protectively, but I can't do much, whether the battle is verbal or physical. Instead, I slip my hand into Carter's, signaling that it's the two of us against Charles, and Carter squeezes my hand warmly. I feel the weight of his gaze and look up at him. His lips lift slightly, and at first, I think he's amused by my silly attempt at protecting him, but there's heat in the depths of his blue eyes that has nothing to do with laughing at me and everything to do with . . . us? He presses a kiss to my forehead, and I sink into him.

Does he know that's my Kryptonite, making me feel like an ooey, gooey s'mores on the inside that someone melted juuust right?

After a bit, we make our way to a formal dining room. Though I wasn't expected, there's the exact number of places set at the long table, including fine China plates, silverware, and crystal glasses. Whoever the house staff is, they're on the ball. Not that I thought the Harringtons would allow for anything other than quick efficiency.

Carter guides me to sit beside him, placing the napkin in my lap again. This time, at least I don't jump.

What are all those forks for? I know one's for salad and one's for the entrée, but there's one at the top of the plate too, and I have no idea on that.

"Where's Jacob?" Grace asks Claire as the first course is served. Cameron looks at Grace questioningly, and Grace explains, "That's her son. He's annoying, but he's funner than being the only kid here."

"Grace!" Cameron says sharply. "We don't call people annoying."

Grace's brow wrinkles. "You call Uncle CJ annoying all the time." She looks to Carter, who's staring at his brother with one brow raised, and repeats, "He does. 'Specially when you whine about work stuffs."

"Is that so?" Carter asks.

Claire clears her throat. "Jacob is home with his father, my husband, Mads. It didn't seem like he'd be needed for a simple dinner." She looks around the table, and somehow, even her gaze is condescending.

"Your husband's name is Mads?" Kayla inquires. "I know a guy named Mads too. Never heard of another one. He wouldn't happen to work at South Peach bar, does he?"

I can't tell whether Kayla is serious or not. Claire can't either, I guess, because she scowls as she answers. "My husband is *not* a bartender. He's a banker. And his name is Madison, but he prefers Mads."

Kayla shrugs. "Understandable. The name thing, not the bartender thing. There's nothing wrong with being a bartender. Mads is my friend. He's cool and got his name because he's a little . . ." She twirls a finger by her ear. "We make sure we don't get him mad."

I doubt Claire's husband is cool. He's probably a stuffy numbers type that wears his socks in bed. I can't imagine she'd have it any other way.

"Harrumph," Claire says as she stabs a crouton and shoves it in her mouth.

From somewhere beneath the table, a phone rings. Everyone looks at each other, eyes questioning.

"Oh, that's me. Excuse me," Cole says, pulling his phone from his pocket. He stands, stepping out of the room, but even in the hallway, we can hear his muffled speaking. "Hello?" He's quiet for a moment, presumably listening, and then says, "Yeah, I got it. No worries. You're saving me from a boring family business dinner. I'll see ya in a few."

When he pokes his head around the corner, I half-expect Charles to demand that Cole sit his butt down for this 'boring family business dinner', but he doesn't get the chance. Cole throws a two-fingered wave and says, "Duty calls. Nice to meet you, Elena, Claire. Make sure my brother takes care of you, Luna. He can be an asshole."

I giggle in surprise as Cole disappears down the hall. Less than a half-second later, the front door opens and closes. Beneath the table, Carter puts his hand on my thigh, squeezing firmly, and my tiny laughter stops instantly. I can feel the weight of his touch, the power in his grip, and the heat spreading from his fingertips to my center. I squirm, not sure whether I want more or for him to stop, and Carter whispers out of the side of his mouth, "You okay?"

No, I'm not okay. This is madness. Complete and utter madness. Does he know what he's doing to me? With his touches, his kisses, his . . . kindness? Is it some sort of joke—look at what I can do to the poor, young, inexperienced weirdo? Watch me wind her up and send her spinning?

If I were sitting on my couch at home, wearing sweats, with my tablet in my hands, watching this dinner on the TV screen, this whole thing would be hilarious. Everyone is cutting each other with verbal knives, the tension is palpable, and we've barely been served our salads.

But I'm not at home and this isn't scripted for television. I'm right in the middle of the drama.

Hell, I'm *part* of the drama.

And that's not usually how I roll. I prefer hiding on the outskirts, but with Carter at my side and his hand on my leg, this craziness seems manageable. Or at least enjoyable in a small, twisted way.

Like improv dinner theater. As long as it doesn't turn into a murder mystery, I'm probably . . . maybe . . . sorta okay.

Maybe I can even help . . . if I talk about the one thing I'm comfortable discussing.

"Elena, did you see the news about the museum's upcoming exhibition? The month-long showing of *Digital Immersion Through Virtual Reality*. It's ground-breaking technology that'll bring art to life in a new way. Maeve—that's my boss—is organizing the installation, and I'll do tours with groups as they approach the pieces in our world and then use VR headsets to dive into them in an immersive way, where it seems as though they're a part the art, able to trace brushstrokes with their fingertips, move about the scene, and more."

Did I breathe at all while rambling that? I'm not sure.

What I am sure of? Carter's pinkie finger is point-oh-two inches higher on my thigh and there's a quiet rumble of approval in his throat.

"That sounds interesting," Elena says uncertainly. "I don't know that I've ever seen a VR anything, much less art."

"I would be delighted to do a private tour for you," I offer. "In addition to experiencing the art, you could see how a short-term exhibition is handled at the museum. See if you're comfortable showcasing some of Thomas's collection."

"What?" Claire screeches, slamming her napkin on the table. "You're giving away Uncle Thomas's art to some museum?"

Her overreaction sends a cold shiver down my spine, and I try to walk it back. "No, no. Not *giving* the museum anything. Only exhibiting, for a short time. To share Thomas's collection in his honor."

"You two want to share in Uncle Thomas's everything, don't you?" Claire snipes.

"Claire!" Elena says harshly. More gently, and with a pat of Claire's hand, Elena adds, "You make it sound like they're trying to steal Thomas away from us. He's gone, dear. I know you were close, and it hurts, but . . . he's gone."

Charles adopts an expression of kind concern. "I think we can all appreciate the pain of losing someone. We certainly don't want to dig in an open wound, but it's also the survivors' responsibility to take the best care of what's left behind. Blue Lake Assets can help with that."

I listen politely as Carter, Charles, and Elena direct the conversation to the Cartwright portfolio. Part of it is because it's totally over my head, given that I have a grand total of three hundred dollars in my bank account and they're talking about millions of dollars. But another reason I stay quietly watchful is Carter. He told me how worried he was about his dad walking over him on this deal, but truthfully, Carter is the one doing the majority of the talking and all the wooing.

I'm not sure Elena even likes Charles, which probably isn't good, I guess. But I'm cheering Carter on with every smile Elena flashes, every concern of hers that Carter alleviates, and every look of approval I see on Cameron's face. Not Charles, because he's staying in deal-mode, but Cameron doesn't have a dog in this fight, so he's watching as a spectator and seems impressed by his brother.

I wonder if Carter knows that Cameron feels that way?

CHAPTER
SEVENTEEN
CARTER

AS THE DINNER plates are swept away from the table, I feel like I'm making some real headway with Elena. Like I expected, Dad is being too much, but I'm doing what I can to balance him out.

What I didn't expect is that having Luna at my side would be more than just an 'in' to discuss art. She hasn't said much since the conversation switched to business, but her gentle support is probably the only thing getting me through this dinner. It has nothing to do with Renoir, brushstrokes, or Thomas Cartwright's collection, but with her unwavering belief that I can do this.

I'm a confident man by nature, but Luna's faith in me makes me feel like I could easily tackle the world. Though I could offer her the entirety of the Earth in my hands and she wouldn't be the slightest bit impressed. That's not what drives her, and needing to be more than a wallet and good looks to interest her excites me in a way I hadn't anticipated.

When dessert is served, she moans in delight at the vanilla mascarpone mousse, and I look over to see that she's got a tiny dollop of it on her lip. Going for broke, I decide to push the line a little bit.

"Babe, come here," I tell her quietly, knowing the whole table can still easily hear me.

Though I'm focused on her lip, I see her swallow thickly. Keeping my eyes open and on hers, I tilt her chin up gently and place a tender kiss right over the wayward mousse, letting the tip of my tongue dance over the sweetness as I remove it.

"Delicious," I whisper as I pull away. She delicately dabs at her lips with her napkin, and for some weird reason, I feel like she's wiping my kiss off and want to mark her again.

"Newlyweds are the cutest, don't you think?" Elena asks Dad, her hand propping up her chin as she looks at Luna and me with hearts in her eyes.

I lick my own lips and then smirk at him, knowing he's stuck.

"Cuter than puppy dog shit," Dad answers. He knows something's up. Almost all of us do, but in a way, I keep forgetting that it's fake with Luna. For the tiniest of seconds, it almost feels . . . not real, exactly, because we're definitely not married, but like a real date?

I do my best to stay focused but find my mind wandering to Luna again and again. I keep checking to make sure she's comfortable, that she's got what she needs, and that no one is eyeballing her in a way that makes her nervous. I keep my hand on her thigh because it lets me feel in-sync with her, and I've noticed that every time she feels uncertain about something, she wiggles her feet, so by touching her, I can respond as soon as I feel the movement.

By the time dinner is done, I feel like we've made our case to Elena. If she doesn't want to work with Blue Lake Assets and me for her portfolio management, then it wasn't meant to be. We've done all we can do. I damn sure know I've done all I can do, and some things I probably shouldn't have.

So when the evening is coming to a close, I feel good about walking Elena and Claire to the front door, even though Mom and Dad follow along. They shake hands, and then I have one last moment to seal the deal.

Elena hugs Luna and me at the same time, her head between us and an arm on each of our shoulders. "Thank you for making a *boring family business dinner* bearable," she whispers, then she winks as she pulls away. She obviously heard Cole's comment and thankfully, found it funny. "Best I've had in ages."

Claire gives me a dead-eyed stare in place of a goodbye and then follows her aunt. Before she gets far, Grace pops her head around the doorframe. "Tell Jacob I said hi!" she shouts, waving her hand as though Jacob can see her. Claire glances over her shoulder. There might be a tiny hint of a smile, or more likely from what I've seen from Claire, it might be a trick of the light. Either way, it disappears when Grace adds, "And that I hope his balls are okay!"

Dad bites his tongue until Elena and Claire are in the car and headed down the long drive, and then he lets loose. "What in the hell are you up to, Son? And who the hell are you?" He scowls at Luna, and I step between them, pulling her behind me. Her hands land flat on my lower back, letting me know she's supporting me, not hiding away.

"Not now. Luna and I are leaving. We'll have this conversation tomorrow, just you and me." I put as much steel in the statement as possible to try to make him accept it and not press the issue.

No dice.

He scoffs. "We'll have a talk right now. I like to know who's sitting at my dining room table."

Mom places a calming hand on Dad's arm. "Charles, I think Carter's right. This might not be the time." She leans left a little, smiling around me to Luna. "Y'all go on, kids."

I'm an adult. I'm a skilled businessman. I'm not scared of anything, not even my father. Mostly. None of those things stop me from grabbing Luna's hand and escaping, at least for tonight.

"Come on!" I shout, and laughingly, she runs with me. She lets out a whooping yell, her heels click-clacking on the drive. It feels wild and reckless, like we're getting away with something naughty. "Get in," I tell her, holding the passenger door of her car open and shooing her inside. She sits down messily, her skirt riding up her thigh, and my eyes zero in on the length of flesh. As much as I'd like to touch it again, I shut the door and run around to the driver's side to make our getaway.

Luna hands me her keys, and with a quick turn of the ignition, we're off into the night.

Still laughing, she turns to look out the back window, but the seatbelt jerks her back into her seat. "I can't believe we pulled that off!"

"Me either," I confess. It's a temporary reprieve, but the fallout will be mine to bear and Luna doesn't need to worry about it.

There's a long moment of easy silence, and when I glance over, she's staring out the window with a soft smile. "Luna?" I ask, checking her out carefully. "You okay?"

The rush is going to wear off quickly, and I want to catch her before she crashes from doing something so far out of her comfort zone. I can't imagine what it took for her to walk into my family home with lies on her lips and a false narrative in her heart. That's not who she is, but she's stretching herself in major ways . . . all for me. Well, mostly for me . . . and a peek at some art.

She closes her eyes for a second, and when she opens them again, they're bright with the glow of the dash lights. "Surprisingly, I'm okay. As long as I don't have to go to that chitty-chat with your dad. If I can skip that, I'm fine." She holds her hand out flat, showing me that she's not shaking, not even a little bit.

I chuckle grimly. "Wish I could skip it too, but that's not gonna be an option for me."

"Sorry, not sorry," she teases.

I don't ask, I don't think. I just drive home, taking Luna with me. I park in the garage and turn the car off. Looking at her, I say, "Thank you for tonight, but I'm not ready for it to be over. You want to come up?"

"Uhm, okay."

Despite the delay in her answer, she sounds sure, and I'm buzzing from the successful dinner and the feeling of her thigh beneath my palm.

Upstairs in my apartment, I hold my arms out. "Welcome to my humble home."

It's different from Luna's for sure. Where hers is colorful and full of personality, mine is inoffensive and lackluster. Everything is quality and designer-selected, but it doesn't have the spark Luna's place has. She looks around politely. "Nice," she surmises. From anyone else, it'd be a bland compliment. From Luna, it's totally an insult.

"You hate it," I guess.

"No!" she gasps. "It's . . ." She looks around again. "Nice. Like a magazine."

A laugh pops out unbidden. "It was in the *Bridgeport Monthly* a couple of years ago," I confess. "It's around here somewhere. The designer gave me a copy, thinking I'd be excited about it."

"Were you?"

"Didn't give a shit in the slightest," I swear, holding up a hand as though testifying. "Have a seat. I'll get us a drink. What would you like?"

"Water, please," she answers as she sits on the couch. "With lemon or lime, if you have any. It makes it seem fancier than plain, and that's how I trick myself into getting fruits and veggies into my diet." A flush rises to her cheeks quickly, and she rushes to assure me, "Not that I eat like crap. It might not look like it, but I eat pretty healthy."

"Luna, I don't care what you do or don't eat. You're beautiful, and in case you didn't notice, I was loving your thigh beneath my palm tonight." I let my gaze drop slowly, methodically over her curves—from her breasts, to her hips, to the thighs in question. When I lift my eyes to hers once more, she's staring at me in surprise, her lips parted in a soft circle.

"Oh." Her cheeks flush even further, but when she shifts on the sofa, it's to show off her legs rather than hide them away. Her dress inches up a bit, and though she places her hand there, she doesn't pull it back down.

Is Luna Starr flirting with me? If so, I am fucked.

I remind myself that she's my best friend's little sister, but when she pushes her glasses up her nose and looks at me through her lashes, I forget too easily. I already know I'm going to hell, but right now, the things I'm thinking of doing to those sweet thighs are enough to send me there on the fast track.

"Water!" I say too loudly, virtually running for the kitchen. This girl has me on edge, and the slightest encouragement from her, when it's only the two of us and my bed is a mere twenty-five steps away—yes, I've counted—is danger waiting to happen.

In the kitchen, I take a couple of deep breaths, not to slow my racing heart but to give my cock a moment to soften. It's not working, but I make her a glass of water, smiling as I drop in a 'fancy' lemon wedge, and a whiskey for myself. I've never hoped for whiskey dick before, but right now, a little help would go a long way.

When I return to the living room, Luna has taken her heels off, leaving them askew under the coffee table, and has her legs folded beneath her. I hand her the water glass and sit down beside her on the couch. "Feet hurt?"

"I don't know who invented heels, but they must've been a sadist. Those things are killer, and I barely walked in them." She throws a dirty look at the offending pain-inducers.

"Or a masochist?" I question.

I lean forward and set my drink on the table and then tap Luna's knee. "Let me help."

There are many, many more things I'd like to do to. Filthy, dangerous things. But rubbing her feet after she dressed up tonight seems *relatively* safe.

"You sure?" Even as she double-checks my willingness, she's rearranging herself so that her legs are outstretched and her feet are in my lap. Thankfully, over my thighs and not touching my cock, which is reminding me that I should've taken that whiskey as a shot.

I take her left foot in my hands, running my thumb along her arch, and she groans. "Ohmagawd, I forget how much I'm on my feet." I do it again to keep her talking. "I love the museum tours, but I'm on my feet for eight hours straight. And when I work at home, I'm usually barefoot, but I have a habit of curling up in weird positions. I don't realize that I've pulled this or crunched that until it hurts."

"Because you're so focused on Alphena?" I guess.

She nods. "Mm-hmm."

"Thank you for coming tonight. I know it was . . ." I search for a word as I press along the ball of her foot.

"Ridiculous?" she suggests. "Over the top? Stupid?"

I chuckle. "Difficult."

She closes her eyes, laying her head over to the back of the couch to enjoy the massage as I find a particularly sensitive spot. "They're not as bad as you made them out to be. Well, other than your dad."

She goes quiet as I switch to her right foot, only the occasional moan and groan coming out as I work my magic. I don't know what witchcraft she's working on me, but words pour forth.

"He's not that bad. Protective, mostly. Of the business, not us kids," I explain. "We're expected to have our shit together by this point and be able to handle it when he pushes us. But when we were young, he was the guy at our practices and games, checking our report cards, and even doctoring our boo-boos. When I was a little older, he'd look out for me, especially when he thought I was going the wrong way or making bad choices. I put him and Mom through the wringer, but they were a dream team, a united front at all times, no matter what I got up to."

"I'm having a hard time picturing you getting into any real trouble." She smiles at whatever image she has created in her mind. "But I can see your being delivered home by the police in the middle of the night for something like partying or trespassing. Maybe shoplifting for the thrill of it."

"I wasn't that kind of bad. I hate to admit it, but I was a douchebag. Entitled, didn't understand hard work . . . lived like the world was my oyster, and I treated it like an all you can eat buffet. Dad warned me about friends, girls, and shit I was doing." I slip my hands a little higher, working her ankles and up to her calves even as I remind myself, "That's why I was glad when I met Zack. He's the real deal. Smart, loyal, creative. I could see what my dad was talking about then, the difference in good people and how they can change everything. Zack helped me grow up."

"He's an okay brother," she agrees. "He was too old to look

out for me at school when I was younger, but he helped me learn that I'm okay exactly how I am. Kids would bully me because I'm weird. The teacher would be up at the board, and I'd be staring off into space, totally in my own world, not hearing a thing she said. But when she'd call on me, I could glance at the board and give the right answer. Stuff like that made other kids mad. And that was before I got into art. Then, I always had paint on my cheeks, charcoal under my nails, and was working on my tablet at a rapid-fire pace most people couldn't understand. But my brain could. If I could get my fingers to move faster to keep up with my mind, I would've. I could look at the blank page and see what it would be, what I could help it become." Her fingers twitch reflexively as she talks, and I wonder if she's subconsciously drawing.

"Zack told me that he was like that . . . only with me. He could see what I would be."

My hands have a mind of their own too, kneading and tracing over Luna's knees and under the hem of her dress. "Luna?"

She opens her eyes, looking at me clear-eyed and focused. Her legs shift open the slightest bit, giving me greater access to her thighs and ultimately, to her core. The scent of her arousal fills my nostrils, and I have to hold myself back from diving into the source of that sweetness.

"Tell me to stop. I'm not strong enough to do it myself." I've already asked so much of her, and now I'm asking more. Not for me this time, but for her.

She smiles a tiny smile of rebellion. "Don't stop."

I should stop anyway, but I don't. I tell myself I'll go a little further . . . that's it. Nothing too bad, I vow, measuring my own wickedness by the inches of Luna's leg I can see. I shift so I can knead the flesh of her inner thighs, working her dress higher and higher, almost immediately breaking my own promise.

Goosebumps break out over her skin, and I tease a fingertip over them. "Cold?"

She bites her lip, shaking her head. "Hot. So hot." Her hips writhe beneath my touch. "Please . . ."

"Please what? More? Stop? Harder? Tell me, Luna. Tell me what you want," I command, my voice a rough whisper.

"More. Harder. Touch me, please." Luna begging me to touch her is nothing I would've expected. It's a beautiful and powerful motivator, and I do exactly what she's demanded of me.

Finding the side of her panties, I pull them down and off her legs in an effortless swoop before urging her legs open. The sight that I behold is unlike anything I've seen before.

"Fucking gorgeous," I tell her as I see her pink, puffy pussy for the first time. I want to touch her, taste her, mark her until that pussy knows who it belongs to. The urge is more caveman than I usually experience, but something about Luna is bringing up primal desires I've never had. I want to possess her, care for her . . . and I haven't even laid a hand on her heaven yet.

I'm so fucked.

Using my thumbs to spread her smooth lips, I gather her juices and smear them up to her clit.

A few small circles there and Luna is already working her hips in time with me. I slip two fingers inside her easily, curling them up to pet her inner walls. "There," she murmurs. "Right there."

Goddamn, Luna telling me what she likes is the sexiest thing I've ever heard. I keep up the strokes, doing just what she asks until she starts panting with a little cry on every exhale. "I'm gonna . . . Can I come?"

Luna asking the same question in that bed at Elena's flashes through my mind, and a dark thought follows it. I press her hips down hard, preventing her from bucking into my hand. "No. Not yet, not till I say you can."

Her eyes pop open, looking at me in shock. We're both frozen for a moment, locked in a silent battle to see if she's going to give in. I stroke that spot inside her, slowly and gently, to encourage her, and a fresh wash of clear fluid coats my hand.

"That's it. Let me see what your body can do. Show me." I swallow thickly as I begin stroking into her harder . . . deeper . . . faster, matching my pace with swipes over her clit. "Show me what a good girl you are."

She cries out as her eyes roll back and her head tosses back and forth, setting her glasses off-kilter. She's coming undone before my very eyes and I want more of it . . . more of her.

Watching her closely, I find the rhythm that she responds to best and push her higher and higher, then back off. She does her best to hold out, but too quickly, she's asking, "I need to . . . Can I?"

It's not enough. "Can you what? Say it. I want to hear you."

She's gone to pleasure, riding the edge so close it might as well be a blade. "Can I come, sir?" she gasps.

"Yes. Fuck, I want to see you wild, Luna. Come now."

The orgasm takes her flying before the words leave my mouth, and I watch, awestruck, as she sings for me with complete abandon. I keep talking, saying dirty things she seems to like, as I tease her clit and feel the pulsing waves of her pussy squeezing my fingers.

"More. You . . . I want you," she pants, wiggling her fingers toward me.

This is a bad idea. Maybe the worst. But I don't have to be told twice. I'm damn near about to spill in my pants.

Quickly, I rip my shirt off, not undoing the buttons but instead pulling it over my head in a rush, and then shove my pants and underwear down my thighs, freeing my leaking cock. I dive for the end table, opening a drawer to grab a condom. I give myself a rough stroke before donning the latex, and then I lean over Luna, one arm on the couch cushion beneath her and one at the base of my dick.

"Tell me you want this. Want *me*. I need to hear you say it."

"Yes," she moans.

It's not what I asked, but it's enough because I've reached the end of my control. I enter her in one thrust, and her pussy envelops me so well that I nearly come right then. But I won't be a one-pump chump, not now, not ever. So I fight my orgasm back, doing what I asked her to do and hold on longer for it to be better.

Luna's back arches as she wraps her hands around my upper arms, her fingernails digging into the backs of my triceps. Her walls flutter again, and I want to help her ride out what seems to be another smaller orgasm.

I stroke into her powerfully. "That's it. Come on my cock, baby."

"I am. I am, Carter."

"Shit," I hiss. Any remaining thread of control I had snaps instantly when she says my name, and I fuck Luna. I fuck her harder and more thoroughly than I should. There's no gentle kindness now, no sweet touches. It's rough and hard as I take her body, and she gives it all to me.

"Are you gonna come for me too? Fill me up?" There's a sparkle in her eye as she says the phrase she called gross before. I get it. Sometimes, the dirtiest things are the sexiest in the moment, and I suspected she liked it before, despite her protest.

"Fuck yeah, I'm gonna fill you up until you can't hold it all and it leaks down your leg, marking you as mine." I emphasize the words by harshly gripping her inner thigh, right beside where I'm entering her. I'm going to do no such thing. When I spill, it'll be in the condom, but the idea of painting her walls with my cum is an image I can't withstand, and I slip off the edge.

I grunt, rutting into Luna as she fucks me back. Her nails dig into my skin, holding on for dear life as our cries become a chorus. I come hard as her pussy squeezes me just right.

When I sag over her, leaning against the back of the couch, I see that her glasses have gone crooked. I straighten them gently. "You look amazing in these. Don't let anyone ever tell you differently."

I smile goofily, enjoying the awestruck look on her face. Her eyes are vacant, dazed as she's in the afterglow.

"That was . . . wow."

Pride builds up in my chest.

"I didn't think people could do it like *that* . . . on their first time."

CHAPTER
EIGHTEEN

LUNA

SILENCE REIGNS for a beat as Carter gawks at me. "Their . . . what?" he snaps.

His utterance brings me back to Earth from the foggy pink haze of bliss I'm floating in. I blink and meet his gaze. He looks horror-stricken and terrified.

"You mean people's first time together, right?" he asks. "Not first-first time. Like you weren't a virgin. For fuck's sake, tell me you weren't a virgin."

He sounds a little hysterical. Offended, I feel my inner Alphena rising up. "Virginity is the patriarchy's attempt to control women's actions through shame. And if you're talking about loss of the hymen, I've had periods for over a decade and used plenty of toys."

I could've left the details out, especially about toys, but Samantha has taught me that they can be a vital part of pleasuring oneself and nothing to be ashamed of. Gritting his teeth, Carter asks again, "You weren't a virgin, though? I mean, you've had sex before?"

"Oral and fingers," I admit, "but not . . . *what we did.*"

It's only when he pulls his now-soft dick out of me and deals with the condom that I realize this conversation has all been with him still inside me, post-orgasm. "Holy fuck, Luna! I would've been more . . . or less . . . if I'd known. That's the sort of thing you tell someone beforehand. You should've told me."

I can feel the heat of a blush creeping up my neck, and lying here with my dress around my waist seems sleazy when he's freaking out and already regretting this. I squirm, trying to shove my dress down, desperately wanting to hide. Or escape.

"I wouldn't have changed a thing, until this moment."

I swing my leg around him, sitting up and reaching for my heels. I dread putting them back on, but I'm going to strut out of here with every piece of my armor in place or die trying.

"Luna, wait. I didn't mean it like that. Your first time—" I hold up a finger to argue, and he begrudgingly corrects himself. "First time *with someone* should be special. Not a rough fuck on a couch. I would've . . ."

I don't wait for him to tell me all the ways that what we did was wrong. Because I know what he really means. "You would've stopped."

We both know it's true. I really don't think first times—with someone—need to be this rose petal covered bed, a special occasion. But Carter does. Or at least he thinks I should think that. Either way, the net result is the same.

I'm wrong. For what I want, for what I've done, even for what I haven't done. I stand, stepping out of reach as he tries to stop me. "Wait. Luna, wait."

"I'm gonna go. Good luck with . . . everything."

———

How dare Carter ruin what we did with a whole preconceived notion about what sex is supposed to be with some 'should'a, could'a, would'a' bullshit? Like I didn't know what I was doing or what I wanted?

I should'a slapped the panic off his freaked-out face.

I would'a if I'd thought of it at the time.

And I still could'a turn this car around and go back and do it.

But I don't. I go where I know I won't be judged.

A few minutes later, I'm pulling into the parking lot of Sam's apartment building. I knock on her door, and she calls out, "Come in."

I open the unlocked door . . . except Samantha's not alone.

"I am not wearing a butt plug with a raccoon tail while he takes me from behind," a female voice says.

I stop, going deer in the headlights frozen at the group of people staring back at me.

"Uh . . ." A noise of uncertainty is all I can muster.

"Luna?" Samantha says in surprise. She's leading the group, sitting crisscross-applesauce on the floor with the circle of people. "Sorry, everyone."

The apology is for the others, but her eyes are locked on me.

"I–I . . . Sorry!" I try to backpedal and close the door.

"Wait!" Samantha says, hurrying over to me. Lowering her voice, she asks, "Are you okay?"

I should say I'm fine and go home. Or at the least, tell Sam to call me later. But what pops out is, "I had sex with Carter."

"Practice group's over, people. Everyone out," Sam says flatly, her eyes wide and jaw hanging open.

There's a mumble of voices, and I think I hear someone say 'what?' and 'can she do that?' But with Sam helping people up, the other group members take the hint and rise, walking past me. I apologize over and over, hating the attention until one girl confides that they're not mad at the interruption. They're mad they're not getting to stay for the tea.

"I don't know your situation, girl, but there ain't no shame in getting some when you need or want it," she reassures me. She cuts her eyes to the man at her side, sassily adding, "As long as he doesn't want you to be a face down-trash bandit while you do the deed."

"It was a fake scenario, Rebecca," he says with an eye roll. To me, he says, "We do those to practice what we'd say when a client says something like that."

I blank for so long that Rebecca pats me on the shoulder and leaves before I can compose a response to her assessment. Way too late, when she's down the hall, I call out, "Thanks!"

She looks back and smiles, but it's in that 'what a weirdo' way that I'm all too familiar with.

Great, the raccoon-obsessed lady thinks I'm the strange one? Seriously?

Once Samantha gets the apartment cleared—promising a makeup session to one guy who doesn't seem to want to leave—she slams the door shut. "Tell me everything."

I start with the dinner—how Carter kissed me in front of everyone and kept his hand on my thigh the whole time. I kick my shoes off as I relive the foot massage with her, sit on the couch as I tell her about letting Carter's fingers do the walking right up to my center, and then mindlessly bounce my knees as I reveal how we had sex.

I look up to judge her reaction, but she's wearing the blank, non-judgmental therapist's face she's been working to perfect, not her bestie face. "What?"

She blinks patiently, letting the quiet grow. "What else?"

"Huh? That's everything."

She tilts her head curiously, still silent. I sigh and confess, "It was so damn good, Sam. Better than I ever dreamed. Carter's got a filthy mouth, and I loved it. He made me ask to co—"

Sam holds up a finger to stop me and asks tightly, "He denied you pleasure?"

My eyes drop to where I'm fidgeting with the hem of my dress. "No, definitely not. It was . . . to show I was a good girl."

"Ooh, I like where this is going!" When I risk glancing up, Samantha's therapist face is completely gone and she's smiling widely. "And were you a good girl?" she teases.

I giggle and nod. "A very good one."

"Then I'm confused. So, why are you here?"

And poof, there goes my good mood again.

"He, uhm . . ." I swallow, not wanting to say it aloud because it'll make it real. Right now, I can pretend it was a nightmare. Why not? It's no different than pretending I'm Carter's wife.

Except the way I felt with Carter inside me. That was real.

"Luna?" Sam says gently as she scoots next to me on the couch.

"Afterward, he flipped out."

She flinches. "Flipped out how, exactly? Are you okay?"

"What? Oh, yeah. Not like *that*," I say quickly. Sam's ride or die, and if I don't call her off, she'd be busting down Carter's door. With a kitchen knife and the Taser she carries on campus.

"Okay." She sighs in relief.

I've told Samantha a lot, nearly everything. We've talked about sex for hours . . . in theory. I've helped her study for countless tests, read her research papers, and we've talked about past partners. Hers, obviously, though I've shared my paltry experiences. I've just never explicitly told her . . .

"I haven't done it with an actual person before tonight. Well, other than oral," I confess quietly.

"*Hadn't*. You have now." The correction is delivered with a waggle of her eyebrows. She doesn't seem shocked in the slightest. When I look at her questioningly, she laughs. "Did you think I didn't know that? It's literally going to be my job to know the things people don't tell me and lead them to discover themselves. For now, that's easiest with people I know well—like my friends."

That makes sense, but I still feel vulnerable that she knew. What else does she know about me that I haven't figured out?

"I guess I thought it was kinda my secret," I agree solemnly. Meeting her eyes, I confess, "It was amazing, Sam. But he regretted it. While he was still inside me."

"*Shit*. Ouch." She's thoughtful for a moment and then asks, "What about you? I don't give a single, solitary fuck about Carter Harrington or his feelings. All I care about is you."

I search my heart, my body, and my mind. "The only thing I regret is that I left my panties on his coffee table."

She glances down at my legs, following them under my dress. "Alexa, remind me to clean my couch before class tomorrow," she blurts to the room.

The automated voice repeats the message.

She laughs in shock, and then we're both laughing. I flop back on the couch, and her eyes go wide as my legs flail.

"Quit acting like I have my bare business on your couch!"

She purses her lips, looking doubtful. "So you did take my advice and wax the wild jungle?"

I swat her leg as I gasp in offense. "It was not *wild* down there."

"Well, obviously, not anymore." She adopts a Steve Irwin documentary-style voice, "What was once natural bush has been tamed and civilized. Like a national park."

"Thanks. I feel better," I tell Sam sarcastically, still laughing a bit. "I think I'm going to go home. I want a shower, my tablet, and maybe a good night's sleep."

"You sure?"

I am. Tonight might've been nothing like I thought it would be, and Carter might be nothing like I thought either, but sex with him was good and I'm going to hold onto that.

"*Let it gooooo . . . let it goooo . . .*" I sing, holding my arms out wide. "I'm good."

Stealing the tune, she suggests, "Maybe try . . . Carter's a *fuckin' hoooo . . . oh noooo . . .*"

About to walk out the door, I pause. "What's the deal with Rebecca and the raccoon tail butt plug?"

Sam zips her lips. "Patient-therapist confidentiality." She winks and adds, "Except it's not a real patient or real group, just a client study where we role play. However, on a completely unrelated note, you know how I said people discover themselves? Have you ever heard of a furry? Because *someone* in my study group has some shit to learn . . . about themselves."

CHAPTER
NINETEEN
CARTER

IT'S time to deal with what I've done. At least in one way, which is why I'm back at my parents' house. The other issue with Luna? I'm not sure what the hell to do about it.

I purposefully guide Dad to the living room for our talk, wanting to avoid his office and the power play inherent to it this time. Sitting on the couch, my hands clasped between my knees, I implore him to understand. "It wasn't supposed to be like this. I told you the whole family dinner song and dance was overkill."

"You think the family dinner was the issue? That's what was overkill?" he barks, leaning forward in the chair with his eyes drilling into me. "Not the lie in the first place?" He presses his finger into the coffee table. "Or not telling us before dinner?" Another finger press.

He shakes his head, obviously frustrated. "What the fuck, Carter? We don't do business this way. You know that."

The disappointment in his eyes cuts deep. As much as I hate to admit it, on some level, I'm still the boy trying to garner his dad's approval. I look down at my shoes, then study the rug between them. It's Persian, with swirling designs in various shades of blue. I think Mom bought it the last time she redecorated, or maybe it was the time before that. But the answers aren't in the fibers beneath me.

I look Dad in the eye, ready to take my lumps. "I wanted the deal. For Elena, for Blue Lake, and mostly, for me. I can bring in clients myself, manage my own accounts. I've been doing it for years. But this one? I knew it was a big deal and wanted it. I was . . . *am* willing to do whatever it takes. Including learning about art or taking in a ringer to seal the deal."

Dad listens, though he huffs in exasperation before he answers snidely, "You think this is how to show me what you're capable of?"

Throwing my arms wide, I shout, "It wasn't just about that. But now that you mention it, well, nothing else was working!"

"Neither is this!" he shouts back.

We glare at each other, matching gritted teeth making our jaws sharp. I give in first. "I disagree. It was well in hand. But what do you want to do now?"

He closes his eyes and pinches the bridge of his nose, and for the first time, I see his age wearing on him. Dad has spent a lot of years at the helm of Blue Lake Assets. Maybe this stunt is the straw that broke the camel's back?

"I don't know," he mutters. "This is your mess. I'm inclined to let you fix it, except that you've dragged Blue Lake and the family into it too."

I bite back a snarky comment that technically, he dragged the family in by forcing the dinner. If he'd stayed out like I'd asked, this would be my issue alone.

"I can fix it, though right now, there's nothing to fix if you think about it." He looks at me doubtfully, and I explain my thinking. "Dinner was fine, and Elena believes Luna is my wife. She likes us and is open to using Blue Lake for portfolio management. I'll meet with Elena and her current finance guy, and we'll go from there. There's no need to *do* anything. I feel bad about it because she seems like a nice lady, and maybe I didn't need to do all of this, but at the time, it seemed like a way in. For now, it is what it is."

"Seriously? You think continuing this charade is the way to go?"

"You think telling her I lied is better?" I counter. "Then it would have all been for nothing."

Dad pushes up from the chair, and I have a split second of wondering if we're about to take this outside again. Thankfully, he paces to the window and stares out at the garden instead. He's got his thinking face on, and that's never a good thing.

"Look, I'm sorry. It all got out of hand so quickly." I'm trying to talk him down and stop whatever mental journey he's going on because it can't bode well for me.

Still gazing out the window, he declares, "You'll tell Elena the truth. If it costs us the deal, so be it."

"What?" I balk. "I can't do that!"

He whirls, glaring at me. "You can, and you will. Even if it succeeded, it'll be found out eventually, and it'll be worse. Or did you plan a fake divorce too?"

He makes it sound ridiculous, and maybe I haven't thought that far ahead yet, but there's no need to be rash about deciding right now, today. But Dad's already settled . . .

"This whole lie is always a bomb waiting to explode in the middle of the relationship you're trying to build with Elena. I won't have our reputation sullied. It's not how we operate. Can I trust you to fix your fuck up? Or do I need to do it for you?"

I shoot to my feet, facing him angrily. He's tying my hands. And however this plays out, I've changed his opinion of me for the worse, exactly the opposite of what I was desperately trying to do.

Tightly, I bite out, "I'll handle it."

———

I don't know why I go to Luna's. She doesn't want to see me, but there's no one else who'll understand, and she did tell me good luck with everything, so maybe she will want to know what's happened. It's an excuse and I know it, but it doesn't stop me from knocking on her door.

"Carter?" She opens the door with her brow already furrowed in confusion at seeing me. "What are you doing here?"

She's wearing baggy purple sweats with a smattering of stars along the left leg. A quick glance and I see the wording says *Rewrite The Stars*. Her cropped T-shirt hangs off one shoulder, and I'm reminded of the first time I came to her door for simple tutoring. It seems so long ago.

"*Greatest Showman?*" I say, pointing at her leg.

She smooths her hand over the print before adjusting the waistband, pulling it up. I think she's trying to hide, but it only serves to accentuate the swooping curve of her hip beneath her smaller waist.

"Yeah."

I walk past her without waiting for an invitation, knowing she won't stop me. "We should talk."

"Carter . . . I don't think . . ." she stammers.

I sit down on her couch, her words—or attempt at them—not swaying me in the slightest. "At least listen, please."

"Fine." She closes the door and comes over to the couch, but she sits as far away from me as possible. "What?"

"I talked to my dad today." That gets her attention, though she doesn't ask questions. "He's angry, of course, and worried about what happens moving forward. If we're found out, what the consequences will be, or if we don't say anything and Elena chooses Blue Lake, there's a perpetual risk of her finding out."

"That makes sense." She shrugs, not seeming particularly concerned either way.

"Which would also affect whether she'd be interested in showcasing Thomas's collection at the museum," I remind her.

"Oh," she says woodenly. "So, what are you going to do?"

I move across the sofa, sitting sideways so our knees touch. "He basically ordered me to tell the truth. He said it's the only way."

She searches my eyes, and I hold her gaze, not wanting to hide anything from her. "Are you going to?" she whispers.

"I have another idea."

I left and came straight to Luna's, but the time in the car was spent playing the whole scenario out in my mind with dozens of different outcomes.

Luna raises her brows questioningly.

"The truth. That's what it's all about. So what if we made it . . . true?" I take Luna's hands in mine, holding them between us. "Marry me. For real."

She laughs in my face, wild and boisterous laughter bubbling up at the absurdity of my idea, which hurts deeply for a reason I can't pinpoint.

I drop her hands in favor of running my fingers through my hair. "It's the only way."

"No, it's not," she says, trying to catch her breath from laughing so hard. "Your father's right and you should tell Elena the truth."

I thought she'd agree with me, or at least consider my idea. But she's dismissing it outright. "No!" I shout. Luna flinches at the volume, and I gather myself. "I can't do that."

"Carter . . ." Luna starts, her voice a calming tone as though she's trying to soothe me. "This is crazy. Things keep getting more and more out of hand. We've gone from a little bit of art tutoring to your asking me to marry you for real? What's next?"

I don't know, but I can't tell her that. I need to have a plan, one we can stick to. People get married for various reasons all the time, so this isn't that crazy. I tell myself to stick to the facts . . .

"We get married. We ride it out and see it through. After, well, we'll figure it out. I'm desperate here, Luna. Whatever you want."

"You'd have to be desperate to want to marry me."

"That's not what I meant and you know it. Don't put words in my mouth," I snap back.

"I'm gonna put my foot in your mouth," she replies, equally snippy.

"Some people happen to like that."

I grab her foot from beneath her leg, pulling it into the air, and Luna falls back to the arm of the couch. "Wha—"

I shut her up by sucking her big toe into my mouth. I've never done this before, but I have to admit . . . it's sexy as fuck.

"Think about it. Think about us. Think about the deal and

the art exhibition." I nibble the flesh of her toe and remind her, "Think about how good we were together."

I'm not talking about at dinner or with Elena, and we both know it. I've also been thinking non-stop about what happened between Luna and me—how amazing it was and then how it ended. I was shocked and didn't handle it well, and I would love a chance to improve on the experience. Not that I'm complaining, but Luna deserves more.

And fuck, I want to be the one to give it to her. I've been feeling a bit Neanderthal about it being me. I'm not proud of it, but there's something about being the one who she let see her in that most vulnerable moment that's special. I'm fucking hard just thinking about it.

"Have you used those toys you told me about since?" I ask as I push her sweats up and kiss her calf, keeping my eyes on hers.

She bites her bottom lip, not answering, but it's answer enough.

"Where are they?"

"My nightstand," she says quietly as I lick behind her knee. That's as far as I can go with her in these pants, and I want more.

I stand and pull her into my arms, carrying her bridal style to the bedroom down the hall.

She is my bride. Or she's going to be.

I gently lay her down on her bed and follow, arranging myself beside her so I can keep my hands on her . . . all over her as I caress and knead her calves, her thighs, her hips, and up to her breasts.

"Carter, we should be talking about how to come clean, not . . . this." She's arguing, but the words are moaned and her eyes have fluttered shut.

"We should fuck now and talk later," I suggest against the sensitive skin of her neck. "You want this, Luna. You want me. No sense in arguing, your body's giving you away." With my hands under her shirt, I pluck her breasts through her bra and she arches into my touch.

"It's a biological reaction," she says. "It'd happen for anyone."

"You think so? What we did, what we're doing now . . . you think it's like this for everyone?" I've pushed her bra up, letting her full breasts free, and I lick her peaked nipple, moaning against her delicious flesh.

She cries out, grabbing my head and holding me to her for more. As if I have any plan to stop.

I'm not lying or telling her sweet nothings to get her to let me fuck her again. Luna might not realize how special what we did was, but I do. Sex that good is a once in lifetime experience. I think that's part of why I was so upset that she didn't tell me about her virginity. I felt like I'd pushed her too far, too fast, or maybe gone too hard on her.

But finally, I realized that sweet, innocent Luna Starr might just be my match. And no matter how dangerous that is, it's a rare gift I won't waste.

I pull her shirt over her head, and she helps get her bra off while I move down to her sweats, teasing them over her hips as I lay kisses to her belly. "I want to see you. I want to touch and taste every inch of you, find every spot that drives you wild and tease it until you're begging me to fill you."

"Uh-huh." Though it's an easy agreement, it's hard won and I know it.

As I get her pants down, I realize . . . "You don't have on any underwear?" I look up her body to see her smiling at me. "You little teasing slut, there was only one thin layer between me and heaven this whole time?"

I throw her leg over me so that I'm centered between her legs and lay a long lick over her seam, tasting the juices pouring from her pussy. I keep licking as I tell her, "You left your panties on my table when you left. Did you realize that?" She moans, her fingers sliding into my hair and scratching my scalp as she grips my head. "I jacked off with them, remembering this tight pussy clamping down on me and how beautiful you looked as you came for me."

"Oh!" she shouts as I slide two fingers into her slippery core.

"You like that image, Luna? You driving me so fucking crazy that I milked myself with your silky panties wrapped around my cock?"

"Show me."

"Good girl, I want you to tell me what you want." I'm praising her as I already move to do her bidding, standing to pull my shirt over my head and shove my shoes off so I can kick out of my pants. I want skin to skin this time, all of Luna and all of me.

On the bed, she's rolled to her side, looking at me through hazy eyes that drop to my cock as I take myself in hand with long, slow strokes. A bead of precum leaks at the top, covering my hand, and Luna licks her lips hungrily.

"Tell me what you want, baby. You wanna suck me?"

In answer, Luna sits up so that she's on the edge of the bed, her legs on either side of mine. I thrust into my hand, showing her up-close what I want to do to her. As my cock peeks out of my fist, she sticks her tongue out a tiny bit, lapping at the precum like a hungry kitten. I grip her head, holding her still. "Stick your tongue out." She does so, and I rub myself over her pink tongue, tip to throat, slow and easy, teasing us both.

She swallows reflexively, trying to take me deeper. "Take my mouth," she whimpers.

I give her what she wants, fucking her face slow and deep as I watch her closely. She moves a hand to her glasses, and I freeze, holding her at the base of my cock. She looks up at me, her eyes watering behind the lenses, and I remind her, "Glasses on. I want you to see what you do to me, how fucking crazy you make me, Luna."

She nods, her nose burying in my trimmed hair, and only then do I release her. I expect her to need a second—to catch her breath or maybe decide if that was too much—but she doesn't lose contact with my cock, immediately finding a rhythm and pace that brings me to the edge faster than she should be able to.

She takes me in and out of the wet heat of her mouth, slurping on me obscenely. She wraps one hand around my base to work in tandem with her mouth, and then the other hand disappears between her legs. She begins to moan, the vibrations driving me crazy, but not nearly as sexy as the idea that sucking on my cock has Luna so turned on that she needs to touch herself.

I lean back, giving her more of my cock, but mostly so that I can watch her touch herself. When her hips start bucking, I warn, "Don't come. Not yet. I'll make it worth it."

She pouts, a sound deep in her throat working over my cock, but she moves her hand away from her pussy. I reach down for it and bring her fingers to my mouth, sucking the cream from them with a groan. She's so delicious that I'm instantly on edge and have to pull my cock from her mouth.

"Wha—" she says, her eyes jumping to mine.

"We come together." I shudder even as I make the vow, my body in sharp disagreement with my mind. I bend down to kiss her, sliding my tongue against hers as I cup her face. "Lie back. My turn to drive you wild."

Nerves flash in her eyes for a split second, but then she smiles and moves back on the bed. She lays out like Snow White —head on the pillow, hands crossed on her belly, and feet together. That's not gonna work for long, but I leave it alone while I open the drawer of her nightstand to see what type of fun we're going to have.

Dildos, vibes, and lubes . . . oh, my! I smile evilly as I hear Luna's voice singing sweetly in my head.

"Fuck, my sweet girl has a naughty side, doesn't she?"

Luna blushes, her eyes dropping in embarrassment, but I reach over and lift her chin with a finger. "I fucking love it, Luna. I'm glad you know your body. I want to know it too."

Her eyes meet mine this time. "The purple one on my clit . . . is my favorite."

Better. Bolder. Luna has a goddess inside her. It's my job to help Luna release her into the world with a lover, not only on her own.

I press the button on the side of the purple rose-shaped vibrator, and it comes to life with a low, almost soundless hum that I can feel in my hand. I press it again, and the vibrations get faster and faster, sometimes in a rhythm and sometimes full-throttle. Oh, this is going to be fun.

"Butterfly your legs," I order. She puts her feet together, letting her knees fall open to expose herself to my gaze. I lie on the bed between her feet, supporting myself on my elbow so I can have both hands free.

I start with the vibe on low, touching it over her skin. Slowly, I work my way to her breasts, and she arches, wanting the vibe there. I press the button, increasing the vibration as I touch the edge to one nipple. The vibe sucks her nipple into the little orifice at the center of the rose, and Luna's breath hitches. I use my free hand to pluck and play with the other nipple, not wanting it to feel left out.

When she's ready, I blow gently over her clit, not touching her with anything other than my breath. "I wonder if I could get you to come like this . . . without even touching your sweet pussy. What do you think?"

Luna squirms, trying to lift her hips to my mouth, but with me lying over her hip, she's pinned down. "I think you're evil." But then she remembers she can tell me what she wants, that I want her to. "Lick me, suck me, use the rose on me . . . something."

I want her on my mouth, but I promised her toys, so I turn the vibe back down to low before pressing it over her clit. It's torturously not enough and I know it, but her pussy pulses beneath the purple toy, spilling more of her juice. That I can taste. Leaving the toy in place, I slide my stiffened tongue inside her, fucking her with it as I increase the intensity of the vibe.

I work her that way, alternating my tongue and my fingers in tandem with the vibe, taking her to the edge time after time until she's a puddled mess, begging for release. I'm humping the bed beneath me, my dick desperate to get inside her.

I can't wait any longer. Neither can she. I'm so close to the point of no return that it'll barely take a stroke and I'll probably spill all over her belly, and I can have her coming in a heartbeat too.

She holds her hands out, a clear invitation of what she wants.

"Are you sure?" I ask. One last chance before I take her.

She nods, and with me lined up with her pussy, she reaches one hand down, guiding me in. I take it slow, not because Luna needs the adjustment time but because I want to feel her envelop every inch of me in her heat. This is a sensation I've never felt before, a loss of my own virginity of a sort.

With Luna. It seems right that it's with her.

When I bottom out, I pull back before sliding in again. Slowly, we pick up the pace, and at some point, her legs end up on my shoulders. Bit by bit, I lean forward, watching her for signs that it's too much, but she must've been telling the truth about doing yoga because her legs are up by her ears and I'm pounding into her raised pussy in minutes.

She tilts her head back and pleads, "Hand necklace."

"Goddamn it, Luna," I grunt. But I wrap a hand around her neck gently. "This what you want?"

"Choke me, please." She smiles as her eyes clear. Luna might not be experienced, but she knows what she wants.

I squeeze gently and feel the corresponding flutter against my cock. Wanting to try something more, I keep one hand around her throat and smack her ass with my other.

"Oh!" she cries out with the sharp sound. I do it again and again, each time the cry becoming more of a guttural moan. Luna's going wild beneath me. She thrashing her head, and I have to press harder to hold her in place. Her calves are digging into my shoulders for leverage as she bucks, making her ass slap my hips as she takes my cock deep. I wrap an arm over her legs, pinning her there, and take control.

I fuck her hard, legs locked and throat pinned, totally at my mercy.

"Do you want to come, Luna?" I grit out through clenched teeth.

"Yes! Please, can I?"

"Good girl," I praise at her remembering to ask. "Can I come too? I promised you we'd come together, and I'm about to fill this pussy up with my cum for real." Fresh tingles run from my balls up to my spine. "I've never done that, Luna. I want to . . . with you."

I want her to understand that this is special to me too. She is special to me.

"Together," she agrees.

We fight to get there, and when she's right on the edge again, I hold her impaled with my cock bottomed out inside her, making shallow thrusts, and manage to grunt out, "Say you're mine, Luna. Say you'll marry me."

"Yes!" she screams as the flutters of her pussy surround me. I'm not sure if she's answering me or crying out her pleasure, but I'm going to hold her to it. Either way, I can't hold back any longer and I spill inside Luna. Hot spurts of cum jet from my cock, and the idea that I'm marking her is ridiculously sexy to a deep, dark, possessive part of my soul.

It might not be right, but it's the truth.

As Luna comes back to consciousness from her orgasm, I keep pumping into her, wanting to keep my cum deep. "God-damn, Luna. You're fucking amazing."

She sags back, taking her legs from my shoulders to let them hang down limp and flopping her arms onto the bed. I trace my hands over her skin, petting her all over. When my now-soft cock slips from her, I use my fingers to push our combined cum back into her.

"You're a slippery mess," I tell her. She squirms, probably thinking it's some sort of insult, and I swat her hip. "Sexiest thing I've ever seen. Your pussy covered in our cum, white cream spilling out but your pussy sucking it back in when I push my thumb inside you. You want it there, don't you?"

I glance up, and she nods silently, her eyes bright with mischief.

I whisper, "Want to know a secret?" I don't wait for her to answer, just tell her, "I want it there too. My cum marking you and then drying over your thighs when it runs down your legs. I want to rub it into your skin like lotion so you know you're mine."

She laughs lightly. "Yours? I'm not yours, Carter. That was just . . . you know, dirty talk."

In an instant, I slam my fingers inside her, impaling her hard and deep and fast, and lean over her, getting right in her face, nose to nose. "Mine. You said yes, Luna. You're going to marry me."

CHAPTER
TWENTY

LUNA

WHAT THE HELL? *Was Carter serious? He couldn't have been serious! It was sex talk, that's it.*

But the stone-cold stare in his eyes tells a different story. He looks dangerously serious, especially as he starts pumping his fingers into me again.

"You said yes." Pump. "We're getting married." He wiggles his fingers deep inside me. "Say it," he orders, finding a new rhythm.

"But—" I cry.

I can't marry him. That's crazy. I also can't come again, not so soon. But Carter doesn't agree with either option.

"You can, and you will, Luna."

That's the last he says of it, thankfully, because when he gives me one more earth-shattering orgasm, I think I would've agreed to anything he said in that moment.

Quack like a duck and call me Spanky!

Deal, Spanky. Shucky-ducky quack-quack!

Paint a landscape with the brush clenched in your asshole!

Sure thing. I'm your girl. I gotchu, no problem!

Marry him . . . fuck my life, I would have said yes.

Afterward, I'm toast. Like call me a croissant because I roll over to my side, curl up, and pass out. Somewhere in my unconsciousness, I know Carter is lying behind me, his arm thrown over me and his fingers tracing gentle circles across my belly beneath the blankets he's pulled over us.

That's how I know this is probably all a dream, anyway. Carter Harrington is not petting my round belly after proposing mid-sex. I'll wake up in the morning alone, the way I always am. I'll get up alone, eat breakfast alone, and go to the museum and then later, work on Alphena . . . alone.

And that's okay. I really don't mind it . . . usually. Even so, I snuggle into Carter's embrace, enjoying this dream a little longer.

———

I wake up to near-blinding sunlight streaming in the window. I stretch out like a cat, feeling deliciously rested.

Man, I slept like the dead last night. And those dreams?

I can't believe I concocted a whole scenario of Carter proposing for real and then fucking me until I said yes.

My brain is such a strange place, so full of strange ideas. It's a good thing they're private because I would be so embarrassed to share that one with Samantha. She'd probably try to write a paper on my delusionary imagination.

I laugh to myself, rolling over and rubbing my eyes. I squint, trying to get the clock into focus. I can't see well enough to tell what time it is, but I can see that there's one too many numbers . . . four, instead of three, which means . . .

"I'm late!"

I grab my glasses off the nightstand and shove them onto my face crookedly. I glare at the clock accusingly, wondering why my alarm didn't wake me at eight like it always does. Now, it's after ten, the museum is already open, and I'm supposed to be on duty.

I roll out of bed, sprinting for the bathroom. There's no time for a shower, so a quick brush of my hair, a quicker brush of my teeth, and a fresh layer of deodorant are all I can do. For once, I'm thankful for the ugly uniform I'm required to wear because it limits my choices, so I get dressed in record time.

"Bag, protein bar, and ooh, phone." I retrace my steps to grab my phone from the nightstand too, giving the clock one more glare.

One step into the living room and I stop in my tracks. "Carter?"

He's here. In my kitchen. Sipping on—I inhale and catch the scent that should've been an automatic tell—fresh coffee from the mug Samantha gave me. The one that says *Hos before Bros*.

"Good morning, sleepyhead," he croons. "Coffee?"

But other than his being here, drinking coffee, the other really weird thing is . . . he's naked. Like full Monty, sausage and biscuits, dick and balls *naked* . . . in my kitchen.

"What're you doing? Why are you . . .?" I point south, keeping my eyes averted north politely.

He chuckles and holds his arms out wide. "Didn't seem like a big deal after last night."

Huh? Last night?

How could he know about my dreams? Oh, duh . . . I'm still asleep.

I pinch my arm sharply. "Ow!"

"What the fuck? Why'd you do that?" Dream Carter comes over, setting the coffee down along the way. He takes my arm in his, rubbing the red mark that's already popping up.

"To wake up. I'm gonna be late for work." The explanation makes perfect sense to me, but Dream Carter doesn't seem to think so.

With a furrowed brow, he speaks slowly as though I couldn't possibly understand regular tempo speech. "You're awake. Your alarm went off, but I didn't realize it was for work, so I turned it off. Sorry. Do you want some coffee to go?"

"I'm . . . awake? And you're naked in my kitchen? With fresh coffee?" I laugh at the ridiculousness.

He grins, a bright glint in his eyes. "Go to work, Luna. I'll call you later. We'll do dinner. And if you're a good girl, maybe a bit of dessert too."

"Oh-kay," I drawl because Dream Me really has to get to

work, but staying here and having an early dinner could be good too.

Dream Carter swats my butt, telling me he'll lock up and to have a good day.

————

When Maeve yells at me for being late, I realize that none of this is a dream. Carter really was naked in my kitchen this morning, which means last night . . . was real too?

I can't examine that too closely without freaking out, so I bury myself in customer service mode. It's not until the end of the day, when I check my phone, that it truly hits me.

Carter: Dinner, 7pm. Capitol Chophouse. Wear a dress.

Bossy and to the point. Infuriating man.

A few minutes after that, he texted again.

Carter: Or wear whatever you want.

A smile steals across my lips at his self-correction. That's the only reason I consider actually going to this dinner.

Who do you think you're kidding? You're totally going. And you should hurry up because you need a shower before you go.

————

Showered, shaved, lotioned, and potioned, I smooth my palms over the skirt of my dress. I considered taking Carter's option to wear whatever I wanted to heart and show up in overalls or baggy jeans just to be ornery, but ultimately, I decided to play along with whatever this dinner plan is. The dress is the same black one I wore to Carter's parents'—freshly steamed after what I did in it last time—but it's the best I could do from my closet on short notice because Samantha borrowed the green dress, not caring that it exposes several more inches of thigh on her long legs than it does on mine.

The hostess at Capitol Chophouse greets me politely, if not a bit stiffly, when I come in. "I'm meeting a friend here . . . Carter Harrington." I see the spark of interest in her eyes at Carter's name, and she looks me up and down more thoroughly. I follow her to the table, expecting to find Carter waiting for me.

Instead, there are two people sitting there . . . Carter and Zack. "Uh, hi." Both men stand as I approach, and then there's a weird moment where they both reach to pull a chair out for me.

Zack chuckles and sits back down, letting Carter get my seat. "Guess it's a good thing you've got manners, huh? Your brother would have you doing one of his seminars if you didn't."

Carter leans my way. "He's talking about Chance. He hosts a podcast called *Two Men and a Mic* that teaches young men how to thrive in our current world, business economy, and beyond. I don't think he mentioned that at dinner."

"Dinner?" Zack echoes, catching that nugget instantly.

"Yeah, things got a little carried away when the old man caught wind of the whole deal. Called a family dinner," Carter explains as if the dinner was no big deal, which it most definitely was. It was more like a Family Dinner with capital letters.

"Glad I missed that." Zack shakes his head knowingly, and I wonder if he's ever gone to a dinner at the Harrington home. I never cared before or even gave it a single thought, but now, I'm curious.

"For sure," Carter agrees. "About that . . . there's something I want, I mean . . . *we* want to talk to you about." Carter reaches over and takes my hand, pressing a soft kiss to the back of it.

Zack catches onto that quick too. "You son of a bitch," he snarls at Carter. He's at least keeping his voice somewhat reasonable considering the place, and I realize Carter smartly planned for that. "Did you sleep with my sister?"

Scratch that . . . because the table next to us totally heard that.

"There wasn't a lotta sleeping going on," I murmur accidentally, and Zack's stony glare shoots to me. "Oops, that was supposed be my inside voice."

Carter squeezes my hand and tries to reassure Zack. "It wasn't some meaningless fuck." He flashes me a private smile, and I blush furiously as I stare at him in wide-eyed horror. And then it gets so much worse. "It was special. A first."

"Could we not?" I whisper angrily, hoping Carter will shut up. The table next to us has given up all pretense of not-listening and is going so far as to lean our way for a better earful.

Zack looks from me to Carter and seems to realize that not only did we sleep together, but that it was a first for me. Apparently, that technicality counts by some societal standard I don't agree with, but I'm sure as hell not discussing my sex life with my brother.

"I'm going to kill you, you motherfucker," Zack shouts, loud enough to stop dinner and conversations at all the surrounding tables. There's a chorus of surprised gasps as every eye in the restaurant locks on us.

Zack's on his feet in an instant, coming around the table in two strides. Carter stands to meet him with his hands held out wide in a placating stance. "Look, man. Calm down."

Why do people say that? It never actually makes the angry person calm down. I don't think anyone has ever stopped in their tracks, thought to themselves, 'yeah, I'm overreacting', and chilled out. But Carter says it anyway.

Zack grabs his shirt, shaking him a bit, and when that doesn't change the past, Zack rears back and throws a punch smack into Carter's nose, which pops red blood that drips to the marble floor.

"Zack! Carter! Stop it!" I shout, but neither of them pays me any mind.

There's a bit of a scuffle, but it's mostly a one punch-and-done deal because Carter isn't really fighting back. When he's released, Carter covers his nose, glaring at Zack. "Feel bedder?"

I'm sure he means 'better', but the bloody nose is giving his voice a bit of a hollow sound.

Zack doesn't seem to care. "Not at all."

The hostess swishes up with more interest in her eyes than anger and says, "Boys, if this isn't over, I'm going to have to ask you to leave." Out of the side of her mouth, she whispers, "You got them fightin' over you?"

I think that's supposed to be a compliment, not a question.

I speak up for all three of us. "Go get cleaned up." I wave Carter off. "And you sit down." I point at Zack's vacated chair.

"I'll be right back," Carter vows. "And we'll handle this."

Ugh, I hope that doesn't mean more fighting! It's not like it's going to save my honor or something antiquated like that. Alphena would kick both Carter and Zack's butts for even thinking something like that, much less acting on it. And the shred of Alphena that resides inside me is considering doing it, too.

Carter stomps away, not giving any mind to the people he passes who are staring at him in disgust. I guess bloody noses aren't really dinner entertainment in a place like this. Maybe some of these people should come to the college bars Sam takes me to? There, a plate of nachos, a beer, and a fight are a typical Friday night.

"What the hell, Zack?" I demand when it's the two of us. I've leaned in close, though we're sitting next to each other at the table. But we've put on enough of a show. This conversation deserves some privacy.

Zack lays his hands over mine, leaning into me too. "I am so sorry for getting you tied up in this, Moony. This isn't what I meant to happen. I never thought he'd take advantage of you like this."

His eyes are filled with the self-torture he's subjecting himself to. At one point in our lives, I would've let him stew in his own guilt, earned or not. But not now, not this time.

"I'm not sorry," I confess, knowing it's true. "I'm fine, and he didn't take advantage of me. But I'm not discussing my . . ." I pause, looking around to make sure no one is listening, but there are still side-eyes looking our way. I whisper, "*sex life*," and then return to regular volume, "with you. We talk about a lot of things, but that's off-limits. And that goes both ways. I don't want to hear about whose ankles you pinned behind her head, either."

Zack glances toward the restroom and with a tight jaw asks, "Did he?"

"Ah-ah-ah, not doing that," I warn. "You can't go around punching guys I see, even if I have sex with them."

He shrugs. "It's kinda my job."

That stops my argument along with my breath. I know what he's talking about. For all our age difference, the biggest difference was that Zack took on a lot of responsibility when our parents divorced. In some ways, I think he accepted that he was now 'man of the house' and cared for Mom and me. Little things like changing light bulbs, and big things . . . like validating who we dated. I never required much of that 'parenting' because of art and my preference to be by myself. But Zack ran off a couple of Mom's boyfriends he didn't feel passed muster.

In that framework, his overreaction makes sense as years of pent-up worry for me mixed with concern that it's his best friend, with a splash of guilt over his helping to set up the whole fake marriage thing in the first place.

I press a sweet kiss to his cheek. "Thanks, Zack Attack, though I don't know if I should call you that now. It might encourage you to pull stunts like that again." I shoot him a dirty look of disapproval, which he answers with a smirk.

Carter clears his throat, and I jump. His nose is red-tipped and bulbous. "You look like Rudolph," I tell him with a giggle. "You'll go down in his-tor-ryyyy!" I sing, having sung the song in my mind already.

"Glad you think this is funny." His challenging, stone-cold stare is locked on Zack as he places a firm, claiming kiss to my forehead.

Forehead kisses really are the best, I decide, and my feet do a tippy-tap dance of happiness under the table.

Carter sits down, taking my hand and holding it on the table. It's a power move and I know it. Hell, we all know it. But his thumb is doing a sweeping motion across my skin that reminds me of a certain other thing he's done before, and I start to get a little hot.

Zack sighs heavily. "She says you didn't take advantage of her. Not sure I believe that. I've seen how you are in and out of business."

He's talking about me like I'm not sitting right here.

"And, no offense." Zack looks at me. "But you're young, and though you don't want to hear it, naïve. Two things this guy is not. Not that there is a big difference, but there are a lot of life lessons in those years."

He's warning me off, and I've always listened to my brother before. But this time, I'm conflicted. "Do you remember your twenty-seventh birthday?" I ask my brother.

Though he looks confused, he answers in the affirmative.

"I was hiding in a corner, nursing a glass of champagne I wasn't supposed to have and trying to be invisible, as per usual. I was watching people talk and laugh, and I was happy to see you so happy with your friends. I think you know, I've never really liked Carter." I squeeze his hand, telling him to wait because there's a point here. "It's because of that night."

I disappear into the memory as I tell the story, it feeling like reality to me.

"You were dancing, and Carter was talking to a guy. I was listening. I didn't intend to, but they were close by and I couldn't help it, especially when I heard your name. Carter was telling this guy how you thought you were a whiz but didn't have the skills to back it up. This was well after you'd gone into business with him, but he was laughing at you. It pissed me off so badly. I wanted to defend you, tell Carter and the other guy they could stick their arrogance right up their asses. But I . . ."

Zack frowns. "You wouldn't do that."

I shake my head. "I couldn't. I just walked away." I blink hard, remembering how disappointed I'd been in myself. I'd told Zack that I was leaving, and he'd asked me to stay a little longer, but I'd left anyway. "And you got deeper and deeper into business with Carter, always talking about how you couldn't do it without him and saying how much you looked up to him."

"This is why you've always hated him?" Zack asks, and I nod. "Was the guy he was talking to a redheaded guy with a beard?"

"Simmons?" Carter asks hotly. "*That* asshole?"

Zack grins. "Luna, Carter had my back with that guy. Simmons was, and still is, an opportunistic weasel in a thrift store suit. He was always trying to horn in on my leads, undercut me. Carter was trying to run him off my coattails by telling him I was a crap developer. He wasn't betraying me."

And that's it . . . betrayal. All these years, I've thought Carter betrayed my brother. Even through this whole fake marriage thing, even when he's been giving me pleasure I've never known, I didn't trust him because I knew what he was capable of. It wasn't actively in my mind, but a feeling I've had of him since. If he could betray my brother, the most loyal person I know, Carter could betray anyone. So despite Zack thinking I'm naïve, I've maybe been harsher on Carter than I should've been.

Because if he didn't betray Zack and was, in fact, helping him . . . what does that mean?

I've felt the changes in Carter. I've seen a completely different side of him as he works and deals with his family. I've experienced how generous he can be. None of which made sense with my preconceived notions about him. I guess, in a way, I was letting those notions go as I've gotten to know Carter better already, but knowing he didn't betray Zack makes me a *little* more comfortable in continuing down this path with Carter. If he's not and never was a two-faced liar, then he really is trying to do something good for Blue Lake and for Elena.

I'm quiet for a long moment, and Carter gives me the time to process all that. When I look at him with an apology in my eyes, he places a sweet, soft peck to my lips. *Apology accepted*, his kiss says.

"Now that we've handled all that," Carter starts, and when he pauses, Zack dips his chin once, apparently over the bro-code drama already. "Will you be my best man?"

Stupidly, I think he's asking me at first, and I look up from our connected hands and say, "Huh?" But he's looking at Zack with the hope of their history in his eyes.

Carter and I haven't talked about his whole 'real proposal' and my sex-induced answer, but that doesn't seem to be an issue for him. He's going full-steam ahead like this is actually happening.

Is it happening?

I mean, I know it's for the Cartwright deal and to save face with his dad, but that doesn't mean it's fake. Not like it has been. Does Carter really mean for us to sign a marriage certificate, stand up with a best man and maid of honor, and say vows? Move in together like he suggested last night and keep having sex? Like . . . married-married?

That's a very different situation than I ever agreed to. Technically.

And though I always imagined myself getting married, I assumed it would be for love. Not for art or business. Even so, when I see how earnestly Carter is looking at Zack, as though this is an actual moment honoring their friendship, I can't help but be moved.

I kick Zack under the table and he flinches. "Oww!" Rubbing his shin, he looks at me angrily. In return, I shoot daggers at him.

I drop my voice, trying to sound like Zack. *"I'd be honored.* Say it, numb nuts."

Zack and Carter chuckle, both of their heads dropping in disbelief.

Holding out a hand to Carter across the table, Zack sighs. "Apparently, I'd be honored." I have to admit, my imitation was close. Most folks wouldn't have even heard the difference in our two voices. "Though I reserve the right to kick your ass again. One punch hardly seems fair."

"Zack!" I shout too loudly.

But Carter nods. "Deal."

Men are so frustrating.

TWENTY-ONE
LUNA

"ARE YOU SURE ABOUT THIS?" Samantha asks me for the millionth time.

My answer is the same as every time before. "No. I'm not sure about anything at this point!"

My hands are flailing, my heart is racing, and I've probably walked at least a mile in the last ten minutes around Carter's bedroom. I heard about a guy who ran a marathon on his balcony, going back and forth from one end to the other in a nearly never-ending loop of dedicated absurdity. But right now, I have more than enough energy to do that. I could probably high-knee it with the levels of nervous vibes I'm dealing with.

Sam steps in front of me with her hands up to stop my progress across the room. Except it doesn't work because I'm lost in my own mind and walk right into her, boob smacking boob in quite the bumper collision. "Hey!"

"Who would'a thought you'd be hitting second base on your wedding day with someone other than the groom?" Sam laughs. "You're turning into a regular, everyday whore, aren't you?"

"I am no such thing! And keep your voice down!" I clamp my hand over her mouth, looking at the closed door. "Carter and Zack are going to hear."

It's weird, thinking of them getting dressed in Carter's guest bedroom. Carter insisted, though, saying it was only right for me and Samantha to use his primary bedroom with the attached bathroom. The ceremony, if you can call it that, is going to be in the living room.

It's only been two days since the dinner with Zack, and in the interim, he's tried to talk me out of this decision, worrying I'm on some people-pleasing, misguided mission. Meanwhile, Samantha's been trying to talk me into it, waxing poetic about the value of having an adventure and living boldly in my youth as if she's not the same age I am.

And Carter, in full-blown fiancé mode, has been listening to me go back and forth indecisively and then leaving me mindless with back-bowing orgasm after orgasm. After our initial miscommunication, he's been more than happy to help me 'practice' things I've only imagined before. And though I've never been an athlete, I'm starting to understand the value of the 'two-a-days' type practice they do.

Carter's also found time in between orgasms to order dozens of white roses. Samantha and I made a quick trip to the boutique to see Brenda for a white dress, and most surprisingly, Carter suggested that we do our own vows. Which I guess is good because the standard ones aren't exactly appropriate for what we're doing. There's no love, honor, and obey here.

No forever either.

Quick, simple, easy. That's the theme of the day. It's real, but not.

Samantha licks my palm, and I recoil, freeing her to mouth off again. "Who cares? It's not real, remember?"

Samantha's being flippant, but there's a spark of intelligence in her eyes. She knows what she's doing by pushing me. In return, I start pacing again. "I care," I admit. "I didn't always have dreams like other kids, but the day I got married? I imagined that, and it wasn't this."

"But this is a paperwork thing to help a friend, not a real marriage. Like a green card situation," Samantha reasons. "So later, when you meet Mr. Right and want to marry for love, you'll have the dream wedding then. I'll make sure of it."

Her words toss around in my head. *Helping a friend. Like a green card situation.* Which is illegal, but what I'm doing with Carter isn't wrong to that degree. It's just crazy and not the kind of thing that happens to people like me. I'm boring, strange, and close to being a hermit.

But here I am, standing before a floor-length mirror in a white gown with hope in my eyes and confusion in my heart. "This feels real, dangerously so," I whisper to Sam. "I don't know if I'm cut out to play pretend wife to this level."

She stands behind me, meeting my gaze in the mirror. "One, say the word and I'll have you out of here in a second. You know that. Today or any day. But two, do you love Carter?"

"I feel like I'm supposed to say yes if we're getting married, but . . ." I shrug, pulling a face. "I like him."

I expect her to be horrified, but she smiles instead. "Perfect. If you said you love him and he was doing this for a work deal, I'd veto the whole shebang myself. But you're not invested in him like that. You like each other, you have great sex, you can live in the lap of luxury, and maybe, just maybe, you'll bring in the biggest and best exhibition the museum's ever seen. You might even end up with a raise or a promotion at work, which would give you the funds to get Alphena to market. It's a win all the way around." She winks and adds, "Plus, it'll be a great story to tell our grandkids when we're old biddies in the nursing home."

She's right, but is it enough? Isn't this still wrong?

"Business is business, babe. Ain't nothing wrong with that," Sam decides, and I find myself nodding, even though I'm still not sure.

———

Carter

"I can't believe you're going through with it," Zack tells me with a grin that shows off too many white teeth. He's like a shark, looking for blood in the water . . . probably mine.

"Are you enjoying this?"

He laughs bitterly, not bothering to shrink his smile in the slightest. Now that I look again, it's maybe more of a baring of his teeth than a smile. "Are you kidding? We've done some stupid shit, but this takes the cake . . . and the pie . . . and the whole damn dessert buffet." He waves his hands around at the wedding setup in my living room. "Still, I wouldn't have missed this for the world."

"You're about to," I warn.

He flicks one of the white roses dangling from the fireplace mantel. "You're not ditching me now."

He's right and he knows it. I want him here, and so does Luna. "Well, you don't have to be so fucking smug about it."

"Man, don't get it twisted. I'm begrudgingly and barely going along with this. For Luna's sake, not yours. This shitshow is gonna blow up, and I want to be right here to catch her when it does. I love you, but you're gonna land on your feet. She's built different than we are." He glances toward my bedroom door, and though I've been hyper-aware of it all day and know it hasn't opened, I look too.

"I'm not going to hurt her," I vow solemnly.

He shakes his head, his lips pressed together into a tight line. He seems to be considering whether to say what he's thinking. With a heavy sigh, he sadly tells me, "I believe that you believe that. I really do, or I'd have her as far away from you and this mess as I could get her. But in the end? You will. It's inevitable."

"Thanks for the vote of confidence." His words were harsh, so mine are spat out in anger.

"As she's reminded me, I can't do anything about it. She's different than we are, but she's stronger than she thinks, and if I told her no, she'd have my balls in a vice. I'm hoping she keeps that energy in dealing with you."

He holds a cupped palm out but then makes a fist and twists. Involuntarily, I flinch and cover myself.

That's when the doorbell rings.

Saved by the bell! "That should be the Justice of the Peace I booked."

"How much did you have to pay for a house call?"

I raise my brows, confiding, "Not as much as I paid to make sure he understood that this is a very *private* situation." Zack chuckles, and I divulge, "I'm pretty sure he thinks Luna's pregnant."

There's a follow-up knock at the door. "Guess he's impatient." I straighten my tie as I open the door, already saying, "Thank you for—"

Except it's not the Justice of the Peace. It's my sister.

"Kayla! What are you doing here?" I demand sharply. She can't be here. No one in my family can know about this.

As usual, Kayla gives zero fucks and walks on in. "You've been avoiding me, so I'm ambushing you to find out what the hell's going on."

"Nothing's going on."

She ignores me completely and focuses on Zack, pointing at me like I'm not even in the room. "Do you believe him when he lies that badly?"

Zack smirks and shakes his head. "He's a shit liar if you know him."

"Right?" she agrees, sounding like she's pitying me for being so bad at lying. Which I'm *not*.

I don't have time for them to be talking shit about me. I've got to get her out of here. "Kayla, Zack and I are meeting for work and you're interrupting."

Kayla rolls her eyes. Or I assume she does, but I can only see the back of her head. But it seems like something she'd do and Zack is fighting back a laugh.

"Hey, Carter . . . if y'all are having a meeting, what's with the roses?" She grins victoriously as she Vanna Whites the arrangement on the mantel.

Zack loses his battle and laughs. "She's got you there."

I sigh and pinch the bridge of my nose. Which is when the bedroom door opens and Samantha peeks out. "If we don't get this show on the road, Luna might hyperventilate. Again."

Samantha and Kayla lock eyes.

"Are you the JP?" Samantha asks.

NEVER MARRY YOUR BROTHER'S BEST FRIEND 191

Kayla smells blood in the water. "The what?"

I've got to slow this runaway train, and that starts with getting Kayla out of here. Taking her elbow in mine, I lead her to the door. "Time to go."

I open the door, intending to throw her out. Gently, of course. But there's an old man standing there with his hand poised to knock.

"Oh! Mr. Harrington! Lovely day for a wedding, isn't it?" he says.

"No!" I shout, trying to cover Kayla's ears, but the cat's outta the bag.

"Wedding?" she echoes.

"Well, shit," I huff in resignation. "Come on in, Judge Warren. You too, Kayla."

Judge Warren removes his hat as he comes in, dipping his chin to Kayla. "Ma'am."

"I knew it!" Kayla crows in delight. "That whole dinner thing was so weird. Were you testing Mom and Dad or something?"

"Testing? Huh?" I have no idea what she's talking about, but I do know how to play host. "Zack, can you—" I jerk my head toward Judge Warren, handing him over to Zack to deal with while I handle Kayla, who's got so many questions, they're basically buzzing around her in speech bubbles.

Samantha cracks the door again, and I hold up a finger, telling her one minute. "Kayla, focus," I demand, pointing at my eyes with V-ed fingers. Quietly and quickly, I explain it all to her —the fake marriage, the Cartwright deal, Dad forcing a dinner against my wishes, which forced my hand into bringing Luna as my fake wife and trusting that the family would go along. And last, that Luna and I are getting married for real to seal the deal with Elena.

"You're tripling down on a losing bet. You know that, right?"

"It's fine. And perfectly logical, given the circumstances." It is, or at least it makes sense to me. Anything for the deal—that's how I live my life.

"We're doing this now or not at all," Samantha says, coming out of the bedroom. She continues speaking, but I don't hear a word of it because Luna is peeking out from behind Samantha.

I gasp as she comes fully into view. "You're beautiful, Luna," I whisper.

My comment is one hundred percent heartfelt. She's beautiful. Her dress is white and flowy, glancing over her curves to puddle on the floor, the bodice highlights her full cleavage, and there are delicate strappy things that drape over her upper arms, giving the whole look a vintage feel. Her hair is pulled back to the nape of her neck, and behind her glasses, her eyes are made up with liner and lashes that give her a doe-eyed look.

"You like it?" She's blushing, the pink flush a tantalizing addition to the white dress that Luna is swishing back and forth anxiously. "I wasn't sure, but I didn't exactly have a lot of time."

"It's perfect. You're perfect." I take her hands in mine, needing to touch her.

"Save it for the vows," Judge Warren suggests with a glint of happiness in his eyes. For all his years and experience with weddings, I think he's still a romantic at heart. Plus, he doesn't know this is fake.

"Good idea," I say agreeably. "Right over here," I say, leading Luna to the fireplace.

In front of the flowers, she smiles as she inhales deeply. "Pretty, and they smell good too. Dare I say, you've got a sentimental bone in your body? Roses for a wedding," Luna teases.

"Keep it up and you'll have a sentimental bone in your body."

"No." Zack's doing great with all this, truthfully, but there are some things you don't want to know about your sister.

I'd be the same way with Kayla. And beyond the 'don't hurt her' routine, the only way he agreed to not continue with his plan to beat the shit out of me was that he doesn't want to hear one single peep about sex. Considering my nose and the remaining slight swelling, it'd seemed an acceptable deal to me.

We get arranged in front of the fireplace with Judge Warren, and I smile down at Luna, taking her hands in mine again. "Ready." I'm talking to the JP, but Luna nods.

"Wait! One last time . . . Luna, are you sure?" Samantha asks. "Option Escape is still on the table if you need it." She assumes a posture that's more linebacker than maid of honor, acting as though she'd fight off anyone who got in her way if Luna wants to bail.

Luna smiles and releases my hands, and for a moment, panic bubbles up inside my gut. But Luna hugs her friend and assures her, "I'm sure."

"Okay, then," the JP starts.

"Wait, me too," Zack says. "Luna, I'm sorry I got you mixed up with this. Please don't do anything you don't want to, including marrying this fucker."

"You're supposed to be my best man," I growl.

"Yeah, but I'm Luna's brother." He has a valid point, so I let it go.

"Zack, it's fine," she tells him. "I want this."

The JP looks to Kayla expectantly, and she leans between Luna and me. "*Blink twice* will always work with me. Always."

I don't know what she's talking about, but Luna opens her eyes wide and stares back at Kayla for an uncomfortably long time.

I clear my throat. "Should I be offended that no one's asking me if I'm sure?"

Zack, Kayla, and Samantha all chuckle. "You're totally getting the better deal here," Zack explains.

Even the JP nods at that. "That's usually the case, son." He clears his throat. "Experience says, at least."

"Can we get started?" I'm a little grumpy about it, but when I look at Luna, whose full lips are tilted up in quiet laughter at the group's assessment of us, I know they're right. To the outside world, I might be the catch—wealthy, good-looking, and with a well-connected family. But the truth is, Luna is the better person. With her art obsession, shy nervousness, and unpredictable fire . . . she's the one who is truly deserving of a beautiful wedding and a happy marriage.

I might not have the luxury of being Luna's husband in her

heart, or for long, but I will do my best to make sure she has all the things she deserves.

"We are gathered here today to honor Mr. Carter Harrington and Miss Luna Starr by witnessing them joining together in wedded bliss . . ."

CHAPTER
TWENTY-TWO

LUNA

THIS IS HAPPENING. Or, it's actually already happened. I'm holding the pen, signing the marriage license with Judge Warren and Carter, and completely in shock. My hand's barely able to make my signature on the paper, and any minute, I swear Ashton Kutcher is going to jump out again and yell 'gotcha'.

That'd probably make this the longest running prank ever, but this is *so not* my life.

Except it is.

"Okay, all looks to be in order. Congratulations, Mr. and Mrs. Harrington." Judge Warren shakes Carter's hand and then leans in to give me a weak, grandfatherly hug with a promise to file the paperwork promptly.

It's official. I'm married. I'm Mrs. Carter Harrington.

"Oh, my God," I mutter, my knees giving out beneath me. Carter catches me easily, supporting me well above the ground.

Whoo, he moves faster than a frat guy going for a free watered-down light beer. Maybe he's a vampire that's cast a spell on me? Wait, vampires don't cast spells. Witches do. Warlocks? Magicians? Too fast, too fast, too fast . . .

"Luna? You okay?" Carter sounds concerned, and when his face comes into view before my wavering vision, he looks freaked out. Distantly, I hear the judge say not to worry, that these things happen in early pregnancy.

I'm not pregnant! I want to yell out, but I can't find the strength. I'm not pregnant, I'm just ass over heels in shock.

Because I'm married . . . to Carter *freaking* Harrington.

For real.

I've played this out a hundred different ways and was sure I could handle it, but I can't seem to get enough air and there's a tornado's worth of wind roaring in my ears.

"Breathe, Luna." Carter's voice is strong and commanding and coming from right in front of me. I open eyes I didn't realize I'd closed and see that we're nearly nose to nose. "Slow it down. In. Out. In. Out."

I am breathing, but it's too shallow and erratic, and the expansive room feels so small, claustrophobic. But Carter's support helps, and slowly, I'm able to find his rhythm and breathe in sync with him.

"I knew this was a bad idea," I hear Zack hiss, and my breath wavers.

"Don't listen to him," Carter snaps, pulling me to him again. "Focus on my voice. In. Out." A few more rounds and I'm back. "There you are. Good girl."

I try to smile, but I'm not sure if it works because my lips are tingling. "Thanks," I huff out, finally breathing more normally, "Dr. Carter."

Samantha shoulders Carter out of the way. "You haven't had a panic attack in ages, babe. What do you need?"

I flick my eyes to her, but they're drawn back to Carter. His blue eyes are what I need, his forehead kiss is what I want, his strong arms wrapped around me are a relief . . . and that's exactly what he gives me. A moment later—or at least it feels like that to me—and I'm truly recovered.

Carter releases me in phases until he's far enough away to search my eyes for clarity. He must be reassured by what he sees because he lets go. I don't know how we got here, but I'm sitting in a chair and Carter is kneeling in front of me. Behind him stand Zack, Samantha, and Kayla. Judge Warren must've made an escape during my panic attack.

"I'm okay now. Sorry," I tell everyone.

Samantha frowns. "Don't do that. No need for apologies. Here." She holds out a glass of water, and I take it, bringing it shakily to my mouth. Sam swats Carter's shoulder. "Help your wife," she orders, pointing at me as if we don't all know who Carter's wife is.

I'm Carter's wife!

But Carter doesn't move toward the glass. He smiles, eyes locked on mine. "She's got it. My girl's strong."

His faith helps me find additional strength, and I manage to drink the water on my own without spilling a drop. "Thanks."

I'm talking to Carter, but Sam makes a *harrumph* noise that means 'you're welcome' and takes the glass back.

"Do you want something to eat? A little sugar, maybe?" Carter suggests. I nod, and Zack disappears, coming back a moment later with a small plate of cheese cubes, crackers, and chocolate squares that he hands to Carter. Delicately, he feeds me a chocolate, and I chew slowly. When I swallow, he smiles and then holds out a small cracker.

He feeds me a few more bites, each going down easier. "Better?" Carter asks.

"Better," I tell him gratefully. "Just tired."

Kayla says quietly to Samantha, "We should go. I think the honeymoon night might be a little difficult with us fussin' about. And I can tell the reception's going to be a bore if those snacks are the spread."

"I'm not going anywhere," Zack tells Kayla.

I glance up to Samantha, a silent communication telling her what she needs to know. She locks her elbow through Zack's and pulls him. "Let's go, stud brother."

He doesn't budge and squirms his arm out of Samantha's clutches. She doesn't give up so easily, though, and shifts behind him, pushing him with both palms on his back. Grunting as she fights against him, she says, "Let's. Go. Dude, what are you made of? Steel and concrete?"

Kayla takes a gentler approach and tells Zack, "I really think Luna needs to rest."

Zack looks at me in question, and I nod, both that I'm okay

and that I do want to rest a bit. "Okay," he relents, though it's reluctant. Jokingly, he pushes back a little to throw Samantha off, chuckling as she stumbles.

I'm smiling at their antics and glance back to Carter to see if he's as amused as I am, but his eyes are still focused only on me. I'm feeling better, but Carter is still worried about me.

I reach up to cup his face, my thumb soothing the worry lines beside his frown. He tilts into my touch and confides, "That scared the shit outta me."

"I'm sorry. It just happens. Sometimes, I don't even know why. But I really am okay," I reassure him.

Carter leans forward and scoops me up into his arms, carrying me bridal style toward the bedroom door. He calls over his shoulder, "Lock up on your way out."

I whisper, "I don't know if I'm *that* okay."

"La-la-la-la," I hear Zack singing.

In the bedroom, Carter sets me down on the side of the bed and bends down, taking one foot and then the other into his hands to pull my shoes off. I put my hands on his shoulders, sighing in relief at being out of the heels. "I really hate those things."

"Then why wear them if you don't like them? Your Converse are adorable on you."

"Can't really wear those with a wedding dress, though."

Carter grunts. "You could've. It would've been cute on you."

"Excuse me," Samantha says from the doorway. "I brought this." She holds up a plate piled with cheese, crackers, and chocolate. She comes in, setting the plate on the nightstand, and then disappears into the bathroom for a moment. She returns with her bag over her shoulder and a knowing smile. "Be good, kids," she says with a wave. "Or even better, be naughty!"

A moment later, the door opens and closes solidly. We're alone and married. Expectations fall heavily onto my shoulders. "Carter—"

"Stay here," Carter orders before he disappears into the bathroom too. I hear water running and smile, realizing he's filling the bathtub. When he comes back, he pulls me to my feet, guiding me to the tub's side. Carter looks me up and down thoroughly. "You look gorgeous in this. I want to remember every detail."

I turn slightly, showing him the back. "This is my favorite part."

Carter smiles. "Not the dress, Luna. I want to remember every detail of you today."

And now I'm smiling too.

Carter helps me take the dress off with delicate fingers, and though I love it, I want it off too. It feels naughty to be naked while he's fully dressed in a suit, but he helps me into the tub and I sit down in the hot water. "You getting in with me?" I ask.

"Don't have to tell me twice." He yanks his shoes off, pulling at his suit to get it off as quickly as possible.

It's endearing, seeing how urgent he is, and I laugh as he nearly leaps into the tub with me, making waves as he plops down. He stretches out, pulling me between his legs, and I lie back against him. "You're a lumpy pillow," I tell him. He shifts a bit, trying to make me more comfortable. "Didn't say I didn't like it," I tease.

He wraps his arms around me, one lying across the top of my chest and the other beneath my breasts. I sink into him, feeling so much better. "Thank you," I say quietly. "For being there."

Honestly, I'm a little embarrassed by my panic attack. Sam was right, I haven't had one in a long time, but today was a lot.

"You don't need to apologize, Luna. I'm sorry if I pushed you too far." Carter's quiet apology is accompanied by a kiss to the top of my head.

Quietly, I think about my reaction, and as I figure out what I'm feeling, I tell Carter, "It's not too far. I think what we did just kinda hit me all at once. How are you not freaking out?"

I feel a rumbling hum against my back as he speaks. "You're a good person, Luna. That makes this easier, I think. You don't understand how rare and special you are, but I'm honored to be your husband—even like this—and see you discover yourself. Marriage aside, I'm just glad to know you now."

Hot tears fill my eyes. I don't know if I've ever felt more seen.

I swallow thickly, not sure what to say to that. But I don't need to say anything. Carter pulls me in tight for a squeezing hug and then grabs the shower gel and a poufy sponge from the deck of the tub, using them to wash me—gently and thoroughly.

Other than the panic attack, my wedding day is turning out pretty good.

"We should'a brought the snacks in here," I murmur, completely relaxed and at peace in Carter's arms. "Seriously, your sister was right. The reception spread sorta sucks."

"Want me to get them?" he asks, but I shake my head.

"Stay here. I'm comfy despite your being a rock-hard pillow. And we can eat later."

With a chuckle, he gathers me back into his embrace. He loops his finger through a strand of my hair that escaped my hairdo hours ago, twirling it over and over, and we . . . relax. As husband and wife.

I tune in to my heart, checking to see if it's racing again, but it doesn't change. There's no panic this time.

Mr. and Mrs. Carter Harrington.

That has a nice ring to it, actually. I fidget with the new band on my left ring finger, expecting it to feel odd. But it feels okay, comfortable even.

CHAPTER
TWENTY-THREE

CARTER

IT'S TECHNICALLY NOT our honeymoon since we're supposed to have already been married, but I wish I could hole up at my place with Luna. *Our* place. She's keeping her apartment, planning to use it as a getaway to work and paint, but for the last week, she's been here with me and it's been amazing.

Waking up every morning in each other's arms.

Having coffee together.

Kissing her goodbye as I go to the office, usually with her curled up on the couch, lost in her tablet as she creates Alphena's world.

And after a busy day, coming home to her, opening the door knowing that she's going to slam into me for a hug.

Her asking how my day was and telling me about her day at the museum.

Cooking and eating dinner while we talk about everything and nothing.

Falling into bed and each other, only to wake up and do it all again the next day.

I don't know what the difference is between this and a real marriage, at this point. All I know is that Luna is on my mind all day when I'm away from her, and when we're together, I want to do everything I can to make her happy. I enjoy seeing her smile. I love seeing her coming out of her shell more and more each day, letting her guard down around me. Listening to her talk about plot points of the story she's working on and the tour groups she had are more fun than I ever would've thought, especially when she starts acting out the book scenes, with her starring as Alphena, of course.

Luna makes my days interesting and my nights hotter than I've ever dreamed, giving me a fresh purpose.

Right now, though, I straighten my tie, staring into the blue eyes in the mirror. Today is the culmination of what all this is for. "You've got this, Harrington. It's just another deal."

If only that were true. Elena's ready to work with Blue Lake if I can get past this finance guy today, and if he's smart and recognizes how far over his head he is, he'll be thrilled to hand off responsibility to me. Because I can handle it. I'm the best man for the job.

"I'm the best man." Saying it aloud gives it meaning and weight.

"I knew you were arrogant, but your hype sessions are a tad egotistical," Luna teases from the doorway, holding her finger and thumb up a big inch apart.

I lean back on the counter with my arms crossed over my chest as I fight back a smirk. She caught me being cocky fair and square. "What would you suggest instead"

She walks toward me, tilting her head the way she does when she's thinking, and then hops onto the counter next to me. I can't wait to hear what she comes up with. "My hype sessions are usually lots of . . . don't freak out, remember to breathe, nobody's staring at you, smile. You're welcome to use whatever feels right to you."

She puts her hand over her heart, her face serious, but her eyes are dancing with humor.

I move in front of her, and she automatically opens her legs for me. I step between them, liking the way her knees squeeze me. "I think I'll go with the smile recommendation. Elena seems charmed by it." I flash Luna a full-strength grin. "What do you think?"

She laughs, rolling her eyes. "Well, it seems to have worked on me."

I plant a sweet kiss on her, wanting to feel her laugh, taste her smile. "I'm glad."

She leans into our kiss, then pulls back reluctantly. She straightens my already perfect tie and then sweeps her hands over my chest to smooth my shirt. "You need to go."

I don't want to leave. I could stay here, crawl back into bed and into Luna. But she's right. I can't be late for this meeting. Grumpy about being responsible, I growl, "Okay, I'm leaving, but I'm not happy about it." I kiss her one more time and reluctantly pull away. "I'll be back this afternoon."

"I'll make a celebration dinner!" She claps her hands in excitement, and I raise a brow. She laughingly clarifies, "And by make dinner, I mean order in."

One of the things I've learned about Luna is that she can't cook for shit. She tries, but she admits she spends more time working than cooking and usually orders take-out. "Maybe the Indian place again?"

She grins, nodding. "I'll set a timer so I remember to call it in."

I can't fight back the deep chuckle she draws out of me too easily with her animated expressions. What's more, I don't want or need to. She doesn't mind when I'm goofy, something I don't know if I've ever actually been.

———

"Good to meet you, Mr. Oleana. I appreciate your taking time to meet with me today." I hold my hand out, shaking the older gentleman's hand.

I've done my research on him. He's an old-school, conservative fiscal manager who has worked with the Cartwrights for years, just like his father did before him. He looks the part too, in a classic navy suit with a white shirt and red tie, thick, black-framed glasses, and wingtip shoes.

To the uninitiated, he might seem like a mere accountant.

The devil is in the details, though. His suit is custom-tailored, his tie one hundred percent silk, his shoes made of fine leather, and the watch I saw on his wrist is a vintage Rolex. Mr. Oleana might be traditional, but he likes the finer things.

"Nice to meet you as well, Mr. Harrington. Though I daresay I've met you once or twice before through Blue Lake's dealings . . . but you were a lad then. Barely knee-high to a grasshopper." He laughs as though sharing a private joke with Elena, who's sitting next to him at the conference table, as he holds a palm toward the floor, indicating I must've been around twenty-four inches tall.

Oh, so that's how we're playing this, then? I'm just a young whipper-snapper?

His angle is that I'm far too young to take over the Cartwright holdings. I'd expected that to be one of the potential concerns, so I'm ready with a quippy answer. "Maybe so. I don't remember much about those days. Guess you can probably relate." I chuckle as I tap my temple.

"Ooh, he's got you there, Pat." Elena gleefully claps her hands, her eyes flicking back and forth as though our verbal volleys are a tennis match.

"Excuse me?" Mr. Oleana frowns, the marionette lines surrounding his thin lips getting deeper and more pronounced.

"Oh, don't be a grumpy ass. You called him a young'un first, so he called you an old fart. Seems like a fair turnaround to me. Now, *boys* . . ." She looks between us both, daring either of us to disagree with the word. When we're both silent, she nods once in approval. "Let's get on with chitty-chatting about my money because the Lord knows, I've got other things to do today."

"Fine," he grumps, tapping his papers on the table. Like actual papers with charts and graphs on them and what appear to be quarterly reports. The man must kill an entire forest a month with the way he conducts business.

I pull my tablet out of my bag, opening it to the presentation I put together to assure Mr. Oleana that I'm the man for the job and then opening another app to take notes.

The difference of a few decades in living color—black and white papers versus full-color technology.

But what he does has been working for Elena, and I don't want to belittle that, even if I'm certain I can improve on it moving forward. "I'm looking forward to hearing how you've managed such a large and diverse portfolio for so long, especially as a one-man show, Mr. Oleana. That's quite impressive."

He narrows his eyes, not believing my bullshit for a second. But when I hold his gaze, he relents. "Fine. Call me Pat, and let's get this thing done. There's a beach calling my name."

"A beach?" I echo.

Elena pats my arm, leaning over to fill me in. "He's retiring to live near his grandkids out on the coast."

I'm surprised. It must take a lot for a man like Pat to hang up his tie and coat to put on flip-flops and a sunhat. I sure as hell can't see my dad doing that anytime soon. But . . . "Why not continue managing the Cartwright portfolio from there?" I gesture to my tablet, the one-stop shop that lets me work anywhere, anytime, and would do the same for him.

He shrugs. "It's time. Me and Elena go way back. Hell, we used to play on the floor while our dads had lunches and meetings."

He looks at her, and together, they say, "Bo-ring!" They seem to share such a bright familiarity, and I wonder if there was ever more than friendship between the two of them, back before Thomas came into the picture.

I smile politely as they laugh.

"What was I saying?" Pat asks.

"You were explaining why you're not going to manage Elena's portfolio from the beach," I prompt, biting back a comment about his forgetfulness and whether it's age-related.

He nods several times, giving himself a moment to collect his thoughts. "Have you ever done the same thing for so long you could do it in your sleep?" he asks. Not waiting for my answer, he continues, "That's what this is for me. It has been the joy of my life to make sure the Cartwright estate is safe and properly managed. And for a long time, I couldn't imagine doing anything else. That's why I've kept on. But it's time for me to retire, and my kids don't have a mathematical bone in their bodies, so I don't have anyone in my family to pass the business on to. But I can't leave Elena in the lurch, not after we've been through so much together."

Elena smiles, but her eyes look glassy and wet. "Don't go making me cry, Pat Oleana. I'll have your ass on my wall as a trophy if you ruin my mascara."

He chuckles and pats her hand. It looks more friendly and platonic than flirtatious, though. "You've worn waterproof mascara since the day you turned twenty-five and cried black rivers down your face when Thomas told your daddy that he would never ask you to change your family name and in fact, changed his to join your family."

Wait, what?

I don't know if I say something or make a noise, but Elena waves a hand at Pat and then explains to me, "Did you not realize that? Cartwright's my given name from my daddy."

I shake my head in confusion. "I definitely didn't know that."

Elena shakes her head, her eyes going distant. "It was quite the scandal back in the day. Everyone thought either I was a bossy heifer who wouldn't let Thomas hold his own balls, or that he was a gold-digging thief who was going to steal my money and leave me buried in the woods off highway fifteen. Neither were true. He loved me and didn't have a family of his own anymore, seeing as his parents has already passed. He was happy to join the Cartwrights and was as proud to bear our name as any born-and-bred Cartwright was. Daddy said he was an adopted son and treated him like family. Never called him an in-law once. Not a single time." Her smile is wistful as she remembers.

Her eyes clear, and she pins me in her gaze. "Family's important to us—to my Daddy, to me and Thomas, and now, to Claire, Mads, and Jacob. They're the next generation. That's why I like you and Luna so much. I can see how much you care for one another. And with the way you two got on with that sweet

Gracie girl, there's a big, full family table in your future. A whole line up of your brothers and sister, nieces and nephews, and babies of your own. I think that's what makes this feel right, you know?"

Elena puts her hand over her heart, and I swear to all that is holy, if she starts saying the Pledge of Allegiance or singing *Amazing Grace*, I'm going to bolt from this room and never return because the guilt of what I'm doing is so heavy with Elena speaking in such a heartfelt way about what family means to her. Not that I'm going to be careless with her money, I legitimately will do her estate well, but because of the means I'm going to 'get the job'.

And what she sees in mine and Luna's future is scary as fuck. Still, I picture Luna big and round with a baby in her belly and it's not a bad image. Luna would be a great mother, I think, remembering her with Grace and the stories she tells about school field trip kids.

It just won't be my baby.

Eventually, this whole thing is going to come to an end. I'll get the deal and get to work proving myself to Elena, and eventually, Luna and I will probably get divorced when it's been appropriately long enough. After that, she'll find someone and fall in love for real, get married for real, and have a baby . . . for real.

My gut roils at the thought of someone else touching her, loving her, creating a family with her. I swallow thickly and agree, "Family is everything. We love each other no matter what."

And isn't that the fucking truth? I'm talking about Luna, but also, my whole family.

We loved Cameron through his darkest days when his wife died, leaving him alone with Grace. We supported Chance starting his own business and the slow days when he wasn't sure it was going to succeed. We defend Cole even though we don't really have any idea what the hell he does. We make sure Kayla gets her turn in the spotlight when she could easily be overshadowed by her numerous brothers. And we accept that Kyle is always going to have one foot in and one foot out of the family, even if we don't understand why. We just welcome him into the fold every time he chooses to come back.

And me too. Look at what they're doing so I can have a shot at this deal. Going along with my crazy lie and this whole created life with Luna? Well, other than Dad.

Pat clears his throat, and I realize that he and Elena are staring at me. "Penny for your thoughts?" Elena asks gently.

At the same time, Pat says, "That's enough blubbering on about nothing. We should get down to the details here. I want to see what you have planned."

He makes it sound as if his shotgun is ready to punch holes in whatever plans I have, but I take Pat's offered rescue from the emotional bend of our conversations, not needing to analyze any of my family drama or feelings for Luna right now. "Great idea. My research shows that you follow a pretty strict eighty-twenty split for assets, leaning heavily into conservative investments. Correct?"

It's the jumping off point we need to discuss all facets of the Cartwright portfolio, from stock holdings to property investments, donations to taxes, and everything in between.

Hours later, Elena is nodding off in her chair, even occasionally snoring, while Pat and I hammer through report after report and I show him where I see potential improvements in the management of the Cartwright estate.

But no matter what I say or what actions I suggest, he's professionally distant, bordering on cold. My charm hasn't worked on him, my plans haven't swayed him, and for someone who purports wanting to retire, I don't think he's ready to release one finger from managing the Cartwright portfolio. Or at least, not let it go to me.

"Being that aggressive is foolhardy," he repeats, despite having seen the projections I compiled. "I don't care what your little cartoon arrow shows, that's not the best strategy." He waves at my tablet presentation, which does indeed have a green arrow showing a dramatic rise in investment returns.

Gritting my teeth to control my frustrations, I assure him

again. "It would play out this way. I've done it before, and it's even how I have some of my own personal funds invested."

"Then you're not a portfolio manager, you're a gambler hoping for the big score. It might even be a good strategy for someone your age, but not in this case." He slams his stack of papers to the table, and dismissing me, he turns to Elena. "I know you trust your gut, but seriously?" He holds a hand out, gesturing toward me and wrinkling his nose.

He's woken her up, and she wipes drool from the corners of her mouth, sputtering, "Wha–what's . . . what's going on?"

"This kid wants to move you into a more aggressive vehicle—"

Elena interrupts to ask, "Like a sports car?" She's smiling like a kid on Christmas morning who got exactly what they asked Santa for.

"No, investment vehicle," I correct. "But if you want an exotic car experience, I know just the place. We took Dad there for his birthday last year and he loved it." I flash my charming smile, wanting to smooth things over because waking up with someone yelling at you can be disconcerting.

"Yes," she answers quickly, "especially if I can have a hot racecar driver teach me." After a little wiggle with her arms held out in front of her like she's gripping a steering wheel—I refuse to think she's imagining otherwise—she asks, more seriously, "What's wrong with an aggressive investment vehicle?"

She's asking Pat, but I need to answer this. It's key to transitioning her to me as the portfolio manager and getting her to trust my judgment. "Mr. Oleana has you heavily invested in very safe stocks, bonds, etc. They're stable, they have a decent interest, and they grow incrementally each year. You make a steady income from them that will support you to the day you die and beyond."

"Morbid," Pat adds. "And safe is good."

I lick my lips, tasting victory. "Good isn't good enough, not for Elena Cartwright. You're leaving potential money on the table."

"Do tell," she orders, leaning forward on the table to rest her chin on her palm.

I explain how Pat does all his planning based on the need for conservativeness at Elena's age, but that based on her available income, she could be much more aggressive. "Yes, there could be losses, or there could be great gains."

"I already have more money than I know what to do with and currently have a double-digit return rate. By your estimations, that would go up approximately eight more percent per investment year?"

Ooh, she is a slick one. She wasn't sleeping a bit. She was quietly listening to me and Mr. Olena's discussion, evaluating me the whole time.

"Yes, creating the type of gains that don't only create generational wealth but also provide an opportunity to donate to the causes and charities that are closest to your heart, spreading those benefits to even more people in need while still carrying on the Cartwright legacy."

Before Pat can interrupt me, I add, "I know you're already donating significant amounts of money, but what if you could do more? An entire wing at the museum in Thomas's name, a children's hospital in all four corners of the state, or whatever you feel called to do. The point is . . . as you said, you have more money than you know what to do with, so why be this careful? You're not going to run out . . . ever."

"She might if you're the one holding the checkbook," Pat interjects.

"Checkbook? That only goes to show how outdated and out-of-touch you're being. No one has a checkbook anymore. There's an app for that," I quip, but my frustration is showing.

"Enough." Elena pushes back from the table a bit, throwing her hands up. "Carter, thank you for coming. I think me and Pat have some things to discuss." She dips her chin, glaring at Pat through her brow.

I know a dismissal cue when I hear it, so I rise. "Thank you for your time, Mr. Oleana, Elena. I hope you'll give some serious thought to my suggestions."

I shake both of their hands, but Elena's is decidedly limper than before. As I wait for the elevator doors to open and let me out of here, I yell at myself.

Did I blow it? Fuck, I hope not. Not after everything I've done to appeal to Elena.

But when the elevator doors open, I'm not prepared for what I see. Claire, Elena's niece, is stepping off, and when she nearly walks into me, she sneers quite obviously. "You!"

I don't know why she's here at Mr. Oleana's office, or why she's so mad at me. But I offer my most charming smile. "Nice to see you, Claire."

"Fuck you," she hisses, bumping my shoulder as she passes me by.

What is her deal?

I don't get a chance to ask because she disappears into Mr. Oleana's office. I consider chasing her, not wanting her to blow my chances any further than what I just did, but my phone rings and when I look at it, my dad's name is on the screen.

"Hello?"

CHAPTER
TWENTY-FOUR
LUNA

"HOPE y'all had fun and maybe learned something cool today?" I let the question hang, hoping for raised hands from the group of kids I've been showing around the museum for the last two hours.

"My favoritest thing I learned is that they made paint with dirts and eggs in the olden days," a little boy informs me.

"Ooh, good one. Yep, paint was made with different types of dirt, colored rocks, minerals, even gemstones." I freeze dramatically, holding out both hands in a 'stop' pose, and look around at the kids with overly wide eyes. "But what's the rule there?" I prompt.

"Don't use jewelry to make paint!" several kids shout in unison.

"Yes!" I pump my fist to celebrate their correct answers. "Because gems and jewelry are . . .?"

"Different!" the kids respond.

I bend down, wanting to make sure this lesson sticks long after they leave the museum. "Or your momma will get mad at you, and you, and you." I point at various kids, and then myself, "And mad at Miss Luna, and we don't want that, do we?"

"Nooooo!"

I hold up my hands, high-fiving the kids. Another successful school field trip tour in the books!

But as I wave goodbye to the group and their teacher, the overhead speaker calls out, "Luna to the front desk, please."

What? I don't have another tour today. I was looking forward to a little time wandering the halls and talking to museum guests. Guess that's changed.

Maybe Carter is here?

When I approach the desk, the receptionist looks at me in surprise even though she's the one who paged me.

"What's up?"

Silently, she points to her right, and I look where she's indicating. "Oh. Ma. Gawd." My first instinct is to duck down behind the desk so I can't be seen, and I immediately drop to the floor. I know what I saw, but I keep repeating, "No, no, no, no."

Josie leans over the desk, and I hear her above me. "You good?"

"I don't know," I confess honestly, looking up into her concerned face. She's not usually very friendly with me, so I must be freaking her out if she's being nice. "How long has she been here?"

"Maeve? She got here this morning, like usual." When I glare at Josie, she smiles back triumphantly, well aware that I'm not talking about Maeve who I saw at the coffee pot in the employee lounge this morning. "Oh! You mean the other lady? She's been here about an hour, just chatting away with Maeve. Who is she?"

Who is she? She's the Elena Cartwright! What is she doing here?

It's not that I don't want to see Elena, but she's supposed to be meeting with Carter and her money guy today, so her being here is unexpected. I don't do well with the unexpected. I like to plan. Prepare.

Screaming in my head, I measure the distance to the nearest hallway, trying to figure out whether I can crawl over there without being seen. I think I can do it and even make it two feet before Josie throws me under the bus.

"Luna, what are you doing on the floor?" she says, intentionally loud enough for Maeve and Elena to hear.

"What? Luna?" I hear Maeve's voice echoing in the lobby.

"Shiiii—" I whisper, but I realize there's nothing to do but stand up and take my lumps. I pop up too quickly, my vision going a little fuzzy, and have to hold on to the counter so I don't fall. "Oh! Hi there!" I say, my voice an octave higher than usual. "What's up?"

Maeve clears her throat, glaring at me in a silent order to pull myself together. But Elena seems more concerned that I've lost my mind, looking from me to the floor. "You okay, dear?"

"Yes, yes," I assure her hastily. "I thought there was something . . . on the floor?"

"There was . . . you," Josie murmurs. Thankfully, I don't think Maeve and Elena hear her.

Finding some semblance of normalcy—or at least what passes for it—I walk toward Elena with my hand out. "Sorry, just surprised to see you. But it's a great surprise."

Instead of shaking my hand, Elena holds her arms out, enveloping me in a hug. I stiffen for a split second but then hug her back warmly.

"Good to see you too."

When she pulls back, I don't know what to do with my arms and end up with them clenched behind my back as my brain yells, *What is she doing here?*

On cue, Maeve tells me, "Mrs. Cartwright was just telling me about your suggestion that she consider an exhibition here of Mr. Cartwright's collection."

She sounds a little put out, and I realize that I probably should've mentioned it to her before, but it was nothing more than a passing hope. Elena hasn't said anything more than 'interesting' about it.

"Are you actually considering it?" I ask Elena excitedly.

She grins. "I thought I'd check the museum out first. Make sure it's a place Thomas would feel like his collection would be at home."

Nodding, I agree. "Absolutely! I'd be happy to show you around."

"I think you have another tour in a few minutes, right, Luna?" Maeve prompts.

I shake my head, pulling out my phone to double-check. "I don't think so. Unless someone booked one since this morning?" I glance to Josie to make sure no one has called in but find she's fighting back a laugh. I don't understand why until I glance back to Maeve, who's trying to silently communicate with me again, and I realize that she probably wants to be the one to show Elena around. "I mean, uh . . . maybe I have . . . another tour?"

Maeve smiles, and I breathe a sigh of relief for getting it right.

Elena's not having it, though. "Surely, there's someone else who could handle that? It'd make me happier than a tick on a fat dog to have Luna show me around. It only seems right since she's the reason I'm here, and I've been wanting to see that Renoir of yours since she told me about it."

"Oh, well, then there you have it," Maeve answers, seemingly decidedly less than enthusiastic about my showing Elena around. She probably wants to get her own moment to shine, and I'm in the way of that. "I'd be happy to speak with you about the exhibition in more detail after Luna shows you around."

"Sure, sure." Elena dismisses Maeve with a wave of her hand, then holds her elbow out to me. I slip mine through hers and she smiles. "Take me places and show me things, dear."

I lead her off toward the Renaissance wing, trying to keep an Elena-appropriate pace and not the run-away speed I'd like to go at to get away from Maeve's sharply raised brow.

"This is one of the most popular areas of the museum," I tell Elena as she looks around. I know she's not as passionate about art as Thomas was, but I naturally drop into tour guide mode as we explore. "A lot of folks like the clear imagery, and the bright colors are very uplifting."

Elena listens as we walk through room after room, but eventually, I pick up a weirdness in the way she's watching me and barely glancing at the displays. I don't think she's here for the museum. She's here for . . . me?

Hopefully, she's scoping me out for the exhibition, but I'm not sure that's it. I swallow thickly, knowing that if she asks any direct questions about Carter and me, she'll be able to see through any awkward answer I give. And I really hate lying to her. She's so sweet and kind, and I feel like we could be friends even though there's a lifetime's worth of years and millions of dollars between the two of us.

It's like she's been waiting patiently for me to catch on that she doesn't care about the museum because when she sees recognition dawning in my eyes, she smiles gently before sitting down on a bench in the middle of the room. She pats the space beside her, and I slowly lower myself beside her. "Elena?"

"What brought you to art?" she asks, looking around at the paintings. We're in the modern art section, an area that people tend to either love or hate.

I stare into the pop art piece in front of me, searching for an answer that will make sense. "You ever felt like you didn't fit in?" I ask her. I recognize how stupid that sounds and don't wait for her answer. "That was me. But art was . . . accepting. It made me feel normal."

"Whatever that is," she teases, and I smile back, relaxing. Maybe this is about the museum and the possibility of an exhibit. Those are safer zones that I can talk about for hours.

"What about Carter? What brought you two together?"

Danger! What do I say?

I wish Carter were here to handle this question. He's better at non-answer answers than I am. But then I remember what I told Carter . . . keep it simple. Stick to the truth. It's easier on your brain, but it's also easier on my heart.

"My brother, Zack. Carter and he are best friends, have been for years."

"Ooh, was it love at first sight? Did your brother pitch a hissy fit or was he on board?" Elena shimmies her shoulders, looking for juicy gossip.

I laugh at her eagerness. "More like hate at first sight. And second, third, and fourth. It was years before I even liked Carter, but his charm got to me, I guess." I smile, thinking back. Though Elena probably assumes it was long ago, I'm truly only thinking of weeks ago.

Weeks? How can that be? It feels like so much longer.

Remembering her other question, I answer, "Oh, and Zack was . . . let's be polite and say 'upset' about it."

Elena shakes her head. "Let's don't and say we did. Skip the politeness and tell me the good stuff."

"He punched Carter in the nose," I confide, almost happy about it now. "And then they talked for like two seconds and it was all good. Men are weird." I shrug my shoulders, still not sure how that worked out so quickly.

"That they are," Elena agrees, patting my hand. "I'm glad they got over it. Are they still friends?"

"Oh, yeah. Zack filmed Carter's proposal right over there." I point toward my favorite Pollock piece. "And then he was Carter's best man."

Elena smacks my thigh . . . hard. *Damn, she keeps her butt whooping hand strong!* Excited, she asks, "He proposed here? How sweet is that?"

I rub at my thigh, soothing the sting. "I guess . . . but honestly, I kinda thought it was awful." Elena's eyes widen in horror, and I rush to explain, "I wasn't expecting it, and there were people all around us, watching and cheering. I was wearing my uniform." I gesture to the unflattering navy suit I have on today too. "But he learned, and the wedding was super tiny. That was *so* much better."

I smile, remembering. Even though I had a whole-ass panic attack after, I'm glad we were at home, with our best friends.

Home? Is that what I'm considering Carter's place now?

"Sounds like it," Elena says kindly.

She peers at me curiously for a moment, and I wonder what other questions she has up her sleeves. Though the conversation has been casual, I realize that it's been slightly interrogative, with Elena playing the good cop.

"You want to look around some more? I could show you the VR exhibit? Or we're displaying a permanent collection that is on loan from another donor. It'd be a great example of what we could provide Thomas's collection." I stand, pointing toward a hall that leads to the exhibition and hoping to redirect us away from Carter and me and back to art.

"I think I'm good. But I'd love for you and Carter to come over for dinner tomorrow night if y'all are available? Totally casual."

"Oh!" I have no idea whether we have plans. We haven't exactly been sharing calendars. We simply come home at the end of each day and spend the night together. But this feels important. For Carter's deal and for the exhibition, though I'm not sure why. "We'd love to. Can I bring anything?"

"I wish you could bring that sweet Gracie girl, but just bring the two of you, and that'll be fine." Elena smiles, gathering both of my hands in hers. It's not a handshake, exactly, though she is shaking my hands, but rather more like a hand-hug, as odd as that sounds, and she pins me with a soul-searching gaze. "You're sweet, Luna. Thomas would've loved to talk art with you."

Hot tears fill my eyes. "I think I would've loved that too."

Elena tells me that she'd like to wander back up front on her own, just her and Thomas, she says with a sad smile and her hand over her heart, and I sit down heavily on the bench as I watch her go.

This whole thing is so confusing and makes me feel icky inside because though everything I told Elena just now was the truth, it's built on the foundation of a lie.

I sit there alone, staring at the floor instead of the art because the bland tile lets me think and process. Sometime later, Maeve finds me. "Luna! Tell me everything!" she demands with a bright smile as she sits down beside me, scooting sexual-harassment close in her excitement. "Josie called me to the desk, and who do I see but Elena Cartwright? How do you know her? Do you know her? She called you Luna Harrington, not Starr, but you're the only Luna I know, so I assumed she meant you, and you seemed pretty close."

I lift my gaze, pushing my hair behind my ears and my glasses up my nose so I can see properly. "It's a kinda long story," I offer, hoping Maeve won't ask any further questions.

There is no way I can piece together any sort of explanation that'll make any sense. Not about being Carter Harrington's fake wife, and definitely not about being his real one.

"Ooh, isn't that intriguing?" She waggles her brows at me. "You know I love a bit of mystery. But for now, you can keep your secrets *if* we can talk about this opportunity for the museum." She takes my silence as agreement and says, "*The* Thomas Cartwright? As in, a Thomas. Cartwright. Exhibition? Here?"

"That's what Elena said."

"Elena? You're on a first-name basis with Elena Cartwright. How in the world?" Maeve asks.

That's part of the whole explanation thing I can't handle, but maybe . . .

Stick to the art, Luna.

"I, uhm, met Elena. And, well, she showed me Thomas's collection. It's amazing, with Renoir, Van Gogh, Picasso, and some lesser-known artists too. I even got to see pieces Mr. Cartwright did himself." I gain steam as I describe Thomas's collection because the joy of seeing it comes back to me. "I've never experienced anything like it. There are pieces I'd never heard of or seen in books. I wanted to sit and stare at them, study them inch by inch. I could've spent hours and hours, and I thought, if I wanted to do that, other people would too. So I suggested the exhibition as a way to honor him, and—"

Maeve interrupts me. "Breathe, Luna. You're turning blue."

Maeve is smiling warmly at my exuberance, but I'm waiting for her to yell at me. For what? I don't know.

For speaking for the museum without permission? For volunteering us for an exhibition? For wanting to be in charge of anything beyond tours? For not answering her question about my last name?

None of that happens. She just expects me to breathe.

I take the breath she ordered me to, and with a wavering smile, I meet her eyes. "Hi," I say unsurely.

"Good job. I'm proud of you for thinking of the museum during what sounds like a really special tour. I'll email Mrs. Cartwright to follow up on her visit today?"

I'm silent until I feel Maeve looking at me expectantly. I

realize she wasn't telling me that, she's asking me . . . as if I'm already in charge of the exhibition. "Oh! Yes, of course."

Maeve nods and stands, tapping away on her phone before she's even out of the room.

This is happening! A Thomas Cartwright collection right here at the museum, and it sounds like I'll get to help coordinate it.

Needing to celebrate this with someone, I grab my phone to text Carter.

You won't believe this! Elena came to the museum today to talk about the exhibition! I gave her a tour!

I should definitely use fewer exclamation points, but I'm so excited that I'm basically vibrating. Texting like a middle-school girl is the least of my worries, so I hit *Send* and wait.

Less than a minute later, I get a response.

Carter: That's awesome. Congratulations! I can't wait to hear all about it tonight.

Me: How was your meeting?

Carter: I don't know yet. He wasn't as receptive as I'd hoped.

Me: Oh, no! I'm sorry. Anything I can do?

The three dots are there for a long time, and I wonder if he's typing a novel. Or more likely, typing something dirty and then deleting it, and I feel a smile steal my lips at the idea.

Carter: All good. I don't give up that easily.

Luna: Me neither.

Carter: Good girl. I'm heading into a meeting. See you tonight?

I send back a quick heart emoji and put my phone away.

It's not till after my next tour that I realize that I didn't text Samantha, Zack, or even my mom when I got the great news about the exhibition. My first and only thought was that I wanted to talk to Carter.

But that doesn't feel like a bad thing at all.

CHAPTER
TWENTY-FIVE
CARTER

AFTER LUNA TELLS me about Elena's weird museum visit with twenty questions and the dinner invitation, I spend the night tossing and turning with my mind running a million miles a minute. I feel three steps behind, and it's not a feeling I like, but staring at the ceiling isn't helping.

What was Claire doing at Oleana's office?

Why did Elena go to the museum after that?

Is this dinner to tell us that it's all a go?

Or to tell us that she's going a different direction with both her money and Thomas's art?

I scoot away from Luna, planning to leave her blissfully sleeping while I go to the living room to plot and plan, obsess and analyze. But she mumbles, "Carter, where're ya goin'?"

If it was only the half-asleep mumble, I could've headed to the living room, but Luna's reaching out for me with grabby fingers and an unhappy moan is too much for me to bear. I lay back down, and she snuggles into me, her head on my chest and body pressed against me. I feel her cheek move and realize that she's smiling in her sleep.

Because of me.

Having Luna in my arms is a joy I never dreamed of having. I honestly don't know that I ever truly saw her before this whole thing. She was my friend's little sister, but now . . . I see her. I know her. I feel her.

I run my fingers over her arm and press a kiss to her hair. Not for her, but to soothe myself. I have a bad feeling about this dinner, but I vow to myself that I won't let anything happen to Luna.

Eventually, I fall asleep from pure exhaustion, but I don't dream of portfolios. No, Luna dances her way through my sleep, and it's better sleep than I've had in years.

The next day, I decide to work from home, burying myself in every bit of information I have on the Cartwright estate and then digging into what I can find on Claire.

There's not a lot.

In shorthand, she's Thomas's niece, but only because I'm too confused by greats, grands, and once removed to figure out her actual connection. It doesn't matter, really, because 'niece' is what they've always called her. She's married to Madison, who prefers Mads, and they have a son, Jacob. All things I knew. My research does show that I was correct about Mads being a suit-type, though he's a mid-level manager, not an accountant like I suspected. From what I can tell, they live on funds from good ol' Uncle Thomas—their house, cars, Jacob's piano lessons, and more.

Who gets that kid to sit still long enough to play piano? Poor teacher.

But there's nothing concerning that I can find. She seems like a woman of means, the same as many others when your family is Cartwright-level wealthy.

"Here, eat something," Luna tells me as she sets a sandwich on the table next to me. She's been working on Alphena all day, making little noises as she writes that I'm guessing correspond to the action on pages of her tablet.

"Can't. I need to figure this out." I keep tapping away, not sure what I'm hoping to find.

Luna plops into the chair she's been curled up in all day, sitting on her feet in a way that makes my legs hurt, and takes a bite of her own sandwich. Around the mouthful, she says, "If you don't eat all day, when Elena puts dinner in front of you, you're gonna act like a ravenous wildebeest."

I still don't reach for the sandwich.

"Your brain needs fuel to figure out whatever you're trying to figure out. You're not going to do it if all your brain is saying is 'feed me'. You're basically a zombie running on caffeine at this point."

Okay, that's a good point. I take a bite, chewing thoughtfully. "Claire is the key here. I don't know why, but her showing up at Oleana's office and then Elena coming to the museum worry me."

Luna takes another bite and then sets her sandwich down in favor of her tablet. "Whatever it is, you'll handle it."

Her faith in me is reassuring. If only I felt the same way.

She goes back to working, and I watch her for a moment before I do the same.

———

Pulling up to Elena's home this time feels just as fraught with possible missteps as it did last time. I've researched, planned, and plotted. Luna and I have done everything to address the money and the art and have even gone so far as getting married for real. There should be nothing they can throw at us to ruin this.

But my heart is pounding so hard I can almost feel it bursting through my shirt.

Holding Luna's hand, I help her out of the car.

"You bring that piss monster with ya this time?" a grouchy voice says.

I look over to see Bernard, the gardener, holding a spray bottle at the ready like he's a cowboy in the Wild West who's going to shoot the bank robber when he runs by. My guess? Nutbuster is his version of the bad guy, and he'd do anything to protect his rosebushes from another round of baptism by dog pee.

"No, not this time," I answer with a forced smile, waving in greeting.

His lip curls in a snarl and then he squirts the water my way with a jerk of his arm. The spray arcs but doesn't reach me. I think he truly meant for it to, though, which would've gotten my favorite suit wet.

"What the fu—"

Luna squeezes my hand. "Thanks again for taking such good care of Peanut Butter last time we were here, Mr. Bernard. I think he misses you too."

What? There's no way that's what the cantankerous old guy is trying to say. But he grunts once more and then walks away, his head hanging low and scanning left and right, as if he's inspecting every blade of grass.

I look at Luna in shock, and she shrugs. Whispering, she says, "Everybody likes dogs, even grumpy people."

Elena opens the door before I get the chance to knock. "Hey, you two! Get on in here!" She's smiling and welcoming, seeming glad to see us, and my heart rate slows incrementally.

She hugs Luna and then me in greeting, making this feel more like a visit to Grandma's house than a business meeting. Though given how close Elena and Mr. Oleana have been for years, maybe that's the type of working relationship I can look forward to with Elena too. I can imagine monthly lunches where we go over finances and catch up about our lives. Like friends, blending personal and professional. I know that can work because that's how Zack and I function too.

Elena shows us into the formal living room, and all hope dies in my chest instantly. Claire is sitting on the couch, looking smugly amused by our arrival. Mads is sitting next to her, examining his nails though his hands haven't seen a lick of hard labor in his lifetime, from what I read. Jacob is sitting sideways in a chair, tilting his Nintendo Switch left and right as he hisses at the game. "Get'im! No! The other guy, stoopid!"

"Hi, Claire, Jacob," I say with a wave. "You must be Mads." I hold my hand out to him, and he glances at Claire first, as though asking permission, before shaking.

"You must be Carter."

His eyes flick to Luna at my side, but as they shake hands politely, his gaze drops to her chest. It's only for a moment, but it's long enough. I take an instinctual step forward, slipping an arm around Luna's shoulders possessively.

"This is my *wife*, Luna," I say sharply, feeling Luna jump at the harshness in my tone as I introduce her.

The caveman in my gut is glad she's wearing a T-shirt and jeans, because if she were wearing a dress, I don't know if I could hold back from popping him for daring to check out Luna's breasts so brazenly.

"Madison!" Claire scolds, jerking his hand so that he falls back to the couch beside her.

"You know I hate that," he tells her. Not 'don't call me that' or anything commanding, but rather a whiny reminder.

They're having a silent conversation of glares, and though I'm paying attention to it, I check in with Luna. She mouths, "Whoa."

There's a flush high on her cheeks and her eyes are full of heat. I think she liked the caveman moment. I bend to press a quick kiss to her cheek and give her a wink, and she fans herself in response.

Elena chuckles, and Luna remembers that we have an audience, going a bit stiff beside me. Though his eyes are glued to his game, I ask Jacob, "Whatcha playing, man?"

"Mario Kart 8 . . . Nooo!!!" he shouts. "You messed me up." The accusation is reminiscent of the tone his dad just had.

"Sorry," I say, not sorry in the slightest.

"Have a seat," Elena says, coming in behind us and sitting down on the other side of Mads. I wait for Luna to sit on the loveseat, then sit beside her, resting my ankle on my knee and holding Luna's hand on my thigh.

"Luna couldn't stop telling me how excited she was to give you a tour of the museum. What'd you think?" I ask.

Elena smiles warmly at Luna. "We had fun. Two ladies talking about art. Thomas would've gotten a kick out of my going to an art museum. He was always trying to drag me here to see this painting and there to see that painting. Like I had a clue about any of it."

She laughs lightly, and Luna smiles. "I had fun, but I think you gave Maeve a heart attack showing up like that. Me too, honestly."

"Well, I'd say you hid it well," Elena replies, but then the straight face she's holding melts, and she and Luna laugh loudly together, leaving the rest of us looking on in confusion.

"Instead of playing nice, could we talk about something actually important?" Claire frowns at Elena, and I can feel the pendulum of doom swinging over my chest.

"Claire!" Elena snaps sharply. "Could you at least pretend to have a sliver of a heart in that hollow void you call a chest? This isn't the kind of thing you dump on someone without a warning. You gotta warm up to it a bit. And I still think you must be mistaken."

"I'm not," Claire insists.

"Uh, not to interrupt, but is everything okay?" I ask.

Claire's frown intensifies and though Elena shakes her head, she waves a hand of permission. "Get on with it, then. Your funeral."

"Right. Well, then . . ." Claire turns her attention to Luna, and I can feel her shrink back into the couch at the unmitigated focus being directed at her.

My protective instincts kick in again, though I'm not sure what's happening. I lean forward, blocking Claire's view. "What's going on?"

"I went to dinner with a friend recently. At a cute place in Bridgeport." She says it as though that should mean something. When I don't react, she continues, "You'll never guess who I saw."

Mads shifts uncomfortably beside Claire, but she doesn't seem to notice or care.

"Can you guess, Luna?" she asks, a smirk on her lips.

"Someone famous?" Luna guesses. I can feel her peeking around me to answer, so I relax back on the couch, letting her handle this herself. Whatever *this* is.

Claire laughs. "No, definitely not. Though you'll probably wish I had. But no, I saw . . . *you*."

"Me?" Luna squeaks.

"With another man." Claire locks eyes on me, hungry for my reaction to finding out my wife was with another man. "She kissed him."

She enunciates it, wanting to make sure there's no room for misunderstanding. Luna barks out a laugh of shock, but fury shoots through me. Not at the idea of Luna kissing another man because I trust Luna, but at Claire taking some kind of sick, twisted pleasure in thinking she's going to hurt me and Luna.

"Did this dinner happen to be at Capitol Chophouse?" I guess, narrowing my eyes to gauge Claire's reaction now. A little turnabout is fair play, I think.

"Yes, it's quite nice there. The sort of place you take someone when you want to impress them. Like a date, maybe?" Claire's suggestion shows that she's given this lots of thought, considering all the different reasons Luna might be having a nice dinner out with someone.

"Oh! I went to Capitol Chophouse with—" Luna starts to explain, but I place my hand on her knee, squeezing hard, and she stops instantly, though she looks at me questioningly.

I look back at Luna gently, trying to tell her to stay with me here, and then turn an angry glare to Claire. Clenching my jaw, I grit out, "Can you tell me what you saw? Exactly."

"Oh, honey. Don't you worry," Elena tries to soothe me, misjudging the target of my anger. Or maybe she's trying to protect her niece, I'm not sure which.

"Of course I can." Claire's delight is obvious, glee filling her eyes and voice. "There I was, minding my own business, when I saw sweet, innocent Luna with another man. He was older than her—guess she has a type, huh? With brown hair and black glasses. Ring any bells?" she asks. When I stay silent, she continues, giving more details. "They were talking very close, almost intimately, I'd say. And then your wife leaned in even closer and kissed the guy on the cheek, sort of lingering there like she wanted more."

She makes it sound salacious, like Luna and this guy were making out at the table, but I seriously doubt that.

"*Blech.*" Luna makes a retching noise beside me. "That's disgusting."

Her outburst interrupts Claire's gloating storytelling, and Claire looks from me to Luna in confusion. I chuckle, and after a pat of Luna's thigh, I pull out my phone and find a picture of Zack and me on a recent night out. I turn the phone around so Claire can see the picture. "This the guy?" When Claire nods eagerly, I laugh a little harder. "This is Zack, my best friend."

"Oh, that's awful," she says, seemingly sympathetic as she shakes her head, but the glint of pleasure in her eyes belies that. "It's always with the best friend, isn't it?"

"Enough," Luna says firmly, standing up and waving her hands to stop Claire. "Zack is Carter's best friend . . . and my brother!"

Elena laughs first, hooting and guffawing loudly. "Claire! I told you there had to be a reasonable explanation for it, but *no* . . . you didn't believe me. I believe you told me I was getting to be a bit gullible in my old age? Now, who's looking like a fool?"

But Luna's channeling her inner Alphena, and she's in full-blown fiery mode. "You really thought I was cheating on Carter? What kind of mean sicko takes pleasure in telling someone that? You weren't doing this for him," Luna charges, pointing at me. And then she turns her finger at Claire accusingly. "You were doing it for you. Did you see me kiss Zack's cheek and then scurry off like a dog with a bone? You must've, because if you'd waited one measly second longer, you would've seen Carter come back from the bathroom and sit down with us for dinner."

Claire's mouth is opening and closing in shock. Mads looks majorly uncomfortable just sitting next to her, or maybe at the idea that he might have to defend his despicable wife. Elena is grinning wide at seeing Claire put in place. Jacob is still staring at his game despite all the madness. And I'm in awe . . . of Luna.

When she's quiet and shy, and when she's loud and

commanding, Luna is gorgeous. And so damn strong. She's amazing.

"I just thought . . ." Claire stammers. "I mean, the two of you aren't exactly . . ."

"Aren't what?" Luna prompts with her hands on her hips.

Claire straightens her back, remembering that she's not someone to be messed with either, and stands to argue eye to eye with Luna. "Look, the two of you are an odd pairing. You must be ten years younger than Carter, and what in the world do you talk about?" She scoffs, then smiles ferally. "Maybe that's the attraction? You're nothing more than a young, stupid girl he can manipulate?" She taps her nose as though she's got us all figured out. "Guess your mouth must be good for something because he's sure not with you for your looks."

"Claire!" Elena shouts.

"What? You know it's true," Claire huffs, not swayed at the reprimand. "There's no way you're actually considering working with these people."

"I don't care if you do think it's true, you don't say it. Carter and Luna have been nothing but kind, and their relationship is none of your business. Lord knows, I stay out of yours and Mads's, biting my tongue when you're mean as a honey badger to that sweet man." She leans to the right, speaking only to Mads, "No offense. And certainly no judgment from me if you like that."

For someone who's promoting keeping their mouth shut, Elena most definitely is not.

Mads shrugs, telling Elena, "None taken. And no, I don't enjoy it when she goes all bitchy."

"Madison!" Claire shouts, whirling to scowl at him angrily. "I am not mean to you. Tell her. And don't you dare call me a bitch!"

For his part, Mads looks at his wife incredulously. "Call. Me. Mads. And do you hear yourself? Yes, you are mean *sometimes*. And *bitchy* sometimes. I keep wishing the not-mean times will outweigh the others, but then you go and pull a stunt like this? I just can't with you, Claire."

She seems shocked that he dared to speak back to her at all, and I wonder if maybe it's the first time he's ever done it.

"I think you owe Luna and Carter an apology," Elena tells Claire. "Especially Luna."

Claire's lips pucker, as if the idea of an apology is a bitter pill to swallow. But in the end, she appeases her aunt. "Sorry." Quieter, and directed at Mads, she murmurs, "You can't blame me for assuming the worst, though. I mean, seriously?" Her eyes flick toward Luna and me.

I note that she doesn't apologize for anything specific, despite there being several things she should be apologizing for. I'm not ready to let this go, feeling like I need to come to Luna's defense in so many ways. Just because Claire doesn't see how amazing Luna is doesn't make her any less so. She's so much more than a young, stupid girl, and I want everyone to know that.

Because I was one of those people who overlooked her too, but now . . . I see her. I'm about to say something when Luna does.

"Apology accepted," Luna says, sitting back down at my side.

It's not enough, not from Claire and not from me, but I can feel the tension in Luna and that takes priority over what some bitch like Claire thinks. If Luna wants to drop this, I will . . . for her.

It feels like we just dodged hundreds of landmines and we haven't even sat down to dinner yet. I never did eat that sandwich, and Luna's right, I'm starving after such a big adrenaline dump and having to forcefully bite my tongue.

"I'm so sorry about all this," Elena adds, though she had nothing to do with it. "Y'all are just cute as peach pie together, so don't listen to Claire a lick."

"It's fine," I answer. It's not, not at all. But it's also not worth blowing up this deal over, especially now that it's semi-handled and I know that Claire is a snake in the grass, waiting to strike. I'll be on high alert with her from now on.

Luna makes a humming noise, and I realize she's clenching and unclenching her hands. "You okay?" I ask, rubbing her back.

Her head falls, her eyes locked on her hands, and a bad feeling sweeps through my gut. "Luna?"

She glances up, meeting my eyes. There are tears on the lenses of her glasses and her lip is quivering. "I'm sorry. I can't do this anymore."

"What?" I have half a second of not understanding before Luna drops a bomb of her own.

"Carter and I aren't really married. Well, we are now, but we weren't. Not before." She's rambling, which is the only saving grace I can hope for. Maybe nobody understands what she's saying?

I grab her knee, squeezing it firmly. "Luna. You don't have to do this."

She shakes her head, effectively shaking off my plea to shut the fuck up.

Elena is looking at Luna with almost parental concern. "Are you okay, dear?"

"No, I'm not. Carter wanted . . . it was supposed to be art tutoring. That's it. And then he proposed. It was a show, all pretend. It wasn't supposed to be like this. I just wanted to help him. And then Thomas's collection. I couldn't . . . I wanted to see it. Selfishly needed to. So we came to dinner. I never meant . . . I didn't want . . . but then it got to . . . here." She waves her hands around, gesturing to the room at large but really meaning this moment.

Her rambling is rapid-fire and all over the place, but Elena understands. We all understand because she's leaving no room for doubt now.

Luna just confirmed Claire's assumption that we couldn't possibly be together for real and more importantly, torpedoing any shot I had at the Cartwright portfolio.

Dad's already furious at me, and when he finds out how much worse I let this get, he's never going to trust me again. At this rate, I'll be lucky to play second fiddle to Cameron. Maybe they'll let me set the tables at his fancy chef's new restaurant?

I can see my entire career bursting into flames before my very eyes. Every hour of overtime I've worked, every sacrifice I've made, even everything Luna and I have done . . . it's all been for nothing. She just annihilated it all.

"Luna! How could you?" I demand angrily, pushing away from her on the couch. I can't believe she's destroying everything like this. We had a deal, a plan, and she's betraying me worse than I would've ever thought possible.

"I hate lying. Especially when Elena is . . ." She looks to Elena, who seems confused as hell. "So sweet. I'm so sorry. Truly, I am. It got so out of control, so fast."

Luna runs from the room, slamming a door shut somewhere in the front hallway.

I'm fuming, a dark and angry pit in my stomach rising quickly to consume me.

"I'm sorry . . ." I start, but Claire is ready to pounce and interrupts.

"Is that true?" she asks.

True? I don't know what's true anymore, but I don't want to answer Claire's question. Anything I say can and will be used against me. Not in a court of law, but in the practice of business.

I stand, straightening my tie until it's damn near choking me. Or maybe it's the words that are stuck in my throat? "We might not be the usual couple or have gotten together in a typical way, but Luna and I are married. None of this means I can't do the job, and I would love to serve as the financial manager for the Cartwright portfolio. I think we could do really good work together, despite any mistakes that I've made."

I'm trying to save face, putting on a stoic mask even though I know it's all over. Even as I turn to go, I can feel my plans turning to rubble and my heart turning to stone.

I follow the sound of Luna's sobs and in the hall, knock on the bathroom door. "Luna? I think we should go."

She sniffles and with a rough voice says, "I called Zack to come get me. He's on his way to take me home."

Home? I'm already going there. Why does she need Zack to give her a ride? And then I realize . . . she means her home . . . her apartment. Not mine.

I grit my teeth at the fresh gut punch. "Fine."

Elena, Claire, and Mads have followed me into the hallway and are listening to our exchange, but I needlessly repeat, "Her brother's coming to get her. Is that okay?"

Elena dips her chin, her eyes seeming extra shrewd as she stares back at me. I can't take any more and stride toward the door.

"Carter?" Elena says, and I stop, looking over my shoulder. "Sometimes, we end up someplace we never intended and it's up to us to decide whether we like where we're at." She nods as though that's something deep and meaningful and not a barely coherent fortune cookie saying.

I definitely didn't start out planning to deceive Elena like this. It all got so carried away, and I kept thinking I could fix it. I would've fixed it . . . eventually. When I was ready, when the deal was done, when it was planned out and made sense. Not like this.

"Thank you. And again, I'm sorry."

Outside, Bernard tries to talk to me about Nutbuster, but I throw up a hand to stop him and climb into my car.

Peeling out down the road, I can't help but feel like I'm leaving behind something important.

Luna.

I tell my brain, or heart, or dick—whatever's speaking right now—to shut up. I didn't leave her. She left me when she told Elena the truth.

Damn the consequences.

In some ways . . . it's admirable. I wish I'd had the guts to do it, but then I wouldn't have had Luna . . . even for this short period of time.

CHAPTER
TWENTY-SIX
LUNA

I HEAR the front door slam and jump even though I knew it was coming. Carter left me. I knew he would eventually. I just couldn't take it anymore—all the lying, being called an ugly cheater, defending myself while Carter sat there silently watching me go ballistic on Claire.

So many lies. To Elena, to Carter, to myself.

I thought there was something good happening between us. Maybe a weird start, but something real. I felt it over the last few weeks, especially since the wedding, but it's all still just a ploy for him. Nothing more than a charade to close a deal.

I sit on the floor with my knees curled to my chest and sob as I watch my brother's little dot move toward me on the app we have to track each other. He can't get here quick enough, and at the same time, he's going to want some answers, but I don't want to talk about this with him or anyone else.

Breathe, Luna. In, 2, 3, 4. Out, 2, 3, 4.

I don't know how long I sit there talking myself off the razor edge of anxiety when there's a gentle knock at the door. "Luna, dear?"

"I'm sorry," I say again. I don't think I can say it enough at this point.

"Everyone else is gone. It's just me and you. Why don't you come out here and let me make you a glass of tea?"

Elena is being too kind, triggering fresh anxiety to shoot through me. I shake my head, though she can't see me.

"You gonna make me bust this door down? I'll do it if I have to. I can also pick a lock if need be. It's a good skill to have," she says conversationally.

What?

"How . . . how do you know how to do that?" I ask. It doesn't matter, but I think that's probably why she threw that information out there to begin with.

"Open the door and I'll tell you while I teach you."

A lockpicking lesson? Now? The absurdity of it makes a small smile creep up my lips.

Almost as if she knows, Elena adds, "These old locks are pretty easy, but I'm not too good with the new-fangled ones. Never had a reason to pick one of those, I guess."

"Why did you pick the old ones?" The question escapes without my even planning to speak.

"Because I'm a nosey old cuss, mostly," she laughs. "Hated being out of the know about a thing, so I used to break into my daddy's office and my momma's bathroom. Oh, and the barn, but that was one of those spinny combination locks. Combination was my parents' anniversary. Easy as pie."

She's totally distracted me with her story, so I jump a foot when the door swings open. Elena stands there, proud as you please, with a bobby pin in her fingers. "You want that lesson or you want some tea before your brother gets here? Either way, you're getting up off that floor."

She holds her hand out to help me up, and though I take it to be polite, I don't pull on her a bit. I get up on my own, and Elena looks at me with something resembling approval. But that can't be right. There's no way after I lied and hid in her bathroom.

"Come on, then. I think I'm gonna take a shot of whiskey in my tea. You too?" She turns and walks off, leaving me to follow or not.

I shuffle after her, my Converse squeaking on the marble floor. "I'm sorry," I tell her again as she pours a shot . . . make that two . . . into a glass sitting on a tray on the coffee table. I guess Nelda's already been here. I feel guilty over her hard work fixing dinner and nobody eating it. Sitting down in the corner of the couch, I wish I could curl up but know better than to get my shoes on the furniture. Still, if I could become one with the arm of the couch, I would.

"Enough apologies, dear. You want a skinny shot or a heavy-handed one like mine?" she asks, holding up the bottle of amber liquid.

"Uh, skinny?" I don't think I've ever had tea and whiskey before. The pour she makes is lighter than her own, but still longer than I would've done.

She holds it out and then clinks her own glass to mine before sitting down. She takes a big sip, swallowing several times, and then sighs in bliss. When she looks at me expectantly, I take a tiny taste. It's not half-bad, just a bit *whooo* on the alcohol. "Thanks."

"Okay, so tell me what all's the truth and what all's a lie. It appears I need a check-up on my bullshit-o-meter."

I take another drink of the tea instead, finding the burn of it going down less painful than the sour acid of the truth of what I've done. Eventually, though, the whiskey works its magic and loosens my tongue. I don't know what all I say to Elena, but this time I know it's all true.

I laugh lightly as I tell her about how bad Carter is at remembering a damn thing about art. I plead with her to understand as I explain how much I wanted to see Thomas's collection and how special it is to someone like me. I cry when I tell her about how Carter took care of me when I had a panic attack. I blush as I share that his kisses make me warm inside, all the way down to my toes, and that when his blue eyes lock onto me, I feel like I'm beautiful.

"Even if that's not really true. I mean, I know what Claire meant. Carter's . . . Carter. And I'm . . . me. We're not exactly a match made in heaven."

"You shut your mouth up. I may not be a walking lie detector, given the current situation, but I can see how that boy looks at you. Nobody needs to understand your love but you two."

I choke out a bitter laugh. "Love? I don't think so. Carter would never fall in love with me. And despite being married to him, I don't think a man who'd go to these lengths for a business deal is right for me, either. Money's never been important to me like that. We don't make sense."

"Never say never," she replies.

The doorbell rings, and Elena gets up. "I've got it, Stanley!" she shouts. Quieter, she tells me, "He's around here somewhere, probably knows everything that's happened. If I'm nosy, that old fella is Pinocchio."

She disappears, then reappears a moment later with Zack in tow. "See, just like I told you, she's fine. Sipping on some truth serum tea." She winks at me, and I realize that her offer of tea wasn't entirely friendly, after all. She had ulterior motives too.

Sitting down beside me, Zack asks, "What happened?"

"Claire saw you and me and thought . . ." A shiver of ick makes my whole body wiggle in revulsion. "We got that straightened out, but I couldn't do it anymore." I look up, hoping he'll understand. "I told Elena the truth."

"Damn, Moony," he whispers. "You really know how to fuck shit up, don't you? What about Carter?"

My eyes fall again as I shrug. "He left."

"He. Left." He's saying the same thing I did, but it sounds quite different. I'm resolved, but Zack's livid and trying to hide it. I know him well enough to recognize it.

"It's okay," I tell him, trying to assuage his anger. "It doesn't matter. Can we go home? I want to go home."

I let Zack and Elena walk me to the door, feeling like a zombie. "Should I have kept my mouth shut?" I wonder aloud, not sure who I'm asking.

"No, dear," Elena answers as she puts an arm around my shoulders. "You did what your heart told you to do, and listening to that beating muscle of self-direction is always the right thing." She pats her chest, right over her heart, and I wonder what it's telling her now. This old woman's damn near Yoda with her levels of wisdom.

But truthfully, she's probably glad to be rid of us. Someone who lies to your face isn't someone you want managing your money. And someone who wants you to lie will lie to you. I should've realized that about Carter sooner. Myself too, because I was too willing to go along with it. And for what?

Seeing Thomas's collection feels tainted now by my own deception. I didn't deserve to see it.

"Thanks for taking care of her, Mrs. Cartwright," Zack tells Elena at the front door.

I take one last look at the Eakin piece in the foyer, recalling the joy I felt seeing it the first time. How can I have disrespected such artwork, created with so much heart and imbued with so much meaning the way I did?

"I'm sorry," I say one more time. This time, it's to Thomas.

I'm quiet in the car after telling Zack that I don't want to talk about it. He got the gist of it, anyway. I blew up Carter's chance at the Cartwright portfolio. Thankfully, he respects my wish and says nothing until we get to my apartment. "Moony?" he says quietly. "I just want you to know, I'm sorry for getting you mixed up in this, and I love you. No matter what."

I nod and give him a small smile. "Thanks."

Walking into my apartment feels strange. I haven't been here in a while, and it seems empty, even with Zack here with me.

"Go put on comfy clothes or take a bath, maybe?" he offers, trying to comfort me, but there's nothing he can do to fix this, and he's not the best at feely stuff, anyway. Of course, neither am I.

"A bath sounds nice," I tell him, knowing I don't have the energy to do any such thing. But I go into the bathroom and plug the drain, turning the water on high. The temperature doesn't matter because I'm not getting in. I just need the noise to cover up what's probably going to be an ugly cry.

Instead, I sit on the toilet lid, hugging my knees to my chest and closing my eyes. But the tears don't come. I just feel hollowed out, a shell of myself that doesn't even have the energy to let go of the pain inside me.

At some point, there's a knock on the door. "I'm okay, Zack.

I'm gonna go to bed after this. You can leave, but uh, thanks for coming to get me."

The door swings open. Damn it, people keep walking in on me in the bathroom tonight! But it's not Zack, it's Samantha.

"See, I told you she wasn't naked in here," Sam informs Zack sassily. Zack has his hand over his eyes, presumably because he thought I was naked in the tub.

"Luna?" Zack's voice is quiet but tight. He's probably upset that I lied to him too. Guess I'm making it a habit. The thought makes tears finally spill over, for some strange reason.

"I got this," Sam tells Zack, as though I'm not right here listening to them. She's pushing him out the door, trying to close it in his face, but he's not going easily.

Despite all evidence to the contrary, I tell him, "I'm okay."

It doesn't matter if he's here or Sam's here. All I'm going to do is sit and stew in my own mental anguish until I fall asleep. At most, I'll paint if I feel up to it so I can get these emotions out onto canvas.

Zack kisses my head, says something to Sam that I don't hear, and then the front door opens and closes. I realize I never heard Sam arrive.

"How long have you been here?" I ask.

"Long enough to know what's going on. Now, come on . . . let's go to bed so we can fantasize about ways to kill Carter Harrington without getting caught." Sam pulls the plug on the tub and takes my hand, pulling me to my feet. I don't even care that her hand is wet, something that would usually bother the hell out of me.

"Shoes off." I kick out of my Converse, leaving them in a pile, and then crawl into my bed, jeans and all, to clutch my pillow. She climbs in beside me, sitting up with her back against the headboard. "Good. Alright, I'm leaning toward taking him to a farm somewhere and letting the pigs have at him. I heard that's a good way to ditch a body."

She says it casually, as if a murder and body dumping fantasy is light conversation. I guess it's normal post-breakup, though I wouldn't know for sure since I've never broken up with some-one. Especially not after something like this.

Is it even a breakup if it was never real in the first place?

I shake my head.

"Too much? Okay, maybe we go the route of making his life hell instead? Normally, I'd say to freak him out with a STI scare, but that's not really possible here." She sounds sad about that fact, but it only reminds me that my only 'real' sexual experience is with Carter. I swear my body clenches at the thought of going back to only toys after knowing the way that Carter can make it sing. "What if we . . ."

I don't know how many ideas Sam comes up with. I think she's trying to make me smile a bit by the time she suggests spraying fart spray into his car's grill, laughing as she assures me it'll make his Mercedes smell like a shit box forever. Eventually, I fall asleep with Sam still making suggestions.

CHAPTER
TWENTY-SEVEN
CARTER

"MR. HARRINGTON WILL SEE YOU NOW."

Dad's assistant is professional as always, but I can sense doom in her almost sonorous voice regardless.

"Any hints on what's up?" I lift my brows, aiming for charming to pull any info from her, but it hurts and I wince sharply. I move to touch the bruise above my left cheek but redirect my hand at the last moment and straighten my tie, not wanting to invite more questions than the ones already in her eyes.

"I'm not at liberty to say," she responds politely, choosing to ignore the black eye like the pro she is.

"Of course."

I stand outside Dad's door for a second, steeling myself. I know this is about the Cartwright opportunity. I haven't told him about the shitshow from last night, but I have no doubt that he knows. Somehow, he always does. Like he can feel the disturbance in the atmosphere when something's up with his children.

And if he doesn't, he's going to know as soon as he sees me. I could have fought back against Zack, but I didn't. I deserved every lump he could dish out.

Entering the sanctum of my doom, I feign a casualness I don't feel. "Hey, Dad, what's up?"

"What the hell happened to you?" Dad hisses, visibly recoiling when he looks at me.

"Oh, it's fine. You should see the other guy." The joke lands flat, and Dad looks at me expectantly, silently demanding more of an explanation. "Zack and I had words. We'll work it out."

"Zack did that?" Dad sounds more impressed than angry. "Why?"

I don't get a chance to explain because Dad's speaker buzzes. "Mr. Harrington, your ten o'clock is here."

"Want me to come back later?" I ask, hoping for an escape.

Dad firmly points to a chair. "This meeting is about you, apparently. Sit down."

Confused, I lower to the chair as the door opens, but when Dad's assistant shows Claire Reynolds in, I stand up quickly. "What are you doing here?"

"Nice to see you too, Carter. Looks like you got a bit of what you deserved last night," she says smugly, gently touching the area below her eye.

"What he deserved?" Dad echoes harshly.

I'd like to think he's on my side and doesn't appreciate anyone suggesting that one of his children deserves a beatdown, but realistically, he probably just wants answers. And wants them now.

"He hasn't told you? Forgive me for letting the cat out of the bag," Claire says obsequiously, clearly gleeful to be the one to slip the knife in between my ribs. "We had dinner together at the Cartwright estate last night. It was *eventful* to say the least."

I see Dad's tiny flinch at hearing the Cartwright name. He thinks he knows what this is all about now. He ordered me to tell Elena the truth and assumes I did as much, making this his opportunity to smooth over the fallout.

Except he has no idea how deep this goes.

Dad turns on his trademark charm. "It's nice to see you again, though the 'eventful' comment has me worried." He stands to offer her a handshake, which she takes with a delicate touch.

"You should be, Mr. Harrington. I'm afraid I'm here with

some serious concerns." As she sits, she side eyes me to make her point clear.

Dad and I sit back down and dread fills my gut. I spent all night trying to figure out a way to fix this, but there's no coming back from it, no matter how much I wish it wasn't so.

When Zack came barreling through my door last night, shouting and throwing a clean hook to my eye followed by a punch to my gut before really getting to work, I let him. I didn't care because the truth was that I was thinking about Luna.

I was bent over and wheezing when Zack snarled at me. "I knew this would fucking happen. I warned you, thinking maybe you'd stop being led around by your dick and use your brain for a change. Especially with my sister."

"Is Luna okay?" I gasp out.

"No thanks to you, but yeah. She's home, bawling her eyes out with Samantha. You should lock your door because Sam's crazy as shit and will probably go for a little light BnE tonight and make what I'm about to do look like love taps."

"Aww, you do care," I grunt, smiling through the pain as he hammers me in the ribs again. Not the face, baby. It's the moneymaker.

"Fuck you, Carter. Leave my sister alone."

Standing but still hunched a bit, I clarify, "We still having lunch later this week?"

"Yeah. Your treat."

Zack had left, but I'd been stuck on the image of Luna crying and hadn't been able to focus properly on what I could do to fix this deal. Now, ready or not, it's showtime.

"I'm happy to hear any concerns you might have," Dad tells Claire, throwing the door wide open for her to fully destroy me.

She smiles evilly but schools her face into something more akin to concern as if she just remembered that she's not supposed to be smug about this situation.

"Dad—" I start, but he holds up a hand, cutting me off.

"Ms. Reynolds," he says, giving her back the floor.

"Thank you. I had concerns from the get-go when Carter approached my aunt, but after last night . . ." She fades off, making a clicking sound with her tongue. "Well, suffice it to say, I'm alarmed at the way he's represented Blue Lake Assets."

She looks around Dad's office as though it's a used car salesman's trailer, playing to Dad's deepest concern—the legacy of the family business.

"What exactly happened?"

"I think you have some idea, given that you also referred to Luna as Carter's wife during the dinner at your home." The accusation is bold, especially given the disappointed tone she adopts.

Dad sighs and shoots me a look of frustration before returning his attention to Claire. "Yes, unfortunately," he starts, weaving his fingers together on his desktop. "After dinner, Carter and I discussed that the *misunderstanding* about his marriage needed to be addressed. I presume this is about that."

Claire narrows her eyes, assessing Dad again. "Yes . . . and no. Carter didn't say anything about his marriage after our initial dinner. But I could feel something was off about them—I'm perceptive that way. And when I happened to see Luna out for a cozy dinner with another man? I knew I was right." She taps a fingernail to her temple as she nods, agreeing with herself.

I try to interrupt to explain, but Dad nearly imperceptibly shakes his head. I inhale deeply, biting back the words . . . for now.

"I tried to get Aunt Elena to see reason. But she'd had a meeting with Carter and our family financial planner and felt it'd gone well."

A tiny jolt of satisfaction shoots through me. I knew I'd aced that meeting.

"She wouldn't listen, no matter how many times I told her. She's gotten a bit stubborn and is quite scatter-brained. But she did talk to Luna and invite them over last night. I joined them, hoping to clear the air—"

"You mean gleefully accuse Luna of cheating on me with her brother?" I can't sit here idly while Claire paints herself as the picture-perfect niece trying to look out for the forgetful old lady. That's not at all what's going on.

"Carter," Dad says sternly.

"There may have been a misunderstanding there. I guess the dinner was with her brother." She rolls her eyes as if that's a mere minor detail, and then she drops another bomb. "But Luna was quite clear—although a bit hysterical—when she explained that their marriage was a sham . . . and then became quite real. Very real, by the looks of it."

Dad leans forward sharply. "Excuse me?" he demands of Claire, but then his eyes jump to me. "Carter, what is she talking about?"

I meet his eyes brazenly. "Lying doesn't suit a Harrington—something you've told me my entire life—so I made it the truth."

"I told you to *tell the truth*, not make it the truth!" he barks. "Did you actually marry Luna Starr?"

"I did." I nod, but then confess, "Though it's not going well right now."

Claire snorts out a laugh. "I'd say."

Dad's had about all he can take and turns on Claire. "I appreciate your bringing this to my attention, Ms. Reynolds. It appears Carter and I need to have a private conversation to discuss some family business."

She balks, probably wanting to see me get smacked down by Dad, but when he stands with his hand out, she has no choice but to follow suit. Claire shakes Dad's hand, again barely and delicately touching him, and then looks down her nose at me.

"Do not contact my aunt again," she orders. "Or I will be forced to take further measures." She lets the threat hang, and then with a steely glare, she whirls and walks out.

As soon as the door closes, Dad collapses into the chair and scrubs his hands over his face. "Carter . . . what the hell have you gotten us into?"

"Yeah, this is all about you," I snarl, done with his shit at least for a moment. "I've been working on this deal for weeks and it just blew up in a blaze of glory, but yeah, let's talk about you."

His eyes clear as they land on me. "Me? Try the company.

That's what I'm worried about, what I'm *always* worried about. And then you go and do something stupid like this and put everything at risk?"

I'm quiet, knowing he's right but unwilling to admit it.

"We'll have to get the marriage annulled," he declares, as if it's his decision to make. "Because I'm sure you didn't bother getting Luna to sign a prenup, right?"

"Luna's not like that. She's not after my money," I tell him coldly. I can't believe he'd even suggest such a thing. "And I don't want an annulment. I want . . ."

What do I want?

I'm not sure I even know. Or maybe I just don't want to admit it, because if I do . . . I can get hurt.

I'm angry at Luna, that's for sure, but I don't want to pretend this never happened. Because it did. I looked into Luna's eyes as we said our vows, I held her in my arms as she shattered in ecstasy, I listened to her dreams about how Alphena can change young women's lives, and more. Yeah, I'm mad, but I can't imagine life without her.

I want her.

I want Luna.

The insight hits me hard. When did that happen? I'm not sure I can pinpoint an exact moment, but somewhere in this crazy mess, I think I fell in love with Luna Starr. No, Luna Harrington. My wife.

And I want the Cartwright deal. I like Elena and her way of looking at the world. She doesn't take herself too seriously and wants to have a positive impact. I've enjoyed researching her portfolio and analyzing ways to maximize her investments so she can leave a legacy she's proud of. It's made me reconsider what I'm doing day-to-day and the legacy I want to have.

Is it living in Cameron's shadow at Blue Lake? Is it fighting to get Dad to see me as a professional peer? Or something else entirely? I do know I've had more fun with this deal than any I've ever worked on, and I don't feel remotely done with it. I want to keep going, keep working with Elena and the full scope of her estate.

Dad takes the opportunity of my quiet realization to jump in. "We don't always get what we want, Carter." He says it as though it's a divine, important lesson. "Let's just hope she'll sign the annulment so you don't lose half of everything." Thinking that's a valid threat or an actual possibility, he looks to the ceiling with a sigh. I don't know if he's praying Luna signs or praying for the patience to restrain from killing me. "I'll call our attorney and have the paperwork prepared. And for fuck's sake, don't tell your mother that you got married without her."

Like that's that, he begins typing on his computer. Probably sending an email to legal.

It's a clear dismissal. He's given the final word, and I'm expected to follow along like a good dog.

But not this time.

"No," I state firmly. "No annulment, and I'm not done with this Cartwright deal. And I'm certainly not done with Luna."

Before he can reply, I stride out of the room, feeling free in a way I haven't in a long time. Maybe ever. I have a mission—two of them.

Luna.

Elena.

In that order.

CHAPTER
TWENTY-EIGHT

LUNA

I HAVEN'T CALLED in sick a single day in the years I've worked at the museum . . . until today. I simply didn't have it in me to 'people' this morning. Instead, before she left for school, Samantha got us coffee and bagels, made sure I showered and put on fresh clothes so I 'felt cute', and then she set me up with my tablet to work. Okay, she called it 'drowning my emotions in a fantasy world' but it's the same difference.

After working on it for hours, I realized that my tablet had been at Carter's. I have no idea how it got here, but I'm glad to have it because I'm almost finished with this edition of Alphena. Writing has been going great, this edition nearly writing itself.

In this part, Alphena's showing a podcast dude the error of his misogynistic ways, and miraculously, he's coming around. Even more extraordinary, it's not because of her breasts but because of her brains.

"See . . . people can change," Alphena proclaims triumphantly on the page.

"Blah, blah, blah," I tell my alter-ego character, irritated that she's 'pro people' at a time I'd rather shut myself off from everyone and become a hermit. I stepped way out of my comfort zone and onto an unstable raft in a storming sea of lies and emotions. Those are two things I suck at the most, but I tried my best. I really did. It still ended up with me a confused and broken mess.

I know better. That's why I stick with scripts at the museum, close friends who know my strengths and respect my boundaries, and a fantasy world of my own design. It's easier that way.

Looking at Alphena's joy in her accomplishment, I consider scratching the last two chapters of happy resolution and instead, have Alphena throw Podcast Dude into a pit of snakes and let them go bitey-bitey on his balls and peen. That'd be more likely.

"Change *that*! Ugh!" I scribble on the tablet with my pen, and with a rumble of frustration, I toss it on the couch next to me. Flopping back, I curl up with a couch pillow in my arms. One-handed, I braid the strings of the pillow's tassels and consider what to do with my story. And my life.

It was fine . . . until Carter.

I'm furious with him but also disappointed in myself, which only makes me angrier for what we did. Last night, I reached my threshold and simply couldn't contain the truth anymore. It bubbled out of me, relieving a heavy pressure I didn't realize I was fighting.

I take a sip of the coffee that's been sitting on the table too long, annoyed that it's gone cold but still willing to drink it since it's sweeter than candy thanks to Samantha's care-taking efforts. The knock at the door annoys me too, as does the blanket that tries to strangle my feet as I get up.

"Let go," I tell the cuddly soft fabric that I usually love to cozy up with, dragging it halfway across the room. Finally, it does just before I throw open the door, annoyed with it too. "What?"

I figured it was Samantha or Zack coming over to check on me. What I don't expect is to see Carter standing there, grinning like a fool with a black eye. "Luna," he sighs right before he scoops me up into his arms.

My feet dangle toward the floor as he hugs me tightly. It feels so good to sink into him for a moment that my mind turns into fluffy fuzz and my whole body relaxes. Then I remember that I'm mad and I flail, kicking my feet and pushing at his shoulders. "Put me down."

My feet touch the floor gently, but Carter doesn't let me go. He cups my face in his hands as his smile grows by the second, and I swear he's a breath away from kissing me like nothing happened. "I missed you."

I shove him off. "No. Don't do that."

I stomp away, picking up the blanket and folding it carelessly. I lay it on the couch and then pick up my tablet, setting it on the table. That takes me to the coffee mug, and I carry it to the kitchen, pouring it out in the sink. Anything that'll get me away from Carter. Except he follows me into the kitchen, trapping me and making me wish I'd chosen an apartment with a more open floor plan.

"Luna, we need to talk." He sounds so sure that I'll do what he wants, but those days are over.

I've done too much for Carter already, and the end result is that I'm mad at myself and mad at him. "You should go." I put the mug into the dishwasher. "I have nothing to say."

"That's not true. You have so much to say, I can see the words jumbling together behind your eyes."

Carter's right, but telling him what I think won't do either of us any good. I want to walk away and pretend this never happened so I can go back to my comfortable, predictable life. "It doesn't matter. Just go."

I try to squeeze past him, but Carter grips my upper arms in his hands. "It matters to me, Luna."

Laughing bitterly, I jerk out of his grasp. "No, it doesn't. If it did, you wouldn't have dragged me into all this."

His eyes go wide. "Dragged you? As soon as I mentioned Thomas's collection, you were all aboard. Remember that?" I cross my arms over my chest, screaming at him with my eyes and hoping the lenses in my glasses amplify it like sunlight through a magnifying glass and he fries like an ant. He looks back at me, frustrated. "It's easier to fully blame me, though, isn't it? Guess you've decided I'm your all-too-convenient scapegoat."

I put some space between us, but there's nothing else I can do to keep my hands busy. I resort to fidgeting, wringing them together as I clarify, "I'm not blaming you. Or not *only* you. I was wrong too. I shouldn't have gone along with your stupid plan so I could see the art collection. No matter how amazing it is, it was wrong."

I've already given myself a hard time for that and don't need Carter to repeat the conversation or talk me out of the self-flagellation.

He takes a deep breath, his blue eyes locked on me. I feel like he sees everything—my nerves, my anger, and even the desire I'm shoving down so deep I can deny it exists. "That's not even why I'm here. I think we're well beyond that, and we both know it. I want to talk about us."

I laugh. "Us? There is no 'us'."

He jumps in immediately, stating, "But there is. We're married . . . *for real*. My dad's talking about annulments and prenups—"

"Is that what you're worried about?" I bark. "Fine. Show me where to sign and I'll put your mind at ease. I just want this whole thing to be over." I wave my hands around, wishing I could wipe this whole thing away with just a signature. If only it were that easy. But I'll never get Carter out of my heart, no matter how many times I sign us away.

"No!" Carter shouts.

The neighbor knocks on the wall and I yell, "Sorry!" Glaring at Carter, I snap, "This is done. Send me the paperwork and we can pretend this never happened. Should be easy for you. You're good at pretending." I know it's a low blow, but I'm too mad to care.

I don't blink, but I don't see him move. Regardless, I'm suddenly pressed against the counter, immoveable in Carter's grip, with him in my face. "This is *not* done. It'll never be done."

"What?"

I don't get to finish my question because Carter kisses me. His touch is powerful, his lips firm and his tongue demanding entry. I squirm, trying to get away, but he moans, and I'd swear it sounds like my name, but that doesn't make sense. This whole thing makes no sense.

He determinedly dances me down the hall, his unyielding mouth on mine the whole way. "It's real," he murmurs, laying a line of kisses along my jaw to my ear. "I don't know when, and I don't fucking care. But this. Is. *Real.*"

"No, it's not," I argue, but unconsciously, I tilt my head to give him better access.

He bites the tendon in my neck sharply, not enough to hurt but to get my attention, and I gasp. "You like that, don't you?"

I shake my head despite the heat pooling at my center. I feel Carter's chuckle more than hear it, the vibration making my heart race.

"Yes, you do. If I touch you right now, you'll be soaked for me, won't you?"

My body's response to him is nothing more than a biological response. How many times have I told myself that to keep my heart protected? But I know . . . it's not true. But just because my heart and my body are stupid doesn't mean I have to be, and their betrayal only makes me angrier. "Let me go, Carter," I command.

He smirks and releases me, except I didn't realize that he'd stepped me into my room, right up to the edge of my bed, and when he lets go, I fall back to the soft surface. I make a noise of surprise and scowl at him accusingly.

He steps between my legs and leans over me, his fingertips denting the mattress. At first, I lean back, trying to stay away from him, but when I see a teasing glint in his eyes, I freeze, stubbornly holding my ground. I expect him to stop too, but he doesn't. He covers my mouth with his again.

I stay still, but after a moment, I can't fight it. I kiss him back, demanding more. "I hate you," I growl into the kiss and then nip his lip with my teeth, knowing it's too hard but wanting to hurt him. "I hate you."

Unfazed, he shrugs. "I love you," Carter says as his hands cup my breasts. I laugh at the absurdity of that, and he pinches my nipples as punishment. Even through my shirt, the pain is sharp and . . . wonderful. I arch into his hands and he does it again. "I love you."

"You don't." I don't know why he's saying he loves me when there's no way it's true. Has he forgotten the truth of this whole situation? It's all for his deal.

We don't even like each other.

Well, I do like what he does to my body. The way he's sucking my nipples. He's pushed me back to the bed, pulled my shirt off, and is licking a long line along my cleavage as he holds my breasts together, and I definitely like that.

But I hate him . . . why was that again?

Oh, yeah, the lies. And when I told the truth . . .

"You left me."

"You left me first. Blew up my whole fucking world with that mouth of yours and then called Zack to come get you." He looms over me, pinning me in my place with his hand twisted up in my hair and a stony stare that reaches into my soul. "You left me first."

I try to shake my head, but it pulls my hair and I wince. Carter doesn't let go. Instead, he places his other hand around my neck and gets nose to nose with me as he squeezes. "I might've gotten us into this, but you made me fall in love with you, and now there's no going back, Luna. You're my wife, and that's fucking real."

"No, I . . ."

I'm so confused. I mean, I know Carter and I are married for real, as in we said vows, but it was all for the Cartwright deal, not so that we'd actually be married. We're too different and make no sense together. He's too old, I'm too young. He's too money-hungry, I'm too artsy. He's my brother's gorgeous best friend, I'm . . . me.

All arguments I've told myself a dozen times, but none of that seems to matter to Carter as he's ripping my sweats off, panties and all, and thrusting two fingers deep inside me. "Ahh!" I cry out, not in pain but in pleasure. "Carter!"

"Told you. Fucking soaked for me. Your husband."

"I hate you," I say again, but this time, there's no venom.

Carter knows exactly why I say it too. "I'll tell you as many times as you want. I love you. I love you. I love you."

Every time he says it, he pets that spot inside me that drives me to the edge near-instantly. I buck, not fighting him off but driving myself deeper onto his fingers, and touch my clit with my own fingers.

"God damn, that's so sexy. Rub that clit, hard and fast." That's already what I'm doing, but he praises me anyway. "Good girl."

A shudder rushes through me, and I feel my nipples pearl up into hard nubs. I'm burning up, but the cold of the room hurts the sensitive peaks. Carter notices and grips my breast firmly, kneading the flesh in his warm palm. "I shouldn't let you come for what you did. I should edge you over and over until you're sorry for leaving me."

I cry out at the idea, so close to coming already.

"But I won't." His fingers slam into me deep and hard. "This is my fault, and I'm sorry." Another stroke, adding a third finger and stretching me deliciously.

I'm going to be bruised and sore tomorrow, but right now, I want him to do it again, so I say the one thing I know for certain will make that happen.

I peer at him through half-glazed eyes and force out, "I hate you."

I see the half-smirk that lifts the right side of his mouth. And then he licks his lips and rapid-fire plunges his fingers into me, over and over. "I love you, Luna Harrington. My wife. Now come for your husband."

For him . . . for Carter freaking Harrington. I fly. Sparkles rush through me, or maybe I am sparkles? I don't know. I just feel like champagne as I soar through the blackness behind my eyes.

I hear a roaring in my ears and think it's my own heartbeat, but as I float back to consciousness, I realize that it's Carter. He's still fingering me so roughly that his knuckles are starting to hurt against my tender parts, but he's yanked his own pants open and he's mindlessly coming all over me as he jacks himself furiously.

His head is thrown back, the tendons at the sides of his neck standing out sharply, and his face is contorted with pleasure. The heat of his cum is hot on my skin, and instead of rubbing my clit now, I swipe my fingers through the fluid, spreading it over my bare pussy and up to my lower belly. "Cover me. Mark me . . . husband."

His head drops, his eyes open and clear as he finds me. I can see what he needs, but I'm still scared to believe him.

"Say it. Tell me the truth. I want your truth," he grits out.

I couldn't deny him even if I wanted to. Much like before, the words I've been fighting down spill out. "I love you."

He grunts approvingly as one last spurt leaks over his hand, and then he climbs on the bed with me. "Turn over," he orders.

I don't hesitate. I rip my shirt the rest of the way off as I lie on my belly, my glasses thrown aside as I press my cheek into the pillow I cried into last night. Carter has quickly stripped his clothes too, and I feel him kneeling behind me. He lifts my hips into the air and then slaps my ass hard enough to leave a handprint.

"Fuck, this ass looks pretty all flushed pink like this."

I wiggle slightly, and he chuckles darkly as he does it again. I'm expecting a third strike, but instead, he thrusts into me. I'm surprised he's still hard, or hard again when he just came, but there's no doubt that he is thick and solid. Despite being a mess of cum, I clench at the invasion. Not because I don't want Carter, but because I want to keep him inside me . . . always. Carter grips my ass, pulling my cheeks apart, and I feel vulnerably exposed. "You should see how well your pussy grips me. Pretty lips clinging to my glistening cock, sucking me back in every time I try to pull out."

He's thrusting in and out of me slowly, as if he has all the time in the world to study what I look like impaled on him. I moan, arching my back to encourage him to go deeper. Take me, mark me, fuck me . . . claim me.

He doesn't take the hint but rather runs his thumb through my juices and spreads them up to my ass. He circles the tiny knot of nerves there, exploring my reaction. "Talk to me. Tell me what you want, what you don't want. I know you know."

I do, but saying it is hard. Embarrassing, even, though it shouldn't be. I haven't tried anal play on my own, but right now . . . "Finger me . . . there." It's all I can manage, but it's enough for Carter.

"Breathe, baby. Relax and let me in." He dips his thumb in gently, and I cry out. There's pain mixed in this time, but it's a good pain? It doesn't make sense, but I don't care. Carter keeps his steady pace of deep strokes in my pussy and shallow dips into my ass, and intuitively, I move my fingers to my clit again.

It soothes the pain, turning it into a deep, pulsing pleasure, and in minutes, I've relaxed enough that we're able to go harder, though I sense Carter is being careful with me, watching for signs that it's too much. But not with his words . . .

"Shit, Luna. We've got forever together, and one day, I'm gonna be the lucky man who fucks your sexy ass. I want to fill you every way you'll let me."

It's too much, and I scream in ecstasy. The neighbor bangs on the wall again, and I think they yell, but I'm too far gone to be sure.

Carter puts two fingers in my mouth to keep me quiet, and I reflexively suck at them. It's like he's already filling me—in my pussy, in my ass, and in my mouth.

And your heart.

That's what truly makes me come harder than I ever have before.

Carter comes a moment later, and I moan around his fingers encouragingly as I feel the pulses deep inside me. He collapses, his chest pressed to my back as he pants heavily. I try to catch my breath too, but it's hard with his weight partially holding me down.

"Carter?"

"Now can we talk about us?" he says. I can hear the smile in his voice.

"There's more to talk about?" I tease.

He slips out, and I roll over so I can see him. Carter stretches out beside me, his head propped on one hand as his other fingers dance gently over my skin. "So much more to talk about, wife."

CHAPTER
TWENTY-NINE
CARTER

I'M SURE ABOUT THIS. In some ways, I'm actually surprised at how sure I feel about this. I'm a planner, someone who plots out points of success and tackles life until I reach each benchmark. But here I am, throwing it all in on what amounts to an underdog bet.

And underdog is not a position I'm accustomed to.

Approaching the door, I hold Luna's hand a little tighter, glad she's here with me because there are going to be questions for us both.

I ring the bell and clear my throat, ready to plead for my life. Or at least my professional one.

"Sir?" Stanley's greeting as he opens the door is less than friendly. In fact, with his expression, I'm ready for him to declare in a booming voice, *UNLEASH THE HOUNDS!*

"Hi, Stanley, good to see you again. How are you?" I'm going all-in with the charm, but he's giving me nothing, staying blank-faced and stone-still. "I was hoping Elena might be available to talk for a few minutes?"

I smile graciously, assuming he'll either say yes or at the least, go check with Elena.

"Sorry, Mr. Harrington. I've been instructed that you are not to see Mrs. Cartwright under any circumstances." His tone is flat, but there's something in it that tells me he's not sorry at all and really wishes I'd vanish from his employer's doorstep.

"Instructed? Who'd do that?" Luna asks, saying what I'm thinking.

He cuts his eyes to Luna, vacantly acknowledging her for the first time, and shrugs nonchalantly.

"Who told you that?" I repeat. But I already know. She told me as much when she came to see Dad and me. "Claire, right?"

He sighs in exasperation, seeming annoyed that we're asking. "Yes, Mrs. Reynolds. She's 'taking over some things here', apparently. Seems to think Elena's judgment is no longer fit."

"What? Elena's sharp as a tack," Luna argues.

"You didn't hear anything from me," he says, pulling a zipper across his lip and throwing away the key. "You'd best be going. I'd hate for Mrs. Reynolds to hear about your visit."

It sounds like a threat, as if he's the one who would do any tattle-tale telling to Claire, and then he shuts the door in our faces.

"What the fuck?" I say quietly.

Luna's eyes are big and round behind her glasses. "Do you think Elena is okay? I mean, Claire's a bit entitled, but this sounds more like . . ."

"A money grab?" I suggest worriedly. If it is, I'm almost tempted to kick in the door and the consequences be damned. Funnily enough, this old lady means something to me.

Luna presses her lips into a flat line, not liking the sound of that any more than I do.

We step off the porch, looking around at the quiet property. Off to the right, I see another familiar face. "Come on, let's ask Bernard."

"Hi, Bernard, how're your roses doing?" I ask. He doesn't even turn around, ignoring us completely. "Bernard? This is ridiculous. We just wanted to talk, see if you knew what's up with Elena and Claire. You don't have to be rude."

Completing trimming the bush he's on, he turns and screeches, jumping a foot into the air when he sees us. "Oh, my good gravy!" he shouts, pulling earbuds from his ears. "You two liketa scared the tar outta me. Why're you skulking about?"

He's angry and scolding us, but I chuckle at his word choice. "Sorry for the scare, didn't realize you had on earbuds. And we're not skulking. We're looking for Elena." I specifically don't mention that Stanley said we weren't welcome here. If Bernard doesn't know, I won't be the one to tell him.

"She's over in the greenhouse. Come on, I'll show ya," he grunts.

Now that I know he didn't hear me earlier, I repeat my question. "How're your roses doing?"

It's the right thing to ask because the whole way to the greenhouse, he talks about soil content and nitrogen levels, sounding more like a mad scientist than a gardener, while Luna and I nod along agreeably. When he opens the door, I can hear Elena singing. "We were swingin'. Just a-swingin'."

There's something about chocolate pie and fried chicken too, but I don't know what song she's singing. Hopefully, it's about an actual swing and not some upside-down-pineapple, swapping type deal.

"Ms. Elena! I found some trespassers out here. Whatcha want me to do with 'em?" Bernard says, his face impassive.

"What?" Elena says, but then she turns. I watch her eyes tick left to me, right to Luna, down to our clasped hands, and then back up to our eyes. "Oh, this I've gotta hear. Get on in here and tell me everything."

She's grinning widely, and her eyes are sparkling with delight as she waves us closer. Perching herself on the edge of a wooden stool, Elena looks like she's more than pleased to see us. She's wearing what probably amounts to her gardening clothes—polyester pants, a designer patterned shirt, and a sunhat. She pulls her dirt-covered gloves off, setting them on the edge of the pot she's working in.

"There's not a lot to tell," I try, but Elena chuckles and then Luna quietly joins in. "Okay, where do I start?"

"How about where you got that shiner?" Bernard suggests. "And was it deserved?"

It's as good a place as any, so I tell them about Zack coming over and popping me for Luna's honor. Luna frowns, seeming surprised by that news, and says she'll talk to him, but I don't need her to do that. Zack did exactly what I would've done, maybe less, if someone hurt my sister. Though Kayla and Luna are worlds apart in personality, and I'd be more scared that Kayla would hurt someone else than vice-versa.

"Then, Claire showed up to Blue Lake Assets to talk with my father about 'my behavior'," I drone, using finger quotes. I know I didn't react well, but running to my dad—and boss—is such a dick move on Claire's part.

Elena balks, her smile disappearing. "Excuse me, that girl did what now?"

"She's understandably concerned," I reply, giving Claire the benefit of the doubt. "So she asked that we no longer contact you."

"Yet, here you are." Elena gestures to Luna and me.

"I don't quit that easily. Plus, I don't follow orders very well, I'm afraid." I'm hoping that's a positive in Elena's estimation.

She grins slyly and elbows Bernard, confessing, "I do like a streak of rebellion in a man." He chuckles gruffly at her joking, sounding like an empty oil can, and I wonder how much of a rebel Thomas was. I think I would've really liked to know him, but learning about him through Elena is still a gift.

"I hope that's true because I have an idea . . ." I trail off, trying to entice her, but I'm not in sales mode. I'm going pure, unadulterated honesty and praying it's enough.

Elena claps her hands. "Let's hear it."

I look deeply into Luna's eyes as I speak to Elena. "First, we'd like to clarify the truth about us. At the minimum, you deserve that." Luna smiles back at me, and I can feel our connection weaving and growing between us.

Luna starts, telling Elena, "I'm sorry for my anxiety-driven info dump. I reached my limit because I don't usually do things like this."

Elena and Bernard laugh. "We couldn't tell," they tease.

The smile that Luna flashes is shy but grows in intensity, and

I enjoy seeing the way she comes out of her shell as she gets comfortable with people. I think I'll enjoy seeing it happen again and again for our whole lives. "Rude," she jokes back, poorly feigning anger before looking at Bernard. "And you weren't even there!"

He frowns. "You think we weren't all gossiping about your hissy fit after you left? Shoot, Stanley had the tea, Nelda made the tea, and I was hanging on every word as I drank every drop." He makes a slurping sound.

"Oh." Luna startles uncomfortably, not sure what to say to that, but she manages to share the facts. "Carter and I did begin as art tutoring, and you could say it didn't go well. He had the idea of bringing me along so I could speak to the art and he could focus on the finances. And then, it went haywire."

I continue the story, taking responsibility for my part. "I sprang the 'wife' thing on my family at the dinner, and my dad went ballistic afterward, ordering me to tell you the truth. I decided that rather than risk this opportunity by confessing, I would make the lie about our marriage true. Luna and I got married—for real—a few weeks ago. It was a tiny ceremony, and though it was with ulterior motives, I meant the vows I gave Luna."

Luna swats my shoulder. "You vowed to always put the toilet seat down and buy me flowers once a month!" Her laugh is high-pitched and happy with the quite reasonable promises.

"*And* that I would support you in your artistic endeavors, making sure that you always have time to create," I add. "And I do put the toilet seat down. I even got you one of those toilet nightlights so you could see if there are snakes in the bowl, despite living on the top floor of a building in the middle of the city."

Luna's worries might not always make sense to me, but if I can allay them with a simple solution, I'll do my best. Hell, even if it's a complicated solution, I'll still pull a rabbit out of a hat for her.

"Ooh, I like that. That's good," Bernard tells Elena, nodding and pointing a bony finger at me.

She shushes him. "Let them finish telling it. But remind me that I might want one of those light things too."

I smile, and when I explain further, I can feel that Elena is falling under my spell again. But this time, the spell is pure and genuine. "I love Luna. She's spun some web, some magic spell, and I'm a hundred percent in love with her. That's the gist of it. And she loves me."

Saying that aloud is powerful, giving this feeling a fresh sense of realness. I can't help myself and bend down to kiss Luna gently. Though my eyes are closed, I can feel Elena and Bernard looking at us, and then Elena lets out a loud '*woooo*' of encouragement that makes Luna laugh into the kiss.

"Sorry," Luna says, her hand covering her mouth.

I lay my arm over her shoulders, pulling her to my side. "I'm not."

Luna blushes adorably but leans into me.

"You two finally figured it out, then?" It's more of a statement than a question, and then Elena delightedly adds, "It's about damn time you pulled your heads out of your asses, because I've seen it since the beginning and was starting to think you were never going to get out of your own way."

"What?" I ask dumbly.

"You two didn't know each other from Adam when you came out here that first time. That much would've been obvious to a blind man, but even then, there was a spark." She flicks her fingers, as if she ignited us herself. "I could see it between you."

"You knew?" Luna's eyes are wide with shock behind her glasses. "Why didn't you say anything?"

Elena smiles slyly. "Of course I knew. You can't fool an old lady like me. I've seen damn near everything at least once in my life, so I was curious to see how it was going to play out. Look, I'm old. And forgive me, but excitement like this is rare. It keeps the world interesting enough that I want to stay around for a bit longer, maybe see a few more things."

I tilt my head. What she just said could come off as cold-hearted. But I get it, and I certainly can't be mad at Elena for letting us play out our own misguided scheme.

"It took a little longer than I thought it would. You two are a little slow on the uptake about matters of the heart, but I didn't want to spoil the moment for you."

"Spoil it for us?" I say flatly, as shocked as Luna.

"Of course. If I'd told you I knew, it would've been game over. If I told you I saw something between you, you would've denied it and bounced off each other like pinballs. It could ruin everything. No, I kept my mouth shut and let you do your thing, and now here we are, just like I knew we'd be." She hops from the stool and comes forward to wrap Luna and me in a simultaneous hug. She presses a grandma kiss to Luna's cheek and then mine before letting us go. "Now what?"

She sits back down, looking from me to Luna, and then leans over to Bernard and whispers, "I think this is gonna be the extra-good part." To us, she twirls a hand. "Well, get on with it."

Her reaction to everything is encouraging, and I hope she feels the same way about this next bit. "Actually, something you said inspired me," I tell Elena. She nods, murmuring that she says brilliant things all the time. I can't argue with that. "You told me that people end up in places they don't intend, and it's up to them to decide if that's where they want to be."

She slaps Bernard's shoulder, pleased with herself. "I did say that."

"When you said it, I thought of Luna and how I didn't intend to be married to her in the midst of this big pretend thing. I felt like you were telling me to decide where I wanted to be. But when I really thought about what you said, I realized I had the opposite issue. I ended up exactly where I always thought I'd be, only . . ." I swallow. This is hard to say, even though it's true, because it's big. A total redirection of my life. Luna leans into me, her shoulder touching mine in quiet support. But I'm ready, I've decided. "I'm not happy with it. I'm not happy with Blue Lake Assets, always feeling like I need to prove myself and coming up short."

A heavy weight lifts off my shoulders, and I feel like I can breathe for the first time. I've known that I would be a part of the Harrington legacy at Blue Lake since I was a boy. It was never a question for me or my family. It wasn't until I began deep diving into the Cartwright portfolio that I considered doing something else. *Being someone else.*

"What are you thinking about doing, then? Lemme guess . . . firefighter? Astronaut?"

"No, nothing like that. I love what I do, just not where I do it. I want a more personal connection with the people I work with."

Bernard snickers. "More personal than family?"

Before I speak it into existence, I search my heart once more for confirmation, but I know this is right. "With my clients. I'd like to be the personal finance manager for the Cartwright estate. Not as a part of Blue Lake Assets but as Carter Harrington. I've enjoyed examining what Mr. Oleana has done for you and figuring out ways to improve returns as you move forward. To be honest" —I grin at the intentional word choice— "your estate is large enough to warrant full-time, hands-on service, and I'd be honored to provide that."

I'm putting all my cards on the table, not holding back a thing, and hoping that Elena can respect that. Hell, I think I respect myself more than ever before, and that's got to count for something.

"Interesting," Elena hums. "You and me, directing everything the way you were talking about with Pat?" She doesn't seem to be asking me but rather repeating my proposal. "You think we could?"

"Absolutely." I'm one hundred percent sure of that. "We'll have to talk to Claire, though. Stanley told us that Claire is 'taking some things over' because your judgment is 'questionable'?"

"She said *what*?" Elena screeches, jumping down from her stool. "She's family, but I'm gonna tan that girl's hide. I've still got my wits about me. No doubt about that."

Elena seems to be determined to hunt Claire down right this minute, but a car engine growls outside and we run to the door to see what's wrong. It's Claire, speeding down the long driveway and then braking so hard the car jerks. The car's barely shut off when she jumps out, speed walking for the front door.

"Claire Luanne Reynolds, get your ass over here," Elena bellows in a voice that seems about twenty decibels too loud for a woman her size and age.

Luna whispers. "Ooh, her whole government name. She's in deep."

Claire doesn't hear Luna, but she damn sure hears Elena's order, and she whirls, the fire in her eyes hitting Elena and then spreading to me and Luna. Bernard seems to be the only one saved from her dirty look. "What are *you* doing here? I told you to stay away from Aunt Elena."

She's talking to me, and I'm quite willing to handle my own fights, but Elena puts a hand on her hip and starts dramatically waving the other one around. "I know you heard me. Get over here. I got some talking to do, and you got some listening to do, missy." Elena doesn't wait for Claire to get closer but rather bulldozes straight into it. "Are you seriously going around telling folks that I'm losing my mind? I'm sharp as a tack and more than willing to put one in your behind if I need to remind you of just how sharp I am."

Claire gives it right back, shouting in return. "Seriously? You must be losing your mind if you're talking to these bozos." She points at me, thankfully, because if her manicured finger had gotten anywhere near to Luna, I don't think I could stop myself from protecting her.

"I prefer Chief Clown Officer, if you don't mind, or CCO for short," I deadpan, which only incites Claire further. "It's a board-level position."

"Shut up," Claire snarls, like she can snap orders at me. To Elena, she says, "You can't work with Blue Lake Assets. I already told Mr. Harrington that any further contact by his office would be referred to our lawyer. Seems like I need to give him a call."

Her threat should worry me, and maybe later it will, but right now, I'm too caught up in the moment and blurt out, "Guess it's a good thing I'm not asking Elena to work with Blue Lake then, isn't it?"

That draws her up short. "What?"

Elena fills her in on my proposal, and Claire's anger grows exponentially with every word. "So you think you can waltz in here and take everything my aunt's earned."

I shake my head, incredulous that she'd suggest such a thing. "Of course not!" I say dangerously. "But isn't that the pot calling the kettle black? Why are you so worried about what your aunt is doing with her money?"

It's a question that keeps coming up in my mind. It makes complete sense for Claire to protect her aunt, but she's not doing that. She's protecting the money. Also logical, but there's something that doesn't sit right about it. "Are you trying to take control of Elena, her money, or both?"

Claire makes a sound that would be worthy of an internet meme for 'pissed off Karen' as she crosses her arms. "How dare you? You don't know anything about me. Like the fact that Mr. Oleana has been showing me how to reconcile the accounts for years."

"He what?" Elena shrieks.

"It's what Uncle Thomas wanted," Claire asserts with smug certainty.

Elena shakes her head vehemently. "Thomas could want in one hand and shit in the other, and see which filled up faster. You were never going to manage the money. It's a conflict of interest. You get your monthly allowance, same as I do, and leave the money-obsessing to someone qualified to do it."

Claire stomps her foot like she's a toddler. "Allowance? Is that what you call the pittance Mr. Oleana gives me? I can't live on that. Nobody can!"

Luna raises her hand. "I bet most people would be quite grateful to be given an allowance when they didn't do a thing to earn it besides be born into the right gene pool. Am I right?"

Luna's asking me, assuming that because my family has money too, I'll have an opinion on this. I do, but we're going to have to address her assumptions later because she's dead wrong. "I haven't gotten an allowance from my family trust since I was twenty-five and started working. Yes, I have a nest egg. It's there if I have an emergency, but I don't depend on it. My parents made sure that we all have a solid work ethic, know the value of a dollar, and that the only one we should spend is the one we earn. Seems like you missed that lesson, Claire."

"Well, at least I learned not to lie my way through life to get what I want," she counters harshly.

She's got a fair point there, so I nod agreeably. "My dad taught me that too. Shame I didn't learn it very well until recently." I noticeably take Luna's hand, unmistakably communicating that we are together. For real and forever this time.

"Wow," Claire sneers. "You must be really good on your knees." She looks at Luna with undisguised condescension, and I half-expect Luna to go feral on Claire. Deservedly so, in my opinion, and I'd grab my popcorn and cheer my girl on if it comes to that. Luna stays still, though, being the better woman she is, and not getting the reaction she wants, Claire casts a cold stare my way. "Or you really need someone who thinks your manipulative asshole act is charming."

"Claire!"

I hold out a hand, stopping Elena from whatever she's about to say in our defense. "It's okay. That's what she thinks. She's completely wrong, but this gives me a chance to correct her thinking." I take a step toward Claire, and she defiantly lifts her chin to return my hard look.

"Luna is good on her knees." Luna squawks behind me, but I quickly continue, "but that's only a small part of why I love her. She's strong, beautiful, chaotic, and sees the world in a way I can only dream about. She makes every day better just by being there. And maybe I am a manipulative asshole, but if so, Luna knows exactly who and what I am. She's probably the only one who does. And I didn't trick her into loving me, but for some reason, she does—all the good and the bad—so I try to be better every day, for her."

Claire huffs, her eyes rolling so far back into her head that she can probably check out her own non-existent ass. "You're not falling for this again, are you?" she asks Elena.

"I have fallen exactly one time in my whole life, and it was for one Mister Thomas Cartwright. I knew something was up with Carter and Luna from the get-go, same as I know you have Mr. Oleana using estate funds to pay for Jacob's piano lessons and several other bills, thinking I don't have a clue. I signed off on the damn charges, Claire. Same as I signed off on your allowance and the 'extra' one Thomas gave you years ago when you asked him and not me, thinking you could get around me."

She stares Claire down, letting that sink in. "You think you're pulling the wool over my eyes with any of that stuff? I know it's all about the money for you, but giving you money kept you away from Thomas because I knew you'd break his heart eventually, and I would do damn near anything to keep that from happening. All he wanted was a family, and you were the only blood he had left. But you're a greedy bitch. That money was a small price to pay to keep you at arm's distance."

Claire's mouth hangs open, her eyes wide in shock. "Why, I never!"

"We know," Bernard says. Quieter, he turns to me and Luna and says, "This has been a long time coming. Looks like I'll be the one with the tea tonight. Stanley'll be so mad he missed out."

Wait . . .

"You came in on squealing tires, running to stop us from talking to Elena. How'd you know we were here?" I already know the answer, but I'm curious to see if she'll fess up.

"What? I was just coming over to check on Aunt Elena and . . . I saw your car." There's an obvious delay as she tries to create a story on the fly.

"Stanley told you, didn't he?" I deduce.

Claire juts her chin out proudly. "He knows who'll inherit the estate eventually, and who'll be taking care of him. Or *not*."

"You did not threaten Stanley," Elena gasps. "That man has given his whole life to the Cartwright family and is basically family himself. How dare you?"

"It's the truth," Claire says. "He knows what's good for him, *who's* good for him."

Luna pipes up to add, "Not you."

I look at her in surprise, and she blinks rapidly. I'm not sure whether she meant to say that or only think it. But Elena's look says she's fully approving, and I suddenly wonder if Alphena might find a mentor in a kind old lady named Elena.

Elena's heard enough.

"Let's go talk to that man right now," she says, brushing off her backside with no shame. "I'm gonna tell him that he doesn't have to do a thing you say. I don't want him so much as getting you a glass of water if you're dying of dehydration. I won't let you stress that poor man out with this nonsense."

She starts toward the house, and we all follow like soldiers into war.

CHAPTER
THIRTY

LUNA

"AUNT ELENA . . . WAIT . . . STOP . . ." Claire is chasing after Elena, which speaks to how fast Elena is hoofing it across the side yard to the house. It doesn't help that Claire is wearing heels that keep sinking into the grass, but still, pretty impressive for a woman Elena's age.

Bernard grumbles, eyeing the holes Claire's leaving behind, and I have no doubt that he's cussing her a blue streak in his mind.

Elena barrels through the side door, already hollering. "Stanley! Stanley! Come here, you old coot!"

Nelda pops in first, clearly surprised and concerned. "Elena?"

"Where's Stanley?" Nelda's eyes widen in shock at Elena's angry tone, and her shoulders jump to her ears quickly. Elena yells again, and Nelda disappears as quickly as she appeared with Bernard following behind her. "Staaan-leeey!"

"Ma'am?" Stanley answers, hurrying down the hall. He's more disheveled than when Carter and I arrived. His hair is standing up as if he's been running his fingers through it, and his tie is pulled down several inches from its proper place. His eyes jump to Claire, and he visibly shrinks away from her.

Elena whirls on Claire. "What in the Sam Hill did you tell him? He's terrified of you!"

Claire flinches, but Elena doesn't really want an answer

anyway. She turns back to Stanley, pointing a finger at him. "You listen and listen good, Stanley Hodgins. Whatever she's told you" —she turns her finger to Claire so that she's crystal clear— "is a big pile of steaming dog shit and nothing more."

"Aunt Elena, you're hysterical," Claire coos. "You should sit. That'll help you calm down."

Claire tries to prod Elena toward a chair, but Elena jerks her arm out of Claire's grip. "Don't talk to me like I've lost my marbles. I'm as clear-headed as I've ever been, and you're the same overbearing meddler you've always been."

Claire makes a noise of disbelief, clutching invisible pearls. I'm starting to see that reaction as a forced move she thinks makes her look innocent. She did it when Jacob said something she didn't like, and now she's doing it when Elena does the same thing.

Elena huffs. "Oh, save the dramatics. You aren't Scarlett O'Hara, that's for damn sure."

"Ma'am?" Stanley leans between the two women. "What's going on?"

"You tell me," Elena counters. "Did Claire tell you that you owed her some sort of loyalty? Threaten you?"

Stanley looks back and forth, seeming unsure what to say or who to speak against. "I . . . uh, I . . ."

Elena shakes her head in disbelief, her eyes sad. "She really did a number on you, didn't she?"

I burrow into Carter's side, not liking the tension, and he takes my hand, running his thumb over the sensitive skin. Between the distraction of his touch and the support of his arm pressed along mine, I settle, but I don't like the arguing.

"Not that you're hysterical, but sitting down to get all this into the open might not be a bad idea." Carter's recommendation is much more well-received than Claire's, mostly because it comes from a well-intended place rather than Claire's condescension. I think he's also suggesting it thinking it'll help me feel more comfortable.

Elena presses her lips together and glares at Claire. "Yeah, let's do that. First, though, Carter, call your father and have him get out here for dinner."

Carter nods. "Sure, when?"

"Tonight. *If* you meant what you said." Elena raises a brow sharply, questioning.

I squeeze Carter's hand supportively. We talked about this last night, Carter's feelings about his family's company, his role there, and his dreams for the future. I listened as Carter analyzed every angle, even deep-diving into the emotions of what being a part of his family means and whether not being at Blue Lake would change that. We didn't come here lightly, and Carter didn't pitch himself to Elena casually.

Carter pulls his phone out of his pocket and calls while Elena herds Claire and Stanley into the front room.

"Hey, Dad, it's a long story, but I need you to come to Elena Cartwright's for dinner. Leave now. I'll explain when you get here."

He's quiet, listening for a moment.

"No. Tonight. It's important. Please."

Carter sighs in relief. "Thanks. See you soon." He hangs up and puts his phone back in his pocket. "He's coming."

"You're really sure?" I ask. "Last chance to make a run for it." I tilt my head toward the front door with a smile, already knowing his answer.

He smiles in return, the full charm version. "Let's check on Claire." I raise my brows in surprise, and he clarifies, "To see if Elena is done raking her over the coals yet. Is it bad that I want to see that?"

I whisper back, "I hope not because I kinda want to see too."

In the front room, we find Elena reigning in a chair, with Claire and Stanley sitting on the couch, each of them hugging the ends to put as much space between them as possible. Claire's cheeks are flushed and her eyes are hard, glinting with barely restrained anger.

Stanley is frozen, other than his eyes pinging back and forth between the two women. He looks, sadly enough, like a beatdown dog that just pissed the rug and is wondering where the whooping's coming from first.

"Carter?" Elena pauses whatever rant she was on to check in. Carter dips his chin affirmatively. "Good. Now, where were we?"

Silently, Carter guides me to the loveseat and then sits beside me, keeping my hand in his. I'm thankful for the distraction as they begin their conversation again, Stanley raising a finger. "You were talking about Thomas's will."

"Right. Thanks." She points at Stanley. "Thomas's will left everything to me, obviously. Mr. Oleana has managed our family estate for decades and only recently decided that he would like to retire. I've got a financial brain, but managing your own estate when it's this large isn't optimal. I'm too close to it. It needs someone with some objectivity, like Carter."

Claire huffs. "Over my dead body."

"That can be arranged," Elena replies, her brows climbing to her forehead with the threat. Claire glares back angrily through narrowed eyes. "As I was saying, Carter is going to coordinate with Pat so that the transition is seamless. And if you're thinking you only have to wait until I kick the bucket, know that my will does not leave everything to *you*." Elena points at Claire this time. "Under no circumstances will you receive any more than what Thomas wanted you to have—a reasonable monthly stipend."

"What?" Claire snaps.

Elena focuses on Stanley. "Exactly like the rest of you."

"Me?" Stanley questions, his brow furrowed in confusion.

"Of course. You, Nelda, Bernard. Y'all are family." Elena's eyes have gone soft as she tells Stanley what he means to her, what he meant to Thomas. "Just as much—if not more—than other people."

"You can't be serious!" Claire shouts as she stands, her hands on her hips. "That's my money! I'm family . . . blood! Not the hired help! I deserve it! It's mine! Uncle Thomas wanted me to have it!"

Every word she says has an exclamation mark after it, and her voice gets louder and higher as she ramps up. I cringe away from the noise, shrinking deeper into the loveseat, and feel voyeuristic. This is a family matter, and I'm not sure Carter and I should be here for this.

Elena stands slowly, her eyes hard. "Claire, you're mistaken. That money is not yours and will never be. And Thomas was a brilliant, loving, amazing man who cared for you very much. But he and I had conversations about this. The estate and you. I truly don't know where you came up with this idea. It was never either of our intentions, and this only solidifies that feeling." The coldness has melted away, leaving Elena seeming more hurt than anything by Claire's actions and expectations.

Trying to intimidate Elena, Claire threatens, "I'll get a lawyer."

Elena chuckles mirthlessly. "With what money, dear? Do you think I'm going to fund a suit against myself?" She tilts her head. "You should be thankful for what you have, Mads, Jacob, and an allowance that lets you live quite comfortably."

Claire presses her lips together, and I can see her mind working behind her eyes. "Increase my allowance by twenty percent or you'll never see Jacob again."

Whoa. Claire's more evil than I thought. Would she really keep Elena's grandchild from her over money?

Elena sighs sadly. "What kind of mother would use her child that way?" But Claire's not giving in. She crosses her arms, standing her ground. Elena walks over to a picture on the mantel, touching the frame gently right below Jacob's face. "I see. You know I love Jacob with all my heart, and of course, I wish to see him."

Claire smiles victoriously and her eyes light up. It's like she's tasting her success. Completely disgusted, I glance to Carter, who's stone-faced and gritting his teeth.

"I don't like extortion, but if that's the game you want to play?" Elena looks over her shoulder, double-checking whether Claire truly wants to go down this road. Claire shrugs, unbothered by the accusation. Elena inhales deeply, pinning Claire with a curious look. "I see. Well, very well, then. Remember, it was your choice to play hardball. I *will* continue to see

Jacob . . . if *you'd* like to continue receiving an allowance. At all."

"What?" Claire exclaims. "You can't do that!" She fists her hands at her sides, angry, but I don't think she'd actually get physical with Elena. Her M.O. doesn't seem to be bold confrontation, given she's been lurking in the shadows of Thomas and Elena's dealings for years.

"I certainly can. It's still my signature on *all* the financial dealings. Guess I've still got some wits about me, don't I?" Elena says. It's a gloat, but she truly seems pretty sad and disheartened by this whole conversation.

Claire seems to have lost her steam because she clamps her mouth shut, glares hellfire and damnation at Elena, and then walks toward the door. As she passes Carter, she sneers at him, "This is all your fault."

Carter flashes his cocky grin, the one that made me hate him for so long, and Claire growls as she stomps out. A few seconds later, the front door slams.

Changing directions, Elena shakes her head woodenly but meets Stanley's eyes. "You, dear friend, have nothing to worry about. You've given your life to this family, and we will take care of you for the rest of yours. I would never subject you to *that*." Elena jerks her head toward the door where Claire disappears. "When you're ready to retire, my friend, just say the word."

"Thank heavens," Stanley says with obvious relief, wiping at his eyes. "Elena, I'm sorry. That woman has been killing me. Tell me this, do that. What she said made sense, and though I'm loyal to you, I didn't want to be isolated from your family."

Elena walks to Stanley, who stands. "You are my family. Me and Thomas always felt that way, and I'm sorry if we didn't let you know that sooner."

She embraces Stanley, who stays still for a moment before wrapping his arms around her too. A quick second later, he pulls back. "Ma'am." He dips his chin once, deferentially. "Should I tell Nelda to expect guests for dinner?"

Elena smiles. "Please."

Stanley escapes, seeming glad to get away from all the drama and shouting, and Elena turns on Carter and me. "First order of business. We need to quadruple-check that every bit of paperwork lists out Claire's access and allowances. That is . . . if you'd still like to work for the Cartwright estate after all that?"

Carter holds his hand out. "It would be my honor."

"Good. I thought maybe that'd scare you off and I'd spend dinner with your daddy telling him that I'm snatching you from his good graces."

Carter chuckles. "No, I'm with you. But fair warning, Dad's probably going to make your little tiff with Claire look like child's play."

CHAPTER
THIRTY-ONE
CARTER

"ALL RIGHT, we're here. And you are not supposed to be, so what the hell is going on?" Dad growls under his breath as he and Mom come in the door. He manages to look both furious and disappointed at the same time. Mom places a calming hand on his arm, and judging by the tension around her eyes, the drive to Elena's wasn't pleasant.

"Good to see you too, Dad."

I'm lying through my teeth again, something I swore to not do. Which is why I'm glad Dad's here. I'm ready to move forward with Elena, but the process to get there is going to be painful at best. It'll be tough love honesty for both of us.

Dad looks past me and sees Luna and Elena, who've been chatting about the various art pieces in the front room. I think Luna is basically on cloud nine, hearing the detailed stories of how Thomas acquired each and every piece directly from Elena, and Elena is enjoying sharing Thomas's excitement with someone who wants to hear every detail.

It's actually been really helpful. After the drama with Claire, I think Elena was wiped out. It's not every day you have to assume a mantle you may not like and handle things with that much cold, hard strength. But Luna's light and joy have steadily filled Elena back up, and she's returning to the whip-smart, funny woman she normally is.

"Carter?" he says in a warning tone.

"Mr. Harrington, it's so good to see you again." Elena approaches with her hand outstretched and a smile the belies the drama of today. "Thank you for coming on such short notice."

Dad raises a brow, side-eyeing me as they shake. "I wasn't exactly given a choice."

"Charles," Mom says, smiling congenially in an attempt to smooth over Dad's gruffness. "We're delighted to come, of course," she tells Elena. "Good to see you too, Luna."

Luna steps forward, offering her hand to Mom. "Thank you."

She returns to my side and gives me an encouraging smile. She knows how worried I am about this conversation with Dad, but also how resolved I am.

"Why don't we come in here and sit down?" Elena says. "Let's eat and talk."

Elena doesn't wait for agreement, simply walking to the formal dining room. She's putting on the mantle again, ready to turn it on Charles Harrington if necessary.

The vibe is very different from the kitchen table where Elena usually eats. It's heavy, formal, as close to regal as we get in America. Following her, we sit around the dark wooden inlay table with Elena at the head, and Nelda appears with a bottle of wine to pour a glass for each of us.

"Ready for salad?" she asks Elena, who nods in answer.

When Nelda disappears back into the kitchen, Dad's patience runs out. "Not to be rude, but what is going on here?"

Elena chuckles. "No worries at all. I understand my niece, Claire, made a visit to you recently?"

"You could say that," Dad agrees warily. "Why?"

"Let's just say she's a bit of a brat, that one," Elena grumbles. "Hasn't met a boundary she didn't want to cross. And that includes coming to see you. She shouldn't have done that, shouldn't have spoken for me or the estate."

Dad's eyes light up. "You mean Blue Lake Assets is still in consideration to manage the Cartwright portfolio?"

Elena looks to me with a warm smile. "Something like that."

Dad jumps right into selling Blue Lake again—how it started, how it's grown, how his leadership has led to a broad base of successful partnerships on several fronts. He might as well be tooting a horn that screams his own name, completely ignoring the fact that I'm the one who sought out Elena, got to know her and her portfolio needs, and has been dealing with her this entire time.

Not once during his impromptu presentation does he mention my name. Not through the salad course, and not as Nelda sets down plates with roast chicken and root vegetables.

"Interesting," Elena says dryly when Dad finishes his one-man show. Thankfully, she's not impressed at all. She might as well be yawning in boredom.

That's why this is going to work between us. I don't want a formal, impersonal relationship with my work. It's my passion, and I want to do my best, confident that it will be recognized and appreciated.

That'll never happen with Dad, but it will with Elena.

"Though Claire might've overstepped, I've decided to go another direction with the management of my portfolio. No hard feelings?" Elena asks, then takes a bite of her carrots.

Dad's smile melts and his eyes jump to mine as he realizes what Elena's saying. There's anger there. Despite his whole riga-marole show, he thinks I'm the one who somehow blew this for Blue Lake Assets. He has no idea what I'm capable of.

"Dad, I've learned so much from you—how to be a man and how to be a businessman. And I will always be grateful for those lessons. But recently, I've been feeling like there's a world out there for me that I haven't explored. A world beyond Blue Lake."

Mom's jaw drops open as she gasps, "Carter?" In contrast, Dad's jaw goes tight as he clenches his teeth.

"Effective immediately, I will begin my own firm—Carter Harrington Asset Management."

"You are not serious," Dad grunts as he rolls his eyes dismissively. "Carter, you're good, and one day, you'll be great. But not yet. You're not ready."

I want to rant and rage, tell him how wrong he is and that I need his support, not condemnation. But that won't help matters. If anything, he'll see it as affirming his thoughts about me. So I take a deep breath and meet his eyes boldly.

"I feel I am. But I can never know for sure as long as I'm in the Blue Lake shadow, always worried about playing second fiddle to my father . . . or my brother," I tell him honestly. "I am doing this, Dad. I'm leaving Blue Lake and striking out on my own. I plan to—"

Luna places her hand on my thigh beneath the table. Her support means everything as I tackle this. I lay my hand over hers, weaving my fingers through hers.

"I'm taking over the Cartwright portfolio for Elena. Luna and I are married for real and staying that way because we're in love."

Boom. Boom. Boom.

I drop all the bombs at once, each feeling so important that I can't hold one back in favor of the other. I want to shout it from every rooftop so that everyone hears.

So that Mom and Dad hear.

Dad laughs disbelievingly. But Mom skips right over the Cartwright part and squeals, "Carter! Luna! You're married? For real?"

Elena leans back in her chair, watching the scene before her like she orchestrated it herself. Hell, maybe she did somehow. "Now that's a proper show-off. Let the games begin," she murmurs.

My parents are the loudest reaction, but my focus is on Luna. I want to protect her from any shrapnel my bombs might have. She's my priority, and this is the type of thing that could make her panic again. I won't let that happen.

I hold up a hand. "Let me explain."

Dad pushes back from the table sharply, standing to try and lean toward me. With his hands planted on either side of his almost-empty plate, he roars, "Explain? There's nothing to explain. You've lost your mind."

He's completely forgotten that Elena is here to witness this breakdown. But I'm doing my best to remember that and behave accordingly—as the strong and professional person she can entrust with her most valuable assets. It's hard when my ego wants me to stand and roar back at my father.

Gritting my teeth, I manage to say, "I'm managing Elena's portfolio. And I love my wife, Luna."

I take her hand from my lap, pressing a kiss to the back of her hand to reiterate, and then give Elena a grateful nod. She was right to keep her nose out of things and see how they played out. Because this is what matters. This is the life I'm creating for myself, the one I'm choosing.

"Charles, let's hear him out," Mom suggests as she tugs at his sleeve, trying to get him to sit back down. "I want to hear about this marriage."

That's Mom.

Both of my parents care, though they show it in such different ways. Mom's always worried about our mental and emotional well-being first, while Dad wants to make sure we're putting food on the table and upholding our reputations.

"The details don't matter, that's between Elena and me. We have worked out how Mr. Oleana will transition responsibility over to me so he can retire. It's done," I declare, shutting the door on the business side of things to focus on what Mom wants to hear about. "The important thing is that Luna and I are together, happy and in love."

"He is so much like you," Mom says out of nowhere, looking at Dad fondly. "Remember when you were full of piss and vinegar like that, so ready to tackle the world that you wouldn't let anything hold you back?" She laughs lightly, and Dad frowns at her. But he can't stay mad at Mom. He's never been able to.

Dad chuckles unintentionally. "I didn't run off and get married for a business deal," he counters as he jerks his head toward me, talking as if I'm not sitting right here to listen. But his tone is much lighter as Mom works her magic on him.

"No, we got married because we had a deal of a different sort and you didn't want to tell your dad. Surprise!" She waggles her eyebrows at Dad, and I realize what she's insinuating.

"I thought Cameron was born early?"

Elena pats my hand, explaining kindly. "That's just what we used to say when the baby was born seven or eight months into the marriage, dear. And polite folks went along with it and told you how nice it was that the baby was so big for being early."

I blink, looking at Mom and Dad in shock. How did I not know this? It doesn't change anything, not really, but there's also a sense of satisfaction that maybe Dad wasn't always perfect.

Dad fidgets with his fork, examining his plate and his thoughts. When he looks up at me, he asks, "Are you sure?"

I don't know if he's asking about the portfolio management or Luna. It doesn't matter because the answer's the same either way. "Absolutely."

Dad turns his eyes to Luna, who surprisingly meets his and holds his gaze. "Are you sure about this idiot?" There's no hate in the name-calling. It's more of a tease.

Luna frowns, but there's a glint of humor in her eyes. "There's a fine line between love and hate, but yeah, I'm sure."

She grins at me, proud of herself for the dig. In reply, I lean in, closing the gap between us and placing a sweet kiss to her lips. We did it. Together, we've gotten through a gauntlet of battles today, and I couldn't have done it without her at my side. Too quickly, she pulls back and I can see her blushing furiously at the public display.

"Y'all are too cute," Elena declares.

I nod and tell Luna, "Yes, you are."

CHAPTER
THIRTY-TWO
LUNA

"ARE YOU SURE?" Samantha asks me, triggering a sense of déjà vu.

But this time, there are butterflies of a totally different sort. "You asked me that last time I got married too."

Samantha tilts her head. "Yeah, and you told me no. Now?"

I take a moment, searching my head, heart, and soul. It's been a few weeks since the big dinner at Elena's. During that time, so much has changed, but it all feels . . . *right*, which is unusual for me. I typically hate change, but moving in with Carter, living as husband and wife, and exploring our love for one another in many ways and many positions have been revolutionary. For us both.

I meet Samantha's eyes in the mirror and smile. "I've never been surer of anything."

"Ooh, I like that confidence!" she replies with a shoulder shimmy. "Let's do this thing, then."

'This thing' is a vow renewal. Melinda mentioned wishing she'd been present for our first wedding, and Carter and I had talked about it. After we realized that we would like to include our families in our wedding, we've worked to pull together a small, intimate celebration.

Samantha and I walk downstairs into the front room of

Elena's home. It'd seemed the perfect place to have the ceremony because it's what brought us together in the first place.

"I'll be right back. Let me check to see how close to showtime we are," Samantha tells me as she hustles out of the room, leaving me alone.

I look at the painting over the mantel, one of Thomas Cartwright done by the subject himself. His self-portrait seems to look back at me. "Thank you for all this," I tell him. "As much as Elena brought Carter and me together, it was you, too. Your art, your collection . . . if it weren't for you, there would've been no need for us to pretend to be married in the first place." I step closer, laying gentle fingers on the corner of the frame, careful not to touch the canvas. "Thank you."

"Hey, honey, I think we're ready if you are!" my mom says brightly as she comes in the room. She looks up at the painting, smiling happily. She doesn't understand my love of art, but she's always supported it, and finding me staring at a painting on one of the most important days of my life doesn't surprise her in the slightest.

"I'm ready, and thanks, Mom. For everything." I wrap my arms around her, and she hugs me back gently so as not to mess up my dress or hers. She's been amazing with all of this, welcoming Carter with open arms as my husband, already having heard all about him from the years of Zack working with him.

"You know she'll do anything for you, Moony," Zack says from behind me.

Mom and I pull apart, turning to face Zack. He's grinning widely, leaning on the doorframe. "Would you look at you two? Absolutely stunning."

Mom's wearing a soft blue cocktail dress that makes her look glowy. It matches the blue shirt that Zack has on. He looks sharp, but casual. My white dress is the same one I wore previously. It felt important to wear it again because though our relationship is different now, the vows that Carter and I spoke before are still just as true. Today, we're expanding them, not rewriting them.

"Not so bad yourself, Zack Attack," I reply. "And Mom would do anything for either of us."

"That's what moms are for." She shrugs like she's no big deal, but Zack and I both know she's amazing. "We do need to get a move-on. They're ready for you."

Samantha pops her head around the corner. "Yes, they are. Elena sent me to find you." She pauses, her eyes scanning the room. "One question, though . . . all of Carter's family is here, right? There's basically a whole Baywatch cast of blonde, beautiful people out there."

"Oh, I don't think so. Chance is out of town for work, and who knows with Cole. He kinda comes and goes whenever he wants to. But the rest of them should be—his brother Cameron with his daughter Grace, his sister Kayla, and his youngest brother, Kyle—who actually doesn't have blonde hair but his dog, Peanut Butter, does. Plus, Charles and Miranda."

It's a whole gaggle, but I'm learning to love them all. We're going to make a new family, and I can't wait to introduce Mom to all of them. Together, we walk toward the back door. I'm ready for this—to continue my story with Carter.

Grace is standing just outside, holding a white basket tightly in her hands. "Drop the petals. Don't throw the petals," she murmurs to herself urgently. "Drop the petals. Don't throw the petals."

I'm guessing Cameron gave her the mantra to repeat because without it, she'd likely be making it rain white rose petals in a joyous display of youthful exuberance that is Grace. She already managed to talk Carter into letting Peanut Butter be the ring bearer, claiming he's the closest thing to a bear we have. And no amount of explaining that ring bearers aren't actual bears like Smokey could convince her otherwise.

"You're gonna do great," I tell her. When I was her age, walking alone or with a dog down an aisle of people watching me would've been horrifying.

"Of course, I am," she says confidently. Grace is obviously nothing like me. It took me much longer to find anything close to that comfort with myself.

"Go for it, then," Samantha tells the girl, tapping her on the shoulder as the music starts.

Standing off to the side, I see Bernard hand Peanut Butter's leash to Grace and give her a thumbs-up. She sets her shoulders and walks slowly out of view . . . step, together, pause and drop petals, step, together, pause and drop petals.

Zack offers his elbow to Samantha, and they walk out together. Almost too quickly, it's just me and Mom, and I feel like apologizing to her that we didn't get the whole wedding-planning mother-daughter experience, but at the same time, I'm not sure I would've managed all that very well. It's a lot of pressure and a lot of focused attention. Once upon a time, I would've fought my own anxieties to do the expected things for everyone else's comfort, but now? I'm proud of who I am and more confident speaking up about what I want and don't want. And this 'wedding' is perfect. For me.

And that's good enough for Carter.

"I always hoped you'd find someone who would love you exactly as you are, Luna." She takes my elbow and smiles affectionately. "That's not always possible for the easiest of us, and I think we both know that as wonderful as you are, you're not easy. You require people to be more. You see through them otherwise. But you don't open yourself smoothly. You're one step forward, two steps back. Sometimes, a whole leap back." She grins, laughing lightly.

"Wow, thanks. I'm really feeling the love, Mom." My dry delivery undercuts that I know exactly what she's talking about.

"Let me finish," she instructs me. "When you and Carter look at each other, I can see it. He loves you, Luna, and doesn't want you to be anyone other than who you are. And though I never imagined you with a 'suit', when you look at him, I can see how much you love him too."

"Thanks," I say more sincerely.

She wraps her arm through mine, and we step down the aisle together. There's a small gathering—the Harringtons, Samantha, Zack, Elena, Nelda, Stanley, and Bernard—but I don't notice anything except Carter. Mom has to hold me back from running to him. But even with as slow as she's going, in a blink, I'm in front of him.

"Hi," I whisper, waving with my free hand. But I forgot I was holding flowers, so it looks like I'm flapping them around.

"Hi," he answers with a sexy smile that makes me glad he's my husband. He knows me, knows I'm awkward, and loves every second of it.

I hand off my bouquet to Samantha and take Carter's hands. The officiant speaks, but I'm lost in Carter's eyes and don't really register the words until he asks, "Does anyone have any reason these two people shouldn't be married today?"

It's not the question that gets my attention, but Zack clearing his throat. Carter whirls, his eyes wide and incredulous.

Zack grins back. "I was just gonna say that you can't 'be married today' because you're *already* married." He slaps a solid pat to Carter's shoulder. "You're my best friend. You weren't worried I was actually gonna object, were you?"

"No, of course not." Carter totally was.

I kinda was too, even though Carter and Zack are fine now. They've continued their business, with Zack picking up another small property to flip just last week. Though Carter spends all his professional time working on the Cartwright estate, he and Zack spend the occasional lunch or hang out time here and there, talking business and investing what Carter calls 'fun money'. Zack, on the other hand, calls it his livelihood, but it works for them the same way it always has.

"May we continue?" the officiant asks. When Carter and I look back to him, he nods. "I understand you've written your own vows. Please proceed."

Carter licks his lips and for the first time, I see nervousness in his expression. We're already married, so it's not like anything he says here will change that, but this is important to us both.

"Luna, I wish I could offer you pretty words or art that'd make you feel how much I love you because you deserve the moon, the stars, and more. Unfortunately, all I'm offering is me. I hope it's enough because I love you. I will always love you. We started with lies and chaos, things I know you don't like, but they were somehow the perfect beginning to something real. I vow to always be truthful with you and with myself, to protect your heart as if it's my own, and to stand in front of you when you need a moment to hide, beside you as we tackle life together, and behind you when your badass comes out. All versions are equally you and equally beautiful to me."

"Wow," I breathe, and everyone giggles, which makes my cheeks hot. I clear my throat, trying to remember the words I've practiced dozens of times, but they're gone. My mind is completely blank.

"It's okay," Carter says quietly, reading me again. "Look at me. It's just us."

I fall into Carter's blue eyes again, like I have so many times now, and see the warmth and acceptance there. I don't need my practiced words. I know how I feel.

"I hated you, and then you tricked me into this situation that made me uncomfortable. But those aren't bad things. You pushed me to grow and showed me that things aren't always what they seem. And in more ways than one, you made my dreams come true. And now, we have a lifetime to create our future and become whoever we want to be . . . together. I vow to bravely go with you on this journey and enjoy every step along the way . . . even when we have to take a step backward to truly go forward." I glance over at Mom, and she's tearing up that I used her words in my vows.

"Lovely," the officiant says. "And now, you may seal your vows with a—"

Carter doesn't wait for him to say kiss. By the time the officiant says the word, I'm already in Carter's arms with his mouth on mine. His lips move against me, promising even more than his vows did, and I kiss him back with just as many promises.

We did it. Well, we're already doing it since we're technically —legally—already married, but we did it again! I just hope we don't have to keep having wedding ceremonies and proposals because I'm kinda over the public displays. But as Carter lets me go and we smile at our family and friends, I realize . . . this isn't that bad. Not nearly as painful as a school field trip tour, at least.

"Woo-hoo!" I shout, holding our entwined hands up high.

There are shocked faces at my outburst, but then everyone celebrates with us.

"Congratulations!"

"Make sure Luna doesn't pass out again!"

"So happy for y'all!"

"Nutbuster, get your ass over here!"

That last one is Kyle, who's pulling on Peanut Butter's leash as the dog tries to make an escape for the barn. I guess he's hoping to see a particular horse again. He and Ed were good buddies when Peanut Butter visited before, plus the dog knows where the oat cookies are in the barn. Together, he's made up his mind on where he wants to be and even Kyle isn't going to hold him back.

"It's okay, let the mangy mutt run. I'll take him to the barn and meet y'all up at the house." Bernard sounds almost . . . happy? Almost as if he realizes it, he adds, "It'll keep him from tearing up my petunias or pissing on Rosalia."

"Rosalia?" Kyle echoes in confusion, but Carter and I just laugh.

"Long story," I offer.

Inside, Elena has the formal dining table expanded to its maximum capacity, and we all sit down. Carter's at the head of the table, an honor Elena said she would be delighted to extend to him, and I'm on his right.

"I'd like to thank each of you," Carter says, raising his wine for a toast. "Somehow, you each played a part in getting Luna and me here today, and it's exactly where we both belong. We couldn't have done it without you."

We sip, and that begins a round of toasts from almost everyone. Except me. I've had enough time in the spotlight today.

When Elena stands, holding her glass up, she's more serious than I expect on such a joyous occasion. I would think her toasts would include limericks and creative cursing, but rather, she says, "I lost the most important person in my life and was going through the motions of life. Until a charming young man and a passionate young lady showed up on my doorstep for dinner.

And that changed everything. Now, I have an entirely new family."

She looks around the table at each of us, pausing on Stanley. They're good now too, having worked out their feelings about Claire's manipulations. For her part, Claire's been keeping her distance, probably biding her time, but Elena and Carter will figure it out if she pops up like a weed again. And she's held up her end of the bargain, letting Elena see Jacob regularly as long as those allowances keep coming.

"If I may," a polite voice says, interrupting but trying to be polite about it. We turn our eyes to the young chef in a black apron. "Your first course is crab-stuffed mushroom caps with a black pepper cream sauce reduction. Enjoy."

The chef bows lightly and leaves us to taste the delicious course he's prepared. He's sort of connected too, the infamous restauranteur from Cameron's upcoming venture capital deal. The restaurant is scheduled to open in mere weeks, but the chef said cooking tonight so that Nelda could simply be a guest would be his pleasure. I think that's at Cam's request, as a happy send-off for Carter leaving Blue Lake.

And as I taste the mushroom cap, I'm so glad.

"Uhmagawd, thish is ahg-some," I mumble with my mouth full.

"Not nearly as awesome as you are, wife," Carter says, leaning over and placing a soft kiss to the corner of my mouth. I feel his tongue flick over my skin there and realize I must've had a dab of sauce on my lip. Rather than feel embarrassed, I consider painting myself in the stuff so Carter will kiss and lick me all over.

My dirty thoughts must be written all over my face because Carter smirks, raising one brow. "Whatever you're thinking . . . yes."

Later, in the same bed in the same guest room from our first night together at Elena's house, I don't need any help with kitchen-made cream. I've got plenty for Carter and he's got plenty for me.

There is one difference from last time, though.

"Shh," Carter hisses quietly in my ear. "Don't let anyone hear you. Those are my noises. No one gets those from you but me."

He's behind me, my butt lifted high in the air and my chest pressed to the bed. But to whisper in my ear, he leans over me, his front to my back, and I feel caged in the best, sexiest way.

"Ah!" I fight to stay quiet and resort to covering my mouth with my own hand as Carter rolls his hips, driving me wild with his slow thrusts. His fingers grip my hips, digging in. I bet I'll have little pink and purple marks tomorrow when we go on our honeymoon. Carter probably wants it that way considering he's already told me how sexy my tiny bikini is on my whiplash curves.

"Good girl. Can you be quiet when you come?"

I can't risk speaking, so I nod my head furiously, not caring that the pillow is probably knotting my hair. Carter grunts and pulls out of me, leaving me feeling empty without him. He guides me to flip over, pulling my legs over his shoulders so he can get deeper.

"I want to see you."

Carter resumes his punishing pace, slowly rolling his hips until he hits a spot deep inside me that borders on being too much. I feel like I can't breathe with him so far inside me, like he's literally forcing the air out of my lungs.

But I don't need oxygen. I need Carter.

When I fall apart, I keep my eyes locked on his. The blue orbs promise a future I can't wait to experience. "I love you."

"I love you too, Luna." Carter grits out my name as he comes, and his eyes flutter, but he forces them to stay open, pinning me in place with his gaze.

I never would've thought it could be like this. With anyone, but certainly not with Carter Harrington, my brother's best friend. My husband. But I'm so glad someone wise told me to never say never because you might end up regretting those words.

EPILOGUE

CARTER

The museum is abuzz tonight with people coming in from all over the world for this exhibition opening. The pieces contained in it are special, some not being seen for decades.

Together, the women in charge of tonight walk to the podium. Elena and Luna stand together, holding hands as Maeve introduces the lineup.

"To my left, I'd like to introduce Dr. Alice Standford. She's been integral in curating the pieces you'll have the opportunity to see tonight," she says, indicating the woman in a suit.

"To my right is Luna Harrington. This exhibition is a passion project for her, one she designed with Thomas Cartwright's heart in mind. Next to her is Mrs. Elena Cartwright, whose generous loan of Mr. Cartwright's collection made this exhibit possible."

Yeah, Luna isn't in charge of the overall exhibit, but she's not upset about it. Rather, she's been excited to learn about how to curate, design, and see an exhibition from concept to completion. Dr. Standford has been more than willing to teach Luna too, and they've developed a mutual respect for one another.

Luna's still hopeful Alphena takes off and becomes a major graphic novel, or even an anime show, but she's quite happy bouncing between both sides of her art love—digital to paintings, and back again.

The four women move to a ceremonial ribbon set up on the stage, with Maeve as the museum director and Elena as the donor getting center placement. Together, they cut the ribbon with huge gold-plated scissors, officially opening the Thomas Cartwright Collection exhibition.

Inside, Luna leads me through the pieces. I still have no idea what she's talking about most of the time, not able to tell a Rembrandt from a Renoir, but I happily listen to her chatter away about the thing she loves most—art.

Well, other than me.

I hum agreeably as she dissects the subtle nuances between someone's darker period of painting, having already lost the thread of who she's talking about because all I can focus on is her. She's in her element here, with people coming up to shake her hand and ask her thoughts on different pieces. There are no nerves, no scripts, just Luna and her heart, and it shines for everyone to see. What seems like hours later, we walk around a final corner in the exhibition, and Luna gasps.

She's seen my surprise. Maeve and Dr. Standford helped me place it after Elena insisted it be included, at least for tonight's opening.

"That's . . . it can't be . . . that's me!" Luna whispers in shock as it sinks in that the woman on the wall is indeed her.

In the portrait, her glasses have slid down her nose as she stares at a sketchbook in her lap, nibbling her bottom lip. She's curled up on the couch, wearing a bra and shorts that accentuate her curves and socks that slouch above her ankles. The light from the window makes her glow, something I don't know how he captured. Then again, if he can capture Luna so perfectly, sunlight must be easy.

"I had it commissioned," I explain. "Eakin has been working on it for months, going off a picture I sent of you."

The piece is large, at least four feet wide, and shows a pencil sketch in the same style as the one Luna loves in Elena's foyer.

It's stunning, if I do say so myself, though I might be biased because of the subject matter.

"Oh, my God, thank you!" Luna's crying, her hands covering half her face, but I can see the smile in her teary eyes. "It's amazing. He made me beautiful."

I frown in confusion. "This looks exactly like you, photorealism from an actual picture I took," I repeat. "This is what you look like. *Beautiful.*"

And she is. Inside and out.

Luna is my beautiful, passionate, smart, neurotic weirdo of a wife. And I wouldn't have it any other way. Because I'm the lucky bastard who gets to be her husband.

"Once we get home, I think you need a reminder of just how gorgeous you are," I promise in her ear. "I think I'll fuck you in front of the mirror, make you watch how your sexy tits drop into my waiting hands, how your ass bounces when I slam into you, and how gorgeous you are when your mouth's open, panting through your climax. You'll see how you drive me wild with that tight pussy of yours and your filthy mouth that only I get to hear."

Fuck, I'm trying to dirty talk her into feeling beautiful, but I've talked myself into an uncomfortable situation in my slacks. Not caring who sees when I'm standing with my wife in front of an equally sexy drawing of her, I adjust my rock-hard cock.

Luna smiles, shyly dipping her chin so I won't see how much she likes my words. "Again? We just did it before the opening."

She's so fucking cute, thinking that what we did earlier will be enough for me. She's got our combined cum in her panties right now, but I'll never get enough of her. I want her body, her mind, her heart, her soul all the time.

"Never be enough . . . for me!" I sing quietly. I don't think I'd seen a single musical in my life before Luna, but now I can sing along with her. I usually don't because I prefer listening to her, but dropping her favorite lyrics into conversation is a sure-fire smile-getter.

And she does. Her bright smile turns up her lips as her eyes widen. But instead of singing the next line of the song, she grabs my hand and tugs me toward the exit. "Let's go home."

The End

ABOUT THE AUTHOR

Big Fat Fake Series:
My Big Fat Fake Wedding || My Big Fat Fake Engagement || My Big Fat Fake Honeymoon

Standalones:
The French Kiss || One Day Fiance || Drop Dead Gorgeous || The Blind Date || Risky Business

Truth Or Dare:
The Dare || The Truth

Bennett Boys Ranch:
Buck Wild || Riding Hard || Racing Hearts

The Tannen Boys:
Rough Love || Rough Edge || Rough Country

Dirty Fairy Tales:
Beauty and the Billionaire || Not So Prince Charming || Happily Never After

Pushing Boundaries:
Dirty Talk || Dirty Laundry || Dirty Deeds || Dirty Secrets

Made in the USA
Middletown, DE
24 May 2024

54803877R00169